W9-BHV-978

Galileo's Children

Galileo's Children
Tales of Science vs. Superstition

STORIES BY ARTHUR C. CLARKE, GREG EGAN,
URSULA K. LE GUIN, GEORGE R. R. MARTIN,
MIKE RESNICK, ROBERT SILVERBERG, AND OTHERS

Edited by GARDNER DOZOIS

an imprint of **Prometheus Books**
Amherst, NY

Published 2005 by PYR™, an imprint of Prometheus Books

Inquiries should be addressed to
PYR
59 John Glenn Drive
Amherst, New York 14228–2197
VOICE: 716–691–0133, ext. 207
FAX: 716–564–2711
WWW.PYRSF.COM

09 08 07 06 05   5 4 3 2 1

Library of Congress Cataloging-in-Publication Data

Galileo's children : tales of science vs. superstitition / edited by Gardner Dozois.
    p. cm.
  ISBN 1–59102–315–7 (alk. paper)
   1. Science fiction, American. 2. Superstition—Fiction. 3. Persecution—Fiction.
4. Scientists—Fiction. I. Dozois, Gardner R.

PS648.S3G35 2005
813'.0876208—dc22

2005010181

Printed in Canada on acid-free paper

Acknowledgments

A cknowledgment is made for permission to reprint the following material:

"The Stars Below," by Ursula K. Le Guin. Copyright © 1974, 1975 by Ursula K. Le Guin. First published in *Orbit 14* (Harper & Row), edited by Damon Knight. Reprinted by permission of the author and the author's agent, the Virginia Kidd Literary Agency.

"The Will of God," by Keith Roberts. Copyright © 1991 by Davis Publications, Inc. First published in *Asimov's Science Fiction*, July 1991. Reprinted by permission of the author's estate and the agent for the estate, the Owlswick Literary Agency.

"The Way of Cross and Dragon," by George R. R. Martin. Copyright © 1979 by Omni International Ltd. First published in *Omni*, June 1979. Reprinted by permission of the author.

"The Pope of the Chimps," by Robert Silverberg. Copyright © 1982 by Robert Silverberg. First appeared in *Perpetual Light* (Warner Books), edited by Alan Ryan. Reprinted by permission of the author.

"The World Is a Sphere," by Edgar Pangborn. Copyright © 1973 by Terry Carr. First published in *Universe 3* (Random House), edited by Terry Carr. Reprinted by permission of the author's estate and the agent for the estate, Richard Curtis Associates.

"Written in Blood," by Chris Lawson. Copyright © 1999 by Dell Magazines. First published in *Asimov's Science Fiction*, June 1999. Reprinted by permission of the author.

"Falling Star," by Brendan DuBois. Copyright © 2004 by Brendan DuBois. First published in *Space Stations* (DAW), edited by Martin H. Greenberg and John Helfers. Reprinted by permission of the author.

"Three Hearings on the Existence of Snakes in the Human Bloodstream," by James Alan Gardner. Copyright © 1997 by Dell Magazines. First published in *Asimov's Science Fiction*, February 1997. Reprinted by permission of the author.

"The Star," by Arthur C. Clarke. Copyright © 1955 by Royal Publications, Inc. First published in *Infinity Science Fiction*, November 1955. Reprinted by permission of the author and his agents.

"The Last Homosexual," by Paul Park. Copyright © 1996 by Dell Magazines. First published in *Asimov's Science Fiction*, June 1996. Reprinted by permission of the author.

"The Man Who Walked Home," by James Tiptree Jr. Copyright © 1972 by Ultimate Publishing Co. First published in *Amazing Science Fiction Stories*, May 1972. Reprinted by permission of the author's estate and the agent for the estate, the Virginia Kidd Literary Agency.

Contents

"It Still Moves!"
Preface

> I do not feel obligated to believe that the
> same God who endowed us with sense, reason,
> and intellect intended us to forgo their use.
>
> —Galileo Galilei

"**E**ppur si muove!" ("It still moves!" or "But it does move!" or "And yet it does move!"—depending on the translator) is what Italian scientist and pioneering astronomer Galileo Galilei is supposed to have muttered defiantly to the Court of the Inquisition in 1633 after having been forced to abjure his belief in heliocentricity, the idea that the Earth rotated around the sun rather than itself being the center of the solar system, as held by the geocentric Tychonian model officially upheld by the Church.

This famous story is almost certainly apocryphal. Galileo would have to have been suicidally rash to make such a remark to the Inquisition after having narrowly missed being sentenced to torture and death (as it was, he would remain under house arrest until his death in 1642), and records suggest instead that he was a careful, even cautious man. In fact, some modern commentators have criticized Galileo for caving in to the Inquisition and agreeing to "abjure, curse, and detest" his work—but then, *they* weren't in the power of the Inquisition, who did send thousands of people to face mutilation and horrible deaths, especially in Spain, and who were then in the full flush of their power. The danger of torture and death that Galileo faced was very real. Giordano Bruno had been burned to death at the stake in 1600 for holding similar heretical beliefs, including a belief in the large, possibly infinite, size of the universe, and theologians such as the Dominican father Caccini were preaching that "geometry is of the devil" and that "mathematicians should be banished as the authors of all heresies." Another theologian declared, of the Copernican model of the solar system that Galileo would be tried for heresy for teaching: "It upsets the whole basis of theology. If the Earth is a planet, and only one among several planets, it cannot be that any such great things have been done specially for it as the Christian doctrine teaches. If there are other planets, since God makes nothing in vain, they must be inhabited; but how can their inhabitants be descended from Adam? How can they trace back their origin to Noah's Ark? How can they have been redeemed by the Saviour?"

And yet, the Earth *was* a planet, and a planet that rotated around the sun, whether those inconvenient facts conflicted with Scripture or not. "Eppur si muove," indeed. And although Galileo probably never said that, he no doubt would have sympathized with the sentiment, since it's clear that his recantation was insincere and that he continued to believe that indeed it did move, whatever the Inquisition said, throughout the rest of his life, toward the end of which he wrote the epigram that opens this preface.

It's easy enough to make Galileo's story an exercise in Catholic-bashing—especially since the Church did not admit that "errors had been made" in the case of Galileo until 1992—but the reality is more multifaceted and contradictory than that. During the Middle Ages, the same Church that later prosecuted Galileo and Giordano Bruno had gathered and collected the secular knowledge of the ancient Romans and Greeks that might otherwise have disappeared, and many theologians then and later, especially the Jesuits, were also noted investigators into scientific mysteries. The Benedictine abbot Benedetto Castelli, a former student of Galileo's and a professor of mathematics, had come to Galileo's defense, an extremely risky thing to do, and part of Galileo's house arrest was spent in the home of the sympathetic archbishop Ascanio of Silva, also a learned man; even the pope, Pope Urban VII, was an old friend of Galileo's—which perhaps explains why it was possible for Galileo to plea-bargain his way out of the rack and the stake. Clearly, many churchmen were sympathetic to Galileo, and perhaps privately believed that he was right—but that didn't matter as long as the power was in the hands of those who were determined to make science conform to Scripture and who refused to look at any facts that didn't agree with the opinions they already held, just as many refused to even *look* through Galileo's telescopes, for fear of seeing "sinful things."

To enforce willful ignorance through terror—that strikes me as superstition, not religion. And it's a kind of superstition that has persisted down through the years, even to the present day, in many different cultures—there's more than one kind of Scripture to which fearful men have tried to make science conform, with persecution and prosecution and proscription, with imprisonment and exile and bloody murder.

The Inquisition has cast the longest and coldest shadow over the imaginations of Western writers, as this anthology will make clear, but it's far from the only time that proscriptions have been set up as to what people were allowed to think, and enforced with law and iron.

About the same time that Galileo was clashing with the Roman Catholic Church, the Anglican Church under Queen Elizabeth I was hunting down Catholics and having them hanged, drawn, and quartered, a fate as gruesome as the bloody tricks the Inquisition was getting up to (and the great Protestant reformer Philipp Melanchthon was being just as fierce in his attacks on the Copernican theory as was the Roman Church, so Galileo might not have fared any better if it had been the Protestants who were running the show). In China, under the Ming dynasty, Grand Eunuch Chêng Ho commanded the mightiest navy the world had ever seen, far in advance in numbers and sophistication of technology than anything Europe would see for a hundred years or more—until the Confusionist factor at court, fearful that new ideas and contact with foreigners with very different customs would shake up the rigidly stratified class structure of Chinese society, convinced the emperor to institute the Great Withdrawal of 1433, disbanding and scuttling the mighty fleets and forbidding his subjects to travel abroad on pain of death. Later, according to Daniel J. Boorstin in *The Discoverers*, the ban was "eventually extended to include coastal shipping, and later even the construction of sea-going junks"—which, to quote Jared Diamond in *Guns, Germs, and Steel*, caused the country to step back "from the verge of an industrial revolution in the 14th Century" that might have made China the master of the world, and instead to fall into centuries of cultural and technological stagnation that ultimately left them at the dubious mercy of the European nations who forced them to break their self-imposed isolation. In Tokugawa Japan in the 1600s, a few decades later, another kind of Great Withdrawal was taking place, and another country would also step back from the brink of an industrial revolution, with dismal results. Firearms had been introduced into Japan in 1543, in the form of two arquebuses, matchlock muskets, that had been sold to a warlord by Portuguese traders hitching a ride on a Chinese junk, and soon, to again quote from *Guns, Germs, and Steel*, the Japanese had "commenced indigenous gun production, greatly improved gun technology, and by AD 1600 owned more and better guns than any other country in the world." The desire to preserve a rigidly stratified class system, super-stition, fear of foreigners, and the distaste of Confusionists for change soon led to the de facto suppression of gun manufacture and the ban-ning of foreign trade—and indeed any foreign contact. This succeeded in keeping Japan frozen at the same cultural and technological level for more than another two hundred years—until the gunboats of Adm. Matthew Perry forced them to open themselves to the world again, in an inferior and disadvantaged position. The very Arabic nations whose extremist factions now rail against "Western science" were largely responsible for passing the basic mathematical and scientific knowl-edge out of which that science was later developed along to the West in the first place. And so on.

Even today, the pope interdicts cloning, the president of the United States pushes to make stem cell research illegal, mention of the theory of evolution is banned from textbooks and explanations of "cre-ation science" are inserted instead, and politicians of both political parties vote against money for space exploration or any other kind of research where the instant up-front financial benefit to the bottom line is not immediately evident.

The battle of science against superstition is still going on, as is the battle to not have to think only what somebody *else* thinks is okay for you to think. In fact, in a society where more people believe in angels than believe in evolution, that battle may be more critical than ever.

One of the major battlefields is science fiction, one of the few forms of literature where rationality, skepticism, the knowledge of the inevitability of change, and the idea that wide-ranging freedom of thought and unfettered imagination and curiosity are *good* things are the default positions, taken for granted by most of its authors.

Oh, it's not quite that clear-cut, of course—transcendentalism has always been a major force in the genre, with even hardheaded rational-ists like Arthur C. Clarke flirting with the mystic in novels such as *Childhood's End*, just as many of today's theological physicists sound more like mystics or theologians than sober scientists, with their talk of the invisible worlds that surround us and the hidden forces that shape the workings and the structure of the universe.

Still, for the moment at least, until some new Inquisition, motivated by ignorance, intolerance, and fear, forces its writers to go underground and mutter "It still moves!" to each other in hiding, science fiction provides one of the few places in modern letters where the battle between science and superstition is openly discussed and debated, and that makes those who write it, as well as those brave characters they write about, embroiled in the age-old struggle to prevent the control of the human mind and the suppression of the human spirit, "Galileo's Children" in a very real way indeed.

The anthology that follows takes us to many different arenas in that struggle—from the past to the present to the future, from worlds that never were and never will be to worlds deep in space that someday may come to pass—and introduces us to many different warriors, male and female, rich and poor, young and old, who, in their different ways— some quietly, some defiantly, some reluctantly—fight the kind of battles that we ourselves might someday have to fight if we want our children and our grandchildren to be allowed to read these words.

Enjoy—and ponder.

Ursula K. Le Guin is probably one of the best known and most universally respected science fiction writers in the world today. Her famous novel *The Left Hand of Darkness* may have been the most influential science fiction novel of its decade, and it shows every sign of becoming one of the enduring classics of the genre—even ignoring the rest of Le Guin's work, the impact of this one novel alone on future science fiction and future science fiction writers would be incalculably strong. (Her 1968 fantasy novel, *A Wizard of Earthsea*, would be almost as influential on future generations of High Fantasy and Young Adult writers.) *The Left Hand of Darkness* won both the Hugo and the Nebula Awards, as did Le Guin's monumental novel *The Dispossessed* a few years later. Her novel *Tehanu* won her another Nebula in 1990, and she has also won three other Hugo Awards and a Nebula Award for her short fiction, as well as the National Book Award for Children's Literature for her novel *The Farthest Shore*, part of her Earthsea sequence. Her other novels include *Planet of Exile, The Lathe of Heaven, City of Illusions, Rocannon's World, The Beginning Place, A Wizard of Earthsea, The Tombs of Atuan, Tehanu, Searoad*, the controversial multimedia novel *Always Coming Home*, and *The Telling*. She has published nine collections: *The Wind's Twelve Quarters, Orsinian Tales, The Compass Rose, Buffalo Gals and Other Animal Presences, A Fisherman of the Inland Sea, Four Ways to Forgiveness, Tales of Earthsea, The Birthday of the World*, and, most recently, *Changing Planes*. Upcoming is a new novel, *Gifts*, and a collection of her critical essays, *The Wave in the Mind: Tales and Essays on the Reader, and the Imagination*. She lives with her husband in Portland, Oregon.

Here she relates the grim but oddly beautiful story of an astronomer who, denied the study of the stars by the agents of ignorance and fear, undertakes a strange and perilous journey into the uncharted hinterland of his own soul.

The wooden house and outbuildings caught fire fast, blazed up, burned down, but the dome, built of lathe and plaster above a drum of brick, would not burn. What they did at last was heap up the wreckage of the telescopes, the instruments, the books and charts and drawings, in the middle of the floor under the dome, pour oil on the heap, and set fire to that. The flames spread to the wooden beams of the big telescope frame and to the clockwork mechanisms. Villagers watching from the foot of the hill saw the dome, whitish against the green evening sky, shudder and turn, first in one direction then in the other, while a black and yellow smoke full of sparks gushed from the oblong slit: an ugly and uncanny thing to see.

It was getting dark, stars were showing in the east. Orders were shouted. The soldiers came down the road in single file, dark men in dark harness, silent.

The villagers at the foot of the hill stayed on after the soldiers had gone. In a life without change or breadth a fire is as good as a festival. They did not climb the hill, and as the night grew full dark they drew closer together. After a while they began to go back to their villages. Some looked back over their shoulders at the hill, where nothing moved. The stars turned slowly behind the black beehive of the dome, but it did not turn to follow them.

About an hour before daybreak a man rode up the steep zigzag, dismounted by the ruins of the workshops, and approached the dome on foot. The door had been smashed in. Through it a reddish haze of light was visible, very dim, coming from a massive support-beam that had fallen and had smoldered all night inward to its core. A hanging, sour smoke thickened the air inside the dome. A tall figure moved there and its shadow moved with it, cast upward on the murk. Sometimes it stooped, or stopped, then blundered slowly on.

The man at the door said: "Guennar! Master Guennar!"

The man in the dome stopped still, looking toward the door. He had just picked up something from the mess of wreckage and half-burnt stuff on the floor. He put this object mechanically into his coat pocket, still peering at the door. He came toward it. His eyes were red and swollen almost shut, he breathed harshly in gasps, his hair and clothes were scorched and smeared with black ash.

"Where were you?"

The man in the dome pointed vaguely at the ground.

"There's a cellar? That's where you were during the fire? By God! Gone to ground! I knew it, I knew you'd be here." Bord laughed, a little crazily, taking Guennar's arm. "Come on. Come out of there, for the love of God. There's light in the east already."

The astronomer came reluctantly, looking not at the gray east but back up at the slit in the dome, where a few stars burned clear. Bord pulled him outside, made him mount the horse, and then, bridle in hand, set off down the hill leading the horse at a fast walk.

The astronomer held the pommel with one hand. The other hand, which had been burned across the palm and fingers when he picked up a metal fragment still red-hot under its coat of cinders, he kept pressed against his thigh. He was not conscious of doing so, or of the pain. Sometimes his senses told him, "I am on horseback," or, "It's getting lighter," but these fragmentary messages made no sense to him. He shivered with cold as the dawn wind rose, rattling the dark woods by which the two men and the horse now passed in a deep lane overhung by teasel and briar; but the woods, the wind, the whitening sky, the cold were all remote from his mind, in which there was nothing but a darkness shot with the reek and heat of burning.

Bord made him dismount. There was sunlight around them now, lying long on rocks above a river valley. There was a dark place, and Bord urged him and pulled him into the dark place. It was not hot and close there but cold and silent. As soon as Bord let him stop he sank down, for his knees would not bear; and he felt the cold rock against his seared and throbbing hands.

"Gone to earth, by God!" said Bord, looking about at the veined walls, marked with the scars of miners' picks, in the light of his lanterned candle. "I'll be back; after dark, maybe. Don't come out. Don't go farther in. This is an old adit, they haven't worked this end of the mine for years. May be slips and pitfalls in these old tunnels. Don't come out! Lie low. When the hounds are gone, we'll run you across the border."

Bord turned and went back up the adit in darkness. When the sound of his steps had long since died away, the astronomer lifted his head and looked around him at the dark walls and the little burning candle. Presently he blew it out. There came upon him the earth-smelling darkness, silent and complete. He saw green shapes, ocherous blots drifting on the black; these faded slowly. The dull, chill black was balm to his inflamed and aching eyes, and to his mind.

If he thought, sitting there in the dark, his thoughts found no words. He was feverish from exhaustion and smoke inhalation and a few slight burns, and in an abnormal condition of mind; but perhaps his mind's workings, though lucid and serene, had never been normal. It is not normal for a man to spend twenty years grinding lenses, building telescopes, peering at stars, making calculations, lists, maps, and charts of things which no one knows or cares about, things which cannot be reached, or touched, or held. And now all he had spent his life on was gone, burned. What was left of him might as well be, as it was, buried.

But it did not occur to him, this idea of being buried. All he was keenly aware of was a great burden of anger and grief, a burden he was unfit to carry. It was crushing his mind, crushing out reason. And the darkness here seemed to relieve that pressure. He was accustomed to the dark, he had lived at night. The weight here was only rock, only earth. No granite is so hard as hatred and no clay so cold as cruelty. The earth's black innocence enfolded him. He lay down within it, trembling a little with pain and with relief from pain, and slept.

Light waked him. Count Bord was there, lighting the candle with flint and steel. Bord's face was vivid in the light: the high color and blue eyes of a keen huntsman, a red mouth, sensual and obstinate. "They're on the scent," he was saying. "They know you got away."

"Why . . ." said the astronomer. His voice was weak; his throat, like his eyes, was still smoke-inflamed. "Why are they after me?"

"Why? Do you still need telling? To burn you alive, man! For heresy!" Bord's blue eyes glared through the steadying glow of the candle.

"But it's gone, burned, all I did."

"Aye, the earth's stopped, all right, but where's their fox? They want their fox! But damned if I'll let them get you."

The astronomer's eyes, light and wide-set, met his and held. "Why?"

"You think I'm a fool," Bord said with a grin that was not a smile, a wolf's grin, the grin of the hunted and the hunter. "And I am one. I was a fool to warn you. You never listened. I was a fool to listen to you. But I liked to listen to you. I liked to hear you talk about the stars and the courses of the planets and the ends of time. Who else ever talked to me of anything but seed corn and cow dung? Do you see? And I don't like soldiers and strangers, and trials and burnings. Your truth, their truth, what do I know about the truth? Am I a master? Do I know the courses of the stars? Maybe you do. Maybe they do. All I know is you have sat at my table and talked to me. Am I to watch you burn? God's fire, they say; but you said the stars are the fires of God. Why do you ask me that, 'Why?' Why do you ask a fool's question of a fool?"

"I am sorry," the astronomer said.

"What do you know about men?" the count said. "You thought they'd let you be. And you thought I'd let you burn." He looked at Guennar through the candlelight, grinning like a driven wolf, but in his blue eyes there was a glint of real amusement. "We who live down on the earth, you see, not up among the stars . . ."

He had brought a tinderbox and three tallow candles, a bottle of water, a ball of peas-pudding, a sack of bread. He left soon, warning the astronomer again not to venture out of the mine.

When Guennar woke again a strangeness in his situation troubled him, not one which would have worried most people hiding in a hole to save their skins, but most distressing to him: he did not know the time.

It was not clocks he missed, the sweet banging of the church bells in the villages calling to morning and evening prayer, the delicate and willing accuracy of the timepieces he used in his observatory and on whose refinement so many of his discoveries had depended; it was not the clocks he missed, but the great clock.

Not seeing the sky, one cannot know the turning of the earth. All the processes of time, the sun's bright arch and the moon's phases, the planet's dance, the wheeling of the constellations around the pole star, the vaster wheeling of the seasons of the stars, all these were lost, the warp on which his life was woven.

Here there was no time.

"O my God," Guennar the astronomer prayed in the darkness under ground, "how can it offend you to be praised? All I ever saw in my telescopes was one spark of your glory, one least fragment of the order of your creation. You could not be jealous of that, my Lord! And there were few enough who believed me, even so. Was it my arrogance in daring to describe your works? But how could I help it, Lord, when you let me see the endless fields of stars? Could I see and be silent? O my God, do not punish me any more, let me rebuild the smaller telescope. I will not speak, I will not publish, if it troubles your holy Church. I will not say anything more about the orbits of the planets or the nature of the stars. I will not speak, Lord, only let me see!"

"What the devil, be quiet, Master Guennar. I could hear you halfway up the tunnel," said Bord, and the astronomer opened his eyes to the dazzle of Bord's lantern. "They've called the full hunt up for you. Now you're a necromancer. They swear they saw you sleeping in your house when they came, and they barred the doors; but there's no bones in the ashes."

"I was asleep," Guennar said, covering his eyes. "They came, the soldiers. . . . I should have listened to you. I went into the passage under the dome. I left a passage there so I could go back to the hearth on cold nights, when it's cold my fingers get too stiff, I have to go warm my hands sometimes." He spread out his blistered, blackened hands and looked at them vaguely. "Then I heard them overhead. . . ."

"Here's some more food. What the devil, haven't you eaten?"

"Has it been long?"

"A night and a day. It's night now. Raining. Listen, Master: there's two of the black hounds living at my house now. Emissaries of the Council, what the devil, I had to offer hospitality. This is my county, they're here, I'm the count. It makes it hard for me to come. And I don't want to send any of my people here. What if the priests asked them, 'Do you know where he is? Will you answer to God you don't know where he is?' It's best they don't know. I'll come when I can. You're all right here? You'll stay here? I'll get you out of here and over the border when they've cleared away. They're like flies now. Don't talk aloud like that. They might look into these old tunnels. You should go farther in. I will come back. Stay with God, Master."

"Go with God, count."

He saw the color of Bord's blue eyes, the leap of shadows up the rough-hewn roof as he took up the lantern and turned away. Light and color died as Bord, at the turning, put out the lantern. Guennar heard him stumble and swear as he groped his way.

Presently Guennar lighted one of his candles and ate and drank a little, eating the staler bread first, and breaking off a piece of the crusted lump of peas-pudding. This time Bord had brought him three loaves and some salt meat, two more candles and a second skin bottle of water, and a heavy duffle cloak. Guennar had not felt cold. He was wearing the coat he always wore on cold nights in the observatory and very often slept in, when he came stumbling to bed at dawn. It was a good sheepskin, filthy from his rummagings in the wreckage in the dome and scorched at the sleeve-ends, but it was as warm as ever, and was like his own skin to him. He sat inside it eating, gazing out through the sphere of frail yellow candlelight to the darkness of the tunnel beyond. Bord's words, "You should go farther in," were in his mind. When he was done eating he bundled up the provisions in the cloak, took up the bundle in one hand and the lighted candle in the other, and set off down the side-tunnel and then the adit, down and inward.

After a few hundred paces he came to a major cross-tunnel, off which ran many short leads and some large rooms or stopes. He turned left and presently passed a big stope in three levels. He entered it. The farthest level was only about five feet under the roof, which was still well timbered with posts and beams. In a corner of the backmost level, behind an angle of quartz intrusion which the miners had left jutting out as a supporting buttress, he made his new camp, setting out the food, water, tinderbox, and candles where they would come under his hand easily in the dark, and laying the cloak as a mattress on the floor, which was of a rubbly, hard clay. Then he put out the candle, already burned down by a quarter of its length, and lay down in the dark.

After his third return to that first side-tunnel, finding no sign that Bord had come there, he went back to his camp and studied his provisions. There were still two loaves of bread, half a bottle of water, and the salt meat, which he had not yet touched; and four candles. He guessed that it might have been six days since Bord had come, but it might have been three, or eight. He was thirsty, but dared not drink, so long as he had no other supply.

He set off to find water.

At first he counted his paces. After a hundred and twenty he saw that the timbering of the tunnel was askew, and there were places where the rubble fill had broken through, half filling the passage. He came to a winze, a vertical shaft, easy to scramble down by what remained of the wooden ladder, but after it, in the lower level, he forgot to count his steps. Once he passed a broken pick handle; farther on he saw a miner's discarded headband, a stump of candle still stuck in the forehead socket. He dropped this into the pocket of his coat and went on.

The monotony of the walls of hewn stone and planking dulled his mind. He walked on like one who will walk forever. Darkness followed him and went ahead of him.

His candle burning short spilled a stream of hot tallow on his fingers, hurting him. He dropped the candle, and it went out.

He groped for it in the sudden dark, sickened by the reek of its smoke, lifting his head to avoid that stink of burning. Before him, straight before him, far away, he saw the stars.

Tiny, bright, remote, caught in a narrow opening like the slot in the observatory dome: an oblong full of stars in blackness.

He got up, forgetting about the candle, and began to run toward the stars.

They moved, dancing, like the stars in the telescope field when the clockwork mechanism shuddered or when his eyes were very tired. They danced, and brightened.

He came among them, and they spoke to him.

The flames cast queer shadows on the blackened faces and brought queer lights out of the bright, living eyes.

"Here, then, who's that? Hanno?"

"What were you doing up that old drift, mate?"

"Hey, who is that?"

"Who the devil, stop him—"

"Hey, mate! Hold on!"

He ran blind into the dark, back the way he had come. The lights followed him and he chased his own faint, huge shadow down the tunnel. When the shadow was swallowed by the old dark and the old silence came again he still stumbled on, stooping and groping so that he was oftenest on all fours or on his feet and one hand. At last he dropped down and lay huddled against the wall, his chest full of fire.

Silence, dark.

He found the candle end in the tin holder in his pocket, lighted it with the flint and steel, and by its glow found the vertical shaft not fifty feet from where he had stopped. He made his way back up to his camp. There he slept; woke and ate, and drank the last of his water; meant to get up and go seeking water again; fell asleep, or into a doze or daze, in which he dreamed of a voice speaking to him.

"There you are. All right. Don't startle. I'll do you no harm. I said it wasn't no knocker. Who ever heard of a knocker as tall as a man? Or who ever seen one, for that matter. They're what you *don't* see, mates, I said. And what we did see was a man, count on it. So what's he doing in the mine, said they, and what if he's a ghost, one of the lads that was caught when the house of water broke in the old south adit, maybe, come walking? Well then, I said, I'll go see that. I never seen a ghost yet, for all I heard of them. I don't care to see what's not meant to be seen, like the knocker folk, but what harm to see Temon's face again, or old Trip, haven't I seen 'em in dreams, just the same, in the ends, working away with their faces sweating same as life? Why not? So I come along. But you're no ghost, no miner. A deserter you might be, or a thief. Or are you out of your wits, is that it, poor man? Don't fear. Hide if you like. What's it to me? There's room down here for you and me. Why are you hiding from the light of the sun?"

"The soldiers . . ."

"I thought so."

When the old man nodded, the candle bound to his forehead set light leaping over the roof of the stope. He squatted about ten feet from Guennar, his hands hanging between his knees. A bunch of candles and his pick, a short-handled, finely shaped tool, hung from his belt. His face and body, beneath the restless star of the candle, were rough shadows, earth-colored.

"Let me stay here."

"Stay and welcome! Do I own the mine? Where did you come in, eh, the old drift above the river? That was luck to find that, and luck you turned this way in the crosscut, and didn't go east instead. Eastward this level goes on to the caves. There's great caves there; did you know it? Nobody knows but the miners. They opened up the caves before I was born, following the old lode that lay along here sunward. I seen the caves once, my dad took me, you should see this once, he says. See the world underneath the world. A room there was no end to. A cavern as deep as the sky, and a black stream falling into it, falling and falling till the light of the candle failed and couldn't follow it, and still the water was falling on down into the pit. The sound of it came up like a whisper without an end, out of the dark. And on beyond that there's other caves, and below. No end to them, maybe. Who knows? Cave under cave, and glittering with the barren crystal. It's all barren stone, there. And all worked out, here, years ago. It's a safe enough hole you chose, mate, if you hadn't come stumbling in on us. What was you after? Food? A human face?"

"Water."

"No lack of that. Come on, I'll show you. Beneath here in the lower level there's all too many springs. You turned the wrong direction. I used to work down there, with the damned cold water up to my knees, before the vein ran out. A long time ago. Come on."

The old miner left him in his camp, after showing him where the spring rose and warning him not to follow down the watercourse, for the timbering would be rotted and a step or sound might bring the earth down. Down there all the timbers were covered with a deep glittering white fur, saltpeter perhaps, or a fungus: it was very strange, above the oily water. When he was alone again Guennar thought he had dreamed that white tunnel full of black water, and the visit of the miner. When he saw a flicker of light far down the tunnel, he crouched behind the quartz buttress with a great wedge of granite in his hand: for all his fear and anger and grief had come down to one thing here in the darkness, a determination that no man would lay hand on him. A blind determination, blunt and heavy as a broken stone, heavy in his soul.

It was only the old man coming, with a hunk of dry cheese for him.

He sat with the astronomer, and talked. Guennar ate up the cheese, for he had no food left, and listened to the old man talk. As he listened the weight seemed to lift a little, he seemed to see a little farther in the dark.

"You're no common soldier," the miner said, and he replied, "No, I was a student once," but no more, because he dared not tell the miner who he was. The old man knew all the events of the region; he spoke of the burning of the Round House on the hill, and of Count Bord. "He went off to the city with them, with those black-gowns, to be tried, they do say, to come before their council. Tried for what? What did he ever do but hunt boar and deer and foxen? Is it the council of the foxen trying him? What's it all about, this snooping and soldiering and burning and trying? Better leave honest folk alone. The count was honest, as far as the rich can be, a fair landlord. But you can't trust them, none of such folk. Only down here. You can trust the men who go down into the mine. What else has a man got down here but his own hands and his mates' hands? What's between him and death, when there's a fall in the level or a winze closes and he's in the blind end, but their hands, and their shovels, and their will to dig him out? There'd be no silver up there in the sun if there wasn't trust between us down here in the dark. Down here you can count on your mates. And nobody comes but them. Can you see the owner in his lace, or the soldiers, coming down the ladders, coming down and down the great shaft into the dark? Not them! They're brave at tramping on the grass, but what good's a sword and shouting in the dark? I'd like to see 'em come down here. . . ."

The next time he came another man was with him, and they brought an oil lamp and a clay jar of oil, as well as more cheese, bread, and some apples. "It was Hanno thought of the lamp," the old man said. "A hempen wick it is, if she goes out blow sharp and she'll likely catch up again. Here's a dozen candles, too. Young Per swiped the lot from the doler, up on the grass."

"They all know I'm here?"

"*We* do," the miner said briefly. "*They* don't."

Some time after this, Guennar returned along the lower, westleading level he had followed before, till he saw the miners' candles dance like stars; and he came into the stope where they were working. They shared their meal with him. They showed him the ways of the mine, and the pumps, and the great shaft where the ladders were and the hanging pulleys with their buckets; he sheered off from that, for the wind that came sucking down the great shaft smelled to him of burning. They took him back and let him work with them. They treated him as a guest, as a child. They had adopted him. He was their secret.

There is not much good spending twelve hours a day in a black hole in the ground all your life long if there's nothing there, no secret, no treasure, nothing hidden.

There was the silver, to be sure. But where ten crews of fifteen had used to work these levels and there had been no end to the groan and clatter and crash of the loaded buckets going up on the screaming winch and the empties banging down to meet the trammers running with their heavy carts, now one crew of eight men worked: men over forty, old men, who had no skill but mining. There was still some silver there in the hard granite, in little veins among the gangue. Sometimes they would lengthen an end by one foot in two weeks.

"It was a great mine," they said with pride.

They showed the astronomer how to set a gad and swing the sledge, how to go at granite with the finely balanced and sharp-pointed pick, how to sort and "cob," what to look for, the rare bright branchings of the pure metal, the crumbling rich rock of the ore. He helped them daily. He was in the stope waiting for them when they came, and spelled one or another on and off all day with the shovel work, or sharpening tools, or running the ore-cart down its grooved plank to the great shaft, or working in the ends. There they would not let him work long; pride and habit forbade it. "Here, leave off chopping at that like a woodcutter. Look: this way, see?" But then another would ask him, "Give me a blow here, lad, see, on the gad, that's it."

They fed him from their own coarse meager meals.

In the night, alone in the hollow earth, when they had climbed the long ladder up "to grass" as they said, he lay and thought of them, their faces, their voices, their heavy, scarred, earth-stained hands, old men's hands with thick nails blackened by bruising rock and steel; those hands, intelligent and vulnerable, which had opened up the earth and found the shining silver in the solid rock. The silver they never held, never kept, never spent. The silver that was not theirs.

"If you found a new vein, a new lode, what would you do?"

"Open her, and tell the masters."

"Why tell the masters?"

"Why, man! We gets paid for what we brings up! D'you think we does this damned work for love?"

"Yes."

They all laughed at him, loud, jeering laughter, innocent. The living eyes shone in their faces blackened with dust and sweat.

"Ah, if we could find a new lode! The wife would keep a pig like we had once, and by God I'd swim in beer! But if there's silver they'd have found it; that's why they pushed the workings so far east. But it's barren there, and worked out here, that's the short and long of it."

Time stretched behind him and ahead of him like the dark drifts and crosscuts of the mine, all present at once, wherever he with his small candle might be among them. When he was alone now the astronomer often wandered in the tunnels and the old stopes, knowing the dangerous places, the deep levels full of water, adept at shaky ladders and tight places, intrigued by the play of his candle on the rock walls and faces, the glitter of mica that seemed to come from deep inside the stone. Why did it sometimes shine out that way? as if the candle found something far within the shining broken surface, something that winked in answer and occulted, as if it had slipped behind a cloud or an unseen planet's disc.

"There are stars in the earth," he thought. "If one knew how to see them."

Awkward with the pick, he was clever with machinery; they admired his skill, and brought him tools. He repaired pumps and windlasses; he fixed up a lamp on a chain for "young Per" working in a long narrow dead end, with a reflector made from a tin candleholder beaten out into a curved sheet and polished with fine rockdust and the sheepskin lining of his coat. "It's a marvel," Per said. "Like daylight. Only, being behind me, it don't go out when the air gets bad, and tell me I should be backing out for a breath."

For a man can go on working in a narrow end for some time after his candle has gone out for lack of oxygen.

"You should have a bellows rigged there."

"What, like I was a forge?"

"Why not?"

"Do ye ever go up to the grass, nights?" asked Hanno, looking wistfully at Guennar. Hanno was a melancholy, thoughtful, softhearted fellow. "Just to look about you?"

Guennar did not answer. He went off to help Bran with a timbering job; the miners did all the work that had once been done by crews of timberers, trammers, sorters, and so on.

"He's deathly afraid to leave the mine," Per said, low.

"Just to see the stars and get a breath of the wind," Hanno said, as if he was still speaking to Guennar.

One night the astronomer emptied out his pockets and looked at the stuff that had been in them since the night of the burning of the observatory: things he had picked up in those hours which he now could not remember, those hours when he had groped and stumbled in the smoldering wreckage, seeking . . . seeking what he had lost. . . . He no longer thought of what he had lost. It was sealed off in his mind by a thick scar, a burn-scar. For a long time this scar in his mind kept him from understanding the nature of the objects now ranged before him on the dusty stone floor of the mine: a wad of papers scorched all along one side; a round piece of glass or crystal; a metal tube; a beautifully worked wooden cogwheel; a bit of twisted blackened copper etched with fine lines; and so on, bits, wrecks, scraps. He put the papers back into his pocket, without trying to separate the brittle half-fused leaves and make out the fine script. He continued to look at and occasionally to pick up and examine the other things, especially the piece of glass.

This he knew to be the eyepiece of his ten-inch telescope. He had ground the lens himself. When he picked it up he handled it delicately, by the edges, lest the acid of his skin etch the glass. Finally he began to polish it clean, using a wisp of fine lambswool from his coat. When it was clear, he held it up and looked at and through it at all angles. His face was calm and intent, his light wide-set eyes steady.

Tilted in his fingers, the telescope lens reflected the lamp flame in one bright tiny point near the edge and seemingly beneath the curve of the face, as if the lens had kept a star in it from the many hundred nights it had been turned toward the sky.

He wrapped it carefully in the wisp of wool and made a place for it in the rock niche with his tinderbox. Then he took up the other things one by one.

During the next weeks the miners saw their fugitive less often while they worked. He was off a great deal by himself: exploring the deserted eastern regions of the mine, he said, when they asked him what he did.

"What for?"

"Prospecting," he said with the brief, wincing smile that gave him a very crazy look.

"Oh, lad, what do you know about that? She's all barren there. The silver's gone; and they found no eastern lode. You might be finding a bit of poor ore or a vein of tin-stone, but nothing worth the digging."

"How do you know what's in the rock under your feet, Per?"

"I know the signs, lad. Who should know better?"

"But if the signs are hidden?"

"Then the silver's hidden."

"Yet you know it is there, if you knew where to dig, if you could see into the rock. And what else is there? You find the metal, because you seek it, and dig for it. But what else might you find, deeper than the mine, if you sought, if you knew where to dig?"

"Rock," said Per. "Rock, and rock, and rock."

"And then?"

"And then? Hellfire, for all I know. Why else does it get hotter as the shafts go deeper? That's what they say. Getting nearer hell."

"No," the astronomer said, clear and firm. "No. There is no hell beneath the rocks."

"What is there, then, underneath it all?"

"The stars."

"Ah," said the miner, floored. He scratched his rough, tallow-clotted hair, and laughed. "There's a poser," he said, and stared at Guennar with pity and admiration. He knew Guennar was mad, but the size of his madness was a new thing to him, and admirable. "Will you find 'em then, the stars?"

"If I learn how to look," Guennar said, so calmly that Per had no response but to heft his shovel and get back to loading the cart.

One morning when the miners came down they found Guennar still sleeping, rolled up in the battered cloak Count Bord had given him, and by him a strange object, a contraption made of silver tubing, tin struts and wires beaten from old headlamp-sockets, a frame of pick handles carefully carved and fitted, cogged wheels, a bit of twinkling glass. It was elusive, makeshift, delicate, crazy, intricate.

"What the devil's that?"

They stood about and stared at the thing, the lights of their headlamps centering on it, a yellow beam sometimes flickering over the sleeping man as one or another glanced at him.

"He made it, sure."

"Sure enough."

"What for?"

"Don't touch it."

"I wasn't going to."

Roused by their voices, the astronomer sat up. The yellow beams of the candles brought his face out white against the dark. He rubbed his eyes and greeted them.

"What would that be, lad?"

He looked troubled or confused when he saw the object of their curiosity. He put a hand on it protectively, yet he looked at it himself without seeming to recognize it for a while. At last he said, frowning and speaking in a whisper, "It's a telescope."

"What's that?"

"A device that makes distant things clear to the eye."

"How come?" one of the miners asked, baffled. The astronomer answered him with growing assurance. "By virtue of certain properties of light and lenses. The eye is a delicate instrument, but it is blind to half the universe—far more than half. The night sky is black, we say: between the stars is void and darkness. But turn the telescope-eye on that space between the stars, and lo, the stars! Stars too faint and far for the eye alone to see, rank behind rank, glory beyond glory, out to the uttermost boundaries of the universe. Beyond all imagination, in the outer darkness, there is light: a great glory of sunlight. I have seen it. I have seen it, night after night, and mapped the stars, the beacons of God on the shores of darkness. And here too there is light! There is no place bereft of the light, the comfort and radiance of the creator spirit. There is no place that is outcast, outlawed, forsaken. There is no place left dark. Where the eyes of God have seen, there light is. We must go farther, we must look farther! There is light if we will see it.

Not with eyes alone, but with the skill of the hands and the knowledge of the mind and the heart's faith is the unseen revealed, and the hidden made plain. And all the dark earth shines like a sleeping star."

He spoke with that authority which the miners knew belonged by rights to the priests, to the great words priests spoke in the echoing churches. It did not belong here, in the hole where they grubbed their living, in the words of a crazy fugitive. Later on, one talking to another, they shook their heads, or tapped them. Per said, "The madness is growing in him," and Hanno said, "Poor soul, poor soul!" Yet there was not one of them who did not, also, believe what the astronomer had told them.

"Show me," said old Bran, finding Guennar alone in a deep eastern drift, busy with his intricate device. It was Bran who had first followed Guennar, and brought him food, and led him back to the others.

The astronomer willingly stood aside and showed Bran how to hold the device pointing downward at the tunnel floor, and how to aim and focus it, and tried to describe its function and what Bran might see: all hesitantly, since he was not used to explaining to the ignorant, but without impatience when Bran did not understand.

"I don't see nothing but the ground," the old man said after a long and solemn observation with the instrument. "And the little dust and pebbles on it."

"The lamp blinds your eyes, perhaps," the astronomer said with humility. "It is better to look without light. I can do it because I have done it for so long. It is all practice—like placing the gads, which you always do right, and I always do wrong."

"Aye. Maybe. Tell me what you see—" Bran hesitated. He had not long ago realized who Guennar must be. Knowing him to be a heretic made no difference but knowing him to be a learned man made it hard to call him "mate" or "lad." And yet here, and after all this time, he could not call him Master. There were times when, for all his mildness, the fugitive spoke with great words, gripping one's soul, times when it would have been easy to call him Master. But it would have frightened him.

The astronomer put his hand on the frame of his mechanism and replied in a soft voice, "There are . . . constellations."

"What's that, constellations?"

The astronomer looked at Bran as if from a great way off, and said presently, "The Wain, the Scorpion, the Sickle by the Milky Way in summer, those are constellations. Patterns of stars, gatherings of stars, parenthoods, semblances . . ."

"And you see those here, with this?"

Still looking at him through the weak lamplight with clear brooding eyes, the astronomer nodded, and did not speak, but pointed downward, at the rock on which they stood, the hewn floor of the mine.

"What are they like?" Bran's voice was hushed.

"I have only glimpsed them. Only for a moment. I have not learned the skill; it is a somewhat different skill. . . . But they are there, Bran."

Often now he was not in the stope where they worked, when they came to work, and did not join them even for their meal, though they always left him a share of food. He knew the ways of the mine now better than any of them, even Bran, not only the "living" mine but the "dead" one, the abandoned workings and exploratory tunnels that ran eastward, ever deeper, toward the caves. There he was most often; and they did not follow him.

When he did appear amongst them and they talked with him, they were more timid with him, and did not laugh.

One night as they were all going back with the last cartload to the main shaft, he came to meet them, stepping suddenly out of a crosscut to their right. As always he wore his ragged sheepskin coat, black with the clay and dirt of the tunnels. His fair hair had gone gray. His eyes were clear. "Bran," he said, "come, I can show you now."

"Show me what?"

"The stars. The stars beneath the rock. There's a great constellation in the stope on the old fourth level, where the white granite cuts down through the black."

"I know the place."

"It's there: underfoot, by that wall of white rock. A great shining and assembly of stars. Their radiance beats up through the darkness. They are like the faces of dancers, the eyes of angels. Come and see them, Bran!"

The miners stood there, Per and Hanno with backs braced to hold the cart from rolling: stooped men with tired, dirty faces and big hands bent and hardened by the grip of shovel and pick and sledge. They were embarrassed, compassionate, impatient.

"We're just quitting. Off home to supper. Tomorrow," Bran said.

The astronomer looked from one face to another and said nothing.

Hanno said in his hoarse gentle voice, "Come up with us, for this once, lad. It's dark night out, and likely raining; it's November now; no soul will see you if you come and sit at my hearth, for once, and eat hot food, and sleep beneath a roof and not under the heavy earth all by yourself alone!"

Guennar stepped back. It was as if a light went out, as his face went into shadow. "No," he said. "They will burn out my eyes."

"Leave him be," said Per, and set the heavy ore-cart moving toward the shaft.

"Look where I told you," Guennar said to Bran. "The mine is not dead. Look with your own eyes."

"Aye. I'll come with you and see. Good night!"

"Good night," said the astronomer, and turned back to the side-tunnel as they went on. He carried no lamp or candle; they saw him one moment, darkness the next.

In the morning he was not there to meet them. He did not come.

Bran and Hanno sought him, idly at first, then for one whole day. They went as far down as they dared, and came at last to the entrance of the caves, and entered, calling sometimes, though in the great caverns even they, miners all their lives, dared not call aloud because of the terror of the endless echoes in the dark.

"He has gone down," Bran said. "Down farther. That's what he said. Go farther, you must go farther, to find the light."

"There is no light," Hanno whispered. "There was never light here. Not since the world's creation."

But Bran was an obstinate old man, with a literal and credulous mind; and Per listened to him. One day the two went to the place the astronomer had spoken of, where a great vein of hard light granite that cut down through the darker rock had been left untouched, fifty years ago, as barren stone. They retimbered the roof of the old stope where the supports had weakened, and began to dig, not into the white rock but down, beside it; the astronomer had left a mark there, a kind of chart or symbol drawn with candleblack on the stone floor. They came on silver ore a foot down, beneath the shell of quartz; and under that— all eight of them working now—the striking picks laid bare the raw silver, the veins and branches and knots and nodes shining among broken crystals in the shattered rock, like stars and gatherings of stars, depth below depth without end, the light.

The Will of God

Keith Roberts

Martyrdom is usually thought of as something reserved for prophets, saints, and missionaries, but as the unsettling story that follows demonstrates, it's perfectly possible to be a martyr for science—particularly if you stubbornly insist on continuing to search for Truth long after more cautious folk would have heeded the warnings and let themselves be turned away.

One of the most powerful talents to enter the field in the last half of the twentieth century, the late Keith Roberts secured an important place in genre history in 1968 with the publication of his classic novel *Pavane*, one of the best books of the sixties and certainly one of the best Alternate History novels ever written, rivaled only by books such as L. Sprague De Camp's *Lest Darkness Fall*, Ward Moore's *Bring the Jubilee*, and Philip K. Dick's *The Man in the High Castle*. Trained as an illustrator—he did work extensively as an illustrator and cover artist in the British science fiction world of the sixties—Roberts made his first sale

to *Science Fantasy* in 1964. Later, he would take over the editor-
ship of *Science Fantasy,* by then called *SF Impulse,* as well as providing many of the magazine's striking covers. But his career as
an editor was short-lived, and most of his subsequent impact on
the field would be as a writer, including the production of some
of the very best short stories of the last three decades.
Roberts's other books include the novels *The Chalk Giants, The
Furies, The Inner Wheel, Molly Zero, Grainne, Kiteworld,* and *The
Boat of Fate,* one of the finest historical novels of the seventies.
His short work can be found in the collections *Machines and
Men, The Grain Kings, The Passing of the Dragons, Ladies from Hell,
The Lordly Ones, Winterwood and Other Hauntings,* and *Kaeti On
Tour.* Roberts died in 2000. Publishers take note: a posthumous
collection of his best work is long overdue.

"Becker-Margareth . . . Becker-Margareth. . . ."

The voice seems to come from a distance. The man is interrupted in
his work. He looks up, listening intently; and the words sound again.

"Becker-Margareth. . . ."

He shakes his head slightly, as if to clear it. It was not the voice
that was far off, but his mind. The thought starts others that are
shadowy, immense; but they too slip away. Too fast, it seems, for the
originating brain to grasp. If indeed the brain originates them at all;
if they are not supplied, by some other being or from some other place.
For who can claim to be the father of a thought? One moment it is not
there; the next it is, and the world has changed.

He shakes his head again. The path is an alluring one, but barren;
he has followed it already times enough. Philosophy perhaps is not his
bent; he must do the work that lies to hand. There is little time; little
enough even for that.

A key grates in a lock. Bolts are withdrawn; the door of the inn creaks open, is slammed shut again. From above, the man hears the dull thump, senses the vibrations that chase and eddy through the fabric of the place. Vibrations, it seems, are entwined with his life, part of its very essence. In his mind he sees them reaching out, spreading as from a focus; meeting others of their kind, diminishing, reacting. A hundred pebbles, a thousand, are dropped into a pond. Its surface twinkles, coruscates, becomes a paradigm perhaps for a great truth barely glimpsed; that life, all being, is itself vibration.

He rubs tiredly at his face. A lifetime is a flickering; too brief to follow such a notion even halfway to its root. The image fades; and he turns back to the bench. The water of the pond is still again.

Downstairs, the girl pulls her headscarf free, shakes at her hair. She leans her back to the door; and as ever a tiny sigh escapes her, a breathing of relief. At first, the leaning building with its smoke-stained walls oppressed; now it has come to seem a haven. Its gloominess is almost welcome, the faint, sour stink that always seems to cling to it and that with time, she is sure, has worked its way into her very clothes. It shuts her from the street, the busy world outside; the endless grind of traffic, gabbing of voices from the marketplace, the shops. Once the town excited, thrilling with its life and bustle; the bright clothes of its citizens, goods brought from halfway round the world by the great ships in the harbor. Now she is less sure. A shadow has fallen on the place, a darkness even sunlight cannot dispel. A menace stalks the streets, formless but to be dreaded; one day, she knows it will seek her out.

She swallows, and brushes at her hair again. Such fears are for children; she should have long outgrown them. She is unimportant; a dust speck merely, in the great scheme of things. Also, she has done no harm; so why should harm come to her? The thing is absurd; absurd as all night fears.

The old woman is already stumping away, down the long corridor toward the kitchen. The girl finds her voice, uncertainly at first. She says, "Is he upstairs?"

The other turns back, sardonically. "Where else?" she says. "Where is he ever?" She jerks her thumb at the tall landing. "Don't be long," she says. "I need you to shop for me, save my legs for a change. So just you don't be long."

The girl nods unhappily, staring after her. The words hang in the air; the words and the threat beneath them, unspoken but no less real. Where would he go, if she turned him out of doors; where would either of them go? His money is useful, sure enough; the customers, what few remain, are old, not caring, or not noticing, that the ale is vinegar-thin. But these are unsure times.

She puts the thought from her, takes a fresh grip on the basket she carries. Though climbing the stairs, she cannot help her nose once more wrinkling with distaste. The odor that pervades the place has itself a quality of oldness; old dirt in the cracks of unscrubbed boards, old draperies fusty with their years. Old sins perhaps. So unlike her mother's house, still fresh in memory. She remembers that other world, with sudden longing. Sweetness of thatch, in which the mice and birds made homes, scents of flowers from the tiny, neat-trimmed garden; also the vividness of sky, seen through diamond-lighted windows. Here, the panes are grubby as the rest; so the light seems always dull, lowering as if at the onset of a storm. Through them, the surrounding buildings loom forbiddingly, shutting away more of the sky. It's an area the police for the most part avoid; the new police she fears so much, with their hard, suspicious faces, the guns strapped to their belts. The few that do venture into the precinct walk in pairs; the rest stay safe inside their vehicles. Though the vehicles are equally to be dreaded. Hearing them pass at night, the girl shivers; waiting for the pounding on a door, the cries of yet another wretch, arrested by the State for crimes unmentionable.

A part of her mind wonders why she came at all, to this alien, con-

fusing place. In one sense, the answer is easy; yet in another, there is
no answer at all. Perhaps there was some notion of security, of hiding
herself in the town with its bustling crowds. Certainly the village,
once so safe, seemed less so after the police first came. Early it was, on
a bright spring day; she saw their vehicles in the little square, the
priest and doctor standing by bemused, the priest wringing his hands.
She heard the shouted questions; and a great hot pang shot through
her, stabbed to her very heart. They were searching for him, without a
doubt; searching for her mentor, who had always been so kind. But
they were disappointed, for he was already gone. Packed his bags by
night, if the village gossip was true, locked his house and fled. To the
town, where such goings-on as his were maybe tolerated. Later she
packed her own things, what few she owned; though the thought of
the journey, and what awaited her, dried her lips, made the phlegm
rise to her throat. She told herself without her he was helpless; none to
fend for him, or see him fed. She knew this to be true; yet it was
another force that drove her.

She sighs, tapping at the low-beamed door. A fine trade, his father
left him; a fine trade and honorable, if he would but follow it. In childhood dreams she worked beside him, kneading at the stiff dough,
laying the pale loaves out on their wooden paddles. Later they were
drawn out from the brick-lined ovens, smoking and golden; and all
was peace. The machines though disrupted peace, whirring and clat-
tering; the machines he built so cleverly, making each part with his
hands. His forge glowed, orange in the night; later a steady rasping
sounded as he shaped and smoothed the work. "The Big Wheels," she
said once when she was young. Clapping her hands, and pointing.
"The Big Wheels. . . ." But he shook his head, and laughed. "No," he
said, "a Drejelad. A turning-lathe. The old folk knew about them, the
writings are in books. But mine is strong, for metal." He took her
hands then, drew her from the bench. "Stand farther off," he said, for
he was always gentle to her. "My lathe bites cruelly, with silver teeth."

He showed her where the tip of his own finger was gone, eaten by the monster he had made; so she backed off, clenching her fists and pouting. Hearing the whick-hiss of leather belts, rumble of other wheels that turned half-seen under the cobwebby stone roof. In her memory, the sounds mix with others; shouts of children splashing in the stream outside, silky roar of water from where the mill race still discharges, making a green-white foam that fans and spreads across the deep green of the pool.

There has been no answer to her knock. But then, she scarcely expected one. Once he is engrossed, the roof might fall. That or the sky; and he would be none the wiser. She told him once, laughing; but that was in the days when laughter came more readily.

She pushes at the door. No lathes now of course; he left such things behind him. Instead, other matters preoccupy his mind. He looks up, seeming to see her vaguely. He is bent, as ever, over his little bench. Before him is a curious device; a sheet of thinnest metal, clamped at its edges to a frame. Round it at intervals are small brass screws; she has seen him turn them, tapping and listening as a musician tunes the stretched skin of a drum. A slender pointer touches a cylinder that itself revolves, driven by the parts of the old clock hanging on the wall. Seeing him repair it her heart jumped with pleasure, thinking he had found a trade that might be profitable; but it was for the machine.

Below the frame, wires are fixed at their ends by more brass screws. They are like silver string, or the false edge that curls back from an oversharpened blade. Other wires he wraps painstakingly with paper, before winding them coil on coil. "To stop the fluid soaking all away," he told her once; and she peered, bemused. Try as she might she could see no fluid, no hint of dampness at all; but he merely laughed, for he was never angered by her lack of understanding. "This fluid is not visible," he said. "Nonetheless it can be stored, and gathered. See, I will show you."

She watched, wondering, as he took sealing wax and wool. "This is the beginning," he said. "By this means the fluid, which is in all things, is taken from the wax. This I call the state of negativity." He sprinkled tiny scraps of paper; and she gasped, seeing them fly by magic to the bright-colored rod. But at that he looked unusually solemn. "No," he said, "never speak of magic. All this is natural, and well known to our ancestors." He held the wax out, and she stepped back a little. "See how eagerly they cling," he said. "Anxious to return some essence of them-selves. Balance must be restored; equilibrium is all." Later he polished a piece of glass with silk. "Now, I add a fluid," he said. "My other fluid, which is positive. See what happens when the two are brought together." And sure enough the paper fragments fluttered down, to lie once more quietly on the bench. "See," he said again. "I have restored what was taken away. The charges cancel; all things are at rest." He looked away, speaking it seemed to himself. "But how to control the fluid?" he said musingly. "How to make it flow, at my command. . . ."

She frowned, not wholly reassured; still half convinced, despite his words, that he was a magician. For some days after, she avoided his home. In time, the mood passed; for she could never remain angry with him for long.

She sets the basket down, stares round the little chamber. The frown returns; also she bites her lip. On the little table by the window lies a plate with uneaten food. "You promised me," she says. "Yes-terday, you promised. But you forgot again."

He has followed the direction of her glance. For a moment he seems puzzled; then he understands, and gives a little guilty smile. "I am sorry," he says simply. "I meant to."

Knowing he is sincere, she smiles in turn; but her eyes remain somber. "You will waste away to nothing," she says, "because of your machines. You will become so thin the breeze will blow you away. Then when I come, you will not be here. You must think of me as well. What would I do, with no one to look after? And no one to look after me?"

He puts his hand out, touches her fingers gently. "You are kind to me," he says. "More kind than I deserve." He sighs, and his eyes stray back to the machine. "So much to do," he says. "But the truth still runs away, like a little child at play."

She pulls away firmly, begins to unpack the basket. "First, you must eat," she says. "See, I have brought you a good stew. There are apples I will leave; but the stew must be eaten now." Her eyes stray round the room again. "Also you will need fuel for your fire," she says. "For the cold nights are coming. Or I shall find you turned into a snowman, with little bits of coal instead of eyes."

"And a turnip for a nose," he says. "Like the snowmen you used to build in winter. Do you remember, I helped you once? And afterward we skated on the pond."

She smiles the ghost of a smile. The memory indeed is clear with her; and of his arms guiding, suddenly so strong and warm. The mill race had also frozen, leaving little ruts; she tumbled over one of them, and he rushed to help. "I was not hurt though," she says. "Do you remember how we laughed, after the frost was dusted from my coat? The old horse was watching, over the hedge. I think he was laughing, too." She takes his arm, with sudden urgency. "Let us go home," she says. "Let us leave this place. Soon, your money will be gone. And then. . . ." She bites her lip again, not knowing how to finish the thought. "Let us go home," she says. "I will be good to you."

He frowns in turn. Always, it seems, pressures are placed on him. He owes a duty to her, that at least is clear. He would give much to see her happy, the shadows gone from her eyes. Yet there are other duties. Vaguer perhaps, less well defined; but duties nonetheless. He glances again, uncertain, at the bench; and she laughs, it seems a little bitterly. "I know," she says. "It is always the machines. They must come first."

"No," he says. "No, I . . . listen." He takes her hands once more. "I am so close," he says. "So very close to . . . something. What, I cannot say. Listen," he says again. "Listen, and I will promise. In two weeks, three . . . before the winter sets in hard . . . we will go away. You will be contented then; I shall see that it is so."

She nods, resigned; for she has heard the words before. He means them, means them with all his heart; but he will forget. As he forgot the food. "Very well," she says. She sits, drawing her skirt across her knees. He has told her many times how useful it is to talk, even if she doesn't understand. Sometimes the words drop in his own brain, notions become clear; and she is nothing if not faithful. "Now," she says, "what has your machine told you? Since I came here last?"

He becomes eager at once. He draws the device forward. "See," he says. "See here." He points to the drum. Round it he has stretched paper, blackened by soot from the lamp. He turned the wick up, till the room was filled with stink and floating smuts; and Becker-Margareth came rushing for the stairs, convinced the place was afire. Later though he fixed the paper unconcerned, adjusted the pointer and the levers that controlled it. The next day he spent shouting at the diaphragm, shouting till his voice was hoarse; nonsense words for the most part, anything that came into his head. The girl became concerned; if the neighbors heard, he was certain to be hauled off as a madman. He brushed her protests aside, staring at the drum, fiddling with the levers and their joints, starting the motor again. Later, he even prevailed on her; now he points proudly to a line of dots and scratchings in the soot. Between them are peaks and hills, like a tiny mountain range. She sees that he has scratched her name beside them. "Your voice," he says. "The machine heard your voice. So. . . ." He hesitates, as if searching for words. "It drew it down," he says. "Drafted the shapes it made in air, as an artist drafts a picture. . . ."

Abruptly, he becomes despondent. Again, something seems to hover at the edge of consciousness. The marks are there; sure and firm, not to be gainsaid. He remembers the joy with which he watched them form, the wonder. Some essence of the girl was captured certainly, by the pointer and the moving drum. The words though are gone; lost in Time, as all words, acts, are lost. How to recall them? To turn the scratchings back to sounds would be to cheat Death itself.

He falls to brooding. Later he once more sets the drum to its slow turning. He touches the pointer, presses its bright tip with his finger. The links, the joinings, are mechanical; no mystery or problem there. Vibrations are transmitted from the thin, stretched disc; the tympan, like the membrane of an ear. Before the disc though there was naught but air; so the ripplings traveled through that medium, too. But that is a fact already known and noted. How else could he himself hear the words she and others speak? Or she him? Vibrations form, and inform, all; all fluids certainly, his mind insists.

So air itself is a fluid; plastic, moving, molding to all things. High buildings, and the masts of ships at sea. Perhaps a fluid made of tiny pieces; as beach sand is a fluid, sculpted by the breezes, rippling with the tide. He remembers how he once sat on a beach the entire day, till folk must have surely thought him mad. The sand intrigued him; he scooped it by the handful, time and again, watching it run liquid through his fingers. Yet the grains that formed it were each discrete and hard. Later, when the tide came in, it became sleek and brown; then, it seemed firm as earth itself. As the air, at times so gentle, can yet become a seeming solid thing. Then, the slates whirl high; and stout masts fracture, crashing to destruction.

He stops, struck by a sudden notion. Why end there? In fact, why end at all? Could the fluid in his wires, the electric fluid as he styles it, be made of fragments, too? Fragments too tiny for the mind to grasp, striking each other with untiring force? Like the model he once made, culled from an ancient book. The little silver globes, each hanging by its thread, intrigued for days; the thought of them intrigues him still. Each touched the next; raise one and let it fall and its fellow at the end leaped out in sympathy, though nothing visible had passed between. Its purpose baffled, though of one thing he was sure; this was no simple toy. Now, the pattern instantly becomes clear. Like the stone dropped into water, it is a paradigm; the shape of something otherwise beyond expression.

He narrows his eyes. Another thought has come, following hard, it seems, on the heels of the first. The airy fluid impinges on the ear; and its inner parts vibrate, he knows that to be true. What then though, just what happens after? What becomes of the vibrations? How do we perceive the words, the thoughts that lie behind them? Of love perhaps, or hate? Could it be . . . could there be *fragments* in the head as well? The electric force itself, coursing to the brain?

He turns. "Listen," he says excitedly. "A new idea has come to me. . . ."

He stops, blinking a little. The room is empty. The girl has gone about her affairs; she has remembered she has to shop, for both their lives.

He stoops over the curious array of instruments; the resonators, magnets, the metal forks of various lengths and sizes. The resonators are ovoid, hollow, fretted with slots and holes. The traveler sold them to him years before, the man from far-off Potsdam. Though as he rapidly discovered, he was no ordinary mendicant; he was a scholar, fallen like so many on hard times. He was bound for England, where he'd heard such as he were honored; maybe even the New World. For many years, the voice had been his study; the voice, and the means of its production. These last few pieces, useless save to a fellow student, were all that were left of his once extensive apparatus. The erstwhile baker paid him handsomely; and he went on his way rejoicing.

His benefactor studied the strange devices. Certainly the forks, struck in random order, made odd and complex tones, approximating sometimes almost to speech. They intrigued him, as the model had intrigued; yet again he sensed a barrier. Thus far, and yet no more; how to proceed beyond?

The man pushes at his hair. It is his custom, when faced with new ideas, to return to the old and proven. Reassurance lies there; also the mind, turning idly, may sometimes light on fresh insights. He twangs the forks more vigorously. Momentarily the room is filled with sound; and despite himself he starts back. For an instant, it was as if the girl herself cried out; called him by name, from some distant place of pain.

There is a tapping at the door. He turns, vaguely. "Heine," he says after a moment. "Did you bring the thing I asked for? Was it ready?"

The lad who enters is tall and strongly built, with dark hair that curls lustrous round his shoulders. He lays a small package on the bench. "He wanted paying first," he says. "Hell's own job talking it out of him."

If the casual blasphemy is noted, the other pays no heed. "Then see to it," he says mildly. "Take him his money; you know where it is kept." He turns aside, begins to unwrap the packet with eager fingers. He lifts out a tiny spring, and sighs with relief. Yes, this is what is needed, he is sure of it. Exactly what is required. He places it reverently on the bench, like a gemstone of rare worth. Once he would have shaped the thing and tempered it himself; now though, he lacks the means. And also perhaps, the skill. His eyes, once keen, have been troubling him increasingly of late; so the watchmaker was pressed unwillingly into service.

The boy crosses the room. He opens a cupboard, takes down an old earthenware jar. He peers inside, and purses his lips. Little enough remains; soon it will be time, perforce, to seek a new master.

He looks up, vaguely troubled; but the other is already immersed in his work. He hesitates; then he extracts a single golden coin. He puts the jar back on its shelf. Let the old slug round the corner wait a day or so; it will do him no harm. As for the rest . . . bad, perhaps, to serve a half-mad master. Worse, if it were to come to certain ears. Cash is cash though, however it may be acquired; more so than ever now. The times are hard for many in the town, but worse for him. He the only breadwinner; his mother ailing, hungry mouths to feed.

He makes for the stairs. On the way down, he flicks the coin jauntily; then he stows it carefully away. At the street door though he pauses. The girl who visits, so pretty and so pale; daughter or lover, he has no idea. Neither does he much care. But he feels, momentarily, the rise of pity; an emotion for the most part strange to him. She should not have come here. From the first, a mark seemed laid on her; he has heard of such things before, but not believed. Secretly he makes the little sigh that wards off the Evil Eye.

He eases the door open, slips through. Outside, a police vehicle grumbles by. His demeanor changes instantly. He darts aside, into one of the alleys with which the place abounds. A second later, he is gone from sight.

The man sits listlessly, staring at the bench. In front of him is the machine; though it now presents a somewhat different appearance. Behind the metal disc, a thick iron rod is held secure by clamps. Round it, delicately suspended, hangs a coil of finest wire. Other wires lead to the curious box he has constructed. On its side, a half-round dial displays a metal needle, like the slim hand of a clock or watch. There is a hastily scrawled scale; at the base of the needle, the tiny spring maintains it in suspension. The machine is delicate; the pointer quivers to the slightest tapping of the bench top. To shield it from such vibrations, he has placed a folded blanket beneath it; but the quiverings he wished so much to see were absent.

He half leans forward, slumps back again. It is useless, he already knows it. Once more he shouted himself hoarse; till a beating came on the wall, a voice, half-heard and thick, demanded quiet. And still the needle had not moved.

He pulls the machine toward him, rubs his eyes. As the tympan trembles so the coil, linked to it, must vibrate; interrupting the etheric force, breaking the lines of power from the magnet. He sees them with his mind, standing out like stiff, fine hair. More of the electric fluid must be generated; this he knows, from the Potsdam man's experiments. But the needle, the measuring device, failed each time to register the flow.

Despite himself, a weariness comes over him. He lies down on the bed. The sky is brightening already; he hears the sounds as the town begins to stir. Rumbling of traffic, the sound of voices, footsteps on the pavements. Once the evidence of other folk around him, other lives being led, would have pleased, albeit obscurely; now such things are no longer his concern. His world is not theirs; it has become a bleak and barren place.

The thoughts still circle in his head. The flow is too weak, or the meter faulty; either way, he has failed. He closes his eyes, knowing he will not sleep. To his surprise, it is full light when he wakes.

The girl has also passed a miserable night. Despite herself, the dreams would come; sometimes as soon as her head touched the pillows. She saw the cottage again, the flowers that always grew up round the porch. The porch itself was thatched with brown-gray straw, drawn up at each side into little points. On them, bird-shapes poised; like the birds that strutted once on the roof of the house itself. Till the wind came, blowing them away; she cried, privately, at the scattering of dark straw feathers.

Beyond, she saw the red roofs of the village. The pond, so still and green, the ancient, rambling mill. Later, her mother's coffin was lowered into the earth; and she walked back to her home dry-eyed. Knowing her fate was sealed; as the doors and windows of the mill were sealed, her one friend fled away.

Half-waking, she remembered what he had often said; that all things are fragmented, the reasons for action seldom wholly clear. Certainly in her case it was true; though at the time one reason had seemed paramount. The *Bürgermeister* needed a new wife; and her uncle, who now had charge of her affairs, was not one to trouble himself unduly over the vaporings of girls. Cash had been exchanged, she knew it for a fact, certain other provisions agreed; so to the *Bürgermeister* she would go. To the gaunt house, standing on its own, where the village worthies roistered after hunting and the blood of hares and deer ran to the kitchen flags. The flags that were never cleaned, save where the dogs licked, and that were deep in filth. It was then, quietly, that she packed her things; only to come to a place that in some respects was worse.

The dream was succeeded by others; images so vile they startled her awake, though later she could not remember them with clearness. Only that there were bones, faces that screeched and shouted. Finally, more blood came; great streams and gouts of it. So that she rose at first light ashen-faced, washed herself in icy water and began to dress.

She is late returning to the inn. The town is busier than she can recall; it is as if folk are flocking in, for some great festival. She is pushed and jostled; she tries to hurry, dodging from side to side along the narrow pavements. She crosses the long bridge, stares down unseeing at the ships, the steel-gray water. She detours twice, glimpsing the police ahead; later, passing the little corner shop, she is sure the watchmaker glowers through the glass. She ducks her head, once more increasing her pace; taps at the wide, studded door, waits nervously for Becker-Margareth's shuffling step. Her hair is covered, decently; nonetheless, she draws the scarf closer round her throat.

It seems her presence has not been missed. Save by the old woman, vituperative as ever. She escapes finally, makes her way upstairs. The man sits gloomily, regarding the apparatus on the bench. He waves the food away, with a dismissive gesture; so she begins to pack the things, knowing words are vain. "If the electric fluid is too weak," she offers without real hope, "could you not make it stronger?"

He stares at her, unseeing; then it is as if a light dawns in his eyes. To her amazement he takes her in his arms, waltzing her round and round the tiny space. Articles are bowled from shelves; his coat and hat, his stick, the resonators and the long metal forks. The place becomes melodious with jangling; but he ignores it. "Fool," he cries, over and again. "Fool, not to have seen the obvious. . . ." At first she thinks he must mean her; but it is not the case. "Fool," he cries again. "Oh, fool, fool, fool. . . ." He rains kisses on her startled face; then, abruptly, he pushes away. "Where is my food?" he demands. "Where is the meal you brought? Why must you forever be tucking things away?" To her fresh amazement he gobbles at the soup, tearing great hunks of bread. "Fool," he says between mouthfuls. "Oh, fool that I am. . . ." He jumps up, grabs her shoulders urgently. "Where is Heine?" he asks. "Where is my assistant? Find him for me, quickly. There is work to be done. . . ."

She scurries on her errand; uncomprehending, but eager to please. To help, in any way she can.

When she returns next day, the place is transformed. The door bangs back against a great glass carboy, nestling, straw-cased, in its cage of iron. She draws her skirts away from it, cautiously. Nearer at hand are squat glass jars, lined inside and out with metal. She shies away again; but the experimenter merely laughs, as he laughed before. She touched one once, snatched her hand back at the sudden hot biting; it was as though some invisible creature had sunk its teeth into her flesh. She stared, expecting to see blood; but there was no mark. She was truly frightened then, for the first time; but he put an arm round her, speaking gently as was his custom. "It is the fluid," he said. "There is no harm in it. See, you can touch the jar safely now; it has leaked away." He held the thing out; but she shrank back.

"No," she said, "take it away. Take it away from me, please."

He set the thing down. "It will not hurt you," he said. "It is a natural essence. The vessels attract and store it; it seeks its freedom eagerly, not wishing to be confined." He did a strange thing then; touched first her forehead, then his own. "I believe," he said, "I believe the fluid flows through all things. Through ourselves, through stones and trees; through this very room." He smiled, and rubbed her fingers. "Come," he said. "We will walk a little; you will soon feel better, and forget."

No time though now, for walking or for talk. He is working feverishly, testing this, checking that. Heine stands at his elbow, handing apparatus at his command; wires and screws, small plates of pink and silver metal. "It is almost ready," says the man. "You will be the first to see."

The girl frowns. On the bench are many glass containers, filled almost to their tops with fluid. Acid perhaps, from the great iron-girded jars. She sees pairs of the plates are immersed in each; from some, strings of tiny bubbles rise steadily. Each is connected to the next by lengths of the shining wire; other wires stretch to the tympan, surround it in loops and coils. Beside it is the box with its white, half-round dial. The pointer is at rest; though at times, as he works, she fancies she sees it jump and quiver.

He is adjusting the pairs of plates, clicking his tongue and frowning, moving some closer to each other, some farther apart. Finally he seems satisfied. He takes her arm and draws her forward. "Speak," he says excitedly. "It doesn't matter what you say, the words are not important. Speak to the machine. You will be the first."

Her lips have dried. She puts a hand to her throat. She opens her mouth, but no words come. "What will happen?" she whispers finally. "What will it do?"

He laughs again. "No, no," he says. "Louder, and more firmly. Look, I will show you." He leans forward. "*O, Fortuna,*" he intones. "*O Fortuna, velut luna; statu variabilis. . . .*"

She cries out. It seems the sound is jerked from her. The little needle has gone mad. With every syllable it leaps and quivers, swinging forward and back across the dial. She tries to pull away. "No, no," he says again. "You do not understand. It is the fluid. This is the strength you spoke of, that set my feet on the way. Now, I control it; control it with my lightest word. Soon, you will be its mistress, too. . . ."

His laughter is pure joy.

The experimenter sits brooding, in front of the new device he has built. From time to time he taps the tiny tympan lightly. The needle of the measuring machine obediently reacts.

He puts his chin in his hands. How the notion came to him, he cannot say; but come it did, between sleeping and waking, arriving it seemed as ever from some place outside himself. Carbon, the quintessential substance; breathed out by lamp flames, rising invisible to the sky, trapped deep in the earth itself. And in all living things; for who had not seen, on broken coal, the shadows of leaves and fronds? Not idle sketches he is certain, made by God to while away His days, but signatures, for those with eyes to see. Once, the strange earth-plants had life; they flowered, and knew the sun. Carbon then, from which all things are made, would be his medium, conduct the essence of his new brainchild.

Beside him, a saucer holds a pile of fine black granules. He stirs them with his finger. The work was long and arduous, straining his meager resources to the limit; but he has succeeded. He touches the little machine again, for the pleasure of seeing the pointer move. The carbon grains, compressed and rarefied, transmit their changing state to the fluid. There is a roundness to the notion, an elegance that satisfies the mind.

He frowns. He pulls a sheet of paper toward him, studies it. The rest of his requirements are clear enough; it seemed once started, the ideas flowed without check. His wires will convey the vibrations, he knows it by experiment; the fluid, once a random, wayward factor, is now his servant. How to receive these corrugations though, turn them back to ripples in the aether?

He begins to draw again. A second tympan will be needed, certainly. Also, he knows the power of his coils. Power though must be opposed. The cannon barrel gives gunpowder force; missing its mark, the axe swings merely against air.

The pencil point moves rapidly. A magnet, he is convinced, will be the answer. Cupped, to concentrate its steady, unseen strength. Within it radiation, the tympan and the coil.

He begins to turn out cupboards. He flings aside the metal forks, the resonators. They helped him, certainly; like signposts, marking out the way. But they are not needed now.

The wire, made with such care, is all but gone; and there will be no more. Also the tympans, beaten thin and thinner between sheets of supple leather; he taught himself the craft, again by painful stages. Trusting no other to aid him.

He sits back, eyes vague, the last coil of wire in his hands. It will be enough, it will suffice. He remembers his experiments. The wire, too, was beaten out at first; but the results were disappointing. Untrustworthy, and brittle. But drawn through dies, of ever-decreasing diameter; he had been amazed at the results. Startled at first. Something happened, at some stage in the process; the metal changed its nature, becoming pliant, strong. By the rearrangement of its fragments perhaps, the tiny particles he now believes make up all things; flowers, a girl's hair, sand grains on the beach that themselves are capable of infinite division.

He starts. Dawn is already in the sky. No time for dreaming; there is far too much to do.

He takes the tympan down and studies it. It has guided his steps securely; in a sense, it has become a trusted friend. He lays it aside, picks it up again. Finally his decision is made. He strips it quickly from its frame, and lays it flat. With a pair of dividers he begins, carefully, to scribe the first of four small circles.

He sits with the little diaphragm in his hands. Once more it seems his purpose has been thwarted. The carbon grains, packed in behind, convey the electric fluid; but the fluctuations he had hoped for have been absent, shout at the thing as he might. He scratches his head, lays the device aside, picks it up again. Once more it seems a barrier has been reached. As one is thrown down so others rear ahead, each more unscalable than the last.

The girl sighs. He has been like this now for days. Impossible to draw more than the odd word from him; and those for the most part make no sense. She glances at the window, the gloomy autumn sky. The shortening days afflict her with a sense of urgency. Many times now she has been tempted to pack her things. Always she has resisted. Together, they have been through much; she cannot leave him now. She wishes though, with intense longing, for the peace of the village again. She sees it in her mind, with dreamlike clarity; the pond, the old mill, the race that chuckles beneath, broadening to the stillness of the water.

The man looks up sharply. "What did you say?" he asks. "What was that, about the mill?"

She is startled, momentarily. "I'm sorry," she says. "I must have been thinking aloud."

He rises, begins to pace the room. Something about the mill race seems of critical importance. He, too, sees the water; quiet at first then furrowed, rushing faster as its energy is concentrated.

He picks the diaphragm up again. If he were to beat it, form a shallow cone; its tip, touching the carbon grains, would surely concentrate its force. As the mill race focuses the strength of water.

He frowns, fingering the thing. How to ensure transmission of that energy? How to make firm contact, with shifting, pulsing grains?

He hurries to the cupboard. Gold, purest of metals; only gold will suffice. He takes the pot down, feels inside. He looks up, stricken. It is empty.

The girl stares at him for a moment. Then she quietly draws the thick ring from her finger, places it on the table.

He hurries back, appalled. Not that, surely; not her mother's gift.

He will not take it from her. But she shakes her head. She says, "I have no more need of it."

He takes the ring up, turns it in his fingers. He swallows. "When this is done," he says, "when this last thing is over, we will go away. Forever." He smiles. "Your dearest treasure for your dearest wish."

She looks up sharply. She knows, with strange certainty, that this time he is speaking the truth. The moment should be a joyous one; instead, it seems an icy hand has settled round her heart.

She stares at the strange box on the wall. From its front, a cone-shaped device juts forward like the black mouth of a trumpet. At the side, a similar contrivance hangs from a metal arm; coiled wires, each wrapped with cloth and paper, connect it to the machine. She steps back a little. She says, "What is it?"

He is excited, with an excitement she has not seen before. His hands shake; she feels the trembling as he takes her arm. "Come," he says. "I will show you."

He lifts the dangling object down. A little click sounds from somewhere. She takes the thing, unwillingly; and he laughs. The sound is high pitched, and a little strained. "Place it to your ear," he says. "This is the part you talk to."

"Talk to?" she says. "*Talk to?*"

He whirls a little handle on the far side of the box. "Speak," he says. "Speak clearly, and do not be afraid."

She moistens her lips. "Hello?" she says stupidly. "Is anyone there?"

Becker-Margareth hears the scream from the kitchen. She waddles through hastily, her hands white with flour, pausing only to snatch up a cudgel; the house has known such disturbances before. She is in time to see the girl run desperately into the street. Her hands are to her ears, shutting out the demon voices. She understands now, knows what he has done; for who but demons speak from empty air?

The man pounds after her. "No," he shouts, "no, wait. Don't be afraid. It was only Heine, in the next room. Come back. . . ."

The demons are all round her now. The faces loom at her, their bulging eyes grotesque, their great tongues lolling. Her sleeve is caught; she screams again, pulls free. "No," says the demons, "come with us. Good times to be had, for a pretty one like you."

Drums bang, trumpets squawk; there are horses, dragons, beasts from vilest nightmare. There is a machine with rank on rank of painted pipes. Noise blasts from it; beside it the showman, also masked, whirls at a great spoked wheel. It is the Carnival; but she is not to know.

Her scarf has gone; her hair, light and lustrous, flies round her face, falls limp across her eyes. She stares up at the man who grips her; at the uniforms that crowd in close, the dark, set faces. "Come," says her captor. "We have been watching for some time. We think you have things to tell us."

There are other footsteps on the stairs. The inventor turns, distraught. The assistant's face is white to the lips. He hurries round the room, grabbing his belongings. "Save yourself," he says. "Run, while you still have legs. I can serve you no more."

His master grips his arm. "Where is she?" he asks, anguished. "I searched; but the crowds, the noise. . . ."

The young man wrenches away. "The police have her," he says. "What else did you expect? It was what they were waiting for. Now they are saying she is mad. . . ."

The other starts back, appalled. "The fault is mine," he cries. "Mine, and no other's." He begins to snatch up apparatus. "I will go to them," he says. "Then they will understand. Come with me, Heine; for you, too, can explain. . . ."

He turns; but the room is empty. The other has already fled. He makes for the door, encumbered by boxes and the trailing wires.

The sky glowers beyond the tall windows of the Council Chamber; an autumn light, flaring and yet dull. The *Oberlandvogt* stares out vaguely, brings his attention back unwillingly to the matter in hand. The Chamber is sparsely occupied. The Emperor's representative of course has shown no interest in the current affair; no rich pickings here, no great estates for seizure. The *Blutschoffen*, the Assistant Judges, seem to have found alternative duties, while the rest of the *Hexenausschuss* are likewise mysteriously absent.

He riffles the papers in his hands, coughs uncomfortably. "Undoubtedly, the man is an eccentric," he says. "Perhaps he may even be mad." He attempts a smile. "Madmen are not necessarily all heretics," he says. "Or we should have a busy time indeed."

The emissary turns to stare. He says, "We shall be busy enough." He is a tall man, black browed and with colorless, cold eyes. Before their gaze, the *Oberlandvogt* quails. Despite his rich robes, the heavy chain of office, he is not an impressive figure; less so than ever now. He is dumpy and balding, beginning to sweat a little. "But," he says, "this talk of pacts with devils. . . ."

The other's voice is as cold as his demeanor. Cold, and pefectly modulated. "The matter seems clear enough to me," he says. "All magical practices effecting more than can reasonably be expected in nature imply a pact. Such an arrangement has therefore been made. These things have been known to us for generations."

The High Sheriff attempts to expostulate. "But the girl," he says. "A simple country girl. . . ."

The priest interrupts him. "The girl has already confessed," he says. "She has spoken with invisible demons. She stands condemned, out of her own mouth."

The other winces. Essentially, his is a kindly nature. "But," he says, "the things they will do. The things they will do to them both. . . ."

The cold voice once more breaks in. "We do nothing," says the emissary. "As you are well aware, *Herr Oberlandvogt*. For punishment, they will be handed to your own authorities. With, as ever, a plea for clemency."

The plump man nods unhappily. He is aware of the fact; as he is aware of others. Clemency is also viewed as the favoring of heretics; and heretic lovers can expect scant pity in a right-thinking world. Thus the Church, at all points, guards her flanks.

The priest rises, gathering his robes about him. "If a man abide not in me," he says, "he is cast forth as a branch; and men gather them and cast them into the fire and they are burned." He appears suddenly to lose patience. "Do you question my rights in this matter, Herr Rotensahe? Do you question my judgment?"

The *Oberlandvogt* spreads his arms, alarmed. "Naturally not. Naturally not, my Lord. . . ."

The other draws a parchment from his scrip. "It is not my will you answer to," he says. "It is the will of God. God, and His representative on earth." He spreads the scroll out, pointing; and the *Oberlandvogt* sees the Great Seal, the Mark that cannot be denied. Beside it, a scrawled signature. Claudio Aquaviva, Grand General of Jesuits; and the date, The Year of Our Lord 1589. The Inquisition has come to Germany.

He feels his shoulders sag. He swallows, moistens his lips with his tongue. "It shall be as you require," he says. "In all respects, we will be seen to do our duty."

He walks from the Chamber, and quietly closes the door.

He stands at the window of his office, high in the old *Rathaus*. Below him, the cobbled square bustles with activity. Some, the out-of-towners, have evidently come to gawk; others are more purposive. A cart passes, loaded high with faggots; beyond, men are busy erecting lines of stakes. There is a constant coming and going of priests and soldiers. And the police, of course; their sinister closed vehicles are everywhere.

The stocky man raises his eyes. Across the square the *Hexenturm*, the prison of the witches, looms darkly. Once, it was the lockup; a relatively mild place, almost homely now, where the local drunks and ne'er-do-wells could cool their heels. But the changing times brought trade to many folk; beside the Tower, masons are still working.

A side table holds a wine carafe and glasses. He had poured himself a cup, almost automatically; now though, the drink has lost its savor. He scowls at the carafe. Reflections burn dully within the crimson liquid.

He looks back to the Tower, the gloomy lines of windows. Almost he expects blood to ooze between the bars, as between the teeth of a wounded mouth.

He clenches his fists. He is surprised at the sudden passion that shakes him. This new Law, coming from the south; it offends him to the core, conflicts with every fiber of his being. Truth, logic, the burden of proof, are things of the past; now, accusation and guilt are one. Well, if justice, sanity itself, are swept aside as heathenish, so be it. A heathen he will remain; a heathen, and a Saxon.

The rage is gone as quickly as it arose. Once more he feels his body droop. He lays aside the chain of office, tiredly. For all his fineries, he knows himself to be a small man; small and insignificant, swept along by the red tide of events. He knows his courage would fail him. For his wife and children to walk into the Tower, to walk in himself. . . . He cannot bear the thought. As he knows he could never bear the pain.

He grabs the wine, drinks it down and dashes the glass away. "*Schmutzig*," he mutters to himself. "A dirty, stinking business. . . ."

He rings a handbell for his secretary to come. He stares at the papers spread before him; then he takes up a quill. "*Fiat justicia*," he says. "Let justice be done." A stamp falls with a crash; and he sits back in his chair. He stares, unseeing, at the closing door. "There'll be trouble over this," he mutters. "One of these centuries. . . ."

The suspect is shown the instruments of the Questioning. He seems confused by them. Their purpose is explained, but he does not respond. He appears lost in some inner reverie. His only concern is for the girl. He explains that she is innocent, and that they must release her.

His hair is cropped, and he is placed on the Ladder. He is stripped, and searched for witch teats. The result is inconclusive.

Alcohol is brought. His hair is burned to the roots. The second examination is more successful. Several marks are found. When needles are applied to them he feels no extra pain.

He denies that he is a witch. Strips of sulphur are placed beneath his arms and set on fire. He makes his denial again. His arms are tied behind him, and he is hoisted by the wrists. No weights are used. The *Oberlandvogt* has expressed a wish that the captives be spared extremes of torture.

At zero nine thirty the Questioners go to breakfast. The magician remains suspended. On their return at eleven hundred hours his spirit is seen to have left him. He is revived with water and hot irons, and the *strappado* is employed again. He agrees he may have been a witch, but on being released recants. Alcohol is thrown onto his back and set alight. The *strappado* is used a third time, and the Questioners break for lunch.

At fourteen hundred hours, *gresillons* are applied to the magician's hands and feet. Later his calves are placed in the vice. For this purpose he is released from the pulley. He says again he may have employed spells, but afterward retracts a second time. He is placed back on the Ladder, and a plank with nails embedded pressed against his body.

The Questioners become impatient. He is hoisted up once more, this time with the weights. Squassation is decided on. His body is allowed to drop from near the ceiling. His arms are dislocated.

The accused of course must always confess. He signifies his willingness but indicates that he can no longer use a pen. This is of no importance; the document has already been prepared. He is asked when he first entered into pacts with demons. He states this was some twenty years before. He is asked where it took place. He says it was in the village where he was born. He is asked if the girl lived in the village. He says she was the daughter of a neighbor.

He is asked the names of the demons. His answers are difficult to make out. Balberith seems certain, and Verrine. Gressil is less clear, which is unfortunate. It is Gressil who is the author of impure thoughts. The name is added anyway, for the sake of completeness. He it must have been who made him lust for the girl. He says this is untrue, and that his love was pure.

He is told he must not lie, that she was his concubine. Also there were monstrous acts, performed with demons.

The accused exhibits signs of distress, rolling his head from side to side. He likens her to certain morning stars. He says she will go to Heaven, and not Hell. He repeats his request that she be instantly released.

This answer is not recorded, as being wholly blasphemous. The questions are repeated, but his responses are the same. Whips are brought; his body becomes bathed with blood.

The session is concluded at eighteen hundred hours. It has been a long day; the Questioners have earned their supper.

Next morning the interrogation is less rough. The Questioners have much experience in these matters; they know that once the answers have begun, the process becomes easier. The accused is asked the names of his accomplices. He says the innkeeper sometimes brought him food. He is asked if he means the woman Becker-Margareth. He says again that she sometimes brought him victuals.

The Questioners smile grimly, making more notes. Her case will be a simple one to prove; her aging body will be a rich source of Marks.

It has been stated a young boy was involved. The accused is asked his name. He says that it was Heinrich, but that he knew nothing of the work. He once more makes a plea for clemency.

The Questioners smile again. They ask if it was Heinrich who robbed the graves.

The magician seems surprised. He states that only one body was involved. He took the head, wishing to examine the bones of the inner ear.

The Questioners become intent. The subject is evidently beyond redemption. The lines of ticks extend themselves. *Affirmat* they write, over and again. The accused says yes.

They return to the subject of the girl. But on that alone that guilty one is obdurate. Her virtues are once more extolled. The magician seems much moved. At one point tears are seen to flow from his eyes.

The key question is reserved till last. He has stated she took no part in his affairs. Yet it is known she gave him gold, when his own supply was gone.

The accused rolls his head miserably. It was not to succor him, it was not for food. It was for the machines. He repeats once more his request that she be freed.

The Questioners are satisfied. The case is proved at last. They wish though to be certain beyond all doubt. Justice must be seen to be done. They become persuasive. He has confessed to having sex with devils, stated certain facts. They show him where it is written down. Their members were cold and painful, affording no pleasure. What was the girl's experience? Did it accord?

The accused is seen to struggle. It seems he attempts to rise, strike out. But his arms and legs already belong to Hell. The rest of him will shortly follow. The execution is fixed for seventeen thirty sharp.

The sunlight batters at his eyelids. He sits atop a cart, his wrists and ankles once more bound. A part of him is puzzled as to why. He could not run away.

The sound in his ears is like the noise of the sea. Also his eyes seem weaker than before. He screws them up against the glare. He sees the people crowding round, the buildings to either side. Tall stakes have been set up by the *Schutting*. Round it the trees are gold with autumn. Bodies hang from them, each suspended by a leg.

He lifts his hands by inches, moves them closer to his face. At first the white bone showed; now it is crusted with dull red. He wonders that a part of him can still feel sorrow. His hands worked for him throughout his life; they will not function now.

The girl appears, in her vehicle. His heart gives a bound. Her upper vestment is black and neat, her hair falls softly to her shoulders. She has been saved; she has not known the fire, the hot irons. Then he sees the eyes of the man beside her, the gun pressed to her neck. He understands that death is still her portion.

The crowd boils round. Her eyes look straight ahead; it seems her gaze is fixed on another place.

The shouts coalesce. By degrees, one word comes to dominate. "*Hexenkonigen . . . Hexenkonigen. . . .*" She does turn at that. Her face is full of something that is almost wonder. "No," she says. "It is for my yellow hair. I kept it covered, as a decent woman should; but they found me out."

Suddenly the visions once more burn and hum within his mind. He sees what he has lost, what both of them have lost. He sees what might have been: the town, the countryside, the whole world laced with magic wires. He hears the people laugh and chatter; by the thousand, by the hundred thousand, by the million. "I could have saved them," he shouts, desperate. "Were I a better man. I could have saved you. Saved your voice, to float and ring on air. I could have saved you, Silke. . . ."

The Executioner moves forward, appalled by blasphemy. The magician's head drops to his chest; and the emissary nods grimly. The Devil does not like his secrets noised abroad; at seventeen twenty hours, he breaks the condemned man's neck. The priest makes a final mark on the clipboard he carries, tucks it beneath his arm. He turns on his heel, and is quickly lost in the crowd.

☀

For three hundred years, the wires are silent by the will of God. While the world continues on its reeling way. Romanoff founds a dynasty in Russia; the first Prague Spring triggers thirty years of war. Magdeburg is sacked, America colonized. Richelieu rises to power, and England kills a king. Stenka Razin's severed head laughs at the Czar; by the Peace of Utrecht, the slave trade is cornered by the English. Persia wages war against the Moguls, and Cavendish proves hydrogen to be an element.

America breaks free of England; Charles and Montgolfier break free of earth. The Directory is established by a whiff of grape; and Boney goes to Egypt. The world's first steamship sails the Scottish Clyde, and Metternich restores the European Royals. Sadowa ensures the supremacy of Bismarck; Napoleon the Third is swept away, and Caesar's warring tribes become a nation.

The witches and their tormentors are long since gone. Spain, so feared and hated by the English, is the first to see the light. The Suprema orders the Questioners to their own racks; and everywhere men wake and rub their eyes. Round them, the Age of Reason has begun to dawn.

In 1860, Johann Reis, unsung and unremembered, begins experiments with membranes from the ears of pigs. In February of 1876, Alexander Graham Bell takes out Patent No. 174465 for the protection of a new device; his electric speaking telephone. A month later, his first transmitted sentence passes to history. "Watson, come here; I want you. . . ."

In 1879, the Reverend Henry Hunnings hits on the idea of treated carbon granules, to modulate the power supplied by batteries. And the inventor Watson devises a magneto cranked by hand. A year later, insulation is finally perfected; and New York City buries eleven thousand miles of wire. In 1959, aided by cable amplifiers, the voices finally plunge beneath the sea; today, the world owns half a billion handsets.

God has relented.

The Way of Cross and Dragon
George R. R. Martin

Born in Bayonne, New Jersey, George R. R. Martin made his first sale in 1971 and soon established himself as one of the most popular science fiction writers of the seventies. He quickly became a mainstay of the Ben Bova *Analog* with stories such as "With Morning Comes Mistfall," "And Seven Times Never Kill Man," "The Second Kind of Loneliness," "The Storms of Windhaven" (in collaboration with Lisa Tuttle, and later expanded by them into the novel *Windhaven*), "Override," and others, although he also sold to *Amazing, Fantastic, Galaxy, Orbit*, and other markets. One of his *Analog* stories, the striking novella "A Song for Lya," won him his first Hugo Award, in 1974.

By the end of the seventies, he had reached the height of his influence as a science fiction writer and was producing his best work in that category with stories such as the famous "Sandkings," his best-known story, which won both the Nebula and the Hugo in 1980 (he'd later win another Nebula in 1985 for his story "Portraits of His Children"); "The Way of Cross and Dragon," which won a Hugo Award in the same year (making Martin the first author ever to receive two Hugo Awards for fiction in the same year); "Bitterblooms"; "The Stone City"; "Starlady"; and others. These stories would be collected in *Sandkings*, one of the strongest collections of the period. By now, he had mostly moved away from *Analog*, although he would have a long sequence of stories about the droll interstellar adventures of Havalend Tuf (later collected in *Tuf Voyaging*) running throughout the eighties in the Stanley Schmidt *Analog*, as well as a few strong individual pieces such as the novella "Nightflyers"—most of his major work of the late seventies and early eighties, though, would appear in *Omni*. The late seventies and eighties also saw the publication of his memorable novel *Dying of the Light*, his only solo science fiction novel, while his stories were collected in *A Song for Lya*, *Sandkings*, *Songs of Stars and Shadows*, *Songs the Dead Men Sing*, *Nightflyers*, and *Portraits of His Children*. By the beginning of the eighties, he'd moved away from science fiction and into the horror genre, publishing the big horror novel *Fevre Dream*, and winning the Bram Stoker Award for his horror story "The Pear-Shaped Man" and the World Fantasy Award for his werewolf novella "The Skin Trade." By the end of that decade, though, the crash of the horror market and the commercial failure of his ambitious horror novel *Armageddon Rag* had driven him out of the print world and to a successful career in television instead, where for more than a decade he worked as story editor or producer on such shows as the new *Twilight Zone* and *Beauty and the Beast*.

After years away, Martin made a triumphant return to the print world with the publication in 1996 of the immensely successful fantasy novel *A Game of Thrones*, the start of his Song of Ice and Fire series. A freestanding novella taken from that work,

"Blood of the Dragon," won Martin another Hugo Award in 1997. Two further books in the Song of Ice and Fire series, *A Clash of Kings* and *A Storm of Swords*, have made it one of the most popular, acclaimed, and best-selling series in all of modern fantasy. Coming up is a new volume in the series, *A Feast for Crows*. His most recent book is a massive retrospective collection spanning the entire spectrum of his career: *GRRM: A RRetrospective*.

Martin has always been a richly romantic writer, clearly a direct descendant of the old *Planet Stories* tradition, probably influenced by Leigh Brackett in particular, although you can see strong traces of writers such as Jack Vance and Roger Zelazny in his work as well, where the emphasis is on color, adventure, exoticism, and lush romance, in a universe crowded and jostling both with alien races and human societies that have evolved toward strangeness in isolation, and where the drama is often generated by the inability of one of these cultures to clearly understand the psychology and values and motivations of another.

Evident in the award-winning story that follows is a powerful and exotic study of the future of religion and of a very special kind of heresy that echoes the age-old question "What is truth?"

"**H**eresy," he told me. The brackish waters of his pool sloshed gently.

"Another one?" I said wearily. "There are so many these days."

My Lord Commander was displeased by that comment. He shifted position heavily, sending ripples up and down the pool. One broke over the side, and a sheet of water slid across the tiles of the receiving chamber. My boots were soaked yet again. I accepted that philosophically. I had worn my worst boots, well aware that wet feet are among the inescapable consequences of paying call on Torgathon Nine-Klariis Tûn, elder of the ka-Thane people, and also Archbishop of Vess, Most

Holy Father of the Four Vows, Grand Inquisitor of the Order Militant of the Knights of Jesus Christ, and councillor to His Holiness, Pope Daryn XXI of New Rome.

"Be there as many heresies as stars in the sky, each single one is no less dangerous, Father," the Archbishop said solemnly. "As Knights of Christ, it is our ordained task to fight them one and all. And I must add that this new heresy is particularly foul."

"Yes, my Lord Commander," I replied. "I did not intend to make light of it. You have my apologies. The mission to Finnegan was most taxing. I had hoped to ask you for a leave of absence from my duties. I need a rest, a time for thought and restoration."

"Rest?" The Archbishop moved again in his pool, only a slight shift of his immense bulk, but it was enough to send a fresh sheet of water across the floor. His black, pupilless eyes blinked at me. "No, Father, I am afraid that is out of the question. Your skills and your experience are vital for this new mission." His bass tones seemed to soften somewhat then. "I have not had time to go over your reports on Finnegan," he said. "How did your work go?"

"Badly," I told him, "though ultimately I think we will prevail. The Church is strong on Finnegan. When our attempts at reconciliation were rebuffed, I put some standards into the right hands, and we were able to shut down the heretics' newspaper and broadcast facilites. Our friends also saw to it that their legal action came to nothing."

"That is not *badly*," the Archbishop said. "You won a considerable victory for the Lord."

"There were riots, my Lord Commander," I said. "More than a hundred of the heretics were killed, and a dozen of our own people. I fear there will be more violence before the matter is finished. Our priests are attacked if they so much as enter the city where the heresy has taken root. Their leaders risk their lives if they leave that city. I had hoped to avoid such hatreds, such bloodshed."

"Commendable, but not realistic," said Archbishop Torgathon. He blinked at me again, and I remembered that among people of his race that was a sign of impatience. "The blood of martyrs must sometimes be spilled, and the blood of heretics as well. What matters it if a being surrenders his life, so long as his soul is saved?"

"Indeed," I agreed. Despite his impatience, Torgathon would lecture for another hour if given a chance. That prospect dismayed me. The receiving chamber was not designed for human comfort, and I did not wish to remain any longer than necessary. The walls were damp and moldy, the air hot and humid and thick with the rancid-butter smell characteristic of the ka-Thane. My collar was chafing my neck raw, I was sweating beneath my cassock, my feet were thoroughly soaked, and my stomach was beginning to churn. I pushed ahead to the business at hand. "You say this new heresy is unusually foul, my Lord Commander?"

"It is," he said.

"Where has it started?"

"On Arion, a world some three weeks distance from Vess. A human world entirely. I cannot understand why you humans are so easily corrupted. Once a ka-Thane has found the faith, he would scarcely abandon it."

"That is well known," I said politely. I did not mention that the number of ka-Thane to find the faith was vanishingly small. They were a slow, ponderous people, and most of their vast millions showed no interest in learning any ways other than their own, or following any creed but their own ancient religion. Torgathon Nine-Klariis Tûn was an anomaly. He had been among the first converts almost two centuries ago, when Pope Vidas L had ruled that nonhumans might serve as clergy. Given his great lifespan and the iron certainty of his belief, it was no wonder that Torgathon had risen as far as he had, despite the fact that less than a thousand of his race had followed him into the Church. He had at least a century of life remaining to him. No doubt he would someday be Torgathon Cardinal Tûn, should he squelch enough heresies. The times are like that.

"We have little influence on Arion," the Archbishop was saying. His arms moved as he spoke, four ponderous clubs of mottled green-gray flesh churning the water, and the dirty white cilia around his breathing hole trembled with each word. "A few priests, a few churches, some believers, but no power to speak of. The heretics already outnumber us on this world. I rely on your intellect, your shrewdness. Turn this calamity into an opportunity. This heresy is so palpable that you can easily disprove it. Perhaps some of the deluded will turn to the true way."

"Certainly," I said. "And the nature of this heresy? What must I disprove?" It is a sad indication of my own troubled faith to add that I did not really care. I have dealt with too many heresies. Their beliefs and their questionings echo in my head and trouble my dreams at night. How can I be sure of my own faith? The very edict that had admitted Torgathon into the clergy had caused a half-dozen worlds to repudiate the Bishop of New Rome, and those who had followed that path would find a particularly ugly heresy in the massive naked (save for a damp Roman collar) alien who floated before me, and wielded the authority of the Church in four great webbed hands. Christianity is the greatest single human religion, but that means little. The non-Christians outnumber us five-to-one and there are well over seven hundred Christian sects, some almost as large as the One True Interstellar Catholic Church of Earth and the Thousand Worlds. Even Daryn XXI, powerful as he is, is only one of seven to claim the title of Pope. My own belief was strong once, but I have moved too long among heretics and nonbelievers, and even my prayers do not make the doubts go away now. So it was that I felt no horror—only a sudden intellectual interest—when the Archbishop told me the nature of the heresy in Arion.

"They have made a saint," he said, "out of Judas Iscariot."

As a senior in the Knights Inquisitor, I command my own starship, which it pleases me to call the *Truth of Christ*. Before the craft was assigned to me it was named the *St. Thomas*, after the apostle, but I did not feel a saint notorious for doubting was an appropriate patron for a ship enlisted in the fight against heresy. I have no duties aboard the *Truth*, which is crewed by six brothers and sisters of the Order of St. Christopher the Far-Travelling, and captained by a young woman I hired away from a merchant trader.

I was therefore able to devote the entire three-week voyage from Vess to Arion to study of the heretical Bible, a copy which had been given to me by the Archbishop's administrative assistant. It was a thick, heavy, handsome book, bound in dark leather, its pages tipped with gold leaf, with many splendid interior illustrations in full color with holographic enhancement. Remarkable work clearly done by someone who loved the all-but-forgotten art of book-making. The paintings reproduced inside—the originals were to be found on the walls of the House of St. Judas on Arion, I gathered—were masterful, if blasphemous, as much high art as the Tammerwens and RoHallidays that adorn the Great Cathedral of St. John in New Rome.

Inside the book bore an imprimatur indicating that it had been approved by Lukyan Judasson, First Scholar of the Order of St. Judas Iscariot.

It was called *The Way of Cross and Dragon*.

I read it as the *Truth of Christ* slid between the stars, at first taking copious notes to better understand the heresy I must fight, but later simply absorbed by the strange, convoluted, grotesque story it told. The words of text had passion and power and poetry.

Thus it was that I first encountered the striking figure of St. Judas Iscariot, a complex, ambitious, contradictory, and altogether extraordinary human being.

He was born of a whore in the fabled ancient city-state of Babylon on the same day that the savior was born in Bethlehem, and he spent his childhood in the alleys and gutters, selling his own body when he had to, pimping when he was older. As a youth he began to experiment with the dark arts, and before the age of twenty he was a skilled necromancer. That was when he became Judas the Dragon-Tamer, the first and only man to bend to his will the most fearsome of God's creatures, the great winged fire-lizards of Old Earth. The book held a marvelous painting of Judas in some great dank cavern, his eyes aflame as he wielded a glowing lash to keep at bay a mountainous green-gold dragon. Beneath his arm is a woven basket, its lid slightly ajar, and the tiny scaled heads of three dragon chicks are peering from within. A fourth infant dragon is crawling up his sleeve. That was in the first chapter of his life.

In the second, he was Judas the Conqueror, Judas the Dragon-King, Judas of Babylon, the Great Usurper. Astride the greatest of his dragons, with an iron crown on his head and a sword in his hand, he made Babylon the Capital of the greatest empire Old Earth had ever known, a realm that stretched from Spain to India. He reigned from a dragon throne amid the Hanging Gardens he had caused to be constructed, and it was there he sat when he tried Jesus of Nazareth, the troublemaking prophet who had been dragged before him bound and bleeding. Judas was not a patient man, and he made Christ bleed still more before he was through with Him. And when Jesus would not answer his questions, Judas—contemptuous—had Him cast back out into the streets. But first he ordered his guards to cut off Christ's legs. "Healer," he said, "Heal thyself."

Then came the Repentance, the vision in the night, and Judas Iscariot gave up his crown and his dark arts and his riches, to follow the man he had crippled. Despised and taunted by those he had tyrannized, Judas became the Legs of the Lord, and for a year carried Jesus on his back to the far corners of the realm he once ruled. When Jesus did finally heal Himself, then Judas walked at his side, and from that time forth he was Jesus' trusted friend and counselor, the first and foremost of the Twelve. Finally Jesus gave Judas the gift of tongues, recalled and sanctified the dragons that Judas had sent away, and sent his disciple forth on a solitary ministry across the oceans, "to spread My Word where I cannot go."

There came a day when the sun went dark at noon, and the ground trembled, and Judas swung his dragon around on ponderous wings and flew back across the raging seas. But when he reached the city of Jerusalem, he found Christ dead on the cross.

In that moment his faith faltered, and for the next three days the Great Wrath of Judas was like a storm across the ancient world. His dragons razed the Temple in Jerusalem, and drove the people forth from the city, and struck as well at the great seats of power in Rome and Babylon. And when he found the others of the Twelve and questioned them and learned of how the one named Simon-called-Peter had three times betrayed the Lord, he strangled Peter with his own hands and fed the corpse to his dragons. Then he sent those dragons forth to start fires throughout the world, funeral pyres for Jesus of Nazareth.

And Jesus rose on the third day, and Judas wept, but his tears could not turn Christ's anger, for in his wrath he had betrayed all of Christ's teachings.

So Jesus called back the dragons, and they came, and everywhere the fires went out. And from their bellies he called forth Peter and made him whole again, and gave him dominion over the Church.

Then the dragons died, and so, too, did all dragons everywhere, for they were the living sigil of the power and wisdom of Judas Iscariot, who had sinned greatly. And He took from Judas the gift of tongues and power of healing He had given, and even his eyesight, for Judas had acted as a man blind (there was a fine painting of the blinded Judas weeping over the bodies of his dragons). And He told Judas that for long ages he would be remembered only as Betrayer, and people would curse his name, and all that he had been and done would be forgotten.

But then, because Judas had loved Him so, Christ gave him a boon; an extended life, during which he might travel and think on his sins and finally come to forgiveness, and only then die.

And that was the beginning of the last chapter in the life of Judas Iscariot, but it was a very long chapter indeed. Once dragon king, once the friend of Christ, now he became only a blind traveler, outcast and friendless, wandering all the cold roads of the Earth, living even when all the cities and people and things he had known were dead. And Peter, the first Pope and ever his enemy, spread far and wide the tale of how Judas had sold Christ for thirty pieces of silver, until Judas dared not even use his true name. For a time he called himself just Wandering Ju', and afterwards many other names. He lived more than a thousand years, and became a preacher, and a healer, and a lover of animals, and was hunted and persecuted when the Church that Peter had founded became bloated and corrupt. But he had a great deal of time, and at last he found wisdom and a sense of peace, and finally Jesus came to him on a long-postponed deathbed, and they were reconciled, and Judas wept once again. And before he died, Christ promised that he would permit a few to remember who and what Judas had been, and that with the passage of centuries the news would spread, until finally Peter's Lie was displaced and forgotten.

Such was the life of St. Judas Iscariot, as related in *The Way of Cross and Dragon*. His teachings were there as well, and the apocryphal books he had allegedly written.

When I had finished the volume, I lent it to Arla-k-Bau, the captain of the *Truth of Christ*. Arla was a gaunt, pragmatic woman of no particular faith, but I valued her opinion. The others of my crew, the good sisters and brothers of St. Christopher, would only have echoed the Archbishop's religious horror.

"Interesting," Arla said when she returned the book to me.

I chuckled. "Is that all?"

She shrugged. "It makes a nice story. An easier read than your Bible, Damien, and more dramatic as well."

"True," I admitted. "But it's absurd. An unbelievable tangle of doctrine, apocrypha, mythology, and superstition. Entertaining, yes, certainly. Imaginative, even daring. But ridiculous, don't you think? How can you credit dragons? A legless Christ? Peter being pieced together after being devoured by four monsters?"

Arla's grin was taunting. "Is that any sillier than water changing into wine, or Christ walking on the waves, or a man living in the belly of a fish?" Arla-k-Bau liked to jab at me. It had been a scandal when I selected a nonbeliever as my captain, but she was very good at her job, and I liked her around to keep me sharp. She had a good mind, Arla did, and I valued that more than blind obedience. Perhaps that was a sin in me.

"There is a difference," I said.

"Is there?" she snapped back. Her eyes saw through my masks. "Ah, Damien, admit it. You rather liked this book."

I cleared my throat. "It piqued my interest," I acknowledged. I had to justify myself. "You know the kind of matter I deal with ordinarily. Dreary little doctrinal deviations, obscure quibblings on theology somehow blown all out of proportion, bald-faced political maneuverings designed to set some ambitious planetary bishop up as a new pope, or wring some concession or other from New Rome or Vess. The war is endless, but the battles are dull and dirty. They exhaust me, spiritually, emotionally, physically. Afterwards I feel drained and guilty." I tapped the book's leather cover. "This is different. The heresy must be crushed, of course, but I admit that I am anxious to meet this Lukyan Judasson."

"The artwork is lovely as well," Arla said, flipping through the pages of *The Way of Cross and Dragon* and stopping to study one especially striking plate. Judas weeping over his dragons, I think. I smiled to see that it had affected her as much as me. Then I frowned.

That was the first inkling I had of the difficulties ahead.

So it was that the *Truth of Christ* came to the porcelain city Ammadon on the world of Arion, where the Order of St. Judas Iscariot kept its House.

Arion was a pleasant, gentle world, inhabited for these past three centuries. Its population was under nine million; Ammadon, the only real city, was home to two of those millions. The technological level was medium high, but chiefly imported. Arion had little industry and was not an innovative world, except perhaps artistically. The arts were quite important here, flourishing and vital. Religious freedom was a basic tenet of the society, but Arion was not a religious world either, and the majority of the populace lived devoutly secular lives. The most popular religion was Aestheticism, which hardly counts as a religion at all. There were also Taoists, Erikaners, Old True Christers, and Children of the Dreamer, plus a dozen lesser sects.

And finally there were nine churches of the One True Interstellar Catholic faith. There had been twelve.

The other three were now houses of Arion's fastest-growing faith, the Order of St. Judas Iscariot, which also had a dozen newly built churches of its own.

The Bishop of Arion was a dark, severe man with close-cropped black hair who was not at all happy to see me. "Damien Har Venis!" he exclaimed in some wonder when I called on him at his residence. "We have heard of you, of course, but I never thought to meet or host you. Our numbers are small here—"

"And growing smaller," I said, "a matter of some concern to my Lord Commander, Archbishop Torgathon. Apparently you are less troubled, Excellency, since you did not see fit to report the activities of this sect of Judas worshippers."

He looked briefly angry at the rebuke, but quickly swallowed his temper. Even a bishop can fear a Knight Inquisitor. "We are concerned, of course," he said. "We do all we can to combat the heresy. If you have advice that will help us, I will be glad to listen."

"I am an Inquisitor of the Order Militant of the Knights of Jesus Christ," I said bluntly. "I do not give advice, Excellency. I take action. To that end I was sent to Arion and that is what I shall do. Now, tell me what you know about this heresy, and this First Scholar, this Lukyan Judasson."

"Of course, Father Damien," the Bishop began. He signaled for a servant to bring us a tray of wine and cheese, and began to summarize the short, but explosive, history of the Judas cult. I listened, polishing my nails on the crimson lapel of my jacket, until the black paint gleamed brilliantly, interrupting from time to time with a question. Before he had half finished, I was determined to vist Lukyan personally. It seemed the best course of action.

And I had wanted to do it all along.

Appearances were important on Arion, I gathered, and I deemed it necessary to impress Lukyan with my self and my station. I wore my best boots, sleek dark handmade boots of Roman leather that had never seen the inside of Torgathon's receiving chamber, and a severe black suit with deep burgundy lapels and stiff collar. Around my neck was a splendid crucifix of pure gold; my collarpin was a matching golden sword, the sigil of the Knights Inquisitor. Brother Denis painted my nails carefully, all black as ebon, and darkened my eyes as well, and used a fine white powder on my face. When I glanced in the mirror, I frightened even myself. I smiled, but only briefly. It ruined the effect.

I walked to the House of St. Judas Iscariot. The streets of Ammadon were wide and spacious and golden, lined by scarlet trees called whisperwinds whose long, drooping tendrils did indeed seem to whisper secrets to the gentle breeze. Sister Judith came with me. She is a small woman, slight of build even in the cowled coveralls of the Order of St. Christopher. Her face is meek and kind, her eyes wide and youthful and innocent. I find her useful. Four times now she has killed those who attempted to assault me.

The House itself was newly built. Rambling and stately, it rose from amid gardens of small bright flowers and seas of golden grass, and the gardens were surrounded by a high wall. Murals covered both the outer wall around the property and the exterior of the building itself. I recognized a few of them from *The Way of Cross and Dragon*, and stopped briefly to admire them before walking on through the main gate. No one tried to stop us. There were no guards, not even a receptionist. Within the walls, men and women strolled languidly through the flowers, or sat on benches beneath silverwoods and whisperwinds.

Sister Judith and I paused, then made our way directly to the House itself.

We had just started up the steps when a man appeared from within, and stood waiting in the doorway. He was blond, and fat, with a great wiry beard that framed a slow smile, and he wore a flimsy robe that fell to his sandaled feet, and on the robe were dragons, dragons bearing the silhouette of a man holding a cross.

When I reached the top of the steps, he bowed to me. "Father Damien Har Veris of the Knights Inquisitor," he said. His smile widened. "I greet you in the name of Jesus, and St. Judas. I am Lukyan."

I made a note to myself to find out which of the Bishop's staff was feeding information to the Judas cult, but my composure did not break. I have been a Knight Inquisitor for a long, long time. "Father Lukyan Mo," I said, taking his hand. "I have questions to ask of you." I did not smile.

He did. "I thought you might," he said.

Lukyan's office was large but Spartan. Heretics often have a simplicity that the officers of the true Church seem to have lost. He did have one indulgence, however. Dominating the wall behind his desk/console was the painting I had already fallen in love with: the blinded Judas weeping over his dragons.

Lukyan sat down heavily and motioned me to a second chair. We had left Sister Judith outside in the waiting chamber. "I prefer to stand, Father Lukyan," I said, knowing it gave me an advantage.

"Just Lukyan," he said. "Or Luke, if you prefer. We have little use for hierarchy here."

"You are Father Lukyan Mo, born here on Arion, educated in the seminary on Cathaday, a former priest of the One True Interstellar Catholic Church of Earth and the Thousand Worlds," I said. "I will address you as befits your station, Father. I expect you to reciprocate. Is that understood?"

"Oh, yes," he said amiably.

"I am empowered to strip you of your right to perform the sacraments, to order you shunned and excommunicated for this heresy you have formulated. On certain worlds I could even order your death."

"But not on Arion," Lukyan said quickly. "We're very tolerant here. Besides, we outnumber you." He smiled. "As for the rest, well, I don't perform those sacraments much anyway, you know. Not for years. I'm First Scholar now. A teacher, a thinker. I show others the way, help them find the faith. Excommunicate me if it will make you happy, Father Damien. Happiness is what all of us seek."

"You have given up the faith then, Father Lukyan," I said. I deposited my copy of *The Way of Cross and Dragon* on his desk. "But I see you have found a new one." Now I did smile, but it was all ice, all menace, all mockery. "A more ridiculous creed I have yet to encounter. I suppose you will tell me that you have spoken to God, that he trusted you with this new revelation, so that you might clear the good name, such that it is, of Holy Judas?"

Now Lukyan's smile was very broad indeed. He picked up the book and beamed at me. "Oh, no," he said. "No, I made it all up."

That stopped me. "What?"

"I made it all up," he repeated. He hefted the book fondly. "I drew on many sources, of course, especially the Bible, but I do think of *Cross and Dragon* mostly as my own work. It's rather good, don't you agree? Of course, I could hardly put my name on it, proud as I am of it, but I did include my imprimatur. Did you notice that? It was the closest I dared come to a by-line."

I was only speechless for a moment. Then I grimaced. "You startle me," I admitted. "I expected to find an inventive madman, some poor self-deluded fool firm in his belief that he had spoken to God. I've dealt with such fanatics before. Instead, I find a cheerful cynic who has invented a religion for his own profit. I think I prefer the fanatics. You are beneath contempt, Father Lukyan. You will burn in hell for eternity."

"I doubt it," Lukyan said, "but you do mistake me, Father Damien. I am no cynic, nor do I profit from my dear St. Judas. Truthfully, I lived more comfortably as a priest of your own church. I do this because it is my vocation."

I sat down. "You confuse me," I said. "Explain."

"Now I am going to tell you the Truth," he said. He said it in an odd way, almost as a cant. "I am a liar," he added.

"You want to confuse me with a child's paradoxes," I snapped.

"No, no," he smiled. "A *Liar*. With a capital. It is an organization, Father Damien. A religion, you might call it. A great and powerful faith. And I am the smallest part of it."

"I know of no such church," I said.

"Oh, no, you wouldn't. It's secret. It has to be. You can understand that, can't you? People don't like being lied to."

"I do not like being lied to," I said.

Lukyan looked wounded. "I told you this would be the truth, didn't I? When a Liar says that, you can believe him. How else could we trust each other?"

"There are many of you," I said. I was starting to think that Lukyan was a madman after all, as fanatic as any heretic, but in a more complex way. Here was a heresy within a heresy, but I recognized my duty; to find the truth of things, and set them right.

"Many of us," Lukyan said, smiling. "You would be surprised, Father Damien, really you would. But there are some things I dare not tell you."

"Tell me what you dare, then."

"Happily," said Lukyan Judasson. "We Liars, like all other religions, have several truths that we take on faith. Faith is always required. There are some things that cannot be proven. We believe that life is worth living. That is an article of faith. The purpose of life is to live, to resist death, perhaps to defy entropy."

"Go on," I said, interested despite myself.

"We also believe that happiness is a good, something to be sought after."

"The Church does not oppose happiness," I said dryly.

"I wonder," Lukyan said. "But let's not quibble. Whatever the Church's position on happiness, it does preach belief in an afterlife, in a supreme being, and a complex moral code."

"True."

"The Liars believe in no afterlife, no God. We see the universe as it *is*, Father Damien, and these naked truths are cruel ones. We who believe in life, and treasure it, will die. Afterwards there will be nothing, eternal emptiness, blackness, nonexistence. In our living there has been no purpose, no poetry, no meaning. Nor do our deaths possess these qualities. When we are gone, the universe will not long remember us, and shortly it will be as if we had never lived at all. Our worlds and our universe will not long outlive us. Ultimately entropy will consume all, and our puny efforts cannot stay that awful end. It will be gone. It has never been. It has never mattered. The universe itself is doomed, transient, uncaring."

I slid back in my chair, and a shiver went through me as I listened to poor Lukyan's dark words. I found myself fingering my crucifix. "A bleak philosophy," I said, "as well as a false one. I have had that fearful vision myself. I think all of us do, at some point. But it is not so, Father. My faith sustains me against such nihilism. It is a shield against despair."

"Oh, I know that, my friend, my Knight Inquisitor," Lukyan said. "I'm glad to see you understand so well. You are almost one of us already."

I frowned.

"You've touched the heart of it," Lukyan continued. "The truths, the great truths—and most of the lesser ones as well—they are unbearable for most men. We find our shield in faith. Your faith, my faith, any faith. It doesn't matter, so long as we *believe*, really and truly believe, in whatever lie we cling to." He fingered the ragged edges of his great blond beard. "Our psychs have always told us that believers are the happy ones, you know. They may believe in Christ or Buddha or Erika Stormjones, in reincarnation or immortality or nature, in the power of love or the platform of a political faction, but it all comes to the same thing. They believe. They are happy. It is the ones who have seen the truth who despair, and kill themselves. The truths are so vast, the faiths so little, so poorly made, so riddled with error and contradiction. We see around them and through them, and then we feel the weight of darkness on us, and we can no longer be happy."

I am not a slow man. I knew, by then, where Lukyan Judasson was going. "Your Liars invent faiths."

He smiled. "Of all sorts. Not only religions. Think of it. We know truth for the cruel instrument it is. Beauty is infinitely preferable to truth. We invent beauty. Faiths, political movements, high ideals, belief in love and fellowship. All of them are lies. We tell those lies, and others, endless others. We improve on history and myth and religion, make each more beautiful, better, easier to believe in. Our lies are not perfect, of course. The truths are too big. But perhaps someday we will find one great lie that all humanity can use. Until then, a thousand small lies will do."

"I think I do not care for your Liars very much," I said with a cold, even fervor. "My whole life has been a quest for truth."

Lukyan was indulgent. "Father Damien Har Veris, Knight Inquisitor, I know you better than that. You are a Liar yourself. You do good work. You ship from world to world, and on each you destroy the foolish, the rebels, the questioners who would bring down the edifice of the vast lie that you serve."

"If my lie is so admirable," I said, "then why have you abandoned it?"

"A religion must fit its culture and society, work with them, not against them. If there is conflict, contradiction, then the lie breaks down, and the faith falters. Your Church is good for many worlds, Father, but not for Arion. Life is too kind here, and your faith is stern. Here we love beauty, and your faith offers too little. So we have improved it. We studied this world for a long time. We know its psychological profile. St. Judas will thrive here. He offers drama, and color, and much beauty—the aesthetics are admirable. His is a tragedy with a happy ending, and Arion dotes on such stories. And the dragons are a nice touch. I think your own Church ought to find a way to work in dragons. They are marvelous creatures."

"Mythical," I said.

"Hardly," he replied. "Look it up." He grinned at me. "You see, really, it all comes back to faith. Can you really know what happened three thousand years ago? You have one Judas, I have another. Both of us have books. Is yours true? Can you really believe that? I have only been admitted to the first circle of the order of Liars, so I do not know all our secrets, but I know that we are very old. It would not surprise me to learn that the gospels were written by men very much like me. Perhaps there never was a Judas at all. Or a Jesus."

"I have faith that is not so," I said.

"There are a hundred people in this building who have a deep and very real faith in St. Judas, and the way of cross and dragon," Lukyan said. "Faith is a very good thing. Do you know that the suicide rate on Arion has decreased by almost a third since the Order of St. Judas was founded?"

I remember rising very slowly from my chair. "You are fanatic as any heretic I have ever met, Lukyan Judasson," I told him. "I pity you the loss of your faith."

Lukyan rose with me. "Pity yourself, Damien Har Veris," he said. "I have found a new faith and a new cause, and I am a happy man. You, my dear friend, are tortured and miserable."

"*That is a lie!*" I am afraid I screamed.

"Come with me," Lukyan said. He touched a panel on his wall, and the great painting of Judas weeping over his dragons slid up out of sight, and there was a stairway leading down into the ground. "Follow me," he said.

In the cellar was a great glass vat full of pale green fluid, and in it a thing was floating, a thing very like an ancient embryo, aged and infantile at the same time, naked, with a huge head and a tiny atrophied body. Tubes ran from its arms and legs and genitals, connecting it to the machinery that kept it alive.

When Lukyan turned on the lights, it opened its eyes. They were large and dark and they looked into my soul.

"This is my colleague," Lukyan said, patting the side of the vat, "Jon Azure Cross, a Liar of the fourth circle."

"And a telepath," I said with a sick certainty. I had led pogroms against other telepaths, children mostly, on other worlds. The Church teaches that the psionic powers are a trap of Satan's. They are not mentioned in the Bible, I have never felt good about those killings.

"Jon read you the moment you entered the compound," Lukyan said, "and notified me. Only a few of us know that he is here. He helps us lie most efficiently. He knows when faith is true, and when it is feigned. I have an implant in my skull. Jon can talk to me at all times. It was he who initially recruited me into the Liars. He knew my faith was hollow. He felt the depth of my despair."

Then the thing in the tank spoke, its metallic voice coming from a speaker-grill in the base of the machine that nurtured it. *"And I feel yours, Damien Har Veris, empty priest. Inquisitor, you have asked too many questions. You are sick at heart, and tired, and you do not believe. Join us, Damien. You have been a Liar for a long, long time!"*

For a moment I hesitated, looking deep into myself, wondering what it was I did believe. I searched for my faith, the fire that had once sustained me, the certainty in the teachings of the Church, the presence of Christ within me. I found none of it, none. I was empty inside, burned out, full of questions and pain. But as I was about to answer Jon Azure Cross and the smiling Lukyan Judasson, I found something else, something I *did* believe in, had always believed in.

Truth.

I believed in truth, even when it hurt.

"He is lost to us," said the telepath with the mocking name of Cross.

Lukyan's smile faded. "Oh, really? I had hoped you would be one of us, Damien. You seemed ready."

I was suddenly afraid, and considered sprinting up the stairs to Sister Judith. Lukyan had told me so very much, and now I had rejected them.

The telepath felt my fear. *"You cannot hurt us, Damien,"* it said. *"Go in peace. Lukyan told you nothing."*

Lukyan was frowning. "I told him a good deal, Jon," he said.

"Yes. But can he trust the words of such a Liar as you?" The small misshapen mouth of the thing in the vat twitched in a smile, and its great eyes closed, and Lukyan Judasson sighed and led me up the stairs.

It was not until some years later that I realized it was Jon Azure Cross who was lying, and the victim of his lie was Lukyan. I *could* hurt them. I did.

It was almost simple. The Bishop had friends in government and media. With some money in the right places, I made some friends of my own. Then I exposed Cross in his cellar, charging that he had used his psionic powers to tamper with the minds of Lukyan's followers. My friends were receptive to the charges. The guardians conducted a raid, took the telepath Cross into custody, and later tried him.

He was innocent, of course. My charge was nonsense; human telepaths can read minds in close proximity, but seldom anything more. But they are rare, and much feared, and Cross was hideous enough so that it was easy to make him a victim of superstition. In the end, he was acquitted, and he left the city Ammadon and perhaps Arion itself, bound for regions unknown.

But it had never been my intention to convict him. The charge was enough. The cracks began to show in the lie that he and Lukyan had built together. Faith is hard to come by, and easy to lose, and the merest doubt can begin to erode even the strongest foundation of belief.

The Bishop and I labored together to sow further doubts. It was not as easy as I might have thought. The Liars had done their work well. Ammadon, like most civilized cities, had a great pool of knowledge, a computer system that linked the schools and universities and libraries together, and made their combined wisdom available to any who needed it.

But when I checked, I soon discovered that the histories of Rome and Babylon had been subtly reshaped, and there were three listings for Judas Iscariot—one for the betrayer, one for the saint, and one for the conqueror/king of Babylon. His name was also mentioned in connection with the Hanging Gardens, and there is an entry for a so-called Codex Judas.

And according to the Ammadon library, dragons became extinct on Old Earth around the time of Christ.

We purged all those lies finally, wiped them from the memories of the computers, though we had to cite authorities on a half-dozen non-Christian worlds before the librarians and academics would credit that the differences were anything more than a question of religious preference.

By then the Order of St. Judas had withered in the glare of exposure. Lukyan Judasson had grown gaunt and angry, and at least half of his churches had closed.

The heresy never died completely, of course. There are always those who believe no matter what. And so to this day *The Way of Cross and Dragon* is read on Arion, in the porcelain city Ammadon, amid murmuring whisperwinds.

Arla-k-Bau and the *Truth of Christ* carried me back to Vess a year after my departure, and Archbishop Torgathon finally gave me the rest I had asked for, before sending me out to fight still other heresies. So I had my victory, and the Church continued on much as before, and the Order of St. Judas Isacriot was crushed and diminished. The telepath Jon Azure Cross had been wrong, I thought then. He had sadly underestimated the power of a Knight Inquisitor.

Later, though, I remembered his words.

You cannot hurt us, Damien.

Us?

The Order of St. Judas? Or the Liars?

He lied, I think, deliberately, knowing I would go forth and destroy the way of cross and dragon, knowing, too, that I could not touch the Liars, would not even dare mention them. How could I? Who would credit it? A grand star-spanning conspiracy as old as history? It reeks of paranoia, and I had no proof at all.

The telepath lied for Lukyan's benefit, so he would let me go. I am cetain of that now. Cross risked much to snare me. Failing, he was willing to sacrifice Lukyan Judasson and his lie, pawns in some greater game.

So I left, and I carried within me the knowledge that I was empty of faith, but for a blind faith in truth. A truth I could no longer find in my Church.

I grew certain of that in my year of rest, which I spent reading and studying on Vess and Cathaday and Celia's World. Finally I returned to the Archbishop's receiving room, and stood again before Torgathon Nine-Klariis Tûn in my very worst pair of boots. "My Lord Commander," I said to him, "I can accept no further assignments. I ask that I be retired from active service."

"For what cause?" Torgathon rumbled, splashing feebly.

"I have lost the faith," I said to him, simply.

He regarded me for a long time, his pupilless eyes blinking. At last he said, "Your faith is a matter between you and your confessor. I care only about your results. You have done good work, Damien. You may not retire, and we will not allow you to resign."

The truth will set us free.

But freedom is cold, and empty, and frightening, and lies can often be warm and beautiful.

Last year the Church finally granted me a new and better ship. I named this one *Dragon*.

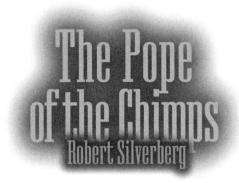

The Pope of the Chimps
Robert Silverberg

Sometimes science itself can become a breeding ground for superstition—especially when the scientists become gods!

Robert Silverberg is one of the most famous science fiction writers of modern times, with dozens of novels, anthologies, and collections to his credit. As both writer and editor (he was editor of the original anthology series New Dimensions, perhaps the most acclaimed anthology series of its era), Silverberg was one of the most influential figures of the Post–New Wave era of the seventies, and continues to be at the forefront of the field to this very day, having won a total of five Nebula Awards and four Hugo Awards, plus SFWA's prestigious Grandmaster Award.

His novels include the acclaimed *Dying Inside, Lord Valentine's Castle, The Book of Skulls, Downward to the Earth, Tower of Glass, Son of Man, Nightwings, The World Inside, Born with the Dead, Shadrack in the Furnace, Thorns, Up the Line, The Man in the Maze, Tom O' Bedlam, Star of Gypsies, At Winter's End, The Face of the*

Waters, Kingdoms of the Wall, Hot Sky at Morning, The Alien Years, Lord Prestimion, Mountains of Majipoor, and two novel-length expansions of famous Isaac Asimov stories, *Nightfall* and *The Ugly Little Boy.* His collections include *Unfamiliar Territory, Capricorn Games, Majipoor Chronicles, The Best of Robert Silverberg, At the Conglomeroid Cocktail Party, Beyond the Safe Zone,* and a massive retrospective collection, *The Collected Stories of Robert Silverberg, Volume One: Secret Sharers.* His reprint anthologies are far too numerous to list here, but include *The Science Fiction Hall of Fame, Volume One* and the distinguished Alpha series, among dozens of others. His most recent books are the novel *The Long Way Home* and the mosaic novel *Roma Eterna.* Upcoming is a major retrospective collection, *Phases of the Moon: Stories from Six Decades.* He lives with his wife, writer Karen Haber, in Oakland, California.

Early last month Vendelmans and I were alone with the chimps in the compound when suddenly he said, "I'm going to faint." It was a sizzling May morning, but Vendelmans had never shown any sign of noticing unusual heat, let alone suffering from it. I was busy talking to Leo and Mimsy and Mimsy's daughter Muffin, and I registered Vendelmans's remark without doing anything about it. When you're intensely into talking by sign language, as we are in the project, you sometimes tend not to pay a lot of attention to spoken words.

But then Leo began to sign the trouble sign at me, and I turned around and saw Vendelmans down on his knees in the grass, white-faced, gasping, covered with sweat. A few of the chimpanzees who aren't as sensitive to humans as Leo is thought it was a game and began to pantomime him, knuckles to the ground and bodies going limp. "Sick—" Vendelmans said. "Feel—terrible—"

I called for help, and Gonzo took his left arm and Kong took his

right and somehow, big as he was, we managed to get him out of the
compound and up the hill to headquarters. By then he was complaining
about sharp pains in his back and under his arms, and I realized that it
wasn't just heat prostration. Within a week the diagnosis was in.

Leukemia.

They put him on chemotherapy and hormones, and after ten days
he was back with the project, looking cocky. "They've stabilized it,"
he told everyone. "It's in remission and I might have ten or twenty
years left, or even more. I'm going to carry on with my work."

But he was gaunt and pale, with a tremor in his hands, and it was
a frightful thing to have him among us. He might have been fooling
himself, though I doubted it, but he wasn't fooling any of us: to us he
was a memento mori, a walking death's-head-and-crossbones. That
laymen think scientists are any more casual about such things than
anyone else is something I blame Hollywood for. It is not easy to go
about your daily work with a dying man at your side—or a dying
man's wife, for Judy Vendelmans showed in her frightened eyes all the
grief that Hal Vendelmans himself was repressing. She was going to
lose a beloved husband unexpectedly soon and she hadn't had time to
adjust to it and her pain was impossible to ignore. Besides, the nature
of Vendelmans's dyingness was particularly unsettling because he had
been so big and robust and outgoing, a true Rabelaisian figure, and
somehow between one moment and the next he was transformed into
a wraith. "The finger of God," Dave Yost said. "A quick flick of Zeus's
pinkie and Hal shrivels like cellophane in a fireplace." Vendelmans was
not yet forty.

The chimps suspected something, too.

Some of them, such as Leo and Ramona, are fifth-generation
signers, bred for alpha intelligence, and they pick up subtleties and
nuances very well. "Almost human," visitors like to say of them. We
dislike that tag, because the important thing about chimpanzees is
that they *aren't* human, that they are an alien intelligent species; but

yet I know what people mean. The brightest of the chimps saw right away that something was amiss with Vendelmans, and started making odd remarks. "Big one rotten banana," said Ramona to Mimsy while I was nearby. "He getting empty," Leo said to me as Vendelmans stumbled past us. Chimp metaphors never cease to amaze me. And Gonzo asked him outright: "You go away soon?"

"Go away" is not the chimp euphemism for death. So far as our animals know, no human being has ever died. Chimps die. Human beings go away. We have kept things on that basis from the beginning, not intentionally at first, but such arrangements have a way of institutionalizing themselves. The first member of the group to die was Roger Nixon, in an automobile accident in the early years of the project long before my time here, and apparently no one wanted to confuse or disturb the animals by explaining what had happened to him, so no explanations were offered. My second or third year here, Tim Lippinger was killed in a ski-lift failure, and again it seemed easier not to go into details with them. And by the time of Will Bechstein's death in that helicopter crack-up four years ago the policy was explicit: we chose not to regard his disappearance from the group as death, but mere going away, as if he had only retired. The chimps do understand death, of course. They may even equate it with going away, as Gonzo's question suggests. But if they do, they surely see human death as something quite different from chimpanzee death—a translation to another state of being, an ascent on a chariot of fire. Yost believes that they have no comprehension of human death at all, that they think we are immortal, that they think we are gods.

Vendelmans now no longer pretends that he isn't dying. The leukemia is plainly acute, and he deteriorates physically from day to day. His original this-isn't-actually-happening attitude has been replaced by a kind of sullen, angry acceptance. It is only the fourth week since the onset of the ailment and soon he'll have to enter the hospital.

And he wants to tell the chimps that he's going to die.

"They don't know that human beings can die," Yost said.

"Then it's time they found out," Vendelmans snapped. "Why perpetuate a load of mythological bullshit about us? Why let them think we're gods? Tell them outright that I'm going to die, the way old Egbert died and Salami and Mortimer."

"But they all died naturally," Jan Morton said.

"And I'm not dying naturally?"

She became terribly flustered. "Of old age, I mean. Their life cycles clearly and understandably came to an end and they died and the chimps understood it. Whereas you—" She faltered.

"—am dying a monstrous and terrible death midway through my life," Vendelmans said, and started to break down and recovered with a fierce effort, and Jan began to cry, and it was generally a bad scene from which Vendelmans saved us by going on, "It should be of philosophical importance to the project to discover how the chimps react to a revaluation of the human metaphysic. We've ducked every chance we've had to help them understand the nature of mortality. Now I propose we use me to teach them that humans are subject to the same laws they are. That we are not gods."

"And that gods exist," said Yost, "who are capricious and unfathomable and to whom we ourselves are as less than chimps."

Vendelmans shrugged. "They don't need to hear all that now. But it's time they understood what we are. Or rather, it's time that we learned how much they already understand. Use my death as a way of finding out. It's the first time they've been in the presence of a human who's actually in the process of dying. The other times one of us has died, it's always been in some sort of accident."

Burt Christensen said, "Hal, have you already told them anything about—"

"No," Vendelmans said. "Of course not. Not a word. But I see them talking to each other. They know."

We discussed it far into the night. The question needed careful examination because of the far-reaching consequences of any change we might make in the metaphysical givens of our animals. These chimps have lived in a closed environment here for decades, and the culture they have evolved is a product of what we have chosen to teach them, compounded by their own innate chimpness plus whatever we have unknowingly transmitted to them about ourselves or them. Any radical conceptual material we offer them must be weighed thoughtfully, because its effects will be irreversible, and those who succeed us in this community will be unforgiving if we do anything stupidly premature. If the plan is to observe a community of intelligent primates over a period of many human generations, studying the changes in their intellectual capacity as their linguistic skills increase, then we must at all times take care to let them find things out for themselves, rather than skewing our data by giving the chimps more than their current concept-processing abilities may be able to handle.

On the other hand, Vendelmans was dying right now, allowing us a dramatic opportunity to convey the concept of human mortality. We had at best a week or two to make use of that opportunity: then it might be years before the next chance.

"What are you worried about?" Vendelmans demanded.

Yost said, "Do you fear dying, Hal?"

"Dying makes me angry. I don't fear it; but I still have things to do, and I won't be able to do them. Why do you ask?"

"Because so far as we know the chimps see death—chimp death—

as simply part of the great cycle of events, like the darkness that comes after the daylight. But human death is going to come as a revelation to them, a shock. And if they pick up from you any sense of fear or even anger over your dying, who knows what impact that will have on their way of thought?"

"Exactly. *Who knows?* I offer you a chance to find out!"

By a narrow margin, finally we voted to let Hal Vendelmans share his death with the chimpanzees. Nearly all of us had reservations about that. But plainly Vendelmans was determined to have a useful death, a meaningful death; the only way he could face his fate at all was by contributing it like this to the project. And in the end I think most of us cast our votes his way purely out of our love for him.

We rearranged the schedules to give Vendelmans more contact with the animals. There are ten of us, fifty of them; each of us has a special field of inquiry—number theory, syntactical innovation, metaphysical exploration, semiotics, tool use, and so on—and we work with chimps of our own choice, subject, naturally, to the shifting patterns of sub-tribal bonding within the chimp community. But we agreed that Vendelmans would have to offer his revelations to the alpha intelligences—Leo, Ramona, Grimsky, Alice, and Attila—regardless of the current structure of the chimp-human dialogues. Leo, for instance, was involved in an ongoing interchange with Beth Rankin on the notion of the change of seasons. Beth more or less willingly gave up her time with Leo to Vendelmans, for Leo was essential in this. We learned long ago that anything important had to be imparted to the alphas first, and they will impart it to the others. A bright chimp knows more about teaching things to his duller cousins than the brightest human being.

The next morning Hal and Judy Vendelmans took Leo, Ramona, and Attila aside and held a long conversation with them. I was busy in a different part of the compound with Gonzo, Mimsy, Muffin, and Chump, but I glanced over occasionally to see what was going on. Hal looked radiant—like Moses just down from the mountain after talking with God. Judy was trying to look radiant, too, working at it, but her grief kept breaking through: once I saw her turn away from the chimps and press her knuckles to her teeth to hold it back.

Afterward Leo and Grimsky had a conference out by the oak grove. Yost and Charley Damiano watched it with binoculars, but they couldn't make much sense out of it. The chimps, when they sign to each other, use modified gestures much less precise than the ones they use with us; whether this marks the evolution of a special chimp-to-chimp argot designed not to be understood by us, or is simply a factor of chimp reliance on supplementary nonverbal ways of communicating, is something we still don't know, but the fact remains that we have trouble comprehending the sign language they use with each other, particularly the form the alphas use. Then, too, Leo and Grimsky kept wandering in and out of the trees, as if perhaps they knew we were watching them and didn't want us to eavesdrop. A little later in the day, Ramona and Alice had the same sort of meeting. Now all five of our alphas must have been in on the revelation.

Somehow the news began to filter down to the rest of them.

We weren't able to observe actual concept transmission. We did notice that Vendelmans, the next day, began to get rather more attention than normal. Little troops of chimpanzees formed about him as he moved—slowly, and in obvious difficulty—about the compound. Gonzo and Chump, who had been bickering for months, suddenly were standing side by side staring intently at Vendelmans. Chicory, normally shy, went out of her way to engage him in a conversation—about the ripeness of the apples on the tree, Vendelmans reported. Anna Livia's young twins, Shem and Shaun, climbed up and sat on Vendelmans's shoulders.

"They want to find out what a dying god is really like," Yost said quietly.

"But look there," Jan Morton said.

Judy Vendelmans had an entourage, too: Mimsy, Muffin, Claudius, Buster, and Kong. Staring in fascination, eyes wide, lips extended, some of them blowing little bubbles of saliva.

"Do they think she's dying, too?" Beth wondered.

Yost shook his head. "Probably not. They can see there's nothing physically wrong with her. But they're picking up the sorrow vibes, the death vibes."

"Is there any reason to think they're aware that Hal is Judy's mate?" Christensen asked.

"It doesn't matter," Yost said. "They can see that she's upset. That interests them, even if they have no way of knowing why Judy would be more upset than any of the rest of us."

"More mysteries out yonder," I said, pointing into the meadow. Grimsky was standing by himself out there, contemplating something. He is the oldest of the chimps, gray-haired, going bald, a deep thinker. He has been here almost from the beginning, more than thirty years, and very little has escaped his attention in that time.

Far off to the left, in the shade of the big beech tree, Leo stood similarly in solitary meditation. He is twenty, the alpha male of the community, the strongest and by far the most intelligent. It was eerie to see the two of them in their individual zones of isolation, like distant sentinels, like Easter Island statues, lost in private reveries.

"Philosophers," Yost murmured.

Yesterday Vendelmans returned to the hospital for good. Before he went, he made his farewells to each of the fifty chimpanzees, even the infants. In the past week he has altered markedly: he is only a shadow of himself, feeble, wasted. Judy says he'll live only another few weeks.

She has gone on leave and probably won't come back until after

Hal's death. I wonder what the chimps will make of her "going away," and of her eventual return.

She said that Leo had asked her if she was dying, too.

Perhaps things will get back to normal here now.

Christensen asked me this morning, "Have you noticed the way they seem to drag the notion of death into whatever conversation you're having with them these days?"

I nodded. "Mimsy asked me the other day if the moon dies when the sun comes up and the sun dies when the moon is out. It seemed like such a standard primitive metaphor that I didn't pick up on it at first. But Mimsy's too young for using metaphor that easily and she isn't particularly clever. The older ones must be talking about dying a lot, and it's filtering down."

"Chicory was doing subtraction with me," Christensen said. "She signed, '*You take five, two die, you have three.*' Later she turned it into a verb: '*Three die one equals two.*'"

Others reported similar things. Yet none of the animals were talking about Vendelmans and what was about to happen to him, nor were they asking any overt questions about death or dying. So far as we were able to perceive, they had displaced the whole thing into metaphorical diversions. That in itself indicated a powerful obsession. Like most obsessives, they were trying to hide the thing that most concerned them, and they probably thought they were doing a good job of it. It isn't their fault that we're able to guess what's going on in their minds. They are, after all—and we sometimes have to keep reminding ourselves of this—only chimpanzees.

They are holding meetings on the far side of the oak grove, where the little stream runs. Leo and Grimsky seem to do most of the talking, and the others gather around and sit very quietly as the speeches are made. The groups run from ten to thirty chimps at a time. We are unable to discover what they're discussing, though of course we have an idea. Whenever one of us approaches such a gathering, the chimps very casually drift off into three or four separate groups and look exceedingly innocent—"We just out for some fresh air, boss."

Charley Damiano wants to plant a bug in the grove. But how do you spy on a group that converses only in sign language? Cameras aren't as easily hidden as microphones.

We do our best with binoculars. But what little we've been able to observe has been mystifying. The chimp-to-chimp signs they use at these meetings are even more oblique and confusing than the ones we had seen earlier. It's as if they're holding their meetings in pig Latin, or double-talk or in some entirely new and private language.

Two technicians will come tomorrow to help us mount cameras in the grove.

Hal Vendelmans died last night. According to Judy, who phoned Dave Yost, it was very peaceful right at the end, an easy release. Yost and I broke the news to the alpha chimps just after breakfast. No euphemisms, just the straight news. Ramona made a few hooting sounds and looked as if she might cry, but she was the only one who seemed emotionally upset. Leo gave me a long deep look of what was almost certainly compassion, and then he hugged me very hard. Grimsky wandered away and seemed to be signing to himself in the new system. Now a meeting seems to be assembling in the oak grove, the first one in more than a week.

The cameras are in place. Even if we can't decipher the new signs, we can at least tape them and subject them to computer analysis until we begin to understand.

Now we've watched the first tapes of a grove meeting, but I can't say we know a lot more than we did before.

For one thing, they disabled two of the cameras right at the outset. Attila spotted them and sent Gonzo and Claudius up into the trees to yank them out. I suppose the remaining cameras went unnoticed; but by accident or deliberate diabolical craftiness, the chimps positioned themselves in such a way that none of the cameras had a clear angle. We did record a few statements from Leo and some give-and-take between Alice and Anna Livia. They spoke in a mixture of standard signs and the new ones, but, without a sense of the context, we've found it impossible to generate any sequence of meanings. Stray signs such as "shirt," "hat," "human," "change," and "banana fly," interspersed with undecipherable stuff, *seem* to be adding up to something, but no one is sure what. We observed no mention of Hal Vendelmans nor any direct references to death. We may be misleading ourselves entirely about the significance of all this.

Or perhaps not. We codified some of the new signs, and this afternoon I asked Ramona what one of them meant. She fidgeted and hooted and looked uncomfortable—and not simply because I was asking her to do a tough abstract thing like giving a definition. She was worried. She looked around for Leo, and when she saw him she made that sign at him. He came bounding over and shoved Ramona away. Then he began to tell me how wise and good and gentle I am. He may be a genius, but even a genius chimp is still a chimp, and I told him I wasn't fooled by all his flattery. Then I asked *him* what the new sign meant.

"Jump high come again," Leo signed.

A simple chimpy phrase referring to fun and frolic? So I thought at first, and so did many of my colleagues. But Dave Yost said, "Then why was Ramona so evasive about defining it?"

"Defining isn't easy for them," Beth Rankin said.

"Ramona's one of the five brightest. She's capable of it. Especially since the sign can be defined by use of four other established signs, as Leo proceeded to do."

"What are you getting at, Dave?" I asked.

Yost said, "'*Jump high come again*' might be about a game they like to play, but it could also be an eschatological reference, sacred talk, a concise metaphorical way to speak of death and resurrection, no?"

Mick Falkenburg snorted. "Jesus, Dave, of all the nutty Jesuitical bullshit—"

"Is it?"

"It's possible sometimes to be too subtle in your analysis," Falkenburg said. "You're suggesting that these chimpanzees have a theology?"

"I'm suggesting that they may be in the process of evolving a religion," Yost replied.

Can it be?

Sometimes we lose our perspective with these animals, as Mick indicated, and we overestimate their intelligence; but just as often, I think, we underestimate them.

Jump high come again.

I wonder. Secret sacred talk? A chimpanzee theology? Belief in life after death? A religion?

They know that human beings have a body of ritual and belief that they call religion, though how much they really comprehend about it is hard to tell. Dave Yost, in his metaphysical discussions with Leo and some of the other alphas, introduced the concept long ago. He drew a hierarchy that began with God and ran downward through human beings and chimpanzees to dogs and cats and onward to insects and frogs, by way of giving the chimps some sense of the great chain of life. They had seen bugs and frogs and cats and dogs, but they wanted Dave to show them God, and he was forced to tell them that God is not actually tangible and accessible, but lives high overhead although His essence penetrates all things. I doubt that they grasped much of that. Leo, whose nimble and probing intelligence is a constant illumination to us, wanted Yost to explain how we talked to God and how God talked to us if He wasn't around to make signs, and Yost said that we had a thing called religion, which was a system of communicating with God. And that was where he left it, a long while back.

Now we are on guard for any indications of a developing religious consciousness among our troop. Even the scoffers—Mick Falkenburg, Beth, to some degree, Charley Damiano—are paying close heed. After all, one of the underlying purposes of this project is to reach an under- standing of how the first hominids managed to cross the intellectual boundary that we like to think separates the animals from humanity. We can't reconstruct a bunch of *Australopithecines* and study them; but we *can* watch chimpanzees who have been given the gift of language build a quasi-protohuman society, and it is the closest thing to trav- eling back in time that we are apt to achieve. Yost thinks, I think, Burt Christensen is beginning to think, that we have inadvertently kindled an awareness of the divine, of the numinous force that must be worshipped, by allowing them to see that their gods—us—can be struck down and slain by an even higher power.

The evidence so far is slim. The attention given Vendelmans and Judy; the solitary meditations of Leo and Grimsky; the large gather- ings in the grove; the greatly accelerated use of modified sign language in chimp-to-chimp talk at those gatherings; the potentially eschato- logical reference we think we see in the sign that Leo translated as "jump high come again." That's it. To those of us who want to interpret that as the foundations of religion, it seems indicative of what we want to see; to the rest, it all looks like coincidence and fantasy. The problem is that we are dealing with nonhuman intelligence and we must take care not to impose our own thought constructs. We can never be certain if we are operating from a value system anything like that of the chimps. The built-in ambiguities of the sign-language grammar we must use with them complicate the issue. Consider the phrase "banana fly" that Leo used in a speech—a sermon?—in the oak grove, and remember Ramona's reference to the sick Vendelmans as "rotten banana." If we take *fly* to be a verb, "banana fly" might be considered a metaphorical description of Vendelmans's ascent to heaven. If we take it to be a noun, Leo might have been talking about the *Drosophila* flies that feed on decaying fruit, a metaphor for the corruption of the flesh after death. On the other hand, he may simply have been making a comment about the current state of our garbage dump.

We have agreed for the moment not to engage the chimpanzees in any direct interrogation about any of this. The Heisenberg principle is eternally our rule here: the observer can too easily perturb the thing observed, so we must make only the most delicate of measurements. Even so, of course, our presence among the chimps is bound to have its impact, but we do what we can to minimize it by avoiding leading questions and watching in silence.

Two unusual things today. Taken each by each, they would be interesting without being significant; but if we use each to illuminate the other, we begin to see things in a strange new light, perhaps.

One thing is an increase in vocalizing, noticed by nearly everyone, among the chimps. We know that chimpanzees in the wild have a kind of rudimentary spoken language—a greeting call, a defiance call, the grunts that mean "I like the taste of this," the male chimp's territorial hoot, and such—nothing very complex, really not qualitatively much beyond the language of birds or dogs. They also have a fairly rich nonverbal language, a vocabulary of gestures and facial expressions. But it was not until the first experiments decades ago in teaching chimpanzees human sign-language that any important linguistic capacity became apparent in them. Here at the research station the chimps communicate almost wholly in signs, as they have been trained to do for generations and as they have taught their young ones to do; they revert to hoots and grunts only in the most elemental situations. We ourselves communicate mainly in signs when we are talking to each other while working with the chimps, and even in our humans-only conferences, we use signs as much as speech, from long habit. But suddenly the chimps are making sounds at each other. Odd sounds, unfamiliar sounds, weird, clumsy imitations, one might say, of human speech. Nothing that we can understand, naturally: the chimpanzee larynx is simply incapable of duplicating the phonemes humans use. But these new grunts, these tortured blurts of sound, seem intended to mimic our speech. It was Damiano who showed us, as we were watching a tape of a grove session, how Attila was twisting his lips with his hands in what appeared unmistakably to be an attempt to make human sounds come out.

Why?

The second thing is that Leo has started wearing a shirt and a hat. There is nothing remarkable about a chimp in clothing; although we have never encouraged such anthropomorphization here, various animals have taken a fancy from time to time to some item of clothing, have begged it from its owner and have worn it for a few days or even weeks. The novelty here is that the shirt and the hat belonged to Hal Vendelmans, and that Leo wears them only when the chimps are gathered in the oak grove, which Dave Yost has lately begun calling the "holy grove." Leo found them in the toolshed beyond the vegetable garden. The shirt is ten sizes too big, Vendelmans having been so brawny, but Leo ties the sleeves across his chest and lets the rest dangle down over his back almost like a cloak.

What shall we make of this?

Jan is the specialist in chimp verbal processes. At the meeting tonight she said, "It sounds to me as if they're trying to duplicate the rhythms of human speech even though they can't reproduce the actual sounds. They're playing at being human."

"Talking the god-talk," said Dave Yost.

"What do you mean?" Jan asked.

"Chimps talk with their hands. Humans do, too, when speaking with chimps, but when humans talk to humans, they use their voices. Humans are gods to chimps, remember. Talking in the way the gods talk is one way of remaking yourself in the image of the gods, of putting on divine attributes."

"But that's nonsense," Jan said. "I can't possibly—"

"Wearing human clothing," I broke in excitedly, "would also be a kind of putting on divine attributes, in the most literal sense of the phrase. Especially if the clothes—"

"—had belonged to Hal Vendelmans," said Christensen.

"The dead god," Yost said.

We looked at each other in amazement.

Charley Damiano said, not in his usual skeptical way, but in a kind of wonder, "Dave, are you hypothesizing that Leo functions as some sort of priest, that those are his sacred garments?"

"More than just a priest," Yost said. "A high priest, I think. A pope. The pope of the chimps."

Grimsky is suddenly looking very feeble. Yesterday we saw him moving slowly through the meadow by himself, making a long circuit of the grounds as far out as the pond and the little waterfall, then solemnly and ponderously staggering back to the meeting place at the far side of the grove. Today he has been sitting quietly by the stream, occasionally rocking slowly back and forth, now and then dipping his feet in. I checked the records: he is forty-three years old, well along for a chimp, although some have been known to live fifty years and more. Mick wanted to take him to the infirmary, but we decided against it; if he is dying, and by all appearances he is, we ought to let him do it with dignity in his own way. Jan went down to the grove to visit him and reported that he shows no apparent signs of disease. His eyes are clear; his face feels cool. Age has withered him and his time is at hand. I feel an enormous sense of loss, for he has a keen intelligence, a long memory, a shrewd and thoughtful nature. He was the alpha male of the troop for many years, but a decade ago, when Leo came of age, Grimsky abdicated in his favor with no sign of a struggle. Behind Grimsky's grizzled forehead there must lie a wealth of subtle and mysterious perceptions, concepts, and insights about which we know practically nothing, and very soon all that will be lost. Let us hope he's managed to teach his wisdom to Leo and Attila and Alice and Ramona.

Today's oddity: a ritual distribution of meat.

Meat is not very important in the diet of chimps, but they do like to have some, and as far back as I can remember, Wednesday has been meat-day here, when we give them a side of beef or some slabs of mutton or something of that sort. The procedure for dividing up the meat betrays the chimps' wild heritage, for the alpha males eat their fill first while the others watch, and then the weaker males beg for a share and are allowed to move in to grab, and finally the females and young ones get the scraps. Today was meat-day. Leo, as usual, helped himself first, but what happened after that was astounding. He let Attila feed, and then told Attila to offer some meat to Grimsky, who is even weaker today and brushed it aside. *Then Leo put on Vendelmans's hat* and began to parcel out scraps of meat to the others. One by one they came up to him in the current order of ranking and went through the standard begging maneuver, hand beneath chin, palm upward, and Leo gave each one a strip of meat.

"Like taking communion," Charley Damiano muttered. "With Leo the celebrant at the Mass."

Unless our assumptions are totally off base, there is a real religion going on here, perhaps created by Grimsky and under Leo's governance. And Hal Vendelmans's faded old blue work hat is the tiara of the pope.

Beth Rankin woke me at dawn and said, "Come fast. They're doing something strange with old Grimsky."

I was up and dressed and awake in a hurry. We have a closed-circuit system now that pipes the events in the grove back to us, and we paused at the screen so that I could see what was going on. Grimsky sat on his knees at the edge of the stream, eyes closed, barely moving. Leo, wearing the hat, was beside him, elaborately tying Vendelmans's shirt over Grimsky's shoulders. A dozen or more of the other adult chimps were squatting in a semicircle in front of them.

Burt Christensen said, "What's going on? Is Leo making Grimsky the assistant pope?"

"I think Leo is giving Grimsky the last rites," I said.

What else could it have been? Leo wore the sacred headdress. He spoke at length using the new signs—the ecclesiastical language, the chimpanzee equivalent of Latin or Hebrew or Sanskrit—and as his oration went on and on, the congregation replied periodically with outbursts of—I suppose—response and approval, some in signs, some with grunting garbled pseudohuman sounds that Dave Yost thought was their version of god-talk. Throughout it all Grimsky was silent and remote, though occasionally he nodded or murmured or tapped both his shoulders in a gesture whose meaning was unknown to us. The ceremony went on for more than an hour. Then Grimsky leaned forward, and Kong and Chump took him by the arms and eased him down until he was lying with his cheek against the ground.

For two, three, five minutes all the chimpanzees were still. At last Leo came forward and removed his hat, setting it on the ground beside Grimsky, and with great delicacy he untied the shirt Grimsky wore. Grimsky did not move. Leo draped the shirt over his own shoulders and donned the hat again.

He turned to the watching chimps and signed, using the old signs that were completely intelligible to us, "Grimsky now be human being."

We stared at each other in awe and astonishment. A couple of us were sobbing. No one could speak.

The funeral ceremony seemed to be over. The chimps were dispersing. We saw Leo sauntering away, hat casually dangling from one hand, the shirt in the other, trailing over the ground. Grimsky alone remained by the stream. We waited ten minutes and went down to the grove. Grimsky seemed to be sleeping very peacefully, but he was dead, and we gathered him up—Burt and I carried him; he seemed to weigh almost nothing—and took him back to the lab for the autopsy.

In midmorning the sky darkened and lightning leaped across the hills to the north. There was a tremendous crack of thunder almost instantly and sudden tempestuous rain. Jan pointed to the meadow. The male chimps were doing a bizarre dance, roaring, swaying, slapping their feet against the ground, hammering their hands against the trunks of the trees, ripping off branches and flailing the earth with them. Grief? Terror? Joy at the translation of Grimsky to a divine state? Who could tell? I had never been frightened by our animals before—I knew them too well, I regarded them as little hairy cousins —but now they were terrifying creatures and this was a scene out of time's dawn, as Gonzo and Kong and Attila and Chump and Buster and Claudius and even Pope Leo himself went thrashing about in that horrendous rain, pounding out the steps of some unfathomable rite.

The lightning ceased and the rain moved southward as quickly as it had come, and the dancers went slinking away, each to his favorite tree. By noon the day was bright and warm and it was as though nothing out of the ordinary had happened.

Two days after Grimsky's death I was awakened again at dawn, this time by Mick Falkenburg. He shook my shoulder and yelled at me to wake up, and as I sat there blinking he said, "Chicory's dead! I was out for an early walk and I found her near the place where Grimsky died."

"Chicory? But she's only—"

"Eleven, twelve, something like that. I know."

I put my clothes on while Mick woke the others, and we went down to the stream. Chicory was sprawled out, but not peacefully—there was a dribble of blood at the corner of her mouth, her eyes were wide and horrified, her hands were curled into frozen talons. All about her in the moist soil of the stream bank were footprints. I searched my memory for an instance of murder in the chimp community and could find nothing remotely like it—quarrels, yes, and lengthy feuds and some ugly ambushes and battles, fairly violent, serious injuries now and then. But this had no precedent.

"Ritual murder," Yost murmured.

"Or a sacrifice, perhaps?" suggested Beth Rankin.

"Whatever it is," I said, "they're learning too fast. Recapitulating the whole evolution of religion, including the worst parts of it. We'll have to talk to Leo."

"Is that wise?" Yost asked.

"Why not?"

"We've kept hands off so far. If we want to see how this thing unfolds—"

"During the night," I said, "the pope and the college of cardinals ganged up on a gentle young female chimp and killed her. Right now they may be off somewhere sending Alice or Ramona or Anna Livia's twins to chimp heaven. I think we have to weigh the value of observing the evolution of chimp religion against the cost of losing irreplaceable members of a unique community. I say we call in Leo and tell him that it's wrong to kill."

"He knows that," said Yost. "He must. Chimps aren't murderous animals."

"Chicory's dead."

"And if they see it as a holy deed?" Yost demanded.

"Then one by one we'll lose our animals, and at the end we'll just have a couple of very saintly survivors. Do you want that?"

We spoke with Leo. Chimps can be sly and they can be manipulative, but even the best of them, and Leo is the Einstein of chimpanzees, does not seem to know how to lie. We asked him where Chicory was and Leo told us that Chicory was now a human being. I felt a chill at that. Grimsky was also a human being, said Leo. We asked him how he knew that they had become human and he said, "They go where Vendelmans go. When human go away, he become god. When chimpanzee go away, he become human. Right?"

"No," we said.

The logic of the ape is not easy to refute. We told him that death comes to all living creatures, that it is natural and holy, but that only God could decide when it was going to happen. God, we said, calls His creatures to Himself one at a time. God had called Hal Vendelmans, God had called Grimsky, God would someday call Leo and all the rest here. But God had not yet called Chicory. Leo wanted to know what was wrong with sending Chicory to Him ahead of time. Did that not improve Chicory's condition? No, we replied. No, it only did harm to Chicory. Chicory would have been much happier living here with us than going to God so soon. Leo did not seem convinced. Chicory, he said, now could talk words with her mouth and wore shoes on her feet. He envied Chicory very much.

We told him that God would be angry if any more chimpanzees died. We told him that *we* would be angry. Killing chimpanzees was wrong, we said. It was not what God wanted Leo to be doing.

"Me talk to God, find out what God wants," Leo said.

We found Buster dead by the edge of the pond this morning, with indications of another ritual murder. Leo coolly stared us down and explained that God had given orders that all chimpanzees were to become human beings as quickly as possible, and this could only be achieved by the means employed on Chicory and Buster.

Leo is confined now in the punishment tank and we have suspended this week's meat distribution. Yost voted against both of those decisions, saying we ran the risk of giving Leo the aura of a religious martyr, which would enhance his already considerable power. But these killings have to stop. Leo knows, of course, that we are upset about them. But if he believes his path is the path of righteousness, nothing we say or do is going to change his mind.

Judy Vendelmans called today. She has put Hal's death fairly well behind her, misses the project, misses the chimps. As gently as I could, I told her what has been going on here. She was silent a very long time—Chicory was one of her favorites, and Judy has had enough grief already to handle for one summer—but finally she said, "I think I know what can be done. I'll be on the noon flight tomorrow."

We found Mimsy dead in the usual way late this afternoon. Leo is still in the punishment tank—the third day. The congregation has found a way to carry out its rites without its leader. Mimsy's death has left me stunned, but we are all deeply affected, virtually unable to proceed with our work. It may be necessary to break up the community entirely to save the animals. Perhaps we can send them to other research centers for a few months, three of them here, five there, until this thing subsides. But what if it doesn't subside? What if the dispersed animals convert others elsewhere to the creed of Leo?

The first thing Judy said when she arrived was, "Let Leo out. I want to talk with him."

We opened the tank. Leo stepped forth, uneasy, abashed, shading his eyes against the strong light. He glanced at me, at Yost, at Jan, as if wondering which one of us was going to scold him; and then he saw Judy and it was as though he had seen a ghost. He made a hollow rasping sound deep in his throat and backed away. Judy signed hello and stretched out her arms to him. Leo trembled. He was terrified. There was nothing unusual about one of us going on leave and returning after a month or two, but Leo must not have expected Judy ever to return, must in fact have imagined her gone to the same place her husband had gone, and the sight of her shook him. Judy understood all that, obviously, for she quickly made powerful use of it, signing to Leo, "I bring you message from Vendelmans."

"Tell tell tell!"

"Come walk with me," said Judy.

She took him by the hand and led him gently out of the punishment area and into the compound and down the hill toward the meadow. I watched from the top of the hill, the tall, slender woman and the compact, muscular chimpanzee close together, side by side, hand in hand, pausing now to talk, Judy signing and Leo replying in a flurry of gestures, then Judy again for a long time, a brief response from Leo, another cascade of signs from Judy, then Leo squatting, tugging at blades of grass, shaking his head, clapping hand to elbow in his expression of confusion, then to his chin, then taking Judy's hand. They were gone for nearly an hour. The other chimps did not dare approach them. Finally Judy and Leo, hand in hand, came quietly up the hill to headquarters again. Leo's eyes were shining and so were Judy's.

She said, "Everything will be all right now. That's so, isn't it, Leo?"

Leo said, "God is always right."

She made a dismissal sign and Leo went slowly down the hill. The moment he was out of sight, Judy turned away from us and cried a little, just a little; then she asked for a drink; and then she said, "It isn't easy, being God's messenger."

"What did you tell him?" I asked.

"That I had been in heaven visiting Hal. That Hal was looking down all the time and he was very proud of Leo, except for one thing, that Leo was sending too many chimpanzees to God too soon. I told him that God was not yet ready to receive Chicory and Buster and Mimsy, that they would have to be kept in storage cells for a long time until their true time came, and that was not good for them. I told him that Hal wanted Leo to know that God hoped he would stop sending him chimpanzees. Then I gave Leo Hal's old wristwatch to wear when he conducts services, and Leo promised he would obey Hal's wishes. That was all. I suspect I've added a whole new layer of mythology to what's developing here, and I trust you won't be angry with me for doing it. I don't believe any more chimps will be killed. And I think I'd like another drink."

Later in the day we saw the chimps assembled by the stream. Leo held his arm aloft and sunlight blazed from the band of gold on his slim hairy wrist, and a great outcry of grunts in god-talk went up from the congregation and they danced before him, and then he donned the sacred hat and the sacred shirt and moved his arms eloquently in the secret sacred gestures of the holy sign language.

There have been no more killings. I think no more will occur. Perhaps after a time our chimps will lose interest in being religious, and go on to other pastimes. But not yet, not yet. The ceremonies continue, and grow ever more elaborate, and we are compiling volumes of extraordinary observations, and God looks down and is pleased. And Leo proudly wears the emblems of his papacy as he bestows his blessing on the worshipers in the holy grove.

The World
Is a Sphere
Edgar Pangborn

In the quietly moving story that follows, we see that even in the darkest of societies, smothered by superstitious fear and political repression, there will always be those who seek the Light—no matter how great the cost.

The late Edgar Pangborn is almost forgotten these days and is rarely ever mentioned even in historical surveys of the fifties and sixties—which is a pity, since he had a depth and breadth of humanity that have rarely been matched inside the field or out. Although he was never a particularly prolific writer (five science fiction novels, one or two mainstream novels, and a baker's dozen or so short pieces), he was nevertheless one of that select crew of underappreciated authors (one thinks of Cordwainer Smith, Fritz Leiber, Jack Vance, Avram Davidson, Richard McKenna) who have had an enormous underground effect on the field simply by impressing the hell out of other writers, and numerous authors-in-the-egg. Pangborn wrote about "little people" for the most part, only rarely focusing on the famous and powerful. He was one of only a handful of science fiction writers capable of writing about small-town or rural people with insight and sympathy (most science fiction is urban in orientation, written by city people *about* city people—or, when it *is* written by people from small towns, they are frequently kids who couldn't wait to get *out* of those small towns and off to the bright lights of the big city, which often amounts to the same thing, as far as sympathies are concerned), and he was also one of the few who could get inside the minds of both the very young and the very old with equal ease and compassion.

Pangborn's masterpiece was *Davy*, which, in spite of a somewhat weak ending (or, at least, a final third that doesn't quite live up to the two-thirds that came before it), may well be the finest postholocaust novel ever written—in my opinion, it is seriously rivaled only by Walter M. Miller's *A Canticle for Leibowitz* and John Wyndham's *Re-Birth*. In any fair world, *Davy* alone ought to be enough to guarantee Pangborn a distinguished place in the history of the genre, but there were also novels like *A Mirror for Observers*—his International Fantasy Award winner, somewhat dated now, but still powerful, in which alien observers from two opposing philosophical camps vie for the soul of a brilliant human boy—and *West of the Sun*, an underrated novel about the efforts of human castaways to survive on an alien world, as well as beautifully crafted short work such as "A Master of Babylon," "Longtooth," "The World Is a Sphere," and "Angel's Egg." Edgar Pangborn's other works include *The Judgment of Eve* and *The Company of Glory*, the mainstream novel *The Trial of Castilla Blake*, the collection *Good Neighbors and Other Strangers*, and the posthumously published collection *Still I Persist in Wondering*. Pangborn died in 1976. He posthumously won the Cordwainer Smith Rediscovery Award at the World Science Fiction Convention in

2003. *Davy* has just been reissued by Old Earth Books as I type these words, with more Pangborn books to follow.

"We have slain bigger monsters," said Ian Moltas, Deliberator of the Ninth Ward of Norlenas. He had spoken aloud within his solitude; the words brought him no consolation, no increase of courage. After a while a man, or a people, will grow weary of slaying monsters, and then back comes the rule of disorder.

He stood by a western window of his museum in the tropic night, his hands pleased by the cool stone sill, his ears accepting the innocent clamor of the dark—insect shrilling, intermittent husky roar of a rutting alligator in the swamp at the border of his parkland, and now and then the trill and chuckle of the nitingal, bird of mystery. They tell us it's good luck to hear that on a clear night of the old moon.

No one ever sees the nitingal, yet it lived in the world at least two hundred years ago in the great time of the Republic, for the poets of that age spoke of it, and by that singing name.

Good luck? Ian Moltas no longer believed in luck of either sort. Out of confusions, sufferings, compromises, you won what you could: let God and the Devil contend for the rest.

"We have cut down monsters like you before," he said, and held up a clotted fist, shutting away the twinkle of lamps in the palace windows half a mile off across the parkland. He did not let his fist obscure the tender brilliance of the old moon declining. Under those lamps the Emperor's clerks might carry the day's toil to midnight or beyond— Musons all, of course, and therefore slaves dependent for life itself on the Emperor's whim. Dwarfish, with delicate hands, high foreheads, often that telltale sixth finger, the poor devils would scratch away at their mean tasks—recording, copying documents and correspondence, above all transcribing to fine vellum the latest imperial rantings and platitudes in the service of Emperor Asta's immortality; and no one would guess from the small pale Muson faces what fires might be ablaze behind their masks. Moltas supposed he knew a little about that; he was not arrogant enough to think that he, a Misipan of the ruling class, could know very much. To know anything at all of it might be regarded as treason to his peers.

The Emperor Asta was already officially a god by act of the Assembly of Deliberators (Moltas concurring—what can one do?), but he would not rest content with that. Two of the three preceding emperors had also been deified, so the bloom was off that peach. No— he meant to be known to eternity as a great thinker, statesman, and literary artist. Unfortunately, he had never had an original idea, and could barely read and write.

"We'll cut you down too." But Moltas, listening for the iron ring of rebellion in his voice, did not hear it. Can you have rebellion without the people? Can rebellion speak in elderly tones with a quaver, almost a note of peevishness? After all, the quarrel was not between him, Deliberator of the Ninth Ward, and the gaunt little egomaniac over there in the palace; it was between the spark of evil in the human world and the spark of good. As for the people—

The Republic! Ah, they said, *the Republic! Yes, we must bring back the Republic, but not just now, because the Emperor (long live the Emperor) has promised to do it himself the first moment it seems practical. Bread and rice! More fights! More fuck-shows in the Stadium! Long live the Emperor! Fights! Fuck-shows! BREAD AND RICE!*

And the Assembly of Deliberators, once the very heart and con-science of the Republic? Moltas thought: *Why, we are mostly old men, and the waves have gone over us. The Republic is not to be brought back only by remembering it with tears.*

The stone sill was paining his hands. He rubbed his fingers and straightened his elderly back, and turned to the spacious quiet of the room he called his museum—like all the house, a little too grand and a little shabby. The spoils of a rich man's curiosity had accumulated here for thirty years. Not wanting to trouble a servant for such a trifle, he touched a taper to a bracket-lamp and carried the flame to a standing lamp on a long table in the center of the room. The table was of mahogany, careful Misipan workmanship of about a hundred and fifty years ago, from the last years of the Republic; but one would not think of it as old compared to the dozen treasures that stood on it, most of them from the American age, the Age of Sorcerers.

Oldest of all, he thought, was a crude two-faced image of blackened stonelike substance, probably clay, male on one side, female on the other, which surely belonged to some period earlier than the Age of Sorcerers, although the mere notion was heresy. A few years ago he had noticed the image in the trashy wares of a peddler from the north, who let it go for one menin, almost a junk price. It really had nothing in common with American relics. However . . .

Time was not, said the priests, until Sol-Amra made the world out of water and air and earth and fire, and gave it to the Americans, the Sorcerers, who became afflicted with the sin of pride, and were destroyed by pestilence and fire, all but a handful. And we, the remote descendants of that handful, are still corrupt, and must continue to bear the divine curses of poverty and mutation until the year 7000, when Sol-Amra comes to judge the world. Poverty is punishment for the sin of greed. Mutation is punishment for our lecherous nature. Most corrupt of all are the Musons, for does not the wrath of God show clearly in their dwarfish size, pallid faces, evil hands? So let them be safely held in slavery, and sacrificed at the Spring Festivals to take upon them the sin of the world.

One knew all that, and knew the necessity of ritual agreement. One also belonged to the not-quite-secret society of the Tera, discreetly smiling in private at the barbarity of the times; even smiling, very privately and rather dangerously, at Sol-Amra and the Lesser Pantheon. These traditions and legends, you know, said the gentlemen of the Tera—excellent stuff for the multitude. Must have something to keep them happy, while we pursue philosophy and pure reason and the quiet life.

If any visitor showed interest in the two-faced image, Ian Moltas would shrug and dismiss it as a curiosity of no importance, most likely made by the little naked savages in that wilderness away up north, west of Penn; or it might even have come from the scarcely explored lake country much farther north. But Moltas had seen enough of the barbarous wooden images and clumsy pottery of those savages to know that this two-faced image was nothing of theirs.

The other treasures on the table were relics of the American age, valuable but not unfamiliar to connoisseurs. A gray metal dish known to have come from the jungle-buried ruins east of Nathes (apparently called Natchez in the Age of Sorcerers, with heaven knows what pronunciation). A tiny cylinder of an unknown bright metal tapered to a hollow point, with part of an inscription still visible, a few of the antique letters that so closely resemble the Misipan alphabet. A disk of heavy glass with the mystic power of magnification. A tray of coins, some of corroded copper, others that appeared untouched by age.

Ian Moltas slumped in one of the massive chairs by the table. At the uncommon age of fifty-eight he was heavy but not fat, not very wrinkled, only somewhat gray. Mild sea blue eyes belied the fierceness of his beaky nose; his flexible orator's mouth was darkly bracketed. He was wearing the scarlet loincloth of the ruling class; his sleeveless white tunic carried on the front the gold-and-green rice-plant symbol of the Assembly of Deliberators. Often if angry or depressed he sought for quiet in the contemplation of the clay image, and often found it. It must have been made, he thought, by fingers alone. How simple the gouges that marked the eyes! The mouths had been achieved by pressure of a thumbnail gone back to dust how many hundreds or thousands of years ago?

He looked up, startled and vague. "Yes, Elkan?" The slave had come silently, or might have been standing in the shadows several moments. He was trained, of course, to go about like a ghost, to be present suddenly whenever needed; but that magical quiet was also a part of the Muson nature.

"A peddler, Deliberator—perhaps not worth your time, but he was insistent. He gives his name as Piet Brun. He apologized for the late hour, saying he didn't wish to carry his treasure in the streets by daylight. This seemed irrational to me—whatever he has is carried in an ordinary sack—and I said so. He replied, with a smile—a rather unpleasant smile, sir, or so I thought—that he felt stronger than others in the dark. I did not like him, Deliberator, but I told him I would bring in his name."

"Does he say what he has?"

"No, sir, only that he thinks you might want to buy it. He says he was Misipan born but has spent most of his time traveling and trading in the barbarous northern countries. His speech suggests it—trader's jargon, quite coarse."

"Well, I'll see him. These people often do have something. But let him wait a few moments—I want to talk to you." Elkan also waited, quiet as the clay image. He was tall for a Muson, nearly five feet, which modified the deceptive childlike proportions that most of them had because of their large heads and stocky bodies, and he was eighty years old, middle-aged for his breed. He stood with arms folded—they never lost an alertness that seemed to cost them no effort—and his pale six-fingered hands spread out over the elbows as if to emphasize their difference. "Elkan, you'll remember that two years ago, two full years, I introduced a measure in the Assembly which would have declared that your people, sharing a common ancestry with humankind, a common language, a history of coexistence—"

"'—are and of right ought to be equal with the human race before the law and in every aspect of our social being.' Forgive the interruption, Deliberator. The words—your own, I believe—have sung in my mind a long time." Elkan's eyes, large and luminous, now and then met Moltas's gaze like the touch of a roving beam of light. "The measure, I presume, has been defeated, sir?"

"Oh, the measure—no, not exactly, not formally. Many times debated, cut to pieces and cobbled together again, saved up in committee for further waste of words, but never quite defeated. I had no hope at any time—as I think I told you—of winning all or even most of what we prayed for. I did hope that by asking for all we might win something. If we had merely won that technical admission of equality, it would have become impossible, by any kind of logic, for the law to say, as it does now, that your people are to exist forever in a state of slavery. The Assembly was almost ready for that simple first step at the time of Asta's accession. No, Elkan, the measure has not been defeated, but—Oh my God, how am I to tell you? . . . Elkan, the best hope of your people was always the Assembly. Nothing good can be expected from any other political source. We Deliberators—we are all that remains of a Republic that once did uphold an ideal of virtue, limited though it was; and it's on my mind tonight that we are not much. And I am obliged to tell you—you must know it for your own safety—the Assembly itself may be dying."

"There have always been passages of failing light." The Muson way, to state anything important as neutrally as possible, not in denial of passion—far from it—but in order to protect rational discourse from the tumults of the heart.

"Elkan, I have allowed myself to think that in talking to you— whom I have come to love as a friend, if I may say it—I am talking to others who cannot hear me directly. I do not want to learn anything about any groups of your people who may be living somehow in the wilderness, because like anyone I might become weak and betray you if my mind disintegrated under torture. However, if any such groups exist I wish them to hear this warning: be more careful than ever in the next few years while Asta lives. Do nothing to stir up the lust of violence. Asta is insecure. He needs a scapegoat, and your people would again be the victims, especially if the Assembly dies. He would not hold back from another Night of Knives—might welcome it."

Elkan said after a while, "The message will be transmitted, Deliberator. The advice may not be followed. Conditions change, my lord. The Night of Knives ten years ago was indecisive."

Moltas looked up, amazed at the overtones. Elkan's face was quiet as always. "Elkan, since the law forbids the freeing of Muson slaves under any conditions, I drew up a will which bequeaths you to my brother-in-law at Nathes. He is a kind soul, a scholar, and fortunate in that he knows almost nothing of the modern world, being concerned with the quarrels and delights of antiquity."

Elkan bowed. "An act of kindness, Deliberator." And it seemed to Moltas that the overtones were saying darkly and jubilantly: *If you die, my lord, I shall be with my people in the wilderness.*

"I'll see that peddler now."

Piet Brun stepped in with the brash grace of a tomcat, a small, bouncing man, gnarled and baldheaded, carrying a green cloth sack. Rudely he hitched a chair nearer the Deliberator's, waiting for no invitation to sit down. When Elkan brought in the second-best wine, Brun tossed off a glass as one swills water, clucked and patted his belly and said, "Very nice, sir. Much obliged." Behind Brun's back, Elkan shared Moltas's amusement with one lifted eyebrow, and faded from sight.

Casually Brun offered autobiography. He had been everywhere and done everything. Born at Alsandra (he said), at thirteen he had run away to join a caravan bound for Penn in the barbarian north. He had served as a mercenary in one of Penn's border wars with the Empire of Katskil (a rising nation, he thought). After that he had a nice thing smuggling spearheads of Katskil steel to the savages in the lake country. He married, but his wife bore a mue, as they called such monstrosities up north, and then another, so he divorced her as Penn law permitted, an action that made her a protected slave of the Amran Church. At mention of that church, Brun automatically made the sign of the wheel over his heart, and scratched his armpit.

Repressing distaste, Moltas inquired, "You became a member of that church, Misur Brun, although Misipan born?"

Brun glanced around the room, maybe looking for eavesdroppers. "Got some nice things here, m'lord. Well, the church—see, I'm a *practical* man, Deliberator. I leave the thinking to the priests—they get paid for it." He laid a grubby finger along his nose, and winked. "Up north, you know, you're a follower of Abraham—I mean, what the church says is the faith of Abraham, or"—he slid the edge of his hand across his throat—"*ssst!*" He gulped more wine. "I had me a junk shop for a while—did all right but sold out. Itching foot, m'lord. Been a bit of a rascal maybe."

Moltas refilled his glass. The politician in him instinctively searched for nuggets of information. "You'd say that Katskil is the major power up north nowadays?"

"Not a doubt of it, sir. They ain't a naval power yet, but they aim to be that, too. Country's riddled with witchcraft, by the way. Church does its best to keep it down, I give 'em credit for that." He glanced at the two-faced image and his eyes skittered away. "That lumin kettle there, that's a nice little piece, m'lord, right out of the Age of the—so-called Sorcerers."

Moltas reflected that the little tramp could be an *agent provocateur* sent by Asta to tempt him into heretical remarks. "So-called, Misur Brun?"

"We, uh, speak in confidence?"

"Certainly, if you wish it so."

"Old slave's gone to bed?"

"Probably. In any case he doesn't eavesdrop."

"Shit, they all do."

"He doesn't eavesdrop, Misur Brun."

"Sorry. Excuse it. Must be your nice wine. No offense, sir—thing is, I been in trouble once or twice before, from speaking out. Now what I mean, it's my opinion them ancient people weren't sorcerers at all, anyhow not like the northern witches. They was just people like us, only they had a lot of knowledge and skill that somehow got lost, that's all."

"I hope you're careful not to say such things openly."

"I ain't thirsting to look down on the fucking world from no cross, Deliberator."

"I have never put anyone in danger of the cross."

"I know that. 'Round the wharves they call you 'The Merciful.'"

"I earned that name," said Ian Moltas.

"Yes, sir—it's one way of looking at things. Me, I can see how the world's all fang and claw. Man's got to look out for himself, nobody else will." He took up his green sack. "Like to see something really good?" Moltas nodded, expecting trash.

The trader took out first a small tripod surmounted by a semi-circular loop a foot high, the whole device one solid or welded piece of one of the ancient silver-gray metals impossible to reproduce in the modern age. He set this on the table, and then brought forth a flabby piece of what must be ancient Plassic in a curious flat harmony of mild colors, mostly blue and green and brown. At both ends of the lump were little metal devices. Brun placed one of these in his mouth, and puffed. Quickly the lump became a softly shining sphere. He placed it in the metal standard and tapped it so that it spun a long moment before quieting into rest. Moltas's mind whirled with it; as motion ceased he blinked and caught his breath.

"Gets you, don't it, sir? I picked it up in Penn from a collector who was afraid of owning it. That's why I could let you have it dirt cheap and still make a penny or two."

"But what is it?"

"A map."

"What are you saying?"

"The Sorcerers, if we got to call them that, knew that the world is round. . . . The way it is up north, Deliberator, people believe that some of the Sorcerers, the Americans, are still around—you know, immortals, haunting devils. Church takes it seriously, or maybe"—his finger was laid again on his nose—"maybe it's just that keeping the devils in their place pays off. Useful things—like that kettle you got there—get the bad magic charmed out of 'em at so much a charm. I understand this was found in the cellar of some ruined building in the area near Fildelfia. The priests would've condemned it, but somebody grabbed it before they got there—"

"Round?"

"Ayah," said Brun with that unpleasant northern twang, and casually, as if dismissing something of no interest, but his eyes were too bright, too amused. "Pick it up if you like, Deliberator. It's not fragile —nor dangerous."

Ian Moltas did so, finding it astonishingly light. He touched the slick surface, so filled with soft splendor from the lamp, and the globe turned at his command. Without the twang, and without that undertone of sniggering laughter, Piet Brun said, "Your hands are holding up the world."

"You disturb me, sir. Naturally I am familiar with—certain philosophical theories."

"Sure." He was mocking again, or seemed to be. "Of course everyone knows the earth is flat."

Moltas was irritated. "On the contrary, there is obviously some curvature. One only need climb a hilltop—"

"Or go to sea, Deliberator, and watch the approach of another ship: first the tip of her mast, and then the tops'l—"

"I know, I know. But after all—" He set the shining thing back on the table. "A map? Perhaps only the creation of an artist, a fanciful mind."

"Speaking of going to sea, Deliberator, what is the shipping situation in Norlenas at present?"

"Shipping? Why, I'm not too well-informed. Normal, I suppose."

"You see, I'm like a stranger here. I just might be interested in buying or chartering some kind of seagoing tub, but I don't know what kind of expense I'll be running into. If I ask around the docks, I won't get an honest answer, so I thought I'd ask you."

The flattery was harmless, and probably sincere. "I don't really know very much, Misur Brun. What sort of ship?"

"She ought to be a hundred-tonner, two-master, I think, with one-level galley and sound slaves—no Musons, I wouldn't give a shit for your Musons in an oar-bank—"

"Misur Brun, all galley rowers of Misipa are freemen. There are no slaves except the Musons."

"Do you tell me!"

"I'm surprised that as a Misipan born you should have forgotten."

"Well, I ran away at thirteen, and before then I didn't take note of much except to wonder when my old man would get drunk again and beat up on my ass. Well, not less than a hundred tons, and I don't want no coastwise crawler. Shorten her masts if I got to, and if her keel's no good I'll go for more ballast." Ian Moltas noticed for the first time that the fellow's clothes were rather good, even expensive, his fingernails clean, and his eyes, when not veiled in slyness, were those of a visionary, a listener to the winds. "Ride low and steady—you got to meet big water on its own terms."

"You think of trading with Velen in the south, perhaps?"

Piet Brun stared beyond him. "Perhaps."

"Well—not much more than guessing, sir—twelve thousand menin might buy you such a ship. About refitting and a cargo, I just don't know, couldn't advise you. . . . And while we are on the subject of money, what would I have to pay for this—relic?"

Brun smiled at him. "Twelve thousand menin." The sphere was a poem of blue and green and brown, floating in the room's silence.

"If," said Moltas presently, "you plan to explore the possibility that the world is a sphere—which of course is not unfamiliar to the philosophers of the Tera, although regarded as far-fetched—won't you need this"—he touched the world and made it spin again—"this map?"

"Made me some tracings," Brun said. The smile was steady on his blunt face; whether the world was a sphere or the footstool of Sol-Amra, Piet Brun had a joke on it. "Made a copy on silk, that I can blow up to size with one of them pig's-bladder toys they make for the kids. Crude, but it'll serve my purpose."

"The thing is certainly a map, as you say. Some of these names I recognize as being old American—almost common knowledge that the City of God Norlenas was once called New Orleans. But your map shows it in the wrong place, and the line of the coast is absurd. The course of the Misipa ends—about here."

"Deliberator, the legends of the Flood are true legends. They know that, up in the north. At the southern end of the Hudson Sea there's a mighty heap of rubble, masses of tumbled masonry, here and there the top of a tower jutting from the water so heavily buttressed by trash and silt that the strongest seas and tides haven't leveled it. They call that place the Black Rocks, but everyone knows it's the ruins of the greatest city in what they call Old Time. The floods came, Deliberator, but they didn't drain away."

"I know the legends. Well, Misur Brun, your price for the relic is outrageous, almost comic, but I will even pay it. If that surprises you, set it down to the whim of an old man who cannot go exploring. I'll write you a draft on my—excuse me." Elkan had appeared in the archway from the hall, looking frightened. Moltas went to him.

"Sir, the Emperor has sent a litter with bearers."

"At this hour?"

Aware of the peddler, Elkan sank his voice to the barely audible. "A lieutenant of the Mavid is with them."

"An escort, no doubt," said Ian Moltas, who knew better. Lieutenants of Asta's secret police were not sent on small errands of courtesy. "I'll go down presently. Has Madam Moltas come back from that banquet?"

"Not yet, sir."

"Bring me my jewel case from the strongbox in my bedroom, Elkan." He returned to his visitor. "Misur Brun, it will be best if I pay you with a jewel of about that value. You've come back to Misipa at a very unstable time. Men go out of favor swiftly, sometimes die swiftly —curious times, very curious. It's possible—so quickly do fortunes change—you might have difficulty cashing a draft tomorrow morning, even though I have plenty of funds to cover it. But jewels will remain negotiable."

"Sir, whatever is convenient." Brun was flushed, still thrown off balance by the incredible success of his errand; it occurred to Moltas that he might have asked that price simply as a piece of impudence, a joke, a conversation piece to introduce genuine bargaining.

"Thank you, Elkan. Here—if you will take this to any appraiser in White Cradle Street, Misur Brun—"

"Sir, I would never question the Deliberator's—"

"I have a litter waiting for me, a late errand. Perhaps I could take you part way to wherever you're staying? Go ahead, please—I'll follow in a moment."

He needed that moment with Elkan, to stand there eye to eye, and hold out his hand as one does to any friend and equal. "I'll return, I suppose," he said. Elkan hesitated long; then the grasp of the six-fingered hand was firm and to Moltas very strange, a bridge between worlds that must somehow communicate with friendship, or die.

The lieutenant of the Mavid politely and correctly pointed out that the litter was small, with no room for anyone but himself and his passenger. A genteel, patient man, in his black loincloth and black tunic with the emblem of crossed spears. Piet Brun spoke a mannerly good-bye, and walked jauntily down the dark street with a green emerald fortune in his pocket that might have bought the virtue of even a Mavid lieutenant. "We are going to the palace, I presume, Lieutenant?"

"Yes, sir. Why are you laughing, my lord, may I ask?"

"I could never explain it," said Ian Moltas.

The scrawny little body of Asta, Appointed of Sol-Amra, Lord of the World, defied the silken ease of his chair, incapable of relaxation; his tight face betrayed a hunger no world could satisfy. The audience room was cool and lovely under the mild lamps, the floor a mosaic of priceless imported marble, gray and rose. A naked Muson girl with a fixed smile held a platter of fruit near his chair, and Asta chewed raisins as if they were the flesh of enemies. "Sit if you wish, Deliberator."

A hundred and fifty years ago, when Ocasta, first of the Emperors, was crowned, the privileges of the Deliberators had been written into statute: an attempt of those who loved the Republic to retain some color of it when the reality was gone. Moltas could have taken the low stool, the only other seat in the room, without need of permission. That Asta had granted it was one of those petty victories the Emperor needed as some need coffee or marawan. And to remain standing would have been bad politics. "Manners, child!" said Asta, and gave the girl a brutal push toward Moltas, who took a fig and nibbled it for politics' sake.

She was small and pretty, like a child indeed at first glance, but Moltas could not guess her age. The platter was heavy, her thin arms in danger of trembling. Asta was known to enjoy the sterile delights of maintaining a harem of Muson women, his Empress being no more to him than a breeder of sons for the dynasty; and rumor had it that any of the girls who survived a few months of his pleasures were given to specially favored members of the ruling clique, as marks of the Emperor's esteem—disposable, in fact, like towels.

"Moltas"—the Emperor sighed with staged patience—"what do you *want*, man? A year ago, we recollect, we offered you a Treasury post—no sinecure, responsible work you could have done very well."

"Majesty, I felt that an elective post was a trust I could not abandon. My talent is in the framing and interpretation of law."

"We know that's what you say. Law and policy, hey?"

A tricky question. In theory, the Assembly might still debate imperial policy; in practice, the Emperor disregarded it. The Emperor proposed measures; if the Assembly did not ratify them they still became law, humorously described as Statutes of Misipa A.D.— Assembly Dissenting. But should the Assembly adopt measures unwelcome to the Emperor, his veto was final. The Assembly was a ghost, a graveyard of honor. One power remained to it, an intangible —the strangely passionate, inarticulate veneration the people still held for it as a symbol of an older time. Even in these sour years memory would not quite die, and A.D. laws were resented—blindly and ineffectively, yet the resentment was real, and the ruler of an explosive people could not wholly disregard it. Moltas said with an evasiveness Asta would understand, "Majesty, the Assembly's position on policy seems to require a day-to-day definition."

Asta smiled clammily and let that pass. "Well—not long ago, we offered you a title. Because we wished to make use of your unquestioned talents on the Advisory Council. You declined. We have been very patient with you, Moltas."

"I felt, Majesty, that a transfer to the Advisory Council would place me out of touch with the people, the citizens—"

Asta leaned forward, waggling a schoolteacher's forefinger. "Are you proposing to instruct us concerning the *people*, Ian Moltas? Don't you understand even yet that the people have one true friend, one only—the Emperor? Why do you think we are known as the Humanitarian, the Light-Bringer of Sol-Amra?"

Moltas thought: *off and running. This could take half an hour.*

It was less than that, but the sentences rolled on like chariot wheels, and a vision appeared of the world as Asta saw it: the Misipan Empire expanding to the utmost, old Velen beyond the Southern Sea crushed, occupied, absorbed as far as the jungles at the lower rim of the world; the northern lands punished for their arrogance by Misipan crossbow and phalanx, Katskil industry harnessed to the Misipan chariot, Misipan law and custom and religion extending at last to all the limits of the earth—one state, one shining whole, dissent unknown and the Humanitarian sitting on top of it. "The state, Moltas—what is there but the state? Do you talk to us of the people, when our vision alone can see them as they are? Ants in a colony, leaves of a tree that perish to enrich the earth." Asta broke off, tightly smiling. "We forget you live on a diet of oratory. To business. We have a special project in mind, Moltas, and we are convinced that there are few other—ants—in the Empire who could do it as well as yourself. We are correct in thinking that you are much concerned with the welfare of the Musons? Even to the point of desiring certain changes in the ancient laws? This is true, sir?"

"It is true, Majesty. I think everyone knows it. Of course, the present temper of the times—"

"My dear Moltas, damn the times. Great men—and deities—make the times. I am the times, Ian Moltas. Now, we have in mind a definitive study of the entire institution of Muson slavery—a work of true scholarship . . . done under our auspices, of course, but without any interference with your scholarly efforts—to serve as a basis for intelligent recommendations leading to improvement. We are quite aware of—let us say, inequities, even cruelties, I'm sorry to say; and you ought to understand that the welfare of the Musons has always been close to our heart. Now we propose that you undertake this study—no restrictions of course, all facilities, any type of assistance you wish, in addition to our promise to give the closest consideration to any recommendations you make." *The tiger invites me to his den for this tainted tidbit—why? What does he want, that requires bringing me here after midnight, when he himself is red-eyed from lack of sleep?* "We have looked into the difficulties, Moltas, and find no legal objection to your assuming this task while retaining your status as Deliberator, with leave of absence."

"Majesty, are there other conditions?"

Asta caught the little slave's buttock and jerked her body to emphasize his words. "See, darling, see how they mistrust me, these everlasting politicians! Notice it, darling? Never fails." She achieved a dutiful giggle, trying to keep her tray of fruit from spilling. A ripe plum rolled and splattered on the floor by Asta's foot. "Clumsy idiot bitch!" The Appointed of Sol-Amra sent the girl staggering to the floor with a blow on the breast; a wave of his arm fetched a guard from the anteroom to pick her up and carry her out of sight. "Some of 'em aren't worth training," Asta said, "but she may do well enough at the farm. Seems healthy. I forget, Moltas," said the Emperor, who never forgot anything, "do you keep a Muson stud?"

Ian Moltas counted to eight. His marriage had not been blessed with children; he thanked God for it. "No, Majesty, that is a project I have never attempted."

"You might find it illuminating for the study we hope you'll undertake. Pity they're so long-lived and come so late to fertility— makes it difficult to experiment with bloodlines. Well, well, you mentioned conditions. Yes, honored Deliberator, we are attaching one condition, and if you suppose the gods themselves could rule men without a little horse-trading, honored Deliberator, your lifetime in politics has been spent in vain. Tomorrow a measure of considerable importance will be presented to the Assembly. It will not be well received, but it happens to be vital to larger considerations of Empire, and an A.D. law, honored Deliberator, will not do! Now, we have noted that some seventeen of the thirty-nine Deliberators have consistently opposed our best efforts toward the welfare of Misipa—obstructionists, reactionaries, selfish old men without vision. Perhaps a dozen others genuinely understand the necessities of the empire that must soon govern the world. The rest—waverers, sheep, *pliable* old men, whom you could sway in the direction of enlightenment. Tomorrow we wish to have your vote on the right side."

"The Emperor would allow a definitive study of Muson slavery to depend on a single political action of one Deliberator?" And Moltas wondered whether the guards would be in for him. He had spoken his unforgivable words in a mild voice; it was even possible that Asta was too stupid to understand all the implications.

Asta had not failed to understand. As he bent forward a flush of blood grew up around his eyes and receded; his voice also was soft. "You may have missed the point, Deliberator Moltas. We ought to have said: we *prefer* to have your vote on the right side—but don't exaggerate your importance. . . . What is your final answer?"

"Majesty, if I may, I should like to consider my answer overnight. Then my vote in the Assembly can be taken as my answer."

"I see. Very well." Asta relaxed, sighing with histrionic patience. "Perhaps you should remember that your vote is not in any way necessary—no more necessary, after all, than the Assembly itself or the continued health of its members. You may go."

Elkan was waiting to open the door, a ritual service he valued. "Elkan, when you spoke with Misur Brun before you brought him up to me, did he mention where he was staying?"

"Yes, sir. The Sign of the Fox, on Dasin Street. It's cheap but respectable."

"Curious fellow. And what a curious thing is a scale of values! The palace is in a poisonous mood, Elkan, and the Assembly may not survive tomorrow."

Elkan stood with folded hands; but when Moltas said no more, he took a torch from a bracket and went ahead to light the Deliberator's way up the marble stairs. "Sir, I ventured to set up another table in the museum."

"Ah, thank you!" Passing through the archway into the museum he saw Elkan's work at once, for the sphere of the world stood on the new table, and before it was the two-faced image. At each end of the table burned a lamp, and all other lamps were extinguished; thus the slave had said: *Here is the world, and here is man, and here is an imperfect light.* "Thank you and good night, Elkan."

He sat before the world in the half-dark, and though the idea of a round earth was perverse, grotesque, even ridiculous, somewhere there might be a truth in it. The sun moves in the heavens, does it not? The sun and the moon? Suppose those orbs are vastly greater than they appear to us. Then imagine some being existing on the surface of one of them: would not our sphere—our *sphere*—seem to his eyes as does the sun or the moon to ours? But if all things are in motion—

It is too much. If all things move and flow—if nothing is ever stable, but all creation is journeying—

Someone entered the museum with a rustling of a skirt—Keva, who would be distressed at his wakefulness. "Ian, aren't you coming to bed? (The banquet was a deadly bore, deadly.) How can you go on without sleep?" He leaned his head back against her breast. "Oh, I suppose it's politics, politics. I wish you wouldn't take so many cares on yourself. No rest?"

"Trouble brewing for the Assembly itself. It may blow over."

"Don't let things distress you so much."

"It's my life, Keva."

"You went to the palace, Elkan told me."

"Asta wishes me to make a scholarly study of Muson slavery."

"Why, that's wonderful!—isn't it? You'd be relieved from the Assembly? And it's something you want to do, isn't it?"

"A condition is attached. And the study itself would end in nothing but one more recommendation."

"I see. I suppose I see."

"What do you see, my dear?"

"I see that in order to satisfy some—some impossible standard of virtue, you're about to throw the Emperor's offer back in his face, never mind if it means your neck, your neck—I can't understand you. I never did understand you. This room, all those old things, dead things—oh, I see you brood and don't know where your mind is. Ian, we must live in the *present*, isn't it so?"

"It's a flash between infinities, a place to be happy and sad. It's not true that the present is the only place we know. I must look beyond, both ways. I can't change myself—"

"Ah, no more, let's not talk about it. Don't stay up much longer, Ian—please? My God, it'll be dawn in an hour or two."

"I'll come to bed soon, Keva."

"What's that absurd round thing?"

"A toy perhaps. Age of the Sorcerers. Go and rest, Keva."

When he was alone again Moltas remembered how some of the stars move, or seem to, like the sun and moon. One lamp was still burning at the palace, a busy, baleful eye; beyond it, the serenity of the dark.

The morning came heavy with wet heat and a hint of storm. In the lobby of the Assembly Hall lounged five of the Mavid with sword and dagger and riot club, neat in their black loincloths and tunics, pointedly disregarding the arriving Deliberators. By every tradition they had no right there; by an even older and graver custom, weapons were forbidden in the Assembly Hall. Moltas felt on his arm the touch of a friend, Amid Anhur; liver spots showed on the crinkled hand—Amid was old, too old, like many here. An evil of the day, no fault of Asta's, that only the rich could afford to try for election in this land that still believed itself to have a representative government, under an emperor who meant to restore the Republic any day; and few of the young were rich. Amid said, "I suppose we must ignore the vermin, Ian? Merely a squad of the wolf's personal fleas."

"How long can we hold out?"

"A day—a week—a year."

"How many of us still possess our souls?"

The building was the work of the middle Republic; Amid Anhur stared at a groove in the threshold of the inner doorway, worn there by more than two hundred years of passage of Misipa's lawmakers. "A year ago I think I could have said twenty-four. Now, Barshon and Menefar dead—possibly of natural causes. The younger Samis murdered in a tavern, the Mavid not curious about his murderers, while his father remembers he has one more son. See Cannon there, pretending not to know I nodded to him. You and I are not safe to know."

"Come to my house this evening. I've bought a curious thing."

"Another antiquity? What about today, Ian?"

"This thing is timeless. I beg you come, have dinner with us. Keva would be happy to see you."

"Oh, I will come, gladly," said the old man, and they entered the hall. "We should concern ourselves with timeless things—while we have a little time."

Kalon Samis, month's Moderator, called them to order, his voice flat and schooled and careful, perhaps in memory of a son. There should have been continuation of a debate on the silk tax, but a sheet of parchment was quivering in Samis's fingers. "There is an imperial message which I am directed to read before the day's business." At the back of the hall a Mavid captain leaned against the bronze doors, his presence unprotested by anything more than angry glances and shocked disdain. "And gentlemen, my reading of this message is to be taken as a motion: formal debate may follow, but perhaps it should be limited. The message reads: 'It is the Imperial intention that the Assembly recognize second and third cousins and cousins by marriage of the Emperor as full members of the Imperial household, entitled to serve not only on the Advisory Council by reason of nobility, but also as consultant members of the Assembly of Deliberators, each to have one vote.' Now as I have said, debate should be limited."

Moltas was on his feet. Some others would soon have broken the stunned and nauseated silence—already he could hear choked words and heavy breathing—but Samis recognized him with a feeble nod. "Deliberators of Misipa, there are occasions when men may find it best not to accept a kick in the groin with murmurs of polite thanks. It is my view—"

It was not difficult, so long as he was on his feet and following the momentum of his own expert and powerful voice. The Assembly had always enjoyed rounded periods and poetic thunder, a part of the style—antique perhaps, but there was a place for it. And now, if a man chose to risk binding himself to the cross in the marketplace with a rope of words, the Assembly would hear him out courteously while he did it. "The cousins, it is true, may find our little gathering a bore at times—dull debates, tax laws, arguments, so many things to interfere with scratching or lifting the tail of a close friend." He introduced other jests and obscenities, although his ears told him that what little laughter responded was merely that of nervousness close to hysteria. Still, in a way they liked it—hanged men dance.

There was relaxation through the mass of well-known faces when he began to speak of the Republic. It was an Assembly cliché, to look toward that lost time with a nostalgia rendered harmless by futility. But then they understood that Moltas was not speaking in that manner. He was speaking of the Republic as if it were a living place almost within the here and now—over a hill; a day's journey. He was asking them to think that what citizens have built once and lost, they may build again, a little better with good fortune. There were times, he said, when human effort appeared to generate nothing but suffering, error, confusion—but maybe even these times add a little to the sum of human understanding. "And there are times," said Ian Moltas, "when the will to struggle against evil seems to be altogether gone. This may be such a time. If the Assembly perishes, there will be no light until, somewhere in the land, you see light from the fires of revolution—not you, perhaps, for most of you will not be there. And now I say, only to a few of you: we need not be ashamed if sometimes there is nothing better to do for an idea than to die for it."

The Assembly voted against Asta, twenty to eighteen. Samis abstained.

The Mavid captain was a trained speaker, too. He strode front, ignoring Moderator Samis, and waited for his correct instant of silence. "By decree of Asta; Appointed of Sol-Amra, Lord of the World, the Assembly of Deliberators now stands dissolved. You will not leave the boundaries of holy Norlenas, and will consider yourselves under the Emperor's displeasure until he has examined certain charges brought against individual members of this body. You will leave the building quietly and go to your homes. That is all."

No longer sustained by the courage of action, his thoughts fluttered like startled doves. *Keva—what can I do?—she has relatives in the Imperial family—maybe—*

Elkan—there is the will—but he will go—money for Elkan—if only—

Sign of the Fox in Dasin Street. Why, I will go and arrange with that fellow—might we not sail—you've got to meet big water on its own terms—

But the Mavid captain had a particular message for him, halting him on the steps of the hall, with two of his men, in case there should be difficulties. Moltas said, "Gentlemen, the world is a sphere."

The captain said neutrally, "You are to come for questioning to the prison in the Seventh Ward."

One of the men was very young, almost a boy. "I will come without resistance, of course," Moltas said, but he wanted to address the boy. "You see, if the world is a sphere, life becomes interesting again—does it not? So much more to know. Do you understand?" The young face showed only alarm.

"We want no difficulty," said the captain, and locked Moltas's wrists behind him.

"Don't you understand, boy? If the world is a sphere, it may also be a star."

Written in Blood
Chris Lawson

Here's an elegant and incisive look at some of the unexpected effects of high-tech bioscience, including a battle between science and faith that may reach all the way down to the very marrow of your bones.

New writer Chris Lawson grew up in Papua New Guinea and now lives in Melbourne with his wife, Andrea. While studying medicine, he earned extra money as a computer programmer, and he has worked as a medical practitioner and as a consultant to the pharmaceutical industry. He's made short fiction sales to *Asimov's Science Fiction*, *Dreaming Down-Under*, *Eidolon*, *Event Horizon*, and *Spectrum SF*, among other places. Some of these stories were gathered in his first collection, *Written in Blood*, in 2003.

CTA TAA CAG TGT AGC GAC GAA TGT CTA CAG AAA CAA
GAA TGT CAT GAG TGT CTA GAT CAT AAC CGA TGT AGC
GAC GAA TGT CTA CAA GAA AGG AAT TAA GAG GGA TAC
CGA TGT AGC GAC GAA TGT CTA AAT CAT CAA CAC AAA
AGT AGT TAA CAT CAG AAA AGC GAA TGC TTC TTT

In the Name of God, the Merciful, the Compassionate.

These words open the Qur'an. They were written in my father's blood. After Mother died, and Da recovered from his chemotherapy, we went on a pilgrimage together. In my usual eleven-year-old curious way, I asked him why we had to go to the Other End of the World to pray when we could do it just fine at home.

"Zada," he said, "there are only five pillars of faith. It is easier than any of the other pillars because you only need to do it once in a lifetime. Remember this during Ramadan, when you are hungry and you know you will be hungry again the next day, but your *haj* will be over."

Da would brook no further discussion, so we set off for the Holy Lands. At eleven, I was less than impressed. I expected to find Paradise filled with thousands of fountains and birds and orchards and blooms. Instead, we huddled in cloth tents with hundreds of thousands of sweaty pilgrims, most of whom spoke other languages, as we tramped across a cramped and dirty wasteland. I wondered why Allah had made his Holy Lands so dry and dusty, but I had the sense even then not to ask Da about it.

Near Damascus, we heard about the bloodwriting. The pilgrims were all speaking about it. Half thought it blasphemous, the other half thought it a path to Heaven. Since Da was a biologist, the pilgrims in our troop asked him what he thought. He said he would have to go to the bloodwriters directly and find out.

On a dusty Monday, after morning prayer, my father and I visited the bloodwriter's stall. The canvas was a beautiful white, and the man at the stall smiled as Da approached. He spoke some Arabic, which I could not understand.

"I speak English," said my father.

The stall attendant switched to English with the ease of a juggler changing hands. "Wonderful, sir! Many of our customers prefer English."

"I also speak biology. My pilgrim companions have asked me to review your product." I thought it very forward of my father, but the stall attendant seemed unfazed. He exuded confidence about his product.

"An expert!" he exclaimed. "Even better. Many pilgrims are distrustful of Western science. I do what I can to reassure them, but they see me as a salesman and not to be trusted. I welcome your endorsement."

"Then earn it."

The stall attendant wiped his mustache, and began his spiel. "Since the Dawn of Time, the Word of Allah has been read by mullahs. . . ."

"Stop!" said Da. "The Qur'an was revealed to Mohammed fifteen centuries ago; the Dawn of Time predates it by several billion years. I want answers, not portentous falsehoods."

Now the man was nervous. "Perhaps you should see my uncle. He invented the bloodwriting. I will fetch him." Soon he returned with an older, infinitely more respectable man with gray whiskers in his mustache and hair.

"Please forgive my nephew," said the old man. "He has watched too much American television and thinks the best way to impress is to use dramatic words, wild gestures, and where possible, a toll-free number." The nephew bowed his head and slunk to the back of the stall, chastened.

"May I answer your questions?" the old man asked.

"If you would be so kind," said Da, gesturing for the man to continue.

"Bloodwriting is a good word, and I owe my nephew a debt of gratitude for that. But the actual process is something altogether more mundane. I offer a virus, nothing more. I have taken a hypo-immunogenic strain of adeno-associated virus and added a special code to its DNA."

Da said, "The other pilgrims tell me that you can write the Qur'an into their blood."

"That I can, sir," said the old man. "Long ago I learned a trick that would get the adeno-associated virus to write its code into bone marrow stem cells. It made me a rich man. Now I use my gift for Allah's work. I consider it part of my *zakât*."

Da suppressed a wry smile. *Zakât*, charitable donation, was one of the five pillars. This old man was so blinded by avarice that he believed selling his invention for small profit was enough to fulfill his obligation to God.

The old man smiled and raised a small ampoule of red liquid. He continued, "This, my friend, is the virus. I have stripped its core and put the entire text of the Qur'an into its DNA. If you inject it, the virus will write the Qur'an into your myeloid precursor cells, and then your white blood cells will carry the Word of Allah inside them."

I put my hand up to catch his attention. "Why not red blood cells?" I asked. "They carry all the oxygen."

The old man looked at me as if he noticed me for the first time. "Hello, little one. You are very smart. Red blood cells carry oxygen, but they have no DNA. They cannot carry the Word."

It all seemed too complicated to an eleven-year-old girl.

My father was curious. "DNA codes for amino acid sequences. How can you write the Qur'an in DNA?"

"DNA is just another alphabet," said the old man. He handed my father a card. "Here is the crib sheet."

My father studied the card for several minutes, and I saw his face change from skeptical to awed. He passed the card to me. It was filled with Arabic squiggles, which I could not understand. The only thing I knew about Arabic was that it was written right-to-left, the reverse of English.

"I can't read it," I said to the man. He made a little spinning gesture with his finger, indicating that I should flip the card over. I flipped the card and saw the same crib sheet, only with Anglicized terms for each Arabic letter. Then he handed me another crib sheet, and said: "This is the sheet for English text."

AAA	a	AGA	q		ATA	[—] dash	ACA	
AAG	b	AGG	r		ATG	[/] slash	ACG	
AAT	c	AGT	s		ATT	{stop}	ACT	
AAC	d	AGC	t		ATC	{stop}	ACC	
GAA	e	GGA	u		GTA	['] apostrophe	GCA {stop}	
GAG	f	GGG	v		GTG	["] quotation mark	GCG	
GAT	g	GGT	w		GTT	[(] open bracket	GCT	0
GAC	h	GGC	x		GTC	[)] close bracket	GCC	1
TAA	i	TGA	y		TTA	[?] question mark	TCA	2
TAG	j	TGG	z		TTG	[!] exclamation	TCG	3
TAT	k	TGT	[ ] space		TTT	[•] end verse	TCT	4
TAC	l	TGC	[.] period		TTC	[¶] paragraph	TCC	5
CAA	m	CGA	[,] comma		CTA	{cap} capital	CCA	6
CAG	n	CGG	[:] colon		CTG		CCG	7
CAT	o	CGT	[;] semi-colon		CTT		CCT	8
CAC	p	CGC	[-] hyphen		CTC		CCC	9

"The Arabic alphabet has 28 letters. Each letter changes form depending on its position in the word. But the rules are rigid, so there is no need to put each variation in the crib sheet. It is enough to know that the letter is *aliph* or *bi*, and whether it is at the start, at the end, or in the middle of the word.

"The [*stop*] commands are also left in their usual places. These are the body's natural commands and they tell ribosomes when to stop making a protein. It only cost three spots and there were plenty to spare, so they stayed in."

My father asked, "Do you have an English translation?"

"Your daughter is looking at the crib sheet for the English language," the old man explained, "and there are other texts one can write, but not the Qur'an."

Thinking rapidly, Da said, "But you could write the Qur'an in English?"

"If I wanted to pursue secular causes, I could do that," the old man said. "But I have all the secular things I need. I have copyrighted crib sheets for all the common alphabets, and I make a profit on them. For the Qur'an, however, translations are not acceptable. Only the original words of Mohammed can be trusted. It is one thing for *dhimmis* to translate it for their own curiosity, but if you are a true believer you must read the word of God in its unsullied form."

Da stared at the man. The old man had just claimed that millions of Muslims were false believers because they could not read the original Qur'an. Da shook his head and let the matter go. There were plenty of imams who would agree with the old man.

"What is the success rate of the inoculation?"

"Ninety-five percent of my trial subjects had identifiable Qur'an text in their blood after two weeks, although I cannot guarantee that the entire text survived the insertion in all of those subjects. No peer-reviewed journal would accept the paper." He handed my father a copy of an article from *Modern Gene Techniques*. "Not because the science is poor, as you will see for yourself, but because Islam scares them."

Da looked serious. "How much are you charging for this?"

"Aha! The essential question. I would dearly love to give it away, but even a king would grow poor if he gave a grain of rice to every hungry man. I ask enough to cover my costs, and no haggling. It is a hundred US dollars or equivalent."

Da looked into the dusty sky, thinking. "I am puzzled," he said at last. "The Qur'an has one hundred and fourteen suras, which comes to tens of thousands of words. Yet the adeno-associated virus is quite small. Surely it can't all fit inside the viral coat?"

At this the old man nodded. "I see you are truly a man of wisdom.

It is a patented secret, but I suppose that someday a greedy industrialist will lay hands on my virus and sequence the genome. So, I will tell you on the condition that it goes no further than this stall."

Da gave his word.

"The code is compressed. The original text has enormous redundancy, and with advanced compression, I can reduce the amount of DNA by over 80 percent. It is still a lot of code."

I remember Da's jaw dropping. "That must mean the viral code is self-extracting. How on Earth do you commandeer the ribosomes?"

"I think I have given away enough secrets for today," said the old man.

"Please forgive me," said Da. "It was curiosity, not greed, that drove me to ask." Da changed his mind about the bloodwriter. This truly was fair *zakât*. Such a wealth of invention for only a hundred US dollars.

"And the safety?" asked my father.

The old man handed him a number of papers, which my father read carefully, nodding his head periodically, and humming each time he was impressed by the data.

"I'll have a dose," said Da. "Then no one can accuse me of being a slipshod reviewer."

"Sir, I would be honored to give a complimentary bloodwriting to you and your daughter."

"Thank you. I am delighted to accept your gift, but only for me. Not for my daughter. Not until she is of age and can make her own decision." Da took a red ampoule in his hands and held it up to the light, as if he was looking through an envelope for the letters of the Qur'an. He shook his head at the marvel and handed it back to the old man, who drew it up in a syringe.

That night, our fellow pilgrims made a fire and gathered around to hear my father talk. As he spoke, four translators whispered their own tongues to the crowd. The scene was like a great theater from the Arabian Nights. Scores of people wrapped in white robes leaned into my father's words, drinking up his excitement. It could have been a meeting of princes.

Whenever Da said something that amazed the gathered masses, you could hear the inbreath of the crowd, first from the English-speakers, and then in patches as the words came out in the other languages. He told them about DNA, and how it told our bodies how to live. He told them about introns, the long stretches of human DNA that are useless to our bodies, but that we carry still from viruses that invaded our distant progenitors, like ancestral scars. He told them about the DNA code, with its triplets of adenine, guanine, cytosine, and thymine, and he passed around copies of the bloodwriter's crib sheet. He told them about blood, and the white cells that fought infection. He talked about the adeno-associated virus and how it injected its DNA into humans. He talked about the bloodwriter's injection and the mild fever it had given him. He told them of the price.

And he answered questions for an hour.

The next day, as soon as the morning prayers were over, the blood-writing stall was swamped with customers. The old man ran out of ampoules by midmorning, and only avoided a riot by promising to bring more the following day.

I had made friends with another girl. She was two years younger than I was, and we did not share a language, but we still found ways to play together to relieve the boredom.

One day, I saw her giggling and whispering to her mother, who looked furtively at me and at Da. The mother waved over her companions, and spoke to them in solemn tones. Soon a very angry-looking phalanx of women descended on my unsuspecting father. They stood before him, hands on hips, and the one who spoke English pointed a finger at me.

"Where is her mother?" asked the woman. She was taller than the others, a weather-beaten woman who looked like she was sixty, but must have been younger because she had a child only two years old. "This is no place for a young girl to be escorted by a man."

"Zada's mother died in a car accident back home. I am her father, and I can escort her without help, thank you."

"I think not," said the woman.

"What right have you to say such a thing?" asked Da. "I am her father."

The woman pointed again. "Ala says she saw your daughter bathing, and she has not had the *khitan*. Is this true?"

"It is none of your business," said Da.

The woman screamed at him. "I will not allow my daughter to play with harlots. Is it true?"

"It is none of your business."

The woman lurched forward and pulled me by my arm. I squealed and twisted out of her grasp and ran behind my father for protection. I wrapped my arms around his waist and held on tightly.

"Show us," demanded the woman. "Prove she is clean enough to travel with this camp."

Da refused, which made the woman lose her temper. She slapped him so hard she split his lip. He tasted the blood, but stood resolute. She reached around and tried to unlock my arms from Da's waist. He pushed her away.

"She is not fit to share our camp. She should be cut, or else she will be shamed in the sight of Allah," the woman screamed. The other women were shouting and shaking their fists, but few of them knew English, so it was as much in confusion as anger.

My father fixed the woman with a vicious glare. "You call my daughter shameful in the sight of Allah? I am a servant of Allah. Prove to me that Allah is shamed and I will do what I can to remove the shame. Fetch a mullah."

The woman scowled. "I will fetch a mullah, although I doubt your promise is worth as much as words in the sand."

"Make sure the mullah speaks English," my father demanded as she slipped away. He turned to me and wiped away tears. "Don't worry, Zada. No harm will come to you."

"Will I be allowed to play with Ala?"

"No. Not with these old vultures hanging around."

By the evening, the women had found a mullah gullible enough to mediate the dispute. They tugged his sleeves as he walked toward our camp, hurrying him up. It was obvious that his distaste had grown with every minute in the company of the women, and now he was genuinely reluctant to speak on the matter.

The weathered woman pointed us out to the mullah and spat some words at him that we did not understand.

"Sir, I hear that your daughter is uncircumcised. Is this true?"

"It is none of your business," said Da.

The mullah's face dropped. You could almost see his heart sinking. "Did you not promise . . . ?"

"I promised to discuss theology with you and that crone. My daughter's anatomy is not your affair."

"Please, sir . . ."

Da cut him off abruptly. "Mullah, in your considered opinion, is it necessary for a Muslim girl to be circumcised?"

"It is the accepted practice," said the mullah.

"I do not care about the accepted practice. I ask what Mohammed says."

"Well, I'm sure that Mohammed says something on the matter," said the mullah.

"Show me where."

The mullah coughed, thinking of the fastest way to extract himself. "I did not bring my books with me," he said.

Da laughed, not believing that a mullah would travel so far to mediate a theological dispute without a book. "Here, have mine," Da said as he passed the Qur'an to the mullah. "Show me where Mohammed says such a thing."

The mullah's shoulders slumped. "You know I cannot. It is not in the Qur'an. But it is *sunnah*."

"*Sunnah*," said Da, "is very clear on the matter. Circumcision is *makrumah* for women. It is honorable but not compulsory. There is no requirement for women to be circumcised."

"Sir, you are very learned. But there is more to Islam than a strict reading of the Qur'an and *sunnah*. There have even been occasions when the word of Mohammed has been overturned by later imams. Mohammed himself knew that he was not an expert on all things, and he said that it was the responsibility of future generations to rise above his imperfect knowledge."

"So, you are saying that even if it was recorded in the Qur'an, that would not make it compulsory." Da gave a smile—the little quirk of his lips that he gave every time he had laid a logical trap for someone.

The mullah looked grim. The trap had snapped shut on his leg, and he was not looking forward to extricating himself.

"Tell these women so we can go back to our tents and sleep," said Da.

The mullah turned to the women and spoke to them. The weathered woman became agitated and started waving her hands wildly. Her voice was an overwrought screech. The mullah turned back to us.

"She refuses to share camp with you, and insists you leave."

Da fixed the mullah with his iron gaze. "Mullah, you are a learned man in a difficult situation, but surely you can see the woman is half-mad. She complains that my daughter has not been mutilated, and would not taint herself with my daughter's presence. Yet she is tainted herself. Did she tell you that she tried to assault my daughter and strip her naked in public view? Did she tell you that she inflicted this wound on me when I stood between her and my daughter? Did she tell you that I have taken the bloodwriting, so she spilled the Word of God when she drew blood?"

The mullah looked appalled. He went back to the woman, who started screeching all over again. He cut her off and began berating her. She stopped talking, stunned that the mullah had turned on her. He kept berating her until she showed a sign of humility. When she bowed her head, the mullah stopped his tirade, but as soon as the words stopped she sent a dagger-glance our way.

That night, three families pulled out of our camp. Many of the others in camp were pleased to see them go. I heard one of the grandmothers mutter "Taliban" under her breath, making a curse of the words.

The mood in camp lifted, except for mine. "It's my fault Ala left," I said.

"No, it is not your fault," said Da. "It was her family's fault. They want the whole world to think the way they think and to do what they do. This is against the teaching of the Qur'an, which says that there shall be no coercion in the matter of faith. I can find the sura if you like."

"Am I unclean?"

"No," said Da. "You are the most beautiful girl in the world."

By morning, the camp had been filled by other families. The faces were more friendly, but Ala was gone. It was my first lesson in intolerance, and it came from my own faith.

In Sydney, we sat for hours, waiting to be processed. By the third hour, Da finally lost patience and approached the customs officer.

"We are Australian citizens, you know?" Da said.

"Please be seated. We are still waiting for cross-checks."

"I was born in Brisbane, for crying out loud! Zada was born in Melbourne. My family is Australian four generations back."

His protests made no difference. Ever since the Saladin Outbreak, customs checked all Muslims thoroughly. Fifty residents of Darwin had died from an outbreak of a biological weapon that the Saladins had released. Only a handful of Saladins had survived, and they were all in prison, and it had been years ago, but Australia still treated its Muslims as if every single one of us was a terrorist waiting for the opportunity to go berserk.

We were insulted, shouted at, and spat on by men and women who then stepped into their exclusive clubs and talked about how uncivilized we were. Once it had been the Aborigines, then it had been the Italian and Greek immigrants; a generation later it was the Asians; now it was our turn. Da thought that we could leave for a while, go on our pilgrimage and return to a more settled nation, but our treatment by the customs officers indicated that little had changed in the year we were away.

They forced Da to strip for a search, and nearly did the same for me, until Da threatened them with child molestation charges. They took blood samples from both of us. They went through our luggage ruthlessly. They x-rayed our suitcases from so many angles that Da joked they would glow in the dark.

Then they made us wait, which was the worst punishment of all.

Da leaned over to me and whispered, "They are worried about my blood. They think that maybe I am carrying a deadly virus like a Saladin. And who knows? Maybe the Qur'an is a deadly virus." He chuckled.

"Can they read your blood?" I asked.

"Yes, but they can't make sense of it without the code sheet."

"If they knew it was just the Qur'an texts, would they let us go?"

"Probably," said Da.

"Why don't you give it to them, then?"

He sighed. "Zada, it is hard to understand, but many people hate us for no reason other than our faith. I have never killed or hurt or stolen from anyone in my life, and yet people hate me because I pray in a church with a crescent instead of a cross."

"But I want to get out of here," I pleaded.

"Listen to me, daughter. I could show them the crib sheet and explain it to them, but then they would know the code, and that is a terrifying possibility. There are people who have tried to design illnesses that attack only Jews or only blacks, but so far they have failed. The reason why they have failed is that there is no serological marker for black or Jewish blood. Now we stupid Muslims, and I count myself among the fools, have identified ourselves. In my blood is a code that says that I am a Muslim, not just by birth, but by active faith. I have marked myself. I might as well walk into a neo-Nazi rally wearing a Star of David.

"Maybe I am just a pessimist," he continued. "Maybe no one will ever design an anti-Muslim virus, but it is now technically possible. The longer it takes the *dhimmis* to find out how, the better."

I looked up at my father. He had called himself a fool. "Da, I thought you were smart!"

"Most of the time, darling. But sometimes faith means you have to do the dumb thing."

"I don't want to be dumb," I said.

Da laughed. "You know you can choose whatever you want to be. But there is a small hope I have for you. To do it you would need to be very, very smart."

"What?" I asked.

"I want you to grow up to be smart enough to figure out how to stop the illnesses I'm talking about. Mark my words, racial plagues will come one day, unless someone can stop them."

"Do you think I could?"

Da looked at me with utter conviction. "I have never doubted it."

Da's leukemia recurred a few years later. The chemotherapy had failed to cure him after all, although it had given him seven good years: just long enough to see me to adulthood, and enrolled in genetics. I tried to figure out a way to cure Da, but I was only a freshman. I understood less than half the words in my textbooks. The best I could do was hold his hand as he slowly died.

It was then that I finally understood what he meant when he said that sometimes it was important not to be smart. At the climax of our *haj* we had gone around the Kaabah seven times, moving in a human whirlpool. It made no sense at all intellectually. Going around and around a white temple in a throng of strangers was about as pointless a thing as you could possibly do, and yet I still remember the event as one of the most moving in my life. For a brief moment I felt a part of a greater community, not just of Muslims, but of the Universe. With that last ritual, Da and I became *haji* and *hajjah*, and it felt wonderful.

But I could not put aside my thoughts the way Da could. I had to be smart. Da had *asked* me to be smart. And when he died, after four months and two failed chemo cycles, I no longer believed in Allah. I wanted to maintain my faith, as much for my father as for me, but my heart was empty.

The event that finally tipped me, although I did not even realize it until much later, was seeing his blood in a sample tube. The oncology nurse had drawn 8 mls from his central line, then rolled the sample tube end over end to mix the blood with the anticoagulant. I saw the blood darken in the tube as it deoxygenated, and I thought about the blood cells in there. The white cells contained the suras of the Qur'an, but they also carried the broken code that turned them into cancer cells.

Da had once overcome leukemia years before. The doctors told me it was very rare to have a relapse after seven years. And this relapse seemed to be more aggressive than the first one. The tests, they told me, indicated this was a new mutation.

Mutation: a change in genetic code. Mutagen: an agent that promotes mutation.

Bloodwriting, by definition, was mutagenic. Da had injected one hundred and fourteen suras into his own DNA. The designer had been very careful to make sure that the bloodwriting virus inserted itself somewhere safe so it would not disrupt a tumor suppressor gene or switch on an oncogene—but that was for normal people. Da's DNA was already damaged by leukemia and chemotherapy. The virus had written a new code over the top, and I believe the new code switched his leukemia back on.

The Qur'an had spoken to his blood, and said: "He it is Who created you from dust, then from a small lifegerm, then from a clot, then He brings you forth as a child, then that you may attain your maturity, then that you may be old—and of you there are some who are caused to die before—and that you may reach an appointed term, and that you may understand. / He it is who gives life and brings death, so when He decrees an affair. He only says to it: *Be*, and it is."

I never forgave Allah for saying *"Be!"* to my father's leukemia. An educated, intelligent biologist, Da must have suspected that the Qur'an had killed him. Still, he never missed a prayer until the day he died. My own faith was not so strong. It shattered like fine china on concrete. Disbelief is the only possible revenge for omnipotence.

An infidel I was by then, but I had made a promise to my father, and for my postdoc I solved the bloodwriting problem. He would have been proud.

I abandoned the crib sheet. In my scheme the codons were assigned randomly to letters. Rather than preordaining *TAT* to mean *zen* in Arabic or "k" in English, I designed a process that shuffled the letters into a new configuration every time. Because there are 64 codons, with three {stop} marks and eight blanks, that comes to about 5×10^{83} or 500,000,000,000,000,000,000,000,000,000,000,000, 000,000,000,000,000,000,000,000,000,000,000,000,000,000 combinations. No one could design a virus specific to the Qur'an suras anymore. The *dhimmi* bastards would need to design a different virus for every Muslim on the face of the Earth. The faith of my father was safe to bloodwrite.

In my own blood I have written the things important to me. There is a picture of my family, a picture of my wedding, and a picture of my parents from when they were both alive. Pictures can be encoded just as easily as text.

There is some text: Crick and Watson's original paper describing the double-helix of DNA, and Martin Luther King's "I Have a Dream" speech. I also transcribed Cassius's words from *Julius Caesar*:

> *The fault, dear Brutus, is not in our stars,*
> *But in ourselves, that we are underlings.*

For the memory of my father, I included a Muslim parable, a *sunnah* story about Mohammed: One day, a group of farmers asked Mohammed for guidance on improving their crop. Mohammed told the farmers not to pollinate their date trees. The farmers recognized Mohammed as a wise man, and did as he said. That year, however, none of the trees bore any dates. The farmers were angry, and they returned to Mohammed demanding an explanation. Mohammed heard their complaints, then pointed out that he was a religious man, not a farmer, and his wisdom could not be expected to encompass the sum of human learning. He said, "You know your worldly business better."

It is my favorite parable from Islam, and is as important in its way as Jesus' Sermon on the Mount.

At the end of my insert, I included a quote from the *dhimmi* Albert Einstein, recorded the year after the atomic bombing of Japan.

He said, "The release of atom power has changed everything but our way of thinking," then added, "The solution of this problem lies in the heart of humankind."

I have paraphrased that last sentence into the essence of my new faith. No God was ever so succinct.

My artificial intron reads:

8 words, 45 codons, 135 base pairs that say:

CTA AGC GAC GAA TGT AGT CAT TAC GGA AGC TAA
CAT CAG TGT TAC TAA GAA AGT TGT TAA CAG TGT
AGC GAC GAA TGT GAC GAA AAA AGG AGC TGT
CAT GAG TGT GAC GGA CAA AAA CAG TAT TAA CAG
AAC TGC

The solution lies in the heart of humankind.

I whisper it to my children every night.

Falling Star

Brendan DuBois

We like to compliment ourselves on the bright, tidy rationality of our technological civilization, but the fact is, as the bittersweet story that follows demonstrates, that that technological civilization is fragile, easy to break—and, once broken, the Old Days and the Old Ways, with all of their bigotry, intolerance, and fear, are waiting to sweep in again, miring and dragging down even those who've always had their eyes on the stars.

Brendan DuBois has twice received the Shamus Award from the Private Eye Writers of America and has been nominated three times for the Edgar Allan Poe Award given by the Mystery Writers of America. He's made sales to *Playboy*, *Ellery Queen's Mystery Magazine*, *Alfred Hitchcock's Mystery Magazine*, *Space Stations*, *Civil War Fantastic*, *Pharaoh Fantastic*, *Knight Fantastic*, *The Mutant Files*, and *Alternate Gerrysburgs*, among other markets. His mystery novels include the Lewis Cole series, *Dead Sand*, *Black Tide*, *Shattered Shell*, *Killer Waves*, and *Buried Dreams*.

His science fiction novels include *Resurrection Day* and *Six Days*. His most recent novel is the suspense thriller *Betrayed*. He lives in Exeter, New Hampshire, with his family, and maintains a Web site at http://www.BrendanDuBois.com.

On a late July day in Boston Falls, New Hampshire, Rick Monroe, the oldest resident of the town, sat on a park bench in the town common, waiting for the grocery and mail wagon to appear from Greenwich. The damn thing was supposed to arrive at two PM, but the Congregational Church clock had just chimed three times and the road from Greenwich remained empty. Four horses and a wagon were hitched up to the post in front of the Boston Falls General Store, some bare-chested kids were playing in the dirt road, and flies were buzzing around his face.

He stretched out his legs, saw the dirt stains at the bottom of the old overalls. Mrs. Chandler, his once-a-week house cleaner, was again doing a lousy job with the laundry, and he knew he should say something to her, but he was reluctant to do it. Having a cleaning woman was a luxury and a bad cleaning woman was better than no cleaning woman at all. Even if she was a snoop and sometimes raided his icebox and frowned whenever she reminded him of the weekly church services.

Some of the kids shouted and started running up the dirt road. He sat up, shaded his eyes with a shaking hand. There, coming down slowly, two tired horses pulling the wagon that had high wooden sides and a canvas top. He waited as the wagon pulled into the store, waited still until it was unloaded. There was really no rush, no rush at all. Let the kids have their excitement, crawling in and around the wagon. When the wagon finally pulled out, heading to the next town over, Jericho, he slowly got up, wincing as his hips screamed at him. He went across the cool grass and then the dirt road, and up to the wooden porch. The children moved away from him, except for young Tom

Cooper, who stood there, eyes wide open. Glen Roundell, the owner of the General Store and one of the town's three selectmen, came up to him with a paper sack and a small packet of envelopes, tied together with a piece of twine.

"Here you go, Mister Monroe," he said, his voice formal, wearing a starched white shirt, black tie, and white store apron that reached the floor. "Best we can do this week. No beef, but there is some bacon there. Should keep if you get home quick enough."

"Thanks, Glen," he said. "On account, all right?"

Glen nodded. "That's fine."

He turned to step off the porch, when a man appeared out of the shadows. Henry Cooper, Tom's father, wearing a checked flannel shirt and blue jeans, his thick black beard down to midchest. "Would you care for a ride back to your place, Mister Monroe?"

He shifted the bag in his hands, smiled. "Why, that would be grand." And he was glad that Henry had not come into town with his wife, Marcia, for even though she was quite active in the church, she had some very un-Christian thoughts toward her neighbors, especially an old man like Rick Monroe, who kept to himself and wasn't a churchgoer.

Rick followed Henry and his boy outside, and he clambered up on the rear, against a couple of wooden boxes and a barrel. Henry said, "You can sit up front, if you'd like," and Rick said, "No, that's your boy's place. He can stay up there with you."

Henry unhitched his two-horse team, and in a few minutes, they were heading out on the Town Road, also known as New Hampshire Route 12. The rear of the wagon jostled and was bumpy, but he was glad he didn't have to walk it. It sometimes took him nearly an hour to walk from home to the center of town, and he remembered again— like he had done so many times—how once in his life it only took him ninety minutes to travel thousands of miles.

He looked again at the town common, at the stone monuments clustered there, commemorating the war dead from Boston Falls, those who had fallen in the Civil War, the Spanish-American War, World Wars I and II, Korea, Vietnam, and even the first and second Gulf Wars. Then, the town common was out of view, as the horse and wagon made its way out of a small New Hampshire village, hanging on in the sixth decade of the twenty-first century.

When the wagon reached his home, Henry and his boy came down to help him, and Henry said, "Can I bring some water out for the horses? It's a dreadfully hot day," and Rick said, "Of course, go right ahead." Henry nodded and said, "Tom, you help Mister Monroe in with his groceries. You do that."

"Yes, sir," the boy said, taking the bag from his hands, and he was embarrassed at how he enjoyed being helped. The inside of the house was cool—but not cool enough, came a younger voice from inside, a voice that said, remember when you could set a switch and have it cold enough to freeze your toes?—and he walked into the dark kitchen, past the coal-burning stove. From the grocery sack he took out a few canned goods—their labels in black and white, glued sloppily on— and the wax paper with the bacon inside. He went to the icebox, popped it open quickly and shut it. Tom was there, looking on, gazing around the room, and he knew what the boy was looking at: the framed photos of the time when Rick was younger and stronger, just like the whole damn country.

"Tom?"

"Yessir?"

"Care for a treat?"

Tom scratched at his dirty face with an equally dirty hand. "Momma said I shouldn't take anything from strangers. Not ever."

Rick said, "Well, boy, how can you say I'm a stranger? I live right down the road from you, don't I?"

"Unh-hunh."

"Then we're not strangers. You sit right there and don't move."

Tom clambered up on a wooden kitchen chair and Rick went over to the counter, opened up the silverware drawer, took out a spoon. Back to the icebox he went, this time opening up the freezer compartment, and he quickly pulled out a small white coffee cup with a broken handle. He placed the cold coffee cup down on the kitchen table and gave the boy the spoon.

"Here, dig in," he said.

Tom looked curious but took the spoon and scraped against the icelike confection in the bottom of the cup. He took a taste and his face lit up, like a lightbulb behind a dirty piece of parchment. The next time the spoon came up, it was nearly full, and Tom quickly ate everything in the cup, and then licked the spoon and tried to lick the inside of the cup.

"My, that was good!" he said. "What was it, Mister Monroe?"

"Just some lemonade and sugar, frozen up. Not had, hunh?

"It was great! Um, do you have any more? Sir?"

Rick laughed, thinking of how he had made it this morning, for a dessert after dinner. Not for a boy not even ten, but so what? "No, 'fraid not. But come back tomorrow. I might have some then, if I can think about it."

At the kitchen sink he poured water into the cup, and the voice returned. *Why not*, it said. *Tell the boy what he's missing. Tell him how it was like, back when a kid his age would laugh rather than eat frozen, sugary lemonade. That with the change in his pocket, he could walk outside and meet up with an ice cream cart that sold luxuries unknown today in the finest restaurants. Tell him that, why don't you?*

He coughed and turned, saw Tom was looking up again at the photos. "Mister Monroe . . ."

"Yes?"

"Mister Monroe, did you really go to the stars? Did you?"

Rick smiled, glad to see the curiosity in the boy's face, and not fear. "Well, I guess I got as close as anyone could, back then. You see—"

The boy's father yelled from outside. "Tom! Time to go! Come on out!"

Rick said, "Guess you have to listen to your dad, son. Tell you what, next time you come back, I'll tell you everything you want to know. Deal?"

The boy nodded and ran out of the kitchen. His hips were still aching and he thought about lying down before going through the mail, but he made his way outside, where Tom was up on the wagon. Henry came up and offered his hand, and Rick shook it, glad that Henry wasn't one to try the strength test with someone as old as he. Henry said, "Have a word with you, Mister Monroe?"

"Sure," he said. "But only if you call me Rick."

From behind the thick beard, he thought he could detect a smile. "All right . . . Rick."

They both sat down on old wicker rocking chairs and Henry said, "I'll get right to it, Rick."

"Okay."

"There's a town meeting tonight. I think you should go."

"Why?"

"Because . . . well, there's some stirrings. That's all. About a special committee being set up. A morals committee, to ensure that only the right people live here in Boston Falls."

"And who decides who are the right people?" he asked, finding it hard to believe this conversation was actually taking place.

Henry seemed embarrassed. "The committee and the selectmen, I guess . . . you see, there's word down south, about some of the towns there, they still got trouble with refugees and transients rolling in from Connecticut and New York. Some of those towns, the natives, they're being overwhelmed, outvoted, and they're not the same anymore. And since you, um—"

"I was born here, Henry. You know that. Just because I lived some-place else for a long time, that's held against me?"

"Well, I'm just sayin' it's not going to help . . . with what you did back then, and the fact you don't go to church, and other things, well . . . it might be worthwhile if you go there. That's all. To defend yourself."

Even with the hot weather, Rick was feeling a cold touch upon his hands. *Now we're really taking a step back,* he thought. *Like the Nuremberg laws, in Nazi Germany. Ensuring that only the ethnically and racially pure get to vote, to shop, to live . . .*

"And if this committee decides you don't belong? What then? Arrested? Exiled? Burned at the stake?"

Now his neighbor looked embarrassed as he stepped up from the wicker chair. "You should just be there, Mister uh, I mean, Rick. It's at eight o'clock. At the town hall."

"That's a long walk in, when it's getting dark. Any chance I could get a ride?"

Even with his neighbor's back turned to him, Rick could sense the humiliation. "Well, I, well, I don't think so, Rick. I'm sorry. You see, I think Marcia wants to visit her sister after the meeting, and I don't know what time we might get back, and, well, I'm sorry."

Henry climbed up into the wagon, retrieved the reins from his son, and Rick called out. "Henry?"

"Yes?"

"Any chance your wife is on this committee?"

The expression on his neighbor's face was all he needed to know, as the wagon turned around on his brown lawn and headed back up to the road.

Back inside, he grabbed his mail and went upstairs, to the spare bed-room that he had converted into an office during the first year he had made it back to Boston Falls. He went to unlock the door and found that it was already open. Damn his memory, which he knew was starting to show its age, just like his hips. He was certain he had locked it the last time. He sat down at the desk and untied the twine, knowing he would save it. What was that old Yankee saying? Use it up, wear it out, or do without? Heavy thrift, one of the many lessons being relearned these years.

One envelope he set aside to bring into Glen Roundell, the General Store owner. It was his Social Security check, only three months late, and Glen—who was also the town's banker—would take it and apply it against Rick's account. Not much being made for sale nowadays, so whatever tiny amount his Social Security check was this month was usually enough to keep his account in good shape.

There was an advertising flyer for the Grafton County Fair, set to start next week. Another flyer announcing a week-long camp revival at the old Boy Scout camp on Conway Lake, during the same time. Competition, no doubt. And a thin envelope, postmarked Houston, Texas, which he was happy to see. It had only taken a month for the envelope to get here, which he thought was a good sign. Maybe some things were improving in the country.

Maybe.

He slit open the envelope with an old knife, saw the familiar handwriting inside.

Dear Rick,

Hope this sees you doing well in the wilds of New Hampshire.

Down here what passes for recovery continues. Last month, two whole city blocks had their power restored. It only comes on for a couple of hours a day, and no a/c is allowed, but it's still progress, eh?

Enclosed are the latest elements for Our Boy. I'm sorry to say the orbit degradation is continuing. Latest guess is that Our Boy may be good for another five years, maybe six.

Considering what was spent in blood and treasure to put him up there, it breaks my heart.

If you get bored and lonely up there, do consider coming down here. I understand that with Amtrak coming back, it should only take four weeks to get here. The heat is awful but at least you'll be in good company with those of us who still remember.

Your pal,

Brian

With the handwritten sheet was another sheet of paper, with a listing of dates and times, and he shook his head in dismay. Most of the sightings were for early mornings, and he hated getting up in the morning. But tonight—how fortunate!—there was going to be a sighting at just after eight o'clock.

Eight o'clock. Why did that sound familiar?

Now he remembered. The town meeting tonight, where supposedly his fate and those of any other possible sinners was to be decided. He carefully folded up the letter, put it back in the envelope. He decided one more viewing was more important, more important than whatever chatter session was going to happen later. And besides, knowing what he did about the town and its politics, the decision had already been made.

He looked around his small office, with the handmade bookshelves and books, and more framed photos on the cracked plaster wall. One of the photos was of him and his friend, Brian Poole, wearing blue-zippered jumpsuits, standing in front of something large and complex, built ages ago in the swamps of Florida.

"Thanks, guy," he murmured, and he got up and went downstairs, to think of what might be for dinner.

Later that night he was in the big backyard, a pasture that he let his other neighbor, George Thompson, mow for hay a couple of times each summer, for which George gave him some venison and smoked ham over the long winters in exchange. He brought along a folding lawn chair, its bright plastic cracked and faded away, and he sat there, stretching out his legs. It was a quiet night, like every night since he had come here, years ago. He smiled in the darkness. What strange twists of fate and fortune had brought him back here, to his old family farm. He had grown up here, until his dad had moved the family south, to a suburb of Boston, and from there, high school and Air Force ROTC, and then many, many years traveling, thousands upon thousands of miles, hardly ever thinking about the old family farm, now owned by a second or third family. And he would have never come back here, until the troubles started, when—

A noise made him turn his head. Something crackling out there, in the underbrush.

"Who's out there?" he called out, wondering if some of the more hot-blooded young'uns in town had decided not to wait until the meeting was over. "Come out and show yourself."

A shape came out from the wood line, ambled over, small, and then there was a young boy's voice, "Mister Monroe, it's me, Tom Cooper."

"Tom? Oh, yes, Tom. Come on over here."

The young boy came up, sniffling some, and Rick said, "Tom, you gave me a bit of a surprise. What can I do for you?"

Tom stood next to him, and said slowly, "I was just wondering . . . well, that cold stuff you gave me earlier, that tasted really good. I didn't know if you had any more left . . ."

He laughed. "Sorry, guy. Maybe tomorrow. How come you're not with your mom and dad at the meeting?"

Tom said, "My sister Ruth is supposed to be watching us, but I snuck out of my room and came here. I was bored."

"Well, boredom can be good, it means something will happen. Tell you what, Tom, wait a couple of minutes, I'll show you something special."

"What's that?"

"You just wait and I'll show you."

Rick folded his hands together in his lap, looked over at the southeast. Years and years ago, that part of the night sky would be a light yellow glow, the lights from the cities in that part of the state. Now, like every other part of the night sky, there was just blackness and the stars, the night sky now back where it had once been, almost two centuries ago.

There. Right there. A dot of light, moving up and away from the horizon.

"Take a look, Tom. See that moving light?"

"Unh-hunh."

"Good. Just keep your eye on it. Look at it go."

The solid point of light rose up higher and seemed brighter, and he found his hands were tingling and his chest was getting tighter. Oh, God, how beautiful, how beautiful it had been up there, looking down on the great globe, watching the world unfold beneath you, slow and majestic and lovely, knowing that as expensive and ill-designed and overbudget and late in being built, it was there, the first permanent outpost for humanity, the first step in reaching out to the planets and stars that were humanity's destiny . . .

The crickets seemed louder. An owl out in the woods hoo-hoo'ed, and beside him, Tom said, "What is it, Mister Monroe?"

The light seemed to fade some, and then it disappeared behind some tall pines, and Rick found that his eyes had gotten moist. He wiped at them and said, "What do you think it was?"

"I dunno. I sometimes see lights move at night, and Momma tells me that it's the Devil's work, and I shouldn't look at 'em. Is that true?"

He rubbed at his chin, thought for a moment about just letting the boy be, letting him grow up with his illusions and whatever misbegotten faith his mother had put in his head, letting him think about farming and hunting and fishing, to concentrate on what was real, what was necessary, which was getting enough food to eat and a warm place and—

No! the voice inside him shouted. *No, that's not fair, to condemn this boy and the others to a life of peasantry, just because of some wrong things that had been done, years before the child was even born.* He shook his head and said, "Well, I can see why some people would think it's the Devil's work, but the truth is, Tom, that was a building up there. A building made by men and women and put up in the sky, more than a hundred miles up."

Tom sounded skeptical. "Then how come it doesn't fall down?"

Great, the voice said. *Shall we give him a lecture about Newton? What do you suggest?*

He thought for a moment and said, "It's complex, and I don't want to bore you, Tom. But trust me, it's up there. In fact, it's still up there and will be for a while. Even though nobody's living in it right now."

Tom looked up and said, "Where is it now?"

"Oh, I imagine it's over Canada by now. You see, it goes around the whole globe in what's called an orbit. Only takes about ninety minutes or so."

Tom seemed to think about that and said shyly, "My dad. He once said you were something. A spaceman. That you went to the stars. Is that true?"

"True enough. We never made it to the stars, though we sure thought about it a lot."

"He said you flew up in the air. Like a bird. And the places you went, high enough, you had to carry your own air with you. Is that true, too?"

"Yes, it is."

"Jeez. You know, my momma, well . . ."

"Your momma, she doesn't quite like me, does she?"

"Unh-hunh. She says you're not good. You're unholy. And some other stuff."

Rick thought about telling the boy the truth about his mother, decided it could wait until the child got older. God willing, the boy would learn soon enough about his mother. Aloud Rick said, "I'm going back to my house. Would you like to get something?"

"Another cold treat?" came the hopeful voice.

"No, not tonight. Maybe tomorrow. Tonight, well, tonight I want to give you something that'll last longer than any treat."

A few minutes later they were up in his office, Tom talking all the while about the fishing he had done so far this summer, the sleep-outs in the back pasture, and about his cousin Lloyd, who lived in the next town over, Hancock, and who died of something called polio. Rick shivered at the matter-of-fact way Tom had mentioned his cousin's death. A generation ago, a death like that never would have happened. Hell, a generation ago, if somebody of Tom's age had died, the poor kid would have been shoved into counseling sessions and group therapies, trying to get closure about the damn thing. And now? Just part of growing up.

In his office Tom oohed and aaahed over the photos on his wall, and Rick explained as best he could what they were about. "Well, that's the dot of light we just saw. It's actually called a space station. Over there, that's what you used to fly up to the space station. It's called a space shuttle. Or a rocket, if you prefer. This . . . this is a picture of me, up in the space station."

"Really?" Tom asked. "You were really there?"

He found he had to sit down, so he did, his damn hips aching something fierce. "Yes, I was really up there. One of the last people up there, to tell you the truth, Tom. Just before, well . . . just before everything changed."

Tom stood before a beautiful photo of a full moon, the craters and

mountains and flat seas looking as sharp as if they were made yesterday. He said, "Momma said that it was God who punished the
world back then, because men were evil, because they ignored God. Is
that true, Mister Monroe? What really happened back then?"

His fists suddenly clenched, as if powered by memory. Where to
begin, young man, he thought. Where to begin. Let's talk about a time
when computers were in everything, from your car to your toaster to
your department store cash register. Everything linked up and intercon-
nected. And when the systems got more and more complex, the childish
ones, the vandals, the destructive hackers, they had to prove that they
had the knowledge and skills and wherewithal to take down a system.
Oh, the defenses grew stronger and stronger, as did the viruses, and the
evil ones redoubled their efforts, like the true Vandals coming into
Rome, burning and destroying something that somebody else created.
The defenses grew more in-depth, the attacks more determined, until
one bright soul—if such a creature could be determined to have a soul—
came up with the ultimate computer virus. No, not one that wormed its
way into software through backdoors or anything fancy like that. No sir.
This virus was one that attacked the hardware, the platforms, that spread
God knows how—theories ranged from human touch to actual impulses
over fiber optics—and destroyed the chips. That's all. Just ate the chips
and left burned-out crumbs behind, so that in days, almost every thing
in the world that used a computer was silent, dark, and dead.

Oh, he was a smart one—for the worst of the hackers were always
male—whoever he was, and Rick often wished that the designer of the
ultimate virus (called the Final Virus, for a very good reason) had been
on an aircraft or an operating room table when it had struck. For when
the computers sputtered out and died, the chaos that was unleashed
upon the world . . . cars, buses, trains, trucks. Dead, not moving. Hundreds of thousands of people, stranded far from home. Aircraft falling
out of the skies. Ships at sea, slowly drifting, unable to maneuver. Stock
markets, banks, corporations, everything and anything that stored the

wealth of a nation in electronic impulses, silent. All the interconnections that fed and clothed and fueled and protected and sheltered most of the world's billions had snapped apart, like brittle rubber bands. Within days the cities had become uninhabitable, as millions streamed into the countryside. Governments wavered and collapsed. Communications were sparse, for networks and radio stations and the cable stations were off the air as well. Rumors and fear spread like a plague itself, and the Four Horsemen of the Apocalypse—called out from retirement at last—swept through almost the entire world.

There were a few places that remained untouched: Antarctica and a few remote islands. But for the rest of the world . . . sometimes the only light on the nightside of the planet were the funeral pyres, where the bodies were being burned.

He grew nauseous, remembering what had happened to him and how it took him months to walk back here, to his childhood home, and he repressed the memory of eating something a farmer had offered him—it hadn't looked exactly like dog, but God, he had been so hungry—and he looked over to young Tom. How could he even begin to tell such a story to such an innocent lad?

He wouldn't. He composed himself and said, "No, God didn't punish us back then. We did. It was a wonderful world, Tom, a wonderful place. It wasn't perfect and many people did ignore God, did ignore many good things . . . but we did things. We fed people and cured them and some of us, well, some of us planned to go to the stars."

He went up to the wall, took down the picture of the International Space Station, the Big Boy himself, and pointed it out to Tom. "Men and women built that on the ground, Tom, and brought it up into space. They did it for good, to learn things, to start a way for us to go back to the Moon and to Mars. To explore. There was no evil there. None."

Tom looked at the picture and said, "And that's the dot of light we saw? Far up in the sky?"

"Yes."

"And what's going to happen to it?"

He looked at the framed photo, noticed his hands shaking some. He put the photo back up on the wall. "One of these days, it's going to get lower and lower. It just happens. Things up in orbit can't stay up there forever. Unless somebody can go up there and do something . . . it'll come crashing down."

He sat down in the chair, winced again at the shooting pains in his hips. There was a time when he could have had new hips, new knees, or—if need be—new kidneys, but it was going to take a long time for those days to ever come back. From his infrequent letters from Brian, he knew that work was still continuing in some isolated and protected labs, to find an answer to the Final Virus. But with people starving and cities still unlit, most of the whole damn country had fallen back to the late 1800s, when power was provided by muscles, horses, or steam. Computers would just have to wait.

Tom said, "I hope it doesn't happen, Mister Monroe. It sounds really cool."

Rick said, "Well, maybe when you grow up, if you're really smart, you can go up there and fix it. And think about me when you're doing it. Does that sound like fun?"

The boy nodded and Rick remembered why he had brought the poor kid up here. He got out of his chair, went over to his bookshelf, started moving around the thick volumes and such, until he found a slim book, a book he had bought once for a future child, for one day he had promised Kathy Meserve that once he left the astronaut corps, he would marry her. . . . Poor Kathy, in London on a business trip, whom he had never seen or heard from ever again after the Final Virus had broken out.

He came over to Tom and gave him the book. It was old but the cover was still bright, and it said, *MY FIRST BOOK ON SPACE TRAVEL*. Rick said, "You can read, can't you?"

"Unh-hunh, I sure can."

"Okay." He rubbed at the boy's head, not wanting to think of Kathy Meserve or the children he never had. "You take this home and read it. You can learn a lot about the stars and planets and what it was like, to explore space and build the first space station. Maybe you can get back up there, Tom." Or your children's children, he thought, but why bring that depressing thought up. "Maybe you can be what I was, a long time ago."

Tom's voice was solemn. "A star man?"

Rick shook his head. "No, nothing fancy like that. An astronaut. That's all. Look, it's getting late. Why don't you head home."

And the young boy ran from his office, holding the old book in his hands, as if scared Rick was going to change his mind and take it away from him.

It was the sound of the horses that woke him, neighing and moving about in his yard, early in the morning. He got out of bed, cursed his stiff joints, and slowly got dressed. At the foot of the bed was a knapsack, for he knew a suitcase would not work. He picked up the knapsack—which he had put together last night—and walked downstairs, walked slowly, as he noticed the woodwork and craftsmanship that a long forgotten great-great-great-grandfather had put into building this house, which he was now leaving.

He went out on the front porch, shaded his eyes from the hot morning sun. There were six or seven horses in his front yard, three horse-drawn wagons, and a knot of people in front. Some children were clustered out under the maple tree by the road, their parents no doubt telling them to stay away. He recognized all of the faces in the crowd, but was pleased to see that Glen Roundell, the store owner and one of the three selectmen, was not there, nor was Henry Cooper. Henry's wife Marcia was there, thin-lipped and perpetually angry, and she strode forward, holding something at her side. She wore a long cotton skirt and long-sleeve shirt—and that insistent voice inside his head wondered why again, with technology having tumbled two hundred years, why did fashion have to follow suit?—and she announced loudly, "Rick Monroe, you know why we're here, don't you."

"Mrs. Cooper, I'm sure I have some idea, but why don't you inform me, in case I'm mistaken. I know that of your many fine attributes, correcting the mistakes of others is your finest."

She looked around the crowd, as if seeking their support, and she pressed on, even though there was a smile or two at his comment. "At a special town meeting last night, it was decided by a majority of the town to suspend your residency here, in Boston Falls, due to your past crimes and present immorality."

"Crimes?" In the crowd he noticed a man in a faded and patched uniform, and he said, "Chief Godin. You know me. What crimes have I committed?"

Chief Sam Godin looked embarrassed. A kid of about twenty-two or thereabouts, he was the Chief because he had strong hands and was a good shot. The uniform shirt he wore was twice as old as he was, but he wore it proudly, since it represented his office.

Today, though, he looked like he would rather be wearing anything else. He seemed to blush and said, "Gee, Mister Monroe . . . no crimes here, since you've moved back. But there's been talk of what you did, back then, before . . . before the change. You were a scientist or something. Worked with computers. Maybe had something to do with the change, that's the kind of crimes that we were thinking about."

Rick sighed. "Very good. That's the crime I've been accused of, of being educated. That I can accept. But immoral? Where's your proof?"

"Right here," Marcia Cooper said triumphantly. "See? This old magazine, with depraved photos and lustful women . . . kept in your house, to show any youngster that came by. Do you deny having this in your possession?"

And despite it all, he felt like laughing, for Mrs. Cooper was holding up—and holding up tight so nothing inside would be shown, of course—an ancient copy of *Playboy* magazine. The damn thing had been in his office, and sometimes he would just glance through the slick pages and sigh at a world—and a type of woman—long gone. Then something came to him and he saw another woman in the crowd, arms folded tight, staring in distaste toward him. It all clicked.

"No, I don't deny it," Rick said, "and I also don't deny that Mrs. Chandler, for once in her life, did a good job cleaning my house. Find anything else in there, Mrs. Chandler, you'd like to pass on to your neighbors?"

She just glared, said nothing. He looked up at the sun. It was going to be another hot day.

The Chief stepped forward and said, "We don't want any trouble, Mister Monroe. But it's now the law. You have to leave."

He picked up his knapsack, shrugged his arms through the frayed straps, almost gasped at the heavy weight back there. "I know."

The Chief said, "If you want, I can get you a ride to one of the next towns over, save you—"

"No," he said, not surprised at how harshly he responded. "No, I'm not taking any of your damn charity. By God, I walked into this town alone years ago, and I'll walk out of this town alone as well."

Which is what he started to do, coming down the creaky steps, across the unwatered lawn. The crowd in front of him slowly gave way, like they were afraid he was infected or some damn thing. He looked at their dirty faces, the ignorant looks, the harsh stares, and he couldn't help himself. He stopped and said, "You know, I pity you. If it hadn't been for some unknown clown, decades ago, you wouldn't be here. You'd be on a powerboat in a lake. You'd be in an air-conditioned mall, shopping. You'd be talking to each other over frozen drinks about where to fly to vacation this winter. That's what you'd be doing."

Marcia Cooper said, "It was God's will. That's all."

Rick shook his head. "No, it was some idiot's will, and because of that, you've grown up to be peasants. God save you and your children."

They stayed silent, but he noticed that some of the younger men were looking fidgety, and were glancing to the Chief, like they were wondering if the Chief would intervene if they decided to stone him or some damn thing. Time to get going, and he tried not to think of the long miles that were waiting for him. Just one step after another, that's all. Maybe, if his knees and hips held together, he could get to the train station in Concord. Maybe. Take Brian up on his offer. He made it out to the dirt road, decided to head left, up to Greenwich, for he didn't want to walk through town. Why tempt fate?

He turned and looked one last time at his house, and then looked over to the old maple tree, where some of the children, bored by what had been going on, were now scurrying around the tree trunk.

But not all of the children.

One of them was by himself, at the road's edge. He looked nervous, and he raised his shirt, and even at this distance, he could make out young Tom Cooper, standing there, his gift of a book hidden away in the waistband of his jeans. Tom lowered his shirt and then waved, and Rick, surprised, smiled and waved back.

And then he turned his back on his home and his town, and started walking away.

Three Hearings on the Existence of Snakes in the Human Bloodstream

James Alan Gardner

James Alan Gardner has made many fiction sales to the *Magazine of Fantasy & Science Fiction*, *Asimov's Science Fiction*, *Amazing*, *Tesseracts*, *On Spec*, *Northern Stars*, and other markets. His books include the science fiction novels *Expendable*, *Commitment Hour*, *Vigilant*, *Hunted*, *Ascending*, and *Trapped*. His most recent novel is *Radiant*.

In the fascinating and ingenious story that follows, he takes us to a world where history has worked out a little differently than it did in our own—but where the fundamental things, particularly the battle between science and superstition, have really not changed at all.

1. Concerning an Arrangement of Lenses, So Fashioned as to Magnify the View of Divers Animalcules, Too Tiny to Be Seen with the Unaided Eye:

His Holiness, Supreme Patriarch Septus XXIV, was an expert on chains.

By holy law, chains were required on every defendant brought to the Court Immaculate. However, my Lord the Jailer could exercise great latitude in choosing which chains went on which prisoners. A man possessed of a healthy fortune might buy his way into nothing more than a gold link necklace looped loosely around his throat; a beautiful woman might visit the Jailer privately in his chambers and emerge with thin and glittering silver bracelets—chains, yes, but as delicate as thread. If, on the other hand, the accused could offer neither riches nor position nor generous physical charms . . . well then, the prison had an ample supply of leg-irons, manacles, and other such fetters, designed to show these vermin the grim weight of God's justice.

The man currently standing before Patriarch Septus occupied a seldom-seen middle ground in the quantity of restraints: two solid handcuffs joined by an iron chain of businesslike gauge, strong enough that the prisoner had no chance of breaking free, but not so heavy as to strain the man's shoulders to the point of pain. Clearly, my Lord the Jailer had decided on a cautious approach to this particular case; and Septus wondered what that meant. Perhaps the accused was nobody himself but had sufficient connections to rule out unwarranted indignities . . . a sculptor or musician, for example, who had won favor with a few great households in the city. The man certainly had an artistic look—fierce eyes in an impractical face, the sort of high-strung temperament who could express passion but not use it.

"Be it known to the court," cried the First Attendant, "here stands one Anton Leeuwenhoek, a natural philosopher who is accused of heresy against God and Our Lady, the Unbetombed Virgin. Kneel, Supplicant, and pray with his Holiness, that this day shall see justice."

Septus waited to see what Leeuwenhoek would do. When thieves and murderers came before the court, they dropped to their knees immediately, making gaudy show of begging God to prove their innocence. A heretic, however, might spit defiance or hurl curses at the Patriarchal throne—not a good way to win mercy, but then, many heretics came to this chamber intent on their own martyrdom. Leeuwenhoek had the eyes of such a fanatic, but apparently not the convictions; without so much as a grimace, he got to his knees and bowed his head. The Patriarch quickly closed his own eyes and intoned the words he had recited five times previously this morning: "God grant me the wisdom to perceive the truth. Blessed Virgin, grant me the judgment to serve out meet justice. Let us all act this day to the greater glory of Thy Divine Union. Amen."

Amens sounded around the chamber: attendants and advocates following the form. Septus glanced sideways toward Satan's Watchboy, an ominous title for a cheerfully freckle-faced youth, the one person here excused from closing his eyes during the prayer. The Watchboy nodded twice, indicating that Leeuwenhoek had maintained a proper attitude of prayer and said Amen with everyone else. Good—this had just become a valid trial, and anything that happened from this point on had the strength of heavenly authority.

"My Lord Prosecutor," Septus said, "state the charges."

The prosecutor bowed as deeply as his well-rounded girth allowed, perspiration already beading on his powdered forehead. It was not a hot day, early spring, nothing more . . . but Prosecutor ben Jacob was a man famous for the quantity of his sweat, a trait that usually bothered his legal adversaries more than himself. Many an opposing counsel had been distracted by the copious flow streaming down ben

Jacob's face, thereby overlooking flaws in the prosecutor's arguments. One could always find flaws in ben Jacob's arguments, Septus knew—dear old Abraham was not overly clever. He was, however, honest, and could not conceive of winning personal advancement at the expense of those he prosecuted; therefore, the Patriarch had never dismissed the man from his position.

"Your Holiness," ben Jacob said, "this case concerns claims against the Doctrine of the, uhh . . . Sleeping Snake."

"Ah." Septus glanced over at Leeuwenhoek. "My son, do you truly deny God's doctrine?"

The man shrugged. "I have disproved the doctrine. Therefore, it can hardly be God's."

Several attendants gasped loudly. They perceived it as part of their job to show horror at every sacrilege. The same attendants tended to whisper and make jokes during the descriptions of true horrors: murders, rapes, maimings. "The spectators will remain silent," Septus said wearily. He had recited those words five times this morning, too. "My Lord Prosecutor, will you please read the text?"

"Ummm . . . the text, yes, the text."

Septus maintained his composure while ben Jacob shuffled through papers and parchments looking for what he needed. It was, of course, standard procedure to read any passages of scripture that a heretic denied, just to make sure there was no misunderstanding. It was also standard procedure for ben Jacob to misplace his copy of the relevant text in a pile of other documents. With any other prosecutor, this might be some kind of strategy; with ben Jacob, it was simply disorganization.

"Here we are, yes, here we are," he said at last, producing a dog-eared page with a smear of grease clearly visible along one edge. "Gospel of Susannah, chapter twenty-three, first verse." Ben Jacob paused while the two Verification Attendants found the passage in their own scripture books. They would follow silently as he read the text aloud, ready to catch any slips of the tongue that deviated from the holy word. When the attendants were ready, ben Jacob cleared his throat and read:

After the procession ended, they withdrew to a garden outside the walls of Jerusalem. And in the evening, it happened that Matthias beheld a serpent there, hidden by weeds. He therefore took up a stone that he might crush the beast; but Mary stayed his hand, saying, "There is no danger, for look, the beast sleeps."

"Teacher," Matthias answered, "it will not sleep forever."

"Verily," said Mary, "I promise it will sleep till dawn; and when the dawn comes, we will leave this place and all the serpents that it holds."

Yet still, Matthias kept hold of the stone and gazed upon the serpent with fear.

"O ye of little faith," said Mary to Matthias, "why do you concern your-self with the sleeping creature before you, when you are blind to the serpents in your own heart? For I tell you, each drop of your blood courses with a legion of serpents, and so it is for every Child of Dust. You are all poisoned with black venoms, poisoned unto death. But if you believe in me, I will sing those serpents to sleep; then will they slumber in peace until you leave this flesh behind, entering into the dawn of God's new day."

Ben Jacob lowered his page and looked to the Verifiers for their confirmation. The Patriarch turned in their direction, too, but he didn't need their nods to tell him the scripture had been read correctly. Septus knew the passage by heart; it was one of the fundamental texts of Mother Church, the Virgin's promise of salvation. It was also one of the most popular texts for heretics to challenge. The presumption of original sin, of damnation being inherent in human flesh . . . that was anathema to many a fiery young soul. *What kind of God*, they asked, *would damn an infant to hell merely for being born?* It was a good question, its answer still the subject of much subtle debate; but the Virgin's words were unequivocal, whether or not theologians had reasoned out all the implications.

"Anton Leeuwenhoek," Septus said, "you have heard the verified word of scripture. Do you deny its truth?"

Leeuwenhoek stared directly back. "I must," he answered. "I have examined human blood in meticulous detail. It contains no serpents."

The toadies in the courtroom had their mouths open, ready to gasp again at sacrilege; but even they could hear the man was not speaking in deliberate blasphemy. He seemed to be stating . . . a fact.

How odd.

Septus straightened slightly in the Patriarchal throne. This had the prospect of more interest than the usual heresy trial. "You understand," he said to Leeuwenhoek, "this passage is about original sin. The Blessed Virgin states that all human beings are poisoned with sin and can only be redeemed through her."

"On the contrary, Your Holiness." Leeuwenhoek's voice was sharp. "The passage states there are snakes in human blood. I know there are not."

"The snakes are merely . . ." Septus stopped himself in time. He had been on the verge of saying the snakes were merely a metaphor; but this was a public trial, and any pronouncements he made would have the force of law. To declare that any part of scripture was not the literal truth . . . no Patriarch had ever done so in open forum, and Septus did not intend to be the first.

"Let us be clear on this point," Septus said to Leeuwenhoek. "Do you deny the Doctrine of Original Sin?"

"No—I could never make heads or tails of theology. What I understand is blood; and there are no snakes in it."

One of the toadies ventured a small gasp of horror, but even a deaf man could have told the sound was forced.

Prosecutor ben Jacob, trying to be helpful, said, "You must appreciate that the snakes would be very, very small."

"That's just it," Leeuwenhoek answered with sudden enthusiasm. "I have created a device that makes it possible to view tiny things as if they were much larger." He turned quickly toward Septus. "Your Holiness is familiar with the telescope? The device for viewing objects at long distances?"

The Patriarch nodded in spite of himself.

"My device," Leeuwenhoek said, "functions on a similar principle —an arrangement of lenses that amplify one's vision to reveal things too small to see with the naked eye. I have examined blood in every particular; and while it contains numerous minute animalcules I cannot identify, I swear to the court there are no snakes. Sleeping or otherwise."

"Mm." Septus took a moment to fold his hands on the bench in front of him. When he spoke, he did not meet the prisoner's eyes. "It is well known that snakes are adept at hiding, are they not? Surely it is possible that a snake could be concealed behind . . . behind these other minute animalcules you mention."

"A legion of serpents," Leeuwenhoek said stubbornly. "That's what the text said. A legion of serpents in every drop of blood. Surely they couldn't *all* find a place to hide; and I have spent hundreds of hours searching, Your Holiness. Days and weeks and months."

"Mm."

Troublesome to admit, Septus didn't doubt the man. The Patriarch had scanned the skies with an excellent telescope, and had seen a universe of unexpected wonders—mountains on the moon, hair on the sun, rings around the planet Cronus. He could well believe Leeuwenhoek's magnifier would reveal similar surprises . . . even if it didn't show serpents in the bloodstream. The serpents were merely a parable anyway; who could doubt it? Blessed Mary often spoke in poetic language that every educated person recognized as symbolic rather than factual.

Unfortunately, the church was not composed of educated persons. No matter how sophisticated the clergy might be, parishioners came from humbler stock. Snakes in the blood? If that's what Mary said, it must be true; and heaven help a Patriarch who took a less dogmatic stance. The bedrock of the church was Authority: ecclesiastic authority, scriptural authority. If Septus publicly allowed that some doctrines could be interpreted as mere symbolism—that a fundamental teaching was metaphor, not literal fact—well, all it took was a single hole in a wineskin for everything to leak out.

On the other hand, truth was truth. If there were no snakes, there were no snakes. God made the world and all the people in it; if the Creator chose to fashion human lifeblood a certain way, it was the duty of Mother Church to accept and praise Him for it. Clinging to a lie in order to preserve one's authority was worse than mere cowardice; it was the most damning blasphemy.

Septus looked at Leeuwenhoek, standing handcuffed in the dock. A living man with a living soul; and with one word, Septus could have him executed as a purveyor of falsehood.

But where did the falsehood truly lie?

"This case cannot be decided today," Septus announced. "Mother Church will investigate the claims of the accused to the fullest extent of her strength. We will build magnifier devices of our own, properly blessed to protect against Satan's interference." Septus fought back a smile at that; there were still some stuffy inquisitors who believed the devil distorted what one saw through any lens. "We shall see what is there and what is not."

Attendants nodded in agreement around the courtroom, just as they would nod if the sentence had been immediate acquittal or death. But ben Jacob said, "Your Holiness—perhaps it would be best if the court were to . . . to issue instructions that no other person build a magnification device until the church has ruled in this matter."

"On the contrary," Septus replied. "I think the church should make magnifiers available to all persons who ask. Let them see for themselves."

The Patriarch smiled, wondering if ben Jacob understood. A decree suppressing magnifiers would simply encourage dissidents to build them in secret; on the other hand, providing free access to such devices would bring the curious *into* the church, not drive them away. Anyway, the question would only interest the leisured class, those with time and energy to wonder about esoteric issues. The great bulk of the laity, farmers and miners and ostlers, would never hear of the offer. Even if they did, they would hardly care. Minute animalcules might be amusing curiosities, but they had nothing to do with a peasant's life.

Another pause for prayer and then Leeuwenhoek was escorted away to instruct church scholars in how to build his magnification device. The man seemed happy with the outcome—more than escaping a death sentence, he would now have the chance to show others what he'd seen. Septus had met many men like that: grown-up children, looking for colorful shells on the beach and touchingly grateful when someone else took an interest in their sandy little collections.

As for Leeuwenhoek's original magnifier—Septus had the device brought to his chambers when the court recessed at noon. Blood was easy to come by: one sharp jab from a pin and the Patriarch had his sample to examine. Eagerly he peered through the viewing lens, adjusting the focus in the same way as a telescope.

Animalcules. How remarkable.

Tiny, tiny animalcules . . . countless schools of them, swimming in his own blood. What wonders God had made! Creatures of different shapes and sizes, perhaps predators and prey, like the fishes that swam in the ocean.

And were there snakes? The question was almost irrelevant. And yet . . . very faintly, so close to invisible that it might be a trick of the eye, something as thin as a hair seemed to flit momentarily across the view.

Then it was gone.

2. The Origin of Serpentine Analogues in the Blood of Papist Peoples:

Her Britannic Majesty, Anne VI, rather liked the Star Chamber. True, its power had been monstrously abused at times in the past five centuries—secret trials leading to secret executions of people who were probably more innocent than the monarchs sitting on the judgment seat—but even in the glorious Empire, there was a place for this kind of hearing. The queen on this side of the table, one of her subjects on the other . . . it had the air of a private chat between friends: a time when difficulties could get sorted out, one way or another.

"Well, Mr. Darwin," she said after the tea had been poured, "it seems you've stirred up quite a hornet's nest. Have you not?"

The fiercely bearded man across the table did not answer immediately. He laid a finger on the handle of his cup as if to drink or not to drink was some momentous decision; then he said, "I have simply spoken the truth, ma'am . . . as I see it."

"Yes; but different people see different truths, don't they? And a great many are upset by the things you say are true. You are aware there has been . . . unpleasantness?"

"I know about the riots, ma'am. Several times they have come uncomfortably close to me. And of course, there have been threats on my life."

"Indeed." Anne lifted a tiny slice of buttered bread and took what she hoped would seem a thoughtful nibble. For some reason, she always enjoyed eating in front of the accused here in the Star Chamber; they themselves never had any appetite at all. "The threats are one reason We invited you here today. Scotland Yard is growing rather weary of protecting you; and Sir Oswald has long pondered whether your life is worth it."

That got the expected reaction—Darwin's finger froze on the cup handle, the color draining away from his face. "I had not realized. . . ." His eyes narrowed. "I perceive, ma'am, that someone will soon make a decision on this issue."

"Exactly," the queen said. "Sir Oswald has turned to the crown for guidance, and now We turn to you." She took another tiny bite of the bread. "It would be good of you to explain your theories—to lay out the train of reasoning that led to your . . . unsettling public statements."

"It's all laid out in my book, ma'am."

"But your book is for scientists, not queens." Anne set down the bread and allowed herself a small sip of tea. She took her time doing so, but Darwin remained silent. "Please," she said at last. "We wish to make an informed decision."

Darwin grunted . . . or perhaps it was a hollow chuckle of cynicism. An ill-bred sound in either case. "Very well, Your Majesty," he nodded. "It is simply a matter of history."

"History is seldom simple, Mr. Darwin; but proceed."

"In . . . 1430-something, I forget the exact year, Anton Leeuwenhoek appeared before Supreme Patriarch Septus to discuss the absence of snakes in the bloodstream. You are familiar with that, ma'am?"

"Certainly. It was the pivotal event in the Schism between Our church and the Papists."

"Just so."

Anne could see Darwin itching to leap off his chair and begin prowling about the room, like a professor lecturing to a class of dull-lidded schoolboys. His strained impetuosity amused her; but she hoped he would keep his impulses in check. "Pray continue, Mr. Darwin."

"It is common knowledge that the Patriarch's decision led to a . . . a deluge, shall we say, of people peering at their own blood through a microscope. Only the upper classes at first, but soon enough it spread to the lower levels of society, too. Since the church allowed anyone to look into a microscope without cost, I suppose it was a free source of amusement for the peasantry."

"An opiate for the masses," Anne offered. She rather liked the phrase —Mr. Marx had used it when *he* had his little visit to the Star Chamber.

"I suppose that must be it," Darwin agreed. "At any rate, the phenomenon far outstripped anything Septus could have foreseen; and even worse for the Patriarchy, it soon divided the church into two camps— those who claimed to see snakes in their blood and those who did not."

"Mr. Darwin, We are well aware of the fundamental difference between Papists and the Redeemed."

"Begging your pardon, ma'am, but I believe the usual historical interpretation is . . . flawed. It confuses cause and effect."

"How can there be confusion?" Anne asked. "Papists have serpents in their blood; that is apparent to any child looking into a microscope. We Redeemed have no such contaminants; again, that is simple observational fact. The obvious conclusion, Mr. Darwin, is that Christ Herself marked the Papists with Her curse, to show one and all the error of their ways."

"According to the Papists," Darwin reminded her, "the snakes are a sign of God's blessing: a sleeping snake means sin laid to rest."

"Is that what you think, Mr. Darwin?"

"I think it more practical to examine the facts before making any judgment."

"That is why we are here today," Anne said with a pointed glance. "Facts . . . and judgment. If you could direct yourself to the heart of the matter, Mr. Darwin?"

"The heart of the matter," he repeated. "Of course. I agree that *today* any microscope will show that Papists have snakes in their bloodstream . . . or as scientists prefer to call them, serpentine analogues, since it is highly unlikely the observed phenomena are actual reptiles—"

"Let us not bandy nomenclature," Anne interrupted. "We accept that the entities in Papist blood are unrelated to cobras and puff adders; but they have been called snakes for centuries, and the name is adequate. Proceed to your point, Mr. Darwin."

"You have just made my point for me, ma'am. Five centuries have passed since the original controversy arose. What we see *now* may not be what people saw *then*." He took a deep breath. "If you read the literature of that long-ago time, you find there was great doubt about the snakes, even among the Papists. Serpentine analogues were extremely rare and difficult to discern . . . unlike the very obvious entities seen today."

"Surely that can be blamed on the equipment," Anne said. "Microscopes of that day were crude contrivances compared to our fine modern instruments."

"That is the usual argument," Darwin nodded, "but I believe there is a different explanation."

"Yes?"

"My argument, ma'am, is based on my observations of pigeons."

Anne blinked. "Pigeons, Mr. Darwin?" She blinked again. "The birds?" She bit her lip. "The filthy things that perch on statues?"

"Not wild pigeons, Your Majesty, domestic ones. Bred for show. For example, some centuries ago, a squire in Sussex took it into his head to breed a black pigeon from his stock of gray ones."

"Why ever would he want a black pigeon?"

"That remains a mystery to me, too, ma'am; but the historical records are clear. He set about the task by selecting pigeons of the darkest gray he could find, and breeding them together. Over many generations, their color grew darker and darker until today, the squire's descendants boast of pigeons as black as coal."

"They boast of that?"

"Incessantly."

Darwin seized up a piece of bread and virtually stuffed it into his mouth. The man had apparently become so engrossed in talking, he

had forgotten who sat across the table. *Good*, Anne thought; he would
be less guarded.

"We understand the principles of animal husbandry," Anne said.
"We do not, however, see how this pertains to the Papists."

"For the past five centuries, Your Majesty, the Papists have been
going through exactly the same process . . . as have the Redeemed, for
that matter. Think, ma'am. In any population, there are numerous
chance differences between individuals; the squire's pigeons, for
example, had varying shades of gray. If some process of selection
chooses to emphasize a particular trait as desirable, excluding other
traits as undesirable—if you restrict darker birds to breeding with one
another and prevent lighter ones from contributing to the bloodline—
the selected characteristic will tend to become more pronounced with
each generation."

"You are still talking about pigeons, Mr. Darwin."

"No, ma'am," he said triumphantly, "I am talking about Papists
and the Redeemed. Let us suppose that in the times of Patriarch
Septus, some people had almost imperceptible serpentine analogues in
their bloodstream—a chance occurrence, just as some people may have
curls in their hair while others do not."

Anne opened her mouth to say that curls were frequently not a
chance occurrence at all; but she decided to remain silent.

"Now," Darwin continued, "what happened among the people of
that day? Some saw those tiny, almost invisible snakes; others did not.
Those who saw them proclaimed, *This proves the unshakable word of
Mother Church*. Those who saw nothing said, *The scriptures cannot be
taken literally—believers must find the truth in their own hearts*. And so the
Schism split the world, pitting one camp against another."

"Yes, Mr. Darwin, We know all that."

"So, ma'am, you must also know what happened in subsequent generations. The rift in belief created a similar rift in the population. Papists
only married Papists. The Redeemed only married the Redeemed."

"Of course."

"Consequently," Darwin stressed the word, "those who could see so-called snakes in their blood only married those of similar condition. Those who saw nothing married others who saw nothing. Is it any wonder that, generation by generation, snakes became more and more visible in Papist blood? And less and less likely to be seen in the Redeemed? It is simply a matter of selective breeding, ma'am. The Papists are not different from us because the Virgin put her mark on them; they are different because they selected to *make* themselves different. To *emphasize* the difference. And the Redeemed have no snakes in their blood for the same reason—simply a side effect of our ancestors' marital prejudice."

"Mr. Darwin!" Anne said, aghast. "Such claims! No wonder you have angered the Papists as much as your own countrymen. To suggest that God's sacred sign is a mere barnyard accident. . . ." The Queen caught her breath. "Sir, where is your decency?"

"I have something better than decency," he answered in a calm voice. "I have proof."

"Proof? How could you prove such a thing?"

"Some years ago, ma'am," he said, "I took passage on a ship sailing the South Seas; and during that voyage, I saw things that completely opened my eyes."

"More pigeons, Mr. Darwin?"

He waved his hand dismissively. "The birds of the Pacific Islands are hardly fit study for a scientist. What I observed were the efforts of missionaries, ma'am; both Papists and the Redeemed, preaching to the natives who lived in those isles. Have you heard of such missions?"

"We sponsor several of those missions personally, Mr. Darwin."

"And the results, ma'am?"

"Mixed," Anne confessed. "Some tribes are open to Redemption, while others . . ." she shrugged. "The Papists do no better."

"Just so, Your Majesty. As an example, I visited one island where the Papists had been established for thirty years, yet the local priest claimed to have made no *true* converts. Mark that word, *true*. Many of the natives espoused Papist beliefs, took part in Papist worship, and so on . . . but the priest could find no snakes in their blood, so he told himself they had not truly embraced Mother Church."

"You would argue with the priest's conclusion?"

"Certainly," Darwin replied. "In my eyes, the island tribe was simply a closed population that for reasons of chance never developed serpentine analogues in their blood. If you interbreed only white pigeons, you will never develop a black."

Anne said, "But—" then stopped stone-still, as the words of a recent mission report rose in her mind. *We are continually frustrated in our work on this island; although the people bow before God's altar, their blood continues to show the serpent-stain of the Unclean. . . .*

"Mr. Darwin," Anne murmured, "could there possibly be islands where all the people had snakes in their blood regardless of their beliefs?"

"There are indeed, ma'am," Darwin nodded. "Almost all the island populations are isolated and homogeneous. I found some tribes with snakes, some without—no matter which missionaries ministered there. When the Papists land among a people who already have analogues in their bloodstream, they soon declare that they have converted the tribe and hold great celebrations. However, when they land among a people whose blood is clear . . . well, they can preach all they want, but they won't change the effects of generations of breeding. Usually, they just give up and move on to another island where the people are more receptive . . . which is to say, where they have the right blood to begin with."

"Ah."

Anne lowered her eyes. Darwin had been speaking about the Papists, but she knew the same was true of Redeemed missionaries. They tended to stay a year in one place, do a few blood tests, then move on if they could not show results—because results were exclusively measured in blood rather than what the people professed. If missionaries, her own missionaries, had been abandoning sincere believers because they didn't believe the conversions were "true" . . . what would God think of that?

But Darwin hadn't stopped talking. "Our voyage visited many islands, Your Majesty, a few of which had never received missionaries of any kind. Some of those tribes had serpentine analogues in their blood, while some did not . . . and each island was homogeneous. I hypothesize that the potential for analogues might have been distributed evenly through humankind millennia ago; but as populations grew isolated, geographically or socially—"

"Yes, Mr. Darwin, We see your point." Anne found she was tapping her finger on the edge of the table. She stopped herself and stood up. "This matter deserves further study. We shall instruct the police to find a place where you can continue your work without disturbance from outside sources."

Darwin's face fell. "Would that be a jail, ma'am?"

"A comfortable place of sanctuary," she replied. "You will be supplied with anything you need—books, paper, all of that."

"Will I be able to publish?" he asked.

"You will have at least one avid reader for whatever you write." She favored him with the slightest bow of her head. "You have given Us much to think about."

"Then let me give you one more thought, Your Majesty." He took a deep breath, as if he was trying to decide if his next words would be offensive beyond the pale. Then, Anne supposed, he decided he had nothing to lose. "Papists and the Redeemed have been selectively breeding within their own populations for five hundred years. There may come a time when they are too far removed from each other to be . . . cross-fertile. Already there are rumors of an unusually high mortality rate for children with one Papist parent and one Redeemed. In time—millennia perhaps, but in time—I believe the two populations may split into separate species."

"Separate species? Of humans?"

"It may happen, Your Majesty. At this very moment, we may be witnessing the origin of two new species."

Queen Anne pursed her lips in distaste. "The origin of species, Mr. Darwin? If that is a joke, We are not amused."

3. The Efficacy of Trisulphozyymase for Preventing SA Incompatibility Reactions in Births of Mixed-Blood Parentage:

The hearing was held behind closed doors—a bad sign. Julia Grant had asked some of her colleagues what to expect and they all said, *Show trial, Show trial*. Senator McCarthy loved to get his name in the papers. And yet the reporters were locked out today; just Julia and the Committee.

A very bad sign.

"Good afternoon, Dr. Grant," McCarthy said after she had sworn to tell the truth, the whole truth, and nothing but the truth. His voice had a smarmy quality to it; an unpleasant man's attempt at charm. "I suppose you know why you're here?"

"No, senator."

"Come now, doctor," he chided, as if speaking to a five-year-old. "Surely you must know the purpose of this Committee? And it therefore follows that we would take great interest in your work."

"My work is medical research," she replied tightly. "I have no political interests at all." She forced herself to stare McCarthy in the eye. "I heal the sick."

"There's sickness and there's sickness," the senator shrugged. "We can all understand doctors who deal with sniffles and sneezes and heart attacks . . . but that's not your field, is it?"

"No," she answered. "I'm a hematologist, specializing in SA compatibility problems."

"Could you explain that for the Committee?"

The doctor suspected that every man on the Committee—and they were all men—had already been briefed on her research. If nothing else, they read the newspapers. Still, why not humor them?

"All human blood," she began, "is either SA-positive or SA-negative—"

"SA stands for Serpentine Analogue?" McCarthy interrupted.

"Yes. The name comes from the outdated belief—"

"That some people have snakes in their bloodstream," McCarthy interrupted again.

"That's correct."

"*Do* some people have snakes in their bloodstream?" McCarthy asked.

"Snakelike entities," another senator corrected . . . probably a Democrat.

"Serpentine analogues are not present in anyone's bloodstream," Julia said. "They don't appear until blood is exposed to air. It's a specialized clotting mechanism, triggered by an enzyme that encourages microscopic threads to form at the site of an injury—"

"In other words," McCarthy said, "SA-positive blood works differently from SA-negative. Correct?"

"In this one regard, yes," Julia nodded.

"Do you think SA-positive blood is *better* than SA-negative?"

"It provides slightly more effective clotting at wounds—"

"Do you *admire* SA-positive blood, doctor?"

Julia stared at him. Mentally, she counted to ten. "I am fascinated by all types of blood," she answered at last. "SA-positive clots faster . . . which is useful to stop bleeding but gives a slightly greater risk of stroke. Overall, I'd say the good points and the bad even out. If they didn't, evolution would soon skew the population strongly one way or the other."

McCarthy folded his hands on the table in front of him. "So you believe in evolution, Dr. Grant?"

"I'm a scientist. I also believe in gravity, thermodynamics, and the universal gas equation."

Not a man on the Committee so much as smiled.

"Doctor," McCarthy said quietly, "what blood type are you?"

She gritted her teeth. "The Supreme Court ruled that no one has to answer that question."

In sudden fury, McCarthy slammed his fist onto the table. "Do you see the Supreme Court in here with us? Do you? Because if you do, show me those black-robed faggots and I'll boot their pope-loving asses straight out the window." He settled back in his chair. "I don't think you appreciate the seriousness of your situation, Dr. Grant."

"What situation?" she demanded. "I am a medical researcher—"

"And you've developed a new drug, haven't you?" McCarthy snapped. "A new *drug*. That you want to loose on the public. I wonder if the person who invented heroin called herself a medical researcher, too?"

"Mr. McCarthy, trisulphozymase is not a narcotic. It is a carefully developed pharmaceutical—"

"Which encourages miscegenation between Papists and the Redeemed," McCarthy finished. "That's what it does, doesn't it, doctor?"

"No!" She took a deep breath. "Trisulphozymase combats certain medical problems that occur when an SA-positive father and an SA-negative mother—"

"When a Papist man sires his filthy whelp on a Redeemed woman," McCarthy interrupted. "When a Papist *fucks* one of the Saved! *That's* what you want to encourage, doctor? That's how you'll make the world a better place?"

Julia said nothing. She felt her cheeks burn like a child caught in some forbidden act; and she was infuriated that her reaction was guilt rather than outrage at what McCarthy was saying.

Yes, she wanted to say, *it* will *make the world a better place to stop separating humanity into hostile camps.* Most people on the planet had no comprehension of either Papist or Redeemed theology; but somehow, the poisonous idea of blood discrimination had spread to every country of the globe, regardless of religious faith. Insanity! And millions recognized it to be so. Yet the McCarthys of the world found it a convenient ladder on which they could climb to power, and who was stopping them? Look at Germany. Look at Ireland. Look at India and Pakistan.

Ridiculous . . . and deadly, time and again throughout history. Perhaps she should set aside SA compatibility and work on a cure for the drive to demonize those who were different.

"A doctor deals with lives, not lifestyles," she said stiffly. "If I were confronted with a patient whose heart had stopped beating, I would attempt to start it again, whether the victim were an innocent child, a convicted murderer, or even a senator." She leaned forward. "Has anyone here ever seen an SA incompatibility reaction? How a newborn infant dies? How the mother goes into spasm and usually dies, too? Real people, gentlemen; real screams of pain! Only a monster could witness such things and still rant about ideology."

A few Committee members had the grace to look uncomfortable, turning away from her gaze; but McCarthy was not one of them. "You think this is all just ideology, doctor? A lofty discussion of philosophical doctrine?" He shook his head in unconvincing sorrow. "I wish it were . . . I truly wish it were. I wish the Papists weren't trying to rip down everything this country stands for, obeying the orders of their foreign masters to corrupt the spirit of liberty itself. Why should I care about a screaming woman, when she's whored herself to the likes of them? *She* made her decision; now she has to face the consequences. No one in this room invented SA incompatibility, doctor. *God* did . . . and I think we should take the hint, don't you?"

The sharp catch of bile rose in Julia's throat. For a moment, she couldn't find the strength to fight it; but she couldn't be sick, not in front of these men. Swallowing hard, she forced herself to breathe evenly until the moment passed. "Senators," she said at last, "do you actually intend to suppress trisulphozymase? To withhold lifesaving treatment from those who need it?"

"Some might say it's a sign," McCarthy answered, "that a Redeemed man can father a child on a Papist without complications, but it doesn't work the other way around. Doesn't that sound like a sign to you?"

"Senators," she said, ignoring McCarthy, "does this Committee intend to suppress trisulphozymase?"

Silence. Then McCarthy gave a little smile. "How does trisulphozymase work, doctor?"

Julia stared at him, wondering where this new question was going. Warily, she replied, "The drug dismantles the SA factor enzyme into basic amino acids. This prevents a more dangerous response from the mother's immune system, which might otherwise produce antibodies to the enzyme. The antibodies are the real problem, because they may attack the baby's—"

"So what you're saying," McCarthy interrupted, "is that this drug can destroy the snakes in a Papist's bloodstream?"

"I told you, there *are* no snakes! Trisulphozymase temporarily eliminates the extra clotting enzyme that comes from SA-positive blood."

"It's only temporary?"

"That's all that's needed. One injection shortly before the moment of birth—"

"But what about repeated doses?" McCarthy interrupted. "Or a massive dose? Could you *permanently* wipe out the SA factor in a person's blood?"

"You don't administer trisulphozymase to an SA-positive person," Julia said. "It's given to an SA-negative mother to prevent—"

"But suppose you *did* give it to a Papist. A *big* dose. *Lots* of doses. Could it destroy the SA factor forever?" He leaned forward eagerly. "Could it make them like us?"

And now Julia saw it: what this hearing was all about. Because the Committee couldn't really suppress the treatment, could they? Her results were known in the research community. Even if the drug were banned here, other countries would use it; and there would eventually be enough public pressure to force reevaluation. This wasn't about the lives of babies and mothers; this was about clipping the devil's horns.

Keeping her voice steady, she said, "It would be unconscionable to administer this drug or any other to a person whose health did not require it. Large doses or long-term use of trisulphozymase would have side effects I could not venture to guess." The faces in front of her showed no expression. "Gentlemen," she tried again, "in an SA-positive person, the enzyme is *natural*. A natural component of blood. To interfere with a body's natural functioning when there is no medical justification . . ." she threw up her hands. "Do no harm, gentlemen. The heart of the Hippocratic Oath. At the very least, doctors must do no harm."

"Does that mean," McCarthy asked, "that you would refuse to head a research project into this matter?"

"Me?"

"You're the top expert in your field," McCarthy shrugged. "If anybody can get rid of the snakes once and for all, it's you."

"Senator," Julia said, "have you no shame? Have you no shame at all? You want to endanger lives over this . . . triviality? A meaningless difference you can only detect with a microscope—"

"Which means they can walk among us, doctor! Papists can walk *among* us. Them with their special blood, their snakes, their damned inbreeding—they're the ones who care about what you call a triviality! They're the ones who flaunt it in our faces. They say they're God's Chosen. With God's Mark of Blessing. Well, I intend to *erase* that mark, with or without your help."

"Without," Julia told him. "Definitely without."

McCarthy's gaze was on her. He did not look like a man who had just received an absolute no. With an expression far too smug, he said, "Let me tell you a secret, doctor. From our agents in the enemy camp. Even as we speak, the Papists are planning to contaminate our water supply with their damned SA enzyme. Poison us or make us like *them* . . . one way or the other. We need your drug to fight that pollution; to remove the enzyme from our blood before it can destroy us! What about *that*, Dr. Grant? Will your precious medical ethics let you work on a treatment to keep us safe from their damned Papist toxins?"

Julia grimaced. "You know nothing about the human metabolism. People couldn't 'catch' the SA factor from drinking water; the enzyme would just break down in your stomach acid. I suppose it might be possible to produce a methylated version that would eventually work its way into the bloodstream. . . ." She stopped herself. "Anyway, I can't believe the Papists would be so insane as to—"

"Right now," McCarthy interrupted, "sitting in a committee room of some Papist hideaway, there are a group of men who are just as crazy as we are. Believe that, doctor. Whatever *we* are willing to do to them, they are willing to do to *us*; the only question is, who'll do it *first*." McCarthy settled back and cradled his hands on his stomach. "Snakes all 'round, Dr. Grant. You can make a difference in who gets bitten."

It was, perhaps, the only true thing McCarthy had said since the hearing had begun. Julia tried to doubt it, but couldn't. SA-positive or negative, you could still be a ruthless bastard.

She said nothing.

McCarthy stared at her a few moments more, then glanced at the men on both sides of him. "Let's consider this hearing adjourned, all right? Give Dr. Grant a little time to think this over." He turned to look straight at her. "A *little* time. We'll contact you in a few days . . . find out who scares you more, us or them."

He had the nerve to wink before he turned away.

The other senators filed from the room, almost bumping into each other in the hurry to leave. Complicitous men . . . weak men, for all their power. Julia remained in the uncomfortable "Witness Chair," giving them ample time to scurry away; she didn't want to lay eyes on them again when she finally went out into the corridor.

Using trisulphozymase on an SA-positive person . . . what would be the effect? Predictions were almost worthless in biochemistry—medical science was a vast ocean of ignorance dotted with researchers trying to stay afloat in makeshift canoes. The only prediction you could safely make was that a large enough dose of *any* drug would kill the patient.

On the other hand, better to inject trisulphozymase into SA-positive people than SA-negative. The chemical reactions that broke down the SA enzyme also broke down the trisulphozymase—mutual assured destruction. If you didn't have the SA enzyme in your blood, the trisulphozymase would build up to lethal levels much faster, simply because there was nothing to stop it. SA-positive people could certainly tolerate dosages that would kill a . . .

Julia felt a chill wash through her. She had created a drug that would poison SA-negatives but not SA-positives . . . that could selectively massacre the Redeemed while leaving the Papists standing. And her research was a matter of public record. How long would it take before someone on the Papist side made the connection? One of those men McCarthy had talked about, just as ruthless and crazy as the senator himself.

How long would it take before they used her drug to slaughter half the world?

There was only one way out: put all the snakes to sleep. If Julia could somehow wave her hands and make every SA-positive person SA-negative, then the playing field would be level again. No, not the playing field—the killing field.

Insanity . . . but what choice did she have? Sign up with

McCarthy; get rid of the snakes before they began to bite; pray the side effects could be treated. Perhaps, if saner minds prevailed, the process would never be deployed. Perhaps the threat would be enough to force some kind of bilateral enzyme disarmament.

Feeling twenty years older, Dr. Julia Grant left the hearing room. The corridor was empty; through the great glass entryway at the front of the building, she could see late afternoon sunlight slanting across the marble steps. A single protester stood on the sidewalk, mutely holding a sign aloft—no doubt what McCarthy would call a Papist sympathizer, traitorously opposing a duly appointed congressional committee.

The protester's sign read, *"Why do you concern yourself with the sleeping creature before you, when you are blind to the serpents in your own heart?"*

Julia turned away, hoping the building had a back door.

The Star
Arthur C. Clarke

Arthur C. Clarke is perhaps the most famous modern science fiction writer in the world, seriously rivaled for that title only by the late Isaac Asimov and Robert A. Heinlein. Clarke is probably most widely known for his work on Stanley Kubrick's film *2001: A Space Odyssey*, but he is also renowned as a novelist, short story writer, and as a writer of nonfiction, usually on technological subjects such as spaceflight. He has won three Nebula Awards, three Hugo Awards, the British Science Fiction Award, the John W. Campbell Memorial Award, and a Grandmaster Nebula for Life Achievement. His best-known books include the novels *Childhood's End, The City and the Stars, The Deep Range, Rendezvous with Rama, A Fall of Moondust, The Sands of Mars, Earthlight, 2001: A Space Odyssey, 2010: Odyssey Two, 2061: Odyssey Three, Songs of Distant Earth*, and *The Fountains of Paradise* and the collections *The Nine Billion Names of God, Tales of Ten Worlds*, and *The Sentinel*. He has also written many nonfiction books on scientific topics, the best known of which are probably *Profiles of the Future* and *The Wind from the Sun*, and is generally considered to be the man who first came up with the idea of the communications satellite. Among his recent books are the novel *3001: The Final Odyssey*, the nonfiction collection *Greetings, Carbon-Based Bipeds: Collected Works 1944–1998*, the fiction collection *Collected Short Stories*, and two novels written in collaboration with Stephen Baxter, *The Light of Other Days* and *Time's Eye: A Time Odyssey*. Born in Somerset, England, Clarke now lives in Sri Lanka, and was recently knighted.

In the classic story that follows, a Hugo-winner, he shows us that the same set of facts can be interpreted very differently, depending on whose eyes you're seeing them through.

I t is three thousand light-years to the Vatican. Once I believed that space could have no power over faith. Just as I believed that the heavens declared the glory of God's handiwork. Now I have seen that handiwork, and my faith is sorely troubled.

I stare at the crucifix that hangs on the cabin wall above the Mark VI computer, and for the first time in my life I wonder if it is no more than an empty symbol.

I have told no one yet, but the truth cannot be concealed. The data are there for anyone to read, recorded on the countless miles of magnetic tape and the thousands of photographs we are carrying back to Earth. Other scientists can interpret them as easily as I can—more easily, in all probability. I am not one who would condone that tampering with the truth which often gave my order a bad name in the olden days.

The crew is already sufficiently depressed; I wonder how they will take this ultimate irony. Few of them have any religious faith, yet they will not relish using this final weapon in their campaign against me—

that private, good-natured but fundamentally serious war which lasted all the way from Earth. It amused them to have a Jesuit as chief astrophysicist. Dr. Chandler, for instance, could never get over it (why are medical men such notorious atheists?). Sometimes he would meet me on the observation deck, where the lights are always low, so that the stars shine with undiminished glory. He would come up to me in the gloom and stand staring out of the great oval port, while the heavens crawled slowly around us as the ship turned end over end with the residual spin we had never bothered to correct.

"Well, Father," he would say at last. "It goes on forever and forever, and perhaps Something made it. But how you can believe that Something has a special interest in us and our miserable little world— that just beats me." Then the argument would start, while the stars and nebulae would swing around us in silent, endless arcs beyond the flawlessly clear plastic of the observation port.

It was, I think, the apparent incongruity of my position which, yes, *amused* the crew. In vain I would point to my three papers in the *Astrophysical Journal*, my five in the *Monthly Notices of the Royal Astronomical Society*. I would remind them that our order has long been famous for its scientific works. We may be few now, but ever since the eighteenth century we have made contributions to astronomy and geophysics out of all proportion to our numbers.

Will my report on the Phoenix Nebula end our thousand years of history? It will end, I fear, much more than that.

I do not know who gave the nebula its name, which seems to me a very bad one. If it contains a prophecy, it is one which cannot be verified for several thousand million years. Even the word "nebula" is misleading; this is a far smaller object than those stupendous clouds of mist—the stuff of unborn stars—which are scattered throughout the length of the Milky Way. On the cosmic scale, indeed, the Phoenix Nebula is a tiny thing—a tenuous shell of gas surrounding a single star.

Or what is left of a star . . .

The Rubens engraving of Loyola seems to mock me as it hangs there above the spectrophotometer tracings. What would *you*, Father, have made of this knowledge that has come into my keeping, so far from the little world that was all the universe you knew? Would your faith have risen to the challenge, as mine has failed to do?

You gaze into the distance, Father, but I have traveled a distance beyond any that you could have imagined when you founded our order a thousand years ago. No other survey ship has been so far from Earth: we are at the very frontiers of the explored universe. We set out to reach the Phoenix Nebula, we succeeded, and we are homeward bound with our burden of knowledge. I wish I could lift that burden from my shoulders, but I call to you in vain across the centuries and the light-years that lie between us.

On the book you are holding the words are plain to read. "*AD MAIOREM DEI GLORIAM*," the message runs, but it is a message I can no longer believe. Would you still believe it if you could see what we have found?

We knew, of course, what the Phoenix Nebula was. Every year, in our galaxy alone, more than a hundred stars explode, blazing for a few hours or days with thousands of times their normal brilliance before they sink back into death and obscurity. Such are the ordinary novae— the commonplace disasters of the universe. I have recorded the spectrograms and light curves of dozens, since I started working at the lunar observatory.

But three or four times in every thousand years occurs something beside which even a nova pales into total insignificance.

When a star becomes a *supernova*, it may for a little while outshine all the massed suns of the galaxy. The Chinese astronomers watched this happen in AD 1054, not knowing what it was they saw. Five centuries later, in 1572, a supernova blazed in Cassiopeia so brilliantly that it was visible in the daylight sky. There have been three more in the thousand years that have passed since then.

Our mission was to visit the remnants of such a catastrophe, to reconstruct the events that led up to it, and, if possible, to learn its cause. We came slowly in through the concentric shells of gas that had been blasted out six thousand years before, yet were expanding still. They were immensely hot, radiating still with a fierce violet light, but far too tenuous to do us any damage. When the star had exploded, its outer layers had been driven upward with such speed that they had escaped completely from its gravitational field. Now they formed a hollow shell large enough to engulf a thousand solar systems, and at its center burned the tiny, fantastic object which the star had now become—a white dwarf, smaller than the Earth, yet weighing a million times as much.

The glowing gas shells were all around us, banishing the normal night of interstellar space. We were flying into the center of a cosmic bomb that had detonated millennia ago and whose incandescent fragments were still hurtling apart. The immense scale of the explosion, and the fact that the debris already covered a volume of space many billions of miles across, robbed the scene of any visible movement. It would take decades before the unaided eye could detect any motion in these tortured wisps and eddies of gas, yet the sense of turbulent expansion was overwhelming.

We had checked our primary drive hours before and were drifting slowly toward the fierce little star ahead. Once it had been a sun like our own, but it had squandered in a few hours the energy that should have kept it shining for a million years. Now it was a shrunken miser, hoarding its resources as if trying to make amends for its prodigal youth.

No one seriously expected to find planets. If there had been any before the explosion, they would have been boiled into puffs of vapor and their substance lost in the greater wreckage of the star itself. But we made the automatic search, as always when approaching an unknown sun, and presently we found a single small world circling the star at an immense distance. It must have been the Pluto of this vanished solar system, orbiting on the frontiers of the night. Too far from the central sun ever to have known life, its remoteness had saved it from the fate of all its lost companions.

The passing fires had seared its rocks and burned away the mantle of frozen gas that must have covered it in the days before the disaster. We landed, and we found the Vault.

Its builders had made sure that we should. The monolithic marker that stood above the entrance was now a fused stump, but even the first long-range photographs told us that here was the work of intelligence. A little later we detected the continentwide pattern of radioactivity that had been buried in the rock. Even if the pylon above the Vault had been destroyed, this would have remained, an immovable and all but eternal beacon calling to the stars. Our ship fell toward this gigantic bull's-eye like an arrow into its target.

The pylon must have been a mile high when it was built, but now it looked like a candle that had melted down into a puddle of wax. It took us a week to drill through the fused rock, since we did not have the proper tools for a task like this. We were astronomers, not archaeologists, but we could improvise. Our original program was forgotten: this lonely monument, reared at such labor at the greatest possible distance from the doomed sun, could have only one meaning. A civilization which knew it was about to die had made its last bid for immortality.

It will take us generations to examine all the treasures that were placed in the Vault. *They* had plenty of time to prepare, for their sun must have given its first warnings many years before the final detonation. Everything that they wished to preserve, all the fruits of their genius, they brought here to this distant world in the days before the end, hoping that some other race would find them and that they would not be utterly forgotten.

If only they had a little more time! They could travel freely enough between the planets of their own sun, but they had not yet learned to cross the interstellar gulfs, and the nearest solar system was a hundred light-years away.

Even if they had not been so disturbingly human as their sculpture shows, we could not have helped admiring them and grieving for their fate. They left thousands of visual records and the machines for projecting them, together with elaborate pictorial instructions from which it will not be difficult to learn their written language. We have examined many of these records, and brought to life for the first time in six thousand years the warmth and beauty of a civilization which in many ways must have been superior to our own. Perhaps they only showed us the best, and one can hardly blame them. But their worlds were very lovely, and their cities were built with a grace that matches anything of ours. We have watched them at work and play, and listened to their musical speech sounding across the centuries. One scene is still before my eyes—a group of children on a beach of strange blue sand, playing in the waves as children play on Earth.

And sinking into the sea, still warm and friendly and life-giving, is the sun that will soon turn traitor and obliterate all this innocent happiness.

Perhaps if we had not been so far from home and so vulnerable to loneliness, we should not have been so deeply moved. Many of us had seen the ruins of ancient civilizations on other worlds, but they had never affected us so profoundly.

This tragedy was unique. It was one thing for a race to fail and die, as nations and cultures have done on Earth. But to be destroyed so completely in the full flower of its achievement, leaving no survivors—how could that be reconciled with the mercy of God?

My colleagues have asked me that, and I have given what answers I can. Perhaps you could have done better, Father Loyola, but I have found nothing in the *Exercitia spiritualia* that helps me here. They were not an evil people: I do not know what gods they worshiped, if indeed they worshiped any. But I have looked back at them across the centuries, and have watched while the loveliness they used their last strength to preserve was brought forth again into the light of their shrunken sun.

I know the answers that my colleagues will give when they get back to Earth. They will say that the universe has no purpose and no plan, that since a hundred suns explode every year in our galaxy, at this very moment some race is dying in the depths of space. Whether that race has done good or evil during its lifetime will make no difference in the end; there is no divine justice, *for there is no God.*

Yet, of course, what we have seen proves nothing of the sort. Anyone who argues thus is being swayed by emotion, not logic. God has no need to justify His actions to man. He who built the universe can destroy it when He chooses. It is arrogance—it is perilously near blasphemy—for us to say what He may or may not do.

This I could have accepted, hard though it is to look upon whole worlds and peoples thrown into the furnace. But there comes a point when even the deepest faith must falter, and now, as I look at my calculations, I know I have reached that point at last.

We could not tell, before we reached the nebula, how long ago the explosion took place. Now, from the astronomical evidence and the record in the rocks of that one surviving planet, I have been able to date it very exactly. I know in what year the light of this colossal conflagration reached Earth. I know how brilliantly the supernova whose corpse now dwindles behind our speeding ship once shone in terrestrial skies. I know how it must have blazed low in the East before sunrise, like a beacon in that Oriental dawn.

There can be no reasonable doubt: the ancient mystery is solved at last. Yet—O God, there were so many stars you *could* have used.

What was the need to give these people to the fire, that the symbol of their passing might shine above Bethlehem?

The Last Homosexual

Paul Park

Just as the Devil is said to be able to quote scripture for his own purposes, so, too, the tools of science can be misused by the wrong hands. In the harrowing story that follows, Paul Park takes us to a nightmarish but all-too-possible future society where bogus "science" in the service of corrupt politicians and religious extremists has made people afraid that almost everything is "catching"—and where the most contagious things of all are fear and intolerance and hatred.

Paul Park is one of the most critically acclaimed writers of his literary generation, having received rave reviews and wide acceptance for novels such as *Soldiers of Paradise*, *Sugar Rain*, *The Cult of Loving Kindness*, *Celestis*, *The Gospel of Corax*, and *Three Marys*. His most recent novel is *No Traveller Returns*. His short work has appeared in *Asimov's Science Fiction*, the *Magazine of Fantasy & Science Fiction*, *Omni*, *Interzone*, *Omni Online*, *Full Spectrum*, *Strange Plasma*, and elsewhere, and has been collected in *If Lions Could Speak and Other Stories*. He lives with his family in North Adams, Massachusetts.

A̲t my tenth high school reunion at the Fairmont Hotel, I ran into Steve Daigrepont and my life changed.

That was three years ago. Now I am living by myself in a motel room, in the southeast corner of the Republic of California. But in those days I was Jimmy Brothers, and my wife and I owned a house uptown off Audubon Park, in New Orleans. Our telephone number was (504) EXodus-5671. I could call her now. It would be early evening.

I think she still lives there because it was her house, bought with her money. She was the most beautiful woman I ever met, and rich, too. In those days she was teaching at Tulane Christian University, and I worked for the *Times-Picayune*. That was why Steve wanted to talk to me.

"Listen," he said. "I want you to do a story about us."

We had been on the baseball team together at Jesuit. Now he worked for the Board of Health. He was divorced. "I work too hard," he said as he took me away from the bar and made me sit down in a corner of the Sazerac Room, under the gold mural. "Especially now."

He had gotten the idea I had an influence over what got printed in the paper. In fact I was just a copy editor. But at Jesuit I had been the starting pitcher on a championship team, and I could tell Steve still looked up to me. "I want you to do a feature," he said. "I want you to come visit us at Carville."

He was talking about the old Gillis W. Long Center, on River Road between New Orleans and Baton Rouge. Formerly the United States national leprosarium, now it was a research foundation.

"You know they're threatening to shut us down," he said.

I had heard something about it. The New Baptist Democrats had taken over the statehouse again, and as usual they were sharpening the axe. Carville was one of the last big virology centers left in the state.

Doctors from all over Louisiana came there to study social ailments. But Senator Rasmussen wanted the buildings for a new penitentiary.

"She's always talking about the risks of some terrible outbreak," said Steve. "But it's never happened. It can't happen. In the meantime, there's so much we still don't know. And to destroy the stocks, it's murder."

Steve's ex-wife was pregnant, and she came in and stood next to the entrance to the lobby, talking to some friends. Steve hunched his shoulders over the table and leaned toward me.

"These patients are human beings," he said, sipping his orange crush. "That's what they don't understand." And then he went on to tell a story about one of the staff, an accountant named Dan who had worked at Carville for years. Then someone discovered Dan had embezzled two hundred and fifty thousand dollars from the contingency fund, and he was admitted as a patient. "Now I'll never leave you. Now I'm home," he said when he stepped into the ward.

"Sort of like Father Damien," I murmured. While I wasn't sure why my old friend wanted this story in the newspaper, still I admired his passion, his urgency. When we said good-bye, he pressed my hand in both of his, as if he really thought I could help him. It was enough to make me mention the problems at Carville to my boss a few days later, who looked at me doubtfully and suggested I go up there and take a look around on my day off.

"People have different opinions about that place," he said. "Although these days it would be hard for us to question the judgment of a Louisiana state senator."

I didn't tell Melissa where I was going. I drove up alone through the abandoned suburbs and the swamps. Once past the city, I drove with the river on my left, behind the new levee. I went through small towns filled with old people, their trailers and cabins in sad contrast to the towers of the petrochemical and agricultural concerns, which lined the Mississippi between Destrehan and Lutcher.

Carville lay inside an elbow of the river, surrounded by swamps and graveyards and overgrown fields. In the old days, people had grown sugar cane. Now I drove up along a line of beautiful live oaks covered with moss and ferns. At the end of it, a thirty-foot concrete statue of Christ the Redeemer, and then I turned in at the gate beside the mansion, a plantation house before the civil war, and the administration building since the time of the original leprosarium.

At the guardhouse, they examined my medical records and took some blood. They scanned me with the lie detector and asked some questions. Then they called in to Steve, and I had to sign a lot of forms in case I had to be quarantined. Finally they let me past the barricade and into the first of many wire enclosures. Soldiers leaned against the Corinthian columns of the main house.

I don't want to drag this out with a lot of description. Carville was a big place. Once you were inside, past the staff offices, it was laid out in sections, and some were quite pleasant. The security was not oppressive. When he met me at the inner gate, Steve was smiling. "Welcome to our Inferno," he said, when no one else could hear. Then he led me down a series of complicated covered walkways, past the hospital, the Catholic and Protestant chapels, the cafeteria. Sometimes he stopped and introduced me to doctors and administrators, who seemed eager to answer questions. Then there were others who hovered at a respectful distance: patients, smiling and polite, dressed in street clothes. They did not shake hands, and when they coughed or sneezed, they turned their faces away.

"Depression," murmured Steve, and later, "alcoholism. Theft."

It had been around the time I was born that Drs. Fargas and Watanabe, working at what had been LSU, discovered the viral nature of our most difficult human problems. I mean the diseases that even Christ can't heal. They had been working with the quarantined HIV-2 population a few years after independence, during the old Christian

Coalition days. Nothing much had changed since then in most of the world, where New Baptist doctrine didn't have the same clout as in Louisiana. But those former states that had been willing to isolate the carriers and stop the dreadful cycle of contagion had been transformed. Per capita income rates showed a steady rise, and crime was almost nonexistent. Even so, thirty years later there was still much to learn about susceptibility, about immunization, and the actual process of transmission. As is so often the case, political theory had outstripped science, and though it was hard to argue with the results, still, as Steve Daigrepont explained it, there was a need for places like Carville, where important research was being done.

"If only to keep the patients alive," he muttered. His voice had softened as we progressed into the complex, and now I had to lean close to him to understand. After the second checkpoint, when we put our masks on, I had to ask him to speak up.

We put on isolation suits and latex gloves. We stood outside some glassed-in rooms, watching people drink coffee and read newspapers, as they sat on plain, institutional couches. "Obesity," whispered Steve, which surprised me. No one in the room seemed particularly overweight.

"These are carriers," he hissed, angry for some reason. "They aren't necessarily infected. Besides, their diet is strictly controlled."

Later, we found ourselves outside again, under the hot sun. I stared into a large enclosure like the rhinoceros exhibit at the Audubon zoo. A ditch protected us, and in the distance I could see some tarpaper shacks and rotted-out cars. "Poor people," mumbled Steve through his mask. "Chronic poverty." Children were playing in the dirt outside one of the shacks. They were scratching at the ground with sticks.

Again, I don't want to drag this out. I want to move on to the parts that are most painful to me. Now it hurts me to imagine what a terrible place Carville was, to imagine myself walking numbly through. That is a disease as well. In those days, in Louisiana, we were all numb, and we touched things with our deadened hands.

But for me, there was a pain of wakening, as when blood comes to a sleeping limb. Because I was pretending to be a reporter, I asked Steve a lot of questions. Even though as time went on I hoped he wouldn't answer, but he did. "I thought this was a research facility," I said. "Where are the labs?"

"That section is classified. This is the public part. We get a lot of important guests."

We were standing outside a high, wrought-iron fence. I peered at Steve through my mask, trying to see his eyes. Why had he brought me here? Did he have some private reason? I stood in the stifling heat with my gloved hands on the bars of the fence, and then Steve wasn't there. He was called away somewhere and left me alone. I stood looking into a small enclosure, a clipped green lawn and a gazebo. But it was dark there, too. Maybe there were tall trees, or a mass of shrubbery. I remember peering through the bars, wondering if the cage was empty. I inspected a small placard near my eye. "Curtis Garr," it said. "Sodom-ite."

And then suddenly he was there on the other side of the fence. He was a tall man in his midfifties, well-dressed in a dark suit, leaning on a cane. He was very thin, with a famished, bony face, and a wave of gray hair that curled back over his ears. And I noticed that he also was wearing gloves, gray leather gloves.

He stood opposite me for a long time. His thin lips were smiling. But his eyes, which were gray and very large, showed the intensity of any caged beast.

I stood staring at him, my hands on the bars. He smiled. Carefully and slowly, he reached out his gloved forefinger and touched me on my wrist, in a gap between my isolation suit and latex hand.

Then as Steve came up, he gave a jaunty wave and walked away.

Steve nodded. "Curtis is priceless," he muttered behind my ear. "We think he might be the last one left in the entire state. We had two others, but they died."

Last of all, Steve took me back to his air-conditioned office. "We must get together for lunch," he said. "Next time I'm in the city."

Now I can wonder about the Father Damien story he had told me at the Fairmont. I can wonder if in some way he was talking about himself. But at the time I smiled and nodded, for I was anxious to be gone.

I didn't tell Steve the man had touched me. Nor did I tell the doctors who examined me before I was released. But driving back to New Orleans, I found myself examining the skin over my left wrist. Soon it was hot and red from rubbing at it. Once I even stopped the car to look. But I didn't tell Melissa, either, when I got home.

She wouldn't have sympathized. She was furious enough at what she called my "Jesuit liberalism," when I confessed where I had been. I hated when she talked like that. She had been born a Catholic like me and Steve, but her parents had converted after the church split with Rome. As she might have explained it, since the differences between American Catholic and New Baptist were mostly social, why not have the courage to do whatever it took to get ahead? No, that's not fair—she was a true believer. At twenty-eight, she was already a full professor of Creationist biology.

"What if somebody had seen you? What if you had caught something?" she demanded as I rubbed my wrist. I was sitting next to the fireplace, and she stood next to the window with the afternoon light in her hair. All the time she lectured me, I was thinking how much I wanted to make love to her, to push her down and push my penis into her right there on the Doshmelti carpet—"I don't know how you can take such risks," she said. "Or I do know: It's because you don't really believe in any of it. No matter what the proofs, no matter how many times we duplicate the Watanabe results, you just don't accept them."

I sat there fingering my wrist. To tell the truth, there were parts of the doctrine of ethical contagion that no educated person believed.

Melissa herself didn't believe in half of it. But she had to pretend that she believed it, and maybe it was the pretense that made it true.

I didn't want to interrupt her when she was just getting started. "Damn those Jesuits," she said. "Damn them. They ruined you, Jim. You'll never amount to anything, not in Louisiana. Why don't you just go on up to Massachusetts, or someplace where you'd feel at home?"

I loved it when she yelled. Her hair, her eyes. She loved it, too. She was like an actress in a play. The fact is, she never would have married one of those Baptist boys, sickly and small and half-poisoned with salt-peter. No matter how much she told her students about the lechery vaccines, no matter how many times she showed her slides of spiro-chetes attacking the brain, still it was too late for her and me, and she knew it.

The more she yelled at me, the hotter she got. After a while, we went at it like animals.

Two months later, I heard from Steve again. I remember it was in the fall, one of those cool, crisp, blue New Orleans days that seem to come out of nowhere. I had been fired from the paper, and I was standing in my vegetable garden looking out toward the park when I heard the phone ring. I thought it was Melissa, calling back to apologize. She had gone up to Washington, which had been the capital of the Union in the old days, before the states had taken back their rights. She was at an academic conference, and lonely for home. Already that morning she had called me to describe a reception she had been to the night before. When she traveled out of Louisiana, she always had a taste for the unusual—"They have black people here!" she said. "Not just ser-vants; I mean at the conference. And the band! There was a trombone player, you have no idea. Such grace, such raw sexuality."

"I'm not sure I want to hear about that," I said.

She was silent for a moment, and she'd apologized. "I guess I'm a little upset," she confessed.

"Why?"

"I don't like it here. No one takes us seriously. People are very rude, as if *we* were to blame. But we're not the only ones"—she told me about a Dr. Wu from Boise who had given a paper the previous night on Christian genetics. "He showed slides of what he called 'criminal' DNA with all the sins marked on them. As if God had molded them that way. 'With tiny fingers,' as he put it."

I wasn't sure what the New Baptists would say about this. And I didn't want to make a mistake. "That sounds plausible," I murmured, finally.

"You would think that. Plausible and dangerous. It's an argument that leads straight back to Catholicism and original sin. That's fine for you—you want to be guilty when everybody else has been redeemed. But it completely contradicts Fargas and Watanabe, for one thing. Either the soul is uncontaminated at birth or else it isn't. If it isn't, all our immunization research is worthless. What's the point of pretending we can be healed, either by Christ or by science? That's what I said during the Q&A. Everybody hissed and booed, but then I found myself supported by a Jewish gentleman from New York. He said we could not ignore environmental factors, which is not quite a New Baptist point of view the way he expressed it, but what can you expect? He was an old reactionary, but his heart was in the right place. And such a spokesman for his race! Such intelligence and clarity!"

That was the last time I spoke to Melissa, my wife. I wish we had talked about another subject, so that now in California, when I go over her words in my mind, I might not be distracted by these academic arguments. Distracted by my anger, and the guilt that we all shared. I didn't want to hear about the Jewish man. So many Jews had died during the quarantine—I can say that now. But at the time, I thought Melissa was teasing me and trying to make me jealous. "That's the one good thing about you getting yourself canned," she said as she hung up. "I always know where to find you."

Sometimes I wonder what might have happened if I hadn't answered the phone when it rang again a few minutes later. I almost didn't. I sulked in the garden, listening to it, but then at the last moment I went in and picked it up.

But maybe nothing would have been different. Maybe the infection had already spread too far. There was a red spot on my wrist where I'd been rubbing it. I noticed it again as I picked up the phone.

"Jimmy, is that you?" Steve's voice was harsh and confused, and the connection was bad. In the background was a rhythmic banging noise. Melissa, in Washington, had sounded clearer.

After Steve was finished, I went out and stood in my vegetable garden again, in the bright, clean sun. Over in the park, a family was sitting by the pond having a picnic. A little girl in a blue dress stood up and clapped her hands.

What public sacrifice is too great, I thought, to keep that girl free from contamination? Or maybe it's just now, looking back, that I allow myself a thought. Maybe at the time I just stared numbly over the fence, and then went in and drank a Coke. It wasn't until a few hours later that I got in the car and drove north.

Over the past months, I had looked for stories about Carville in the news. And Melissa had told me some of the gossip—there were differences of opinion in Baton Rouge. Some of the senators wanted the hospital kept open, as a showpiece for foreign visitors. But Barbara Rasmussen wanted the patients shipped to a labor camp outside of Shreveport, near the Arkansas border. It was a place both Steve and I had heard of.

Over the phone he'd said, "It's murder,"—a painful word. Then he'd told me where to meet him. He'd mentioned a time. But I knew I'd be late, because of the slow way I was driving. I wasn't sure I wanted to help him. So I took a leisurely, roundabout route, and crossed the river near the ruins of Hahnville. I drove up old Route 18 past Vacherie. It was deserted country there, rising swamps and burned-out towns, and endless cemeteries full of rows of painted wooden markers. Some had names on them, but mostly just numbers.

I passed some old Negroes working in a field.

Once I drove up onto the levee, and sat staring at the great river next to a crude, concrete statue of Christ the Healer. The metal bones of His fingers protruded from His crumbling hands. Then over the Sunshine Bridge, and it was early evening.

I first met them on River Road near Belle-Helene plantation, as they were coming back from Carville. There was a patchy mist out of the swamp. I drove slowly, and from time to time I had to wipe the condensation from the inside of my windshield.

In the middle of the smudged circle I had made with my handkerchief, I saw the glimmer of their Coleman lanterns. The oak trees hung over the car. I pulled over to the grass and turned off the ignition. I rolled down my window and listened to the car tick and cool. Soon they came walking down the middle of the road, their spare, pinched faces, their white, buttoned-up shirts stained dirty from the cinders. One or two wore masks over their mouth and nose. Some wore civil defense armbands. Some carried books, others hammers and wrecking bars.

The most terrifying thing about those New Baptist mobs was their sobriety, their politeness. There was no swagger to them, no drunken truculence. They came out of the fog in orderly rows. There was no laughter or shouting. Most of the men walked by me without even looking my way. But then four or five of them came over and stood by the window.

"Excuse me, sir," said one. He took off his gimme cap and wiped the moisture from his bald forehead. "You from around here?"

"I'm from the *Times-Picayune*. I was headed up to Carville."

"Well," said another, shaking his head. "Nothing to see."

"The road's blocked," offered a third. He had rubber gloves on, and his voice was soft and high. "But right here you can get onto the Interstate. You just passed it. Route 73 from Geismar. It will take you straight back to the city."

Some more men had come over to stand next to me along the driver's side. One of them stooped to peer inside. Now he tapped the roof lightly over my head, and I could hear his fingernails on the smooth plastic.

"I think I'd like to take a look," I said. "Even so."

He smiled, and then looked serious. "You a Catholic, sir? I guess New Orleans is a Catholic town."

I sat for a moment, and then rolled up the window. "Thank you," I murmured through the glass. Then I turned on the ignition, and pulled the car around in a tight semicircle. Darkness had come. I put on my headlights, which snatched at the men's legs as I turned around. Illuminated in red whenever I hit the brakes, the New Baptists stood together in the middle of the road, and I watched them in my rearview mirror. One waved.

Then I drove slowly through the crowd again until I found the connecting road. It led away from the river through a few small, neon-lit stores. Pickup trucks were parked there. I recognized the bar Steve had mentioned, and I slowed up when I passed it. I was too late. From Geismar on, the road was deserted.

Close to I-10 it ran through the cypress swamps, and there was no one. Full dark now, and gusts of fog. I drove slowly until I saw a man walking by the side of the road. I speeded up to pass him, and in my high-beams I caught a glimpse of his furious, thin face as he looked over his shoulder. It was Curtis Garr.

I wish I could tell you how I left him there, trudging on the gravel shoulder. I wish I could tell you how I sped away until the sodomite was swallowed up in the darkness and the fog, how I sped home and found my wife there, unexpectedly waiting. The conference might have let out early. She might have decided to surprise me.

These thoughts are painful to me, and it's not because I can never go back. My friend Rob tells me the borders are full of holes, at least for white people. Passports and medical papers are easy to forge. He spends a lot of time at gun shows and survivalist meetings, where I suppose they talk about these things.

But I left because I had to. Because I changed, and Curtis Garr changed me. Now in California, in the desert night, I still can't forgive him, partly because I took such a terrible revenge. If he's dead or in prison now, God damn him. He broke my life apart, and maybe it was fragile and ready to break. Maybe I was contaminated already, and that's why I stopped in the middle of the road, and backed up, and let him into my car. Melissa's car.

He got into the back seat without a word. But he was angry. As soon as we started driving again, he spoke. "Where were you? I waited at that bar for over an hour."

"I thought I was meeting Steve."

"Yes—he told me. He described your car."

I looked at him in the rearview mirror. His clothes were still immaculate, his dark suit. He was a fierce, thin, handsome man.

"Where are you going?"

He said nothing, but just stared on ahead through the windshield. I wondered if he recognized me. If he felt something in me calling out to him, he didn't show it. At Carville, I'd been wearing a mask over my nose and mouth.

But I wanted to ask him about Steve. "You're Curtis Garr," I said.

Then he looked at me in the mirror, his fierce eyes. "Don't be afraid," I said, though he seemed anything but frightened.

"I thought I was meeting Steve," I said after an empty pause. "He didn't say anything about you."

"Maybe he didn't think you would come." And then: "We had to change our plans after Rasmussen's goons showed up. Don't worry about Steve. You'll see him later. No one on the staff was hurt."

Garr's voice was low and harsh. I drove with my left hand. From time to time I scratched the skin over my left wrist.

Soon we came up to the Interstate. The green sign hung flapping. I-10 was a dangerous road, and ordinarily I wouldn't have taken it. Most of the way it was built on crumbling pontoons over the swamp. In some places the guard rail was down, and there were holes in the pavement. But it bypassed all the towns.

Curtis Garr rolled down his window. There was no one on the road. In time we felt a cool draught off the lake.

Once past the airport, we could go faster, because the road was carefully maintained from Kenner to the bridge. The city lights were comforting and bright. We took the Annunciation exit and drove up St. Charles, the great old houses full of prosperous, happy folk.

In more than an hour, Garr and I had not exchanged a word. But I felt a terrible tension in my stomach, and my wrist itched and ached. I kept thinking the man would tell me where to drop him off. I hoped he would. But he said nothing as I drove down Calhoun toward Magazine, toward Melissa's house on Exposition Boulevard.

"Where are you going?" I asked.

He shrugged.

I felt my guts might burst from my excitement. My fingers trembled on the wheel. "Can I put you up?" I said. "It's past curfew. You'll be safer in the morning."

"Yes. I'm meeting Steve at ten."

And that was all. I pulled into the parking slip and turned off the car. Then I stepped outside into the cool, humid night, and he was there beside me. I listened to him breathe. Almost a hissing sound.

"Nice house."

"It's my wife's. She's a professor at Tulane."

Again that harsh intake of breath. He looked up at the gabled roof. For a moment I was afraid he might refuse to come inside. Something in him seemed to resist. But then he followed me onto the porch.

"You don't lock your doors?"

"Of course not."

"Hunh. When I was in school, New Orleans was the murder capital of the entire country."

"It hasn't all been bad," I said.

Then he was in the living room, standing on the Doshmelti carpet. I excused myself to wash my face and hands in the kitchen bathroom, and when I returned he was looking at the bookcase. "Can I get you something to eat?" I asked. "I'm famished."

"Something to drink," by which he meant alcohol. So I brought out a bottle of white bourbon that we had. I poured him a glass. I really was very hungry. I'd scarcely eaten all day.

"How can you stand it?" he asked suddenly. He had moved over to a case full of biology and medical texts, a collection Melissa had gathered during her trips.

He had one of the books open in his hand. With the other, he gestured with his glass around the room. "All this. You're not a fool. Or are you?"

He put down the book and then walked over to stand in front of me, inches away, his face inches from my own. "I was at Carville," he said. "People died there. Aren't you afraid you're going to catch something?"

But I knew I had caught something already. My heart was shuddering. My face was wet.

I looked up at him, and I thought I could see every pore in his skin. I could see the way his teeth fit into his gums. I could smell his breath and his body when he spoke to me, not just the alcohol but something else. "This state is a sick joke everywhere," he said. "Those people who attacked the Center, they didn't have a tenth-grade education between them. How can you blame them?"

Curtis Garr had black hair in his ears. His lower face was rinsed in gray—he hadn't shaved. I stood looking up at him, admiring the shapes his thin lips formed around his words. "What does your wife teach?"

"Biology."

At that moment, the phone rang. It was on a table in a little alcove by the door. I didn't answer it. Garr and I stood inches apart. After three rings the machine picked up.

"Hi, sweetie," said Melissa. "I just thought I'd try to catch you before you went to bed. Sorry I missed you. I was just thinking how nice it would be to be in bed with you, sucking that big Monongahela. Just a thought. I'll be back tomorrow night."

The machine turned off, and Curtis Garr smiled. "That sounds very cozy." Then he stepped away from me, back to the bookcase again, and I let out my breath.

"A third of the population of Louisiana died during the HIV-2 epidemic," I said. "In just a few years. The feds told them not to worry. The doctors told them it couldn't happen. The New Baptists were the only ones who didn't lie to them. What do you expect?"

"Sin and disease," he said. "I know the history. Not everybody died of HIV. I knew some biology, too—the real kind. And I said something about it. That's why I was at Carville in the first place. The other thing's just an excuse."

He was staring at the books as he spoke. But he must have been watching me as well, must have seen something in my face as he sipped his whiskey, because he lowered the glass and grinned at me over the rim. "You're disappointed, aren't you?"

And then after a moment: "Christ, you are! You hypocrite."

But I was standing with my hands held out, my right hand closed around my wrist. "Please," I said. "Please."

He finished his drink and gave a little burp. He put his glass on one of the shelves of the bookcase, and then sat down in the middle of the couch, stretching his thin arms along the top of it on either side.

"No, you disgust me," he said, smiling. "Everything about you disgusts me."

Often now I'll start awake in bed, wondering where I am. "Melissa," I'll say, still half-asleep, when I get up to go to the bathroom. So Rob tells me on the nights he's there. I used to sleep as soundly as a child. That night, when Curtis Garr stayed in the house on Exposition Boulevard, was the first I remember lying awake.

After I had gone upstairs, he sat up late, reading and drinking whiskey on the couch. From time to time I would get up and stand at the top of the stairs, watching the light through the banisters, listening to the rustle of the pages. Near dawn I masturbated, and then, after I'd washed up, I went downstairs and stood next to him as he slept. He had left the light on and had curled up on the couch, still in his suit. He hadn't even taken off his shoes.

His mouth was open, pushed out of shape by the cushions. I stood next to him, and then I bent down and stretched out my left hand. I almost touched him. My left wrist was a mass of hectic spots. The rash had spread up the inside of my arm.

In my other hand, I carried a knapsack with some clothes. My passport, and a few small personal items. Almost everything in the house that actually belonged to me, I could fit in that one bag. A picture of Melissa, which is on my bedside still. I had the card to her bank account, and I stood by the couch, wondering if I should leave a note.

Instead, I went into the kitchen, and, from the kitchen phone, I dialed a number we all knew in Louisiana, in those days. Together with the numbers for the fire department and the ordinary police, it was typed on a piece of paper which was thumbtacked to the wall. The phone rang for a long time. But then finally someone answered it, and there was nothing in his tone of voice to suggest he'd been asleep.

Within a few minutes, I was on my way. I walked up to St. Charles Avenue just as it got light, toward the streetcar line. The air was full of birds, their voices competing with the soft noise of the cars as they passed a block away, bound toward Melissa's house or somewhere else, I couldn't really tell.

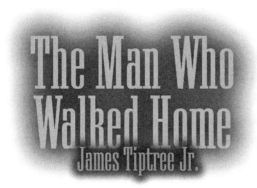

The Man Who Walked Home

James Tiptree Jr.

Here's a vivid and compelling look at how a scientific experiment could *itself* become the basis for a host of superstitions and perhaps even a new religion, given the blurring effect of time—*lots* of time.

As most of you probably know by now, multiple Hugo and Nebula Award–winning author James Tiptree Jr. was actually the pseudonym of the late Dr. Alice Sheldon, a semiretired experimental psychologist and former member of the American intelligence community who also wrote occasionally under the name of Raccoona Sheldon. Dr. Sheldon's tragic death in 1987 put an end to "both" careers, but not before she had won two Nebula and two Hugo Awards as Tiptree, won another Nebula Award as Raccoona Sheldon, and established herself, under whatever name, as one of the very best science fiction writers of our times.

Although "Tiptree" published two reasonably well-received novels—*Up the Walls of the World* and *Brightness Falls from the*

Air—she was, like Damon Knight and Theodore Sturgeon (two writers she aesthetically resembled, and by whom she was strongly influenced), more comfortable with the short story, and more effective with it. She wrote some of the very best short stories of the seventies: "The Screwfly Solution," "The Girl Who Was Plugged In," "The Women Men Don't See," "Beam Us Home," "And I Awoke and Found Me Here on the Cold Hill's Side," "I'm Too Big But I Love to Play," "The Man Who Walked Home," "Slow Music," and "His Smoke Rose Up Forever." Already it's clear that these are stories that will last. They—and a dozen others almost as good—show that Alice Sheldon was simply one of the best short story writers to work in the genre in our times. In fact, with her desire for a high bit-rate, her concern for societal goals, her passion for the novel and the unexpected, her taste for extrapolation, her experimenter's interest in the reactions of people to supernormal stimuli and bizarre situations, her fondness for the apocalyptic, her love of color and sweep and dramatic action, and her preoccupation with the mutability of time and the vastness of space, Alice Sheldon was a natural science fiction writer. I doubt that she would have been able to realize her particular talents as fully in any other genre, and she didn't even seem particularly interested in trying. At a time when many other science fiction writers would be just as happy—or happier—writing "mainstream" fiction, and chaff at the artistic and financial restrictions of the genre, what *she* wanted to be was a *science fiction writer*; that was *her* dream and her passion.

As Tiptree, Dr. Sheldon published ten short story collections, including *Ten Thousand Light Years from Home*, *Warm Worlds and Otherwise*, *Starsongs of an Old Primate*, *Out of the Everywhere*, *Tales of the Quintana Roo*, *Byte Beautiful*, and *The Starry Rift*, and the posthumous retrospective collections, *Crown of Stars*, *Her*

Smoke Rose Up Forever, and *Meet Me at Infinity.* Coming up is a full-dress biography of "Tiptree," by Julie Philips.

*T*ransgression! *Terror! And he thrust and lost there—punched into impossibility, abandoned, never to be known now, the wrong man in the most wrong of all wrong places in that unimaginable collapse of never-to-be-reimagined mechanism—he stranded, undone, his lifeline severed, he in that nanosecond knowing his only tether parting, going away, the longest line to life withdrawing, winking out, disappearing forever beyond his grasp—telescoping away from him into the closing vortex beyond which lay his home, his life, his only possibility of being; seeing it sucked back into the deepest maw, melting, leaving him orphaned on what never-to-be-known shore of total wrongness—of beauty beyond joy, perhaps? Of horror? Of nothingness? Of profound otherness only, only, certainly whatever it was, that place into which he transgressed, certainly it could not support his life there, his violent and violating aberrance; and he, fierce, brave, crazy—clenched into one total protest, one body-fist of utter repudiation of himself there in that place, forsaken there—what did he do? Rejected, exiled, hungering homeward more desperate than any lost beast driving for its unreachable home, his home, his HOME—and no way, no transport, no vehicle, means, machinery, no force but his intolerable resolve aimed homeward along that vanishing vector, that last and only lifeline—he did, what?*

He walked.

Home.

Precisely what hashed up in the work of the major industrial lessee of the Bonneville Particle Acceleration Facility in Idaho was never known. Or rather, all those who might have been able to diagnose the original malfunction were themselves obliterated almost at once in the greater catastrophe which followed.

The nature of this second cataclysm was not at first understood, either. All that was ever certain was that at 1153.6 of May 2, 1989,

Old Style, the Bonneville laboratories and all their personnel were transformed into an intimately disrupted form of matter resembling a high-energy plasma, which became rapidly airborne to the accompaniment of radiating seismic and atmospheric events.

The disturbed area unfortunately included an operational MIRV Watchdog bomb.

In the confusions of the next hours the Earth's population was substantially reduced, the biosphere was altered, and the Earth itself was marked with numbers of more conventional craters. For some years thereafter the survivors were existentially preoccupied and the peculiar dust bowl at Bonneville was left to weather by itself in the changing climatic cycles.

It was not a large crater; just over a kilometer in width and lacking the usual displacement lip. Its surface was covered with a finely divided substance which dried into dust. Before the rains began it was almost perfectly flat. Only in certain lights, had anyone been there to inspect it, a small surface marking or abraded place could be detected almost exactly as the center.

Two decades after the disaster a party of short brown people appeared from the south, together with a flock of somewhat atypical sheep. The crater at this time appeared as a wide shallow basin in which the grass did not grow well, doubtless from the almost complete lack of soil microorganisms. Neither this nor the surrounding vigorous grass were found to harm the sheep. A few crude hogans went up at the southern edge and a faint path began to be traced across the crater itself, passing by the central bare spot.

One spring morning two children who had been driving sheep across the crater came screaming back to camp. A monster had burst out of the ground before them, a huge flat animal making a dreadful roar. It vanished in a flash and a shaking of the earth, leaving an evil smell. The sheep had run away.

Since this last was visibly true, some elders investigated. Finding no sign of the monster and no place in which it could hide, they settled for beating the children, who settled for making a detour around the monster-spot, and nothing more occurred for a while.

The following spring the episode was repeated. This time an older girl was present but she could add only that the monster seemed to be rushing flat out along the ground without moving at all. And there was a scraped place in the dirt. Again nothing was found; an evil-ward in a cleft stick was placed at the spot.

When the same thing happened for the third time a year later, the detour was extended and other charm-wands were added. But since no harm seemed to come of it and the brown people had seen far worse, sheep-tending resumed as before. A few more instantaneous apparitions of the monster were noted, each time in the spring.

At the end of the third decade of the new era a tall old man limped down the hills from the south, pushing his pack on a bicycle wheel. He camped on the far side of the crater, and soon found the monster-site. He attempted to question people about it, but no one understood him, so he traded a knife for some meat. Although he was obviously feeble, something about him dissuaded them from killing him, and this proved wise because he later assisted the men to treat several sick children.

He spent much time around the place of the apparition and was nearby when it made its next appearance. This excited him very much, and he did several inexplicable but apparently harmless things, including moving his camp into the crater by the trail. He stayed on for a full year watching the site and was close by for its next manifestation. After this, he spent a few days making a charmstone for the spot and then left, northward, hobbling, as he had come.

More decades passed. The crater eroded and a rain-gully became an intermittent steamlet across one edge of the basin. The brown people and their sheep were attacked by a band of grizzled men, after which the survivors went away eastward. The winters of what had been Idaho was now frost-free; aspen and eucalyptus sprouted in the moist plain.

Still the crater remained treeless, visible as a flat bowl of grass, and the bare place at the center remained. The skies cleared somewhat.

After another three decades a larger band of black people with ox-drawn carts appeared and stayed for a time, but left again when they, too, saw the thunderclap-monster. A few other vagrants straggled by.

Five decades later a small permanent settlement had grown up on the nearest range of hills, from which men riding on small ponies with dark stripes down their spines herded humped cattle near the crater. A herdsman's hut was built by the streamlet, which in time became the habitation of an olive-skinned, red-haired family. In due course one of this clan again observed the monster-flash, but these people did not depart. The stone the tall man had placed was noted and left undisturbed.

The homestead at the crater's edge grew into a group of three and was joined by others, and the trail across it became a cartroad with a log bridge over the stream. At the center of the still-faintly-discernible crater the cartroad made a bend, leaving a grassy place which bore on its center about a square meter of curiously impacted bare earth and a deeply etched sandstone rock.

The apparition of the monster was now known to occur regularly each spring on a certain morning in this place, and the children of the community dared each other to approach the spot. It was referred to in a phrase that could be translated as "the Old Dragon." The Old Dragon's appearance was always the same; a brief, violent thunder-burst which began and cut off abruptly, in the midst of which a dragonlike creature was seen apparently in furious motion on the earth although it never actually moved. Afterward there was a bad smell and the earth smoked. People who saw it from close by spoke of a shivering sensation.

Early in the second century two young men rode into town from the north. Their ponies were shaggier than the local breed and the equipment they carried included two boxlike objects which the young men set up at the monster-site. They stayed in the area a full year, observing two materializations of the Old Dragon, and they provided much news and maps of roads and trading-towns in the cooler regions to the north. They built a windmill which was accepted by the community and offered to build a lighting machine, which was refused. Then they departed with their boxes after unsuccessfully attempting to persuade a local boy to learn to operate one.

In the course of the next decades other travelers stopped by and marveled at the monster, and there was sporadic fighting over the mountains to the south. One of the armed bands made a cattle-raid into the crater hamlet. It was repulsed, but the raiders left a spotted sickness which killed many. For all this time the bare place at the crater's center remained, and the monster made his regular appearances, observed or not.

The hill-town grew and changed and the crater hamlet grew to be a town. Roads widened and linked into networks. There were gray-green conifers in the hills now, spreading down into the plain, and chirruping lizards lived in their branches.

At century's end a shabby band of skin-clad squatters with stunted milk-beasts erupted out of the west and were eventually killed or driven away, but not before the local herds had contracted a vicious parasite. Veterinaries were fetched from the market-city up north, but little could be done. The families near the crater left, and for some decades the area was empty. Finally cattle of a new strain reappeared in the plain and the crater hamlet was reoccupied. Still the bare center continued annually to manifest the monster and he became an accepted phenomenon of the area. On several occasions parties came from the distant Northwest Authority to observe it.

The crater hamlet flourished and grew into the fields where cattle had grazed and part of the old crater became the town park. A small seasonal tourist industry based on the monster-site developed. The townspeople rented rooms for the appearances and many more-or-less authentic monster-relics were on display in the local taverns.

Several cults now grew up around the monster. Some held that it was a devil or damned soul forced to appear on Earth in torment to expiate the catastrophe of two centuries back. Others believed that it, or he, was some kind of messenger whose roar portended either doom or hope according to the believer. One very vocal sect taught that the apparition registered the moral conduct of the townspeople over the past year, and scrutinized the annual apparition for changes which could be interpreted for good or ill. It was considered lucky, or dangerous, to be touched by some of the dust raised by the monster. In every generation at least one small boy would try to hit the monster with a stick, usually acquiring a broken arm and a lifelong tavern tale. Pelting the monster with stones or other objects was a popular sport, and for some years people systematically flung prayers and flowers at it. Once a party tried to net it and were left with strings and vapor. The area itself had long since been fenced off at the center of the park.

Through all this the monster made his violently enigmatic annual appearance, sprawled furiously motionless, unreachably roaring.

Only as the fourth century of the new era went by was it apparent that the monster had been changing slightly. He was now no longer on the earth but had an arm and a leg thrust upward in a kicking or flailing gesture. As the years passed he began to change more quickly until at the end of the century he had risen to a contorted crouching pose, arms outflung as if frozen in gyration. His roar, too, seemed somewhat differently pitched and the earth after him smoked more and more.

It was then widely felt that the man-monster was about to do something, to make some definitive manifestation, and a series of natural disasters and marvels gave support to a vigorous cult teaching this doctrine. Several religious leaders journeyed to the town to observe the apparitions.

However, the decades passed and the man-monster did nothing more than turn slowly in place, so that he now appeared to be in the act of sliding or staggering while pushing himself backward like a creature blown before a gale. No wind, of course, could be felt, and presently the general climate quieted and nothing came of it all.

Early in the fifth century New Calendar three survey parties from the North Central Authority came through the area and stopped to observe the monster. A permanent recording device was set up at the site, after assurances to the townfolk that no hardscience was involved. A local boy was trained to operate it; he quit when his girl left him but another volunteered. At this time nearly everyone believed that the apparition was a man, or the ghost of one. The record-machine boy and a few others, including the school mechanics teacher, referred to him as the Man John. In the next decades the roads were greatly improved; all forms of travel increased and there was talk of building a canal to what had been the Snake River.

One May morning at the end of Century Five a young couple in a smart green mule-trap came jogging up the high-road from the San-dreas Rift Range to the southwest. The girl was golden-skinned and chatted with her young husband in a language unlike that ever heard by the Man John either at the end or the beginning of his life. What she said to him has, however, been heard in every age and tongue.

"Oh Serli, I'm so glad we're taking this trip now! Next summer I'll be so busy with baby."

To which Serli replied as young husbands often have, and so they trotted up to the town's inn. Here they left trap and bags and went in search of her uncle who was expecting them there. The morrow was the day of the Man John's annual appearance, and her Uncle Laban had come from the MacKenzie History Museum to observe it and to make certain arrangements.

They found him with the town school instructor of mechanics, who was also the recorder at the monster-site. Presently Uncle Laban took them all with him to the town mayor's office to meet with various religious personages. The mayor was not unaware of tourist values, but he took Uncle Laban's part in securing the cultists' grudging assent to the MacKenzie authorities' secular interpretation of the "monster," which was made easier by the fact that they disagreed among themselves. Then, seeing how pretty the niece was, the mayor took them all home to dinner.

When they returned to the inn for the night it was abrawl with holiday makers.

"Whew," said Uncle Laban. "I've talked myself dry, sister's daughter. What a weight of holy nonsense is that Morsha female! Serli, my lad, I know you have questions. Let me hand you this to read; it's a guide book we're giving 'em to sell. Tomorrow I'll answer for it all." And he disappeared into the crowded tavern.

So Serli and his bride took the pamphlet upstairs to bed with them, but it was not until the next morning at breakfast that they found time to read it.

"'All that is known of John Delgano,'" read Serli with his mouth full, "'comes from two documents left by his brother Carl Delgano in the archives of the MacKenzie Group in the early years after the holocaust.' Put some honey on this cake, Mira my dove, 'Verbatim transcript follows; this is Carl Delgano speaking.

"'I'm not an engineer or an astronaut like John. I ran an electronics repair shop in Salt Lake City. John was only trained as a spaceman, he never got to space, the slump wiped all that out. So he tied up with this commercial group who were leasing part of Bonneville. They wanted a man for some kind of hard vacuum tests; that's all I knew about it. John and his wife moved to Bonneville, but we all got together several times a year, our wives were like sisters. John had two kids, Clara and Paul.

"'The tests were all supposed to be secret, but John told me confidentially they were trying for an antigravity chamber. I don't know if it ever worked. That was the year before.

"'Then that winter they came down for Christmas and John said they had something new. He was really excited. A temporal displacement, he called it; some kind of time effect. He said the chief honcho was like a real mad scientist. Bit ideas. He kept adding more angles every time some other project would quit and leave equipment he could lease. No, I don't know who the top company was—maybe an insurance conglomerate, they had all the cash, didn't they? I guess they'd pay to catch a look at the future; that figures. Anyway, John was go, go, go. Katharine was scared; that's natural. She pictured him like, you know, H. G. Wells—walking around in some future world. John told her it wasn't like that at all. All they'd get would be this kind of flicker, like a second or two. All kinds of complications'—Yes, yes, my greedy piglet, some brew for me, too. This is thirsty work!

"So . . . 'I remember I asked him, what about the Earth moving? I mean, you could come back in a different place, right? He said they had that all figured. A spatial trajectory. Katherine was so scared we dropped it. John told her, don't worry, I'll come home. But he didn't. Not that it makes any difference, of course; everything was wiped out. Salt Lake, too. The only reason I'm here is that I went up by Calgary to see Mom, April twenty-ninth. May second it all blew. I didn't find you folks at MacKenzie until July. I guess I may as well stay. That's all I know about John, except that he was an all-right guy. If that accident started all this it wasn't his fault.

"'The second document'—In the name of love, little mother, do I have to read all this! Oh very well; but you will kiss me first, madam. Must you look so ineffable? . . . 'The second document. Dated in the year eighteen, New Style, written by Carl'—see the old handwriting, my plump pigeon. Oh, very well, very well.

"'Written at Bonneville Crater, I have seen my brother John Delgano. When I knew I had the rad sickness I came down here to look around. Salt Lake's still hot. So I hiked up here by Bonneville. You can see the crater where the labs were; it's grassed over. It's different, it's not radioactive, my film's OK. There's a bare place in the middle. Some Indies here told me a monster shows up here every year in the spring. I saw it myself a couple of days after I got here but I was too far away to see much, except I was sure it's a man. In a vacuum suit. There was a lot of noise and dust, took me by surprise. It was all over in a second. I figure it's pretty close to the day, I mean, May second, old.

"'So I hung around a year and he showed up again yesterday. I was on the face side and I could see his face through the faceplate. It's John all right. He's hurt. I saw blood on his mouth and his suit is frayed some. He's lying on the ground. He didn't move while I could see him but the dust boiled up, like a man sliding onto base without moving. His eyes are open like he was looking. I don't understand it anyway, but I know it's John, not a ghost. He was in exactly the same position each time and there's a loud crack like thunder and another sound like a siren, very fast. And an ozone smell, and smoke, I felt a kind of shudder.

"'I know it's John there and I think he's alive. I have to leave here now to take this back while I can still walk. I think somebody should come here and see. Maybe you can help John. Signed. Carl Delgano.'

"'The records were kept by the MacKenzie Group but it was not for several years—' Etcetera, first light-print, etcetera, archives, analysts, etcetera—very good! Now it is time to meet your uncle, my edible one, after we go upstairs for just a moment."

"No, Serli, I will wait for you downstairs," said Mira prudently.

When they came into the town park Uncle Laban was directing the installation of a large durite slab in front of the enclosure around the Man John's appearance-spot. The slab was wrapped in a curtain to await the official unveiling. Townspeople and tourists and children thronged the walks and a Ride-For-Good choir was singing in the bandshell. The morning was warming up fast. Vendors hawked ices and straw toys of the monster and flowers and good-luck confetti to throw at him. Another religious group stood by in dark robes; they belonged to the

Repentance church beyond the park. Their pastor was directing somber glares at the crowd in general and Mira's uncle in particular.

Three official-looking strangers who had been at the inn came up and introduced themselves to Uncle Laban as observers from Alberta Central. They went on into the tent which had been erected over the enclosure, carrying with them several pieces of equipment which the town-folk eyed suspiciously.

The mechanics teacher finished organizing a squad of students to protect the slab's curtain, and Mira and Serli and Laban went on into the tent. It was much hotter inside. Benches were set in rings around a railed enclosure about twenty feet in diameter. Inside the railing the earth was bare and scuffed. Several bunches of flowers and blooming poinciana branches leaned against the rail. The only thing inside the rail was a rough sandstone rock with markings etched on it.

Just as they came in a small girl raced across the open center and was yelled at by everybody. The officials from Alberta were busy at one side of the rail, where the light-print box was mounted.

"Oh, no," muttered Mira's uncle, as one of the officials leaned over to set up a tripod stand inside the rails. He adjusted it and a huge horsetail of fine feathery filaments blossomed out and eddied through the center of the space.

"Oh *no*," Laban said again. "Why can't they let it be?"

"They're trying to pick up dust from his suit, is that right?" Serli asked.

"Yes, insane. Did you get time to read?"

"Oh yes," said Serli.

"Sort of," added Mira.

"Then you know. He's falling. Trying to check his—well, call it velocity. Trying to slow down. He must have slipped or stumbled. We're getting pretty close to when he lost his footing and started to fall. What did it? Did somebody trip him?" Laban looked from Mira to Serli, dead serious now. "How would you like to be the one who made John Delgano fall?"

"Ooh," said Mira in quick sympathy. Then she said, "Oh."

"You mean," asked Serli, "whoever made him fall caused all the, caused—"

"Possible," said Laban.

"Wait a minute," Serli frowned. "He did fall. So somebody had to do it—I mean, he has to trip or whatever. If he doesn't fall the past would all be changed, wouldn't it? No war, no—"

"Possible," Laban repeated. "God knows. All *I* know is that John Delgano and the space around him is the most unstable, improbable, highly charged area ever known on Earth and I'm damned if I think anybody should go poking sticks in it."

"Oh come now, Laban!" One of the Alberta men joined them, smiling. "Our dust-mop couldn't trip a gnat. It's just vitreous monofilaments."

"Dust from the future," grumbled Laban. "What's it going to tell you? That the future has dust in it?"

"If we could only get a trace from that thing in his hand."

"In his hand?" asked Mira. Serli started leafing hurriedly through the pamphlet.

"We've had a recording analyzer aimed at it," the Albertan lowered his voice, glancing around. "A spectroscope. We know there's something there, or was. Can't get a decent reading. It's severely deteriorated."

"People poking at him, grabbing at him," Laban muttered. "You—"

"*Ten minutes!*" shouted a man with a megaphone. "Take your places, friends and strangers."

The Repentance people were filing in at one side, intoning an ancient incantation, "mi-seri-cordia, ora pro nobis!"

The atmosphere suddenly took on tension. It was now very close and hot in the big tent. A boy from the mayor's office wiggled through the crowd, beckoning Laban's party to come and sit in the guest chairs on the second level on the "face" side. In front of them at the rail one of the Repentance ministers was arguing with an Albertan official over his right to occupy the space taken by a recorder, it being his special duty to look into the Man John's eyes.

"Can he really see us?" Mira asked her uncle.

"Blink your eyes," Laban told her. "A new scene every blink, that's what he sees. Phantasmagoria. Blink-blink-blink—for god knows how long."

"Mi-sere-re, pec-cavi," chanted the penitentials. A soprano neighed "May the red of sin pa-aa-ass from us!"

"They believe his oxygen tab went red because of the state of their souls." Laban chuckled. "Their souls are going to have to stay damned a while; John Delgano has been on oxygen reserve for five centuries— or rather, he *will be* low for five centuries more. At a half-second per year his time, that's fifteen minutes. We know from the audio trace he's still breathing more or less normally and the reserve was good for twenty minutes. So they should have their salvation about the year seven hundred, if they last that long."

"*Five minutes!* Take your seats, folks. Please sit down so everyone can see. Sit down, folks."

"It says we'll hear his voice through his suit speaker," Serli whispered. "Do you know what he's saying?"

"You get mostly a twenty-cycle howl," Laban whispered back. "The recorders have spliced up something like *ayt*, part of an old word. Take centuries to get enough to translate."

"Is it a message?"

"Who knows? Could be his word for 'date' or 'hate.' 'Too late,' maybe. Anything."

The tent was quieting. A fat child by the railing started to cry and was pulled back onto a lap. There was a subdued mumble of praying. The Holy Joy faction on the far side rustled their flowers.

"Why don't we set our clocks by him?"

"It's changing. He's on sidereal time."

"One minute."

In the hush the praying voices rose slightly. From outside a chicken cackled. The bare center space looked absolutely ordinary. Over it the recorder's silvery filaments eddied gently in the breath from a hundred lungs. Another recorder could be heard ticking faintly.

For long seconds nothing happened.

The air developed a tiny hum. At the same moment Mira caught a movement at the railing on her left.

The hum developed a beat and vanished into a peculiar silence and suddenly everything happened at once.

Sound burst on them, raced shockingly up the audible scale. The air cracked as something rolled and tumbled in the space. There was a grinding, wailing roar and—

He was there.

Solid, huge—a huge man in a monster suit, his head was a dull bronze transparent globe holding a human face, dark smear of open mouth. His position was impossible, legs strained forward thrusting himself back, his arms frozen in a whirlwind swing. Although he seemed to be in a frantic forward motion nothing moved, only one of his legs buckled or sagged slightly—

—And then he was gone, utterly and completely gone in a thunderclap, leaving only the incredible afterimage in a hundred pairs of staring eyes. Air boomed, shuddering, dust roiled out mixed with smoke.

"Oh, oh my God," gasped Mira, unheard, clinging to Serli. Voices were crying out, choking. "He saw me, he saw me!" a woman shrieked. A few people dazedly threw their confetti into the empty dust-cloud; most had failed to throw at all. Children began to howl. "He *saw* me!" the woman screamed hysterically. "Red, Oh Lord have mercy!" a deep male voice intoned.

Mira heard Laban swearing furiously and looked again into the space. As the dust settled she could see that the recorder's tripod had tipped over into the center. There was a dusty mound lying against it—flowers. Most of the end of the stand seemed to have disappeared or been melted. Of the filaments nothing could be seen.

"Some damn fool pitched flowers into it. Come on, let's get out."

"Was it under, did it trip him?" asked Mira, squeezed in the crowd.

"It was still red, his oxygen thing," Serli said over her head. "No mercy this trip, eh, Laban?"

"Shsh!" Mira caught the Repentance pastor's dark glance. They jostled through the enclosure gate and were out in the sunlit park, voices exclaiming, chattering loudly in excitement and relief.

"It was terrible," Mira cried softly. "Oh, I never thought it was a real live man. There he is, he's *there*. Why can't we help him? Did we trip him?"

"I don't know; I don't think so," her uncle grunted. They sat down near the new monument, fanning themselves. The curtain was still in place.

"Did we change the past?" Serli laughed, looked lovingly at his little wife. He wondered for a moment why she was wearing such odd earrings. Then he remembered he had given them to her at that Indian pueblo they'd passed.

"But it wasn't just those Alberta people," said Mira. She seemed obsessed with the idea. "It was the flowers really." She wiped at her forehead.

"Mechanics or superstition," chuckled Serli. "Which is the culprit, love or science?"

"Shsh." Mira looked about nervously. "The flowers were love, I guess . . . I feel so strange. It's hot. Oh, thank you." Uncle Laban had succeeded in attracting the attention of the iced-drink vendor.

People were chatting normally now and the choir struck into a cheerful song. At one side of the park a line of people were waiting to sign their names in the visitors' book. The mayor appeared at the park gate, leading a party up the bougainvillea alley for the unveiling of the monument.

"What did it say on that stone by his foot?" Mira asked. Serli showed her the guidebook picture of Carl's rock with the inscription translated below: WELCOME HOME, JOHN.

"I wonder if he can see it?"

The mayor was about to begin his speech.

Much later when the crowd had gone away the monument stood alone in the dark, displaying to the moon the inscription in the language of that time and place:

ON THIS SPOT THERE APPEARS ANNUALLY THE FORM OF MAJOR JOHN DEL-GANO, THE FIRST AND ONLY MAN TO TRAVEL IN TIME.

MAJOR DELGANO WAS SENT INTO THE FUTURE SOME HOURS BEFORE THE HOLOCAUST OF DAY ZERO. ALL KNOWLEDGE OF THE MEANS BY WHICH HE WAS SENT IS LOST, PERHAPS FOREVER. IT IS BELIEVED THAT AN ACCIDENT OCCURRED WHICH SENT HIM MUCH FARTHER THAN WAS INTENDED. SOME ANALYSTS SPECULATE THAT HE MAY HAVE GONE AS FAR AS FIFTY THOUSAND YEARS AHEAD. HAVING REACHED THIS UNKNOWN POINT MAJOR DELGANO APPARENTLY WAS RECALLED, OR ATTEMPTED TO RETURN, ALONG THE COURSE IN SPACE AND TIME THROUGH WHICH HE WAS SENT. HIS TRAJECTORY IS THOUGHT TO START AT THE POINT WHICH OUR SOLAR SYSTEM WILL OCCUPY AT A FUTURE TIME AND IS TANGENT TO THE COMPLEX HELIX WHICH OUR EARTH DESCRIBES AROUND THE SUN.

HE APPEARS ON THIS SPOT IN THE ANNUAL INSTANTS IN WHICH HIS COURSE INTERSECTS OUR PLANET'S ORBIT AND HE IS APPARENTLY ABLE TO TOUCH THE GROUND IN THOSE INSTANTS. SINCE NO TRACE OF HIS PASSAGE INTO THE FUTURE HAS BEEN MANIFESTED, IT IS BELIEVED THAT HE IS RETURNING BY A DIFFERENT MEANS THAN HE WENT FORWARD. HE IS ALIVE IN OUR PRESENT. OUR PAST IS HIS FUTURE AND OUR FUTURE IS HIS PAST. THE TIME OF HIS APPEARANCES IS SHIFTING GRADUALLY IN SOLAR TIME TO CONVERGE ON THE MOMENT OF 1153.6 ON MAY 2ND 1989 OLD STYLE, OR DAY ZERO.

THE EXPLOSION WHICH ACCOMPANIED HIS RETURN TO HIS OWN TIME AND PLACE MAY HAVE OCCURRED WHEN SOME ELEMENTS OF THE PAST INSTANTS OF HIS COURSE WERE CARRIED WITH HIM INTO THEIR OWN PRIOR EXISTENCE. IT IS CERTAIN THAT THIS EXPLOSION PRECIPITATED THE WORLDWIDE HOLOCAUST WHICH ENDED FOREVER THE AGE OF HARD-SCIENCE.

—He was falling, losing control, failing in his fight against the terrible momentum he had gained, fighting with his human legs shaking in the inhuman stiffness of his armor, his soles charred, not gripping well now, not enough traction to brake, battling, thrusting as the flashes came, the punishing alternation of light, dark, light, dark, which he had borne so long, the claps of air thickening and thinning against his armor as he skidded through space which was time, desperately braking as the flickers of earth hammered against his feet—only his feet mattered now, only to slow and stay on course—and the pull, the beacon was getting slacker; as he came near home it was fanning out, hard to stay centered; he was becoming, he supposed, more probable; the wound he had punched in time was healing itself. In the beginning it had been so tight—a single ray in a closing tunnel—he had hurled himself after it like an electron flying to the anode, aimed surely along that exquisitely complex single vector of possibility of life, shot and been shot like a squeezed pip into the last clink in that rejecting and rejected nowhere through which he, John Delgano, could conceivably continue to exist, the hole leading to home—had pounded down it across time, across space, pumping with his human legs as the real Earth of that unreal time came under him, his course as certain as the twisting dash of an animal down its burrow, he a cosmic mouse on an interstellar, intertemporal race for his nest with the wrongness of everything closing round the rightness of that one course, the atoms of his heart, his blood, his every well crying Home—HOME!—as he drove himself after that fading breath-hole, each step faster, surer, stronger, until he raced with invincible momentum upon the rolling flickers of Earth as a man might race a rolling log in a torrent! Only the stars stayed constant around him from flash to flash, he looked down past his feet at a million strobes of Crux, of Triangulum; once at the height of his stride he had risked a century's glance upward and seen the Bears weirdly strung out from Polaris—But a Polaris not the Pole Star now, he realized, jerking his eyes back to his racing feet, thinking, I am walking home to Polaris, home! to the strobing beat. He had ceased to remember where he had been, the beings, people or aliens or things he had glimpsed in the impossible moment of being where he could not be; had ceased to see the flashes of worlds *around him, each flash different, the jumble of bodies, walls, landscapes, shapes, colors beyond deciphering—some lasting a breath, some changing pell-mell—the faces, limbs, things poking at him; the nights he had pounded through, dark or lit by strange lamps; roofed or unroofed; the day flashing sun-light, gales, dust, snow, interiors innumerable, strobe after strobe into night again; he was in daylight now, a hall of some kind; I am getting closer at last, he thought, the feel is changing—but he had to slow down, to check; and that stone near his feet, it had stayed there some time now, he wanted to risk a look but he did not dare, he was so tired, and he was sliding, was going out of con-trol, fighting to kill the merciless velocity that would not let him slow down; he was hurt, too, something had hit him back there, they had done something, he didn't know what back somewhere in the kaleidoscope of faces, arms, hooks, beams, centuries of creatures grabbing at him—and his oxygen was going, never mind, it would last—it had to last, he was going home, home! And he had forgotten now the message he had tried to shout, hoping it could be picked up somehow, the important thing he had repeated; and the thing he had car-ried, it was gone now, his camera was gone, too, something had torn it away—but he was coming home! Home! If only he could kill this momentum, could stay on the failing course, could slip, scramble, slide, somehow ride this ava-lanche down to home, to home—and his throat said Home!—said Kate, Kate! And his heart shouted, his lungs almost gone now, as his legs fought, fought and failed, as his feet gripped and skidded and held and slid, as he pitched, flailed, pushed, strove in the gale of timerush across space, across time, at the end of the longest path ever; the path of John Delgano, coming home.*

When the Old Gods Die
Mike Resnick

Mike Resnick is one of the best-selling authors in science fiction, and one of the most prolific. His many novels include *Santiago, The Dark Lady, Stalking the Unicorn, Birthright: The Book of Man, Paradise, Ivory, Soothsayer, Oracle, Lucifer Jones, Purgatory, Inferno, A Miracle of Rare Design, The Widowmaker, The Soul Eater,* and *A Hunger in the Soul*. His award-winning short fiction has been gathered in the collections *Will the Last Person to Leave the Planet Please Turn Off the Sun?, An Alien Land, Kirinyaga, A Safari of the Mind,* and *Hunting the Snark and Other Short Novels*. In the last decade or so, he has become almost as prolific as an anthologist, producing, as editor, *Inside the Funhouse: 17 SF Stories about SF, Whatdunits, More Whatdunits,* and *Shaggy B.E.M. Stories*; a long string of anthologies coedited with Martin H. Greenberg, *Alternate Presidents, Alternate Kennedys, Alternate Warriors, Aladdin: Master of the Lamp, Dinosaur Fantastic, By Any Other Fame, Alternate Outlaws,* and *Sherlock Holmes in Orbit,* among others; as well as two anthologies coedited with Gardner Dozois. He won the Hugo Award in 1989 for "Kirinyaga." He won another Hugo Award in 1991 for another story in the Kirinyaga series, "The Manumouki," and another Hugo and Nebula in 1995 for his novella "Seven Views of Olduvai Gorge." His most recent books include the novel *The Return of Santiago* and the anthologies *Stars: Songs Inspired by the Songs of Janis Ian* (edited with Janis Ian) and *New Voices in Science Fiction*. He lives with his wife, Carol, in Cincinnati, Ohio.

Here, in one of the Kirinyaga stories (which take place on an orbital space colony that has been remade in the image of ancient Kenya as a Utopian experiment, and which were gathered in the collection *Kirinyaga*), he pits science in a head-on battle with superstition, tradition, and hidebound cultural conservatism, with the winner selected on entirely pragmatic grounds: what works, *works*.

N gai, who rules the universe from His golden throne atop the holy mountain Kirinyaga, which men now call Mount Kenya, created the Sun and the Moon, and declared that they should have equal domain over the Earth.

The Sun would bring warmth to the world, and all of Ngai's creatures would thrive and grow strong in the light. But even Ngai must sleep, and when He slept He ordered the Moon to watch over His creations.

But the Moon was duplicitous, and formed a secret alliance with the Lion and the Leopard and the Hyena, and many nights, while Ngai slept, it would turn only a part of its face to the Earth. At such times the predators would go forth to maim and kill and eat their fellow creatures.

Finally one man, a *mundumugu*—a witch doctor—realized that the Moon had tricked Ngai, and he made up his mind to correct the problem. He might have appealed to Ngai, but he was a proud man, and so he took it upon himself to make certain that the flesh eaters would no longer have a partnership with the darkness.

He retired to his *boma* and allowed no visitors. For nine days and nine nights he rolled his bones and arranged his charms and mixed his potions, and when he emerged on the morning of the tenth day, he was ready to do what must be done.

The Sun was overhead, and he knew that there could be no darkness as long as the Sun shone down upon the Earth. He uttered a mystic chant, and soon he was flying into the sky to confront the Sun.

"Halt!" he said. "Your brother the Moon is evil. You must remain where you are, lest Ngai's creatures continue to die."

"What is that to me?" responded the Sun. "I cannot shirk my duty simply because my brother shirks his."

The *mundumugu* held up a hand. "I will not let you pass," he said.

But the Sun merely laughed, and proceeded on its path, and when it reached the *mundumugu* it gobbled him up and spat out the ashes, for even the greatest *mundumugu* cannot stay the Sun from its course.

That story has been known to every *mundumugu* since Ngai created Gikuyu, the first man. Of them all, only one ignored it.

I am that *mundumugu*.

It is said that from the moment of birth, even of conception, every living thing has embarked upon an inevitable trajectory that culminates in its death. If this is true of all living things, and it seems to be, then it is also true of man. And if it is true of man, then it must be true of the gods who made man in their image.

Yet this knowledge does not lessen the pain of death. I had just come back from comforting Katuma, whose father, old Siboki, had finally died, not from disease or injury, but rather from the awful burden of his years. Siboki had been one of the original colonists on our terraformed world of Kirinyaga, a member of the Council of Elders, and though he had grown feeble in mind as well as body, I knew I would miss him as I missed few others.

As I walked back through the village, on the long, winding path by the river that eventually led to my own *boma*, I was very much aware of my own mortality. I was not that much younger than Siboki, and indeed was already an old man when we left Kenya and emigrated to Kirinyaga. I knew my death could not be too far away, and yet I hoped that it was, not from selfishness, but because Kirinyaga was not yet ready to do without me. The *mundumugu* is more than a shaman who utters curses and creates spells; he is the repository of all the moral and civil laws, all the customs and traditions, of the Kikuyu people, and I was not convinced that Kirinyaga had yet produced a competent successor.

It is a harsh and lonely life, the life of a *mundumugu*. He is more feared than loved by the people he serves. This is not his fault, but rather the nature of his position. He must do what he knows to be right for his people, and that means he must sometimes make unpopular decisions.

How strange, then, that the decision that brought me down had nothing at all to do with my people but rather with a stranger.

Still, I should have had a premonition about it, for no conversation is ever truly random. As I was walking past the scarecrows in the fields on the way to my *boma*, I came across Kimanti, the young son of Ngobe, driving two of his goats home from their morning's grazing.

"*Jambo*, Koriba," he greeted me, shading his eyes from the bright overhead sun.

"Jambo, Kimanti," I said. "I see that your father now allows you to tend to his goats. Soon the day will come that he puts you in charge of his cattle."

"Soon," he agreed, offering me a water gourd. "It is a warm day. Would you like something to drink?"

"That is very generous of you," I said, taking the gourd and holding it to my mouth.

"I have always been generous to you, have I not, Koriba?" he said.

"Yes, you have," I replied suspiciously, wondering what favor he was preparing to request.

"Then why do you allow my father's right arm to remain shriveled and useless?" he asked. "Why do you not cast a spell and make it like other men's arms?"

"It is not that simple, Kimanti," I said. "It is not I who shriveled your father's arm, but Ngai. He would not have done so without a purpose."

"What purpose is served by crippling my father?" asked Kimanti.

"If you wish, I shall sacrifice a goat and ask Ngai why He has allowed it," I said.

He considered my offer and then shook his head. "I do not care to hear Ngai's answer, for it will change nothing." He paused, lost in thought for a moment. "How long do you think Ngai will be our god?"

"Forever," I said, surprised at his question.

"That cannot be," he replied seriously. "Surely Ngai was not our god when He was just a *mtoto*. He must have killed the old gods when He was young and powerful. But He has been god for a long time now, and it is time someone killed Him. Maybe the new god will show more compassion toward my father."

"Ngai created the world," I said. "He created the Kikuyu and the Maasai and the Wakamba, and even the Europeans, and He created the holy mountain Kirinyaga, for which our world is named. He has existed since time began, and He will exist until it ends."

Kimanti shook his head again. "If He has been here that long, He is ready to die. It is just a matter of who will kill Him." He paused thoughtfully. "Perhaps I myself will, when I am older and stronger."

"Perhaps," I agreed. "But before you do, let me tell you the story of the King of the Zebras."

"Is this story about Ngai or zebras?" he asked.

"Why don't you listen?" I said. "Then, when I have finished, you can tell *me* what it was about?"

I gently lowered myself to the ground, and he squatted down next to me.

"There was a time," I began, "when zebras did not have stripes. They were as brown as the dried grasses on the savannah, as dull to the eye as the bole of the acacia tree. And because their color protected them, they were rarely taken by the lion and the leopard, who found it much easier to find and stalk the wildebeest and the topi and the impala.

"Then one day a son was born to the King of the Zebras—but it was not a normal son, for it had no nostrils. The King of the Zebras was first saddened for his son, and then outraged that such a thing should be allowed. The more he dwelt upon it, the more angry he became. Finally he ascended the holy mountain, and came at last to the peak, where Ngai ruled the world from His golden throne.

"'Have you come to sing my praises?' asked Ngai.

"'No!' answered the King of the Zebras. 'I have come to tell you that you are a terrible god, and that I am here to kill you.'

"'What have I done to you that you should wish to kill me?' asked Ngai.

"'You gave me a son who has no nostrils, so he cannot sense when the lion and the leopard are approaching him, and because of that they will surely find and kill him when at last he leaves his mother's side. You have been a god too long, and you have forgotten how to be compassionate.'

"'Wait!' said Ngai, and suddenly there was such power in his voice that the King of the Zebras froze where he was. 'I will give your son nostrils, since that is what you want.'

"'Why were you so cruel in the first place?' demanded the King of the Zebras, his anger not fully assuaged.

"'Gods work in mysterious ways,' answered Ngai, 'and what seems cruel to you may actually be compassionate. Because you had been a good and noble king, I gave your son eyes that could see in the dark, that could see through bushes, that could even see around trees, so that he could never be surprised by the lion and the leopard, even should the wind's direction favor them. And because of this gift, he did not need his nostrils. I took them away so that he would not have to breathe in the dust that chokes his fellow zebras during the dry season. But now I have given him back his sense of smell, and taken away his special vision, because you have demanded it.'

"'Then you *did* have a reason,' moaned the King of the Zebras. 'When did I become so foolish?'

"'The moment you thought you were greater than me,' answered Ngai, rising to His true height, which was taller than the clouds. 'And to punish you for your audacity, I decree that from this moment forward you and all your kind shall no longer be brown like the dried grasses, but will be covered with black and white stripes that will attract the lion and the leopard from miles away. No matter where you go on the face of the world, you will never again be able to hide from them.'

"And so saying, Ngai waved a hand and every zebra in the world was suddenly covered with the same stripes you see today."

I stopped and stared at Kimanti.

"That is the end?" he asked.

"That is the end."

Kimanti stared at a millipede crawling in the dirt.

"The zebra was a baby, and could not explain to its father that it had special eyes," he said at last. "My father's arm has been shriveled for many long rains, and the only explanation he has received is that Ngai works in mysterious ways. He has been given no special senses to make up for it, for if he had been he would surely know about them by now." Kimanti looked at me thoughtfully. "It is an interesting story, Koriba, and I am sorry for the King of the Zebras, but I think a new god must come along and kill Ngai very soon."

There we sat, the wise old *mundumugu* who had a parable for every problem, and the foolish young *kehee*—an uncircumcised boy—who had no more knowledge of his world than a tadpole, in total opposition to each other.

Only a god with Ngai's sense of humor would have arranged for the *kehee* to be right.

It began when the ship crashed.

(There are those embittered men and women who would say it began the day Kirinyaga received its charter from the Eutopian Council, but they are wrong.)

Maintenance ships fly among the Utopian worlds, delivering goods to some, mail to others, services to a few. Only Kirinyaga has no traffic with Maintenance. They are permitted to observe us—indeed, that is one of the conditions of our charter—but they may not interfere, and since we have tried to create a Kikuyu Utopia, we have no interest in commerce with Europeans.

Still, Maintenance ships *have* landed on Kirinyaga from time to time. One of the conditions of our charter is that if a citizen is unhappy with our world, he need only walk to that area known as Haven, and a Maintenance ship will pick him up and take him either to Earth or to another Eutopian world. Once a Maintenance ship landed to disgorge two immigrants, and very early in Kirinyaga's existence Maintenance sent a representative to interfere with our religious practices.

I don't know why the ship was so close to Kirinyaga to begin with. I had not ordered Maintenance to make any orbital adjustments lately, for the short rains were not due for another two months, and it was right that the days passed, hot and bright and unchanging. To the best of my knowledge, none of the villagers had made the pilgrimage to Haven, so no Maintenance ship should have been sent to Kirinyaga. But the fact remains that one moment the sky was clear and blue, and the next there was a streak of light plunging down to the surface of the planet. An explosion followed; though I could not see it, I could both hear it and see the results, for the cattle became very nervous and herds of impala and zebra bolted this way and that in panic.

It was about twenty minutes later that young Jinja, the son of Kichanta, ran up the hill to my *boma*.

"You must come, Koriba!" he said as he gasped for breath.

"What has happened?" I asked.

"A Maintenance ship has crashed!" he said. "The pilot is still alive!"

"Is he badly hurt?"

Jinja nodded. "Very badly. I think he may die soon."

"I am an old man, and it would take me a very long time to walk to the pilot," I said. "It would be better for you to take three young men from the village and bring him back to me on a litter."

Jinja raced off while I went into my hut to see what I had that might ease the pilot's pain. There were some qat leaves, if he was strong enough to chew them, and a few ointments if he wasn't. I contacted Maintenance on my computer, and told them that I would apprise them of the man's condition after I examined him.

In years past, I would have sent my assistant to the river to bring back water which I would boil in preparation for washing out the pilot's wounds, but I no longer had an assistant, and the *mundumugu* does not carry water, so I simply waited atop my hill, my gaze turned toward the direction of the crash. A grass fire had started, and a column of smoke rose from it. I saw Jinja and the others trotting across the savannah with the litter; I saw topi and impala and even buffalo race out of their way; and then I could not see them for almost ten minutes. When they once again came into view, they were walking, and it was obvious that they were carrying a man on the litter.

Before they reached my *boma*, however, Karenja came up the long, winding path from the village.

"*Jambo*, Koriba," he said.

"What are you doing here?" I asked.

"The whole village knows that a Maintenance ship has crashed," he replied. "I have never seen a European before. I came to see if his face is really as white as milk."

"You are doomed to be disappointed," I said. "We call them white, but in reality they are shades of pink and tan."

"Even so," he said, squatting down, "I have never seen one."

I shrugged. "As you will."

Jinja and the young men arrived a few minutes later with the litter. On it lay the twisted body of the pilot. His arms and legs were broken, and there was very little skin on him that was not burned. He had lost a lot of blood, and some still seeped through his wounds. He was unconscious, but breathing regularly.

"*Asante sana*," I said to the four young men. "Thank you. You have done well this day."

I had one of them fill my gourds with water. The other three bowed and began walking down the hill, while I went through my various ointments, choosing the one that would cause the least discomfort when placed on the burns.

Karenja watched in rapt fascination. Twice I had to rebuke him for touching the pilot's blond hair in wonderment. As the sun changed positions in the sky, I had him help me move the pilot into the shade.

Then, after I had tended to the pilot's wounds, I went into my hut, activated my computer, and contacted Maintenance again. I explained that the pilot was still alive, but that all of his limbs were broken, his body was covered with burns, and that he was in a coma and would probably die soon.

Their answer was that they had already dispatched a medic, who would arrive within half an hour, and they told me to have someone waiting at Haven to guide the medic to my *boma*. Since Karenja was still looking at the pilot, I ordered him to greet the ship and bring the medic to me.

The pilot did not stir for the next hour. At least, I do not think he did, but I dozed with my back against a tree for a few minutes, so I cannot be sure. What woke me was a woman's voice speaking a language I had not heard for many years. I got painfully to my feet just in time to greet the medic that Maintenance had sent.

"You must be Koriba," she said in English. "I have been trying to communicate with the gentleman who accompanied me, but I don't think he understood a word I said."

"I am Koriba," I said in English.

She extended her hand. "I am Doctor Joyce Witherspoon. May I see the patient?"

I led her over to where the pilot lay.

"Do you know his name?" I asked. "We could not find any identification."

"Samuel or Samuels, I'm not sure," she said, kneeling down next to him. "He's in a bad way." She gave him a perfunctory examination, lasting less than a minute. "We could do much more for him back at Base, but I hate to move him in this condition."

"I can have him moved to Haven within an hour," I said. "The sooner you have him in your hospital, the better."

She shook her head. "I think he'll have to remain here until he's a little stronger."

"I will have to consider it," I said.

"There's nothing to consider," she said. "In my medical opinion, he's too weak to move." She pointed to a piece of his shin bone that had broken through the skin of his leg. "I need to set most of the broken bones, and make sure there's no infection."

"You could do this at your hospital," I said.

"I can do it here at much less cost to the patient's remaining vitality," she said. "What's the problem, Koriba?"

"The problem, *Memsaab* Witherspoon," I said, "is that Kirinyaga is a Kikuyu Utopia. This means a rejection of all things European, including your medicine."

"I'm not practicing it on any Kikuyu," she said. "I'm trying to save a Maintenance pilot who just happened to crash on your world."

I stared at the pilot for a long moment. "All right," I said at last. "That is a logical argument. You may minister to his wounds."

"Thank you," she said.

"But he must leave in three days' time," I said. "I will not risk contamination beyond that."

She looked at me as if she was about to argue, but said nothing. Instead, she opened the medical kit she had brought, and injected something—a sedative, I assumed, or a pain killer, or a combination of the two—into his arm.

"She is a witch!" said Karenja. "See how she punctures his skin with a metal thorn!" He stared at the pilot, fascinated. "Now he will surely die."

Joyce Witherspoon worked well into the night, cleansing the pilot's wounds, setting his broken bones, breaking his fever. I don't remember when I fell asleep, but when I woke up, shivering, in the cold morning air just after sunrise, she was sleeping and Karenja was gone.

I built a fire, then sat near it with my blanket wrapped around me, until the sun began warming the air. Joyce Witherspoon woke up shortly thereafter.

"Good morning," she said when she saw me sitting a short distance away from her.

"Good morning, *Memsaab* Witherspoon," I replied.

"What time is it?" she asked.

"It is morning."

"I mean, what hour and minute is it?"

"We do not have hours and minutes on Kirinyaga," I told her. "Only days."

"I should look at Mr. Samuels."

"He is still alive," I said.

"Of course he is," she replied. "But the poor man will need skin grafts, and he may lose that right leg. He'll be a long time recovering." She paused and looked around. "Uh . . . where do I wash up around here?"

"The river runs by the foot of my hill," I said. "Be sure you beat the water first, to frighten away the crocodiles."

"What kind of Utopia has crocodiles?" she asked with a smile.

"What Eden has no serpents?" I said.

She laughed and walked down the hill. I took a sip from my water gourd, then killed the fire and spread the ashes. One of the boys from the village came by to take my goats out to graze, and another brought firewood and took my gourds down to the river to fill them.

When Joyce Witherspoon returned from the river some twenty minutes later, she was not alone. With her was Kibo, the third and youngest wife of Koinnage, the paramount chief of the village, and in Kibo's arms was Katabo, her infant son. His left arm was swollen to twice it's size, and was badly discolored.

"I found this woman laundering her clothes by the river," said Joyce Witherspoon, "and I noticed that her child had a badly infected arm. It looks like some kind of insect bite. I managed through sign language to convince her to follow me up here."

"Why did you not bring Katabo to me?" I asked Kibo in Swahili.

"Last time you charged me two goats, and he remained sick for many days, and Koinnage beat me for wasting the goats," she said, so terrified she had made me angry that she could not think of a lie.

Even as Kibo spoke, Joyce Witherspoon began approaching her and Katabo with a syringe in her hand.

"This is a broad-spectrum antibiotic," she explained to me. "It also contains a steroid that will prevent itching or any discomfort while the infection remains."

"Stop!" I said harshly in English.

"What's the matter?"

"You may not do this," I said. "You are here to minister to the pilot only."

"This is a baby, and it's suffering," she said. "It'll take me two seconds to give it a shot and cure it."

"I cannot permit it."

"What's the matter with you?" she demanded. "I read your biography. You may dress like a savage and sit in the dirt next to your fire, but you were educated at Cambridge and received your postgraduate degrees from Yale. Surely you know how easily I can end this child's suffering."

"That's not the point," I said.

"Then what *is* the point?"

"You may not medicate this child. It seems like a blessing now— but once before we accepted the Europeans' medicine, and then their religion, and their clothing, and their laws, and their customs, and eventually we ceased to be Kikuyu and became a new race, a race of black Europeans known only as Kenyans. We came to Kirinyaga to make sure that such a thing does not happen to us again."

"*He* won't know why he feels better. You can credit it to your god or yourself for all I care."

I shook my head. "I appreciate your sentiment, but I cannot let you corrupt our Utopia."

"Look at him," she said, pointing to Katabo's swollen arm. "Is Kirinyaga a Utopia for *him*? Where is it written that Utopias must have sick and suffering children?"

"Nowhere."

"Well, then?"

"It is not written," I continued, "because the Kikuyu do not have a written language."

"Will you at least let the mother decide?"

"No," I said.

"Why not?"

"The mother will think only of her child," I answered. "I must think of an entire world."

"Perhaps her child is more important to her than your world is to you."

"She is incapable of making a reasoned decision," I said. "Only *I* can foresee all the consequences."

Suddenly Kibo, who understood not a word of English, turned to me.

"Will the European witch make my little Katabo better?" she asked. "Why are you two arguing?"

"The European witch is here only for the European," I answered. "She has no power to help the Kikuyu."

"Can she not try?" asked Kibo.

"*I* am your *mundumugu*," I said harshly.

"But look at the pilot," said Kibo, pointing to Samuels. "Yesterday he was all but dead. Today his skin is already healing, and his arms and legs are straight again."

"Her god is the god of the Europeans," I answered, "just as her magic is the magic of the Europeans. Her spells do not work on the Kikuyu."

Kibo fell silent, and clutched Katabo to her breast.

I turned to Joyce Witherspoon. "I apologize for speaking in Swahili, but Kibo knows no other language."

"It's all right," she said. "I had no difficulty following it."

"I thought you told me you only spoke English."

"Sometimes you needn't understand the words to translate. I believe you were saying, in essence, 'Thou shalt have no other gods before me.'"

The pilot moaned just then, and suddenly all of her attention was focused upon him. He was coming into a state of semiconsciousness, unfocused and unintelligible but no longer comatose, and she began administering medications into the tubes that were already attached to his arms and legs. Kibo watched in wonderment, but kept her distance.

I remained on my hill most of the morning. I offered to remove the curse from Katabo's arm and give him some soothing lotions, but Kibo refused, saying that Koinnage steadfastly refused to part with any more goats.

"I will not charge you this time," I said, for I wanted Koinnage on my side. I uttered a spell over the child, then treated his arm with a salve made from the pulped bark of the acacia tree. I ordered Kibo to return to her *shamba* with him, and told her that the child's arm would return to normal within five days.

Finally it was time for me to go into the village to bless the scarecrows and give Leibo, who had lost her baby, ointment to ease the pain in her breasts. I would meet with Bakada, who had accepted the bride price for his daughter and wanted me to preside at the wedding, and finally I would join Koinnage and the Council of Elders as they discussed the weighty issues of the day.

As I walked down the long, winding path beside the river, I found myself thinking how much like the European's Garden of Eden this world looked.

How was I to know that the serpent had already arrived?

After I had tended to my chores in the village, I stopped at Ngobe's hut to share a gourd of *pombe* with him. He asked about the pilot, for by now everyone in the village had heard about him, and I explained that the European's *mundumugu* was curing him and would take him back to Maintenance headquarters in two more days.

"She must have powerful magic," he said, "for I am told that the man's body was badly broken." He paused. "It is too bad," he added wistfully, "that such magic will not work for the Kikuyu."

"My magic has always been sufficient," I said.

"True," he said uneasily. "But I remember the day when we brought Tabari's son back after the hyenas had attacked him and chewed off one of his legs. You eased his pain, but you could not save him. Perhaps the witch from Maintenance could have."

"The pilot had broken his legs, but they were not chewed off," I said defensively. "No one could have saved Tabari's son after the hyenas had finished with him."

"Perhaps you are right," he said.

My first inclination was to pounce on the word *"perhaps,"* but then I decided that he meant no insult by it, so I finished my *pombe*, cast the bones and read that he would have a successful harvest, and left his hut.

I stopped in the center of the village to recite a fable to the children, then went over to Koinnage's *shamba* and entered his *boma* for the daily meeting of the Council of Elders. Most of them were already there, grim-faced and silent. Finally Koinnage emerged from his hut and joined us.

"We have serious business to discuss today," he announced. "Perhaps the most serious we have *ever* discussed," he added, staring straight at me. Suddenly he faced his wives' huts. "Kibo!" he shouted. "Come here!"

Kibo emerged from her hut and walked over to us, carrying little Katabo in her arms.

"You all saw my son's arm yesterday," said Koinnage. "It was swollen to twice its normal size, and was the color of death." He took the child and held it above his head. "Now look at him!" he cried.

Katabo's arm was once again a healthy color, and almost all of the swelling had vanished.

"My medicine worked faster than I had anticipated," I said.

"This is not *your* medicine at all!" he said accusingly. "This is the European witch's medicine!"

I looked at Kibo. "I ordered you to leave my *boma* ahead of me!" I said sternly.

"You did not order me not to return," she said, her face filled with defiance as she stood next to Koinnage. "The witch pierced Katabo's arm with a metal thorn, and before I could climb back down your hill the swelling was already half gone."

"You disobeyed my command," I said ominously.

"I am the paramount chief, and I absolve her," interjected Koinnage.

"I am the *mundumugu*, and I do not!" I said, and suddenly Kibo's defiance was replaced by terror.

"We have more important things to discuss," snapped Koinnage. This startled me, for when I am angry, no one has the courage to confront or contradict me.

I pulled some luminescent powder, made from the ground-up bodies of night-stalking beetles, out of my pouch, held it on the palm of my hand, raised my hand to my mouth, and blew the powder in Kibo's direction. She screamed in terror and fell writhing to the ground.

"What have you done to her?" demanded Koinnage.

I have terrified her beyond your ability to comprehend, which is a just and fitting punishment for disobeying me, I thought. Aloud I said, "I have marked her spirit so that all the predators of the Other World can find it at night when she sleeps. If she swears never to disobey her *mundumugu* again, if she shows proper contrition for disobeying me today, then I shall remove the markings before she goes to sleep this evening. If not . . ." I shrugged and let the threat hang in the air.

"Then perhaps the European witch will remove the markings," said Koinnage.

"Do you think the god of the Europeans is mightier than Ngai?" I demanded.

"I do not know," replied Koinnage. "But he healed my son's arm in moments, when Ngai would have taken days."

"For years you have told us to reject all things European," added Karenja, "yet I myself have seen the witch use her magic on the dying pilot, and I think it is stronger that *your* magic."

"It is a magic for Europeans only," I said.

"This is not so," answered Koinnage. "For did the witch not offer it to Katabo? If she can halt the suffering of our sick and our injured faster than Ngai can, then we must consider accepting her offer."

"If you accept her offer," I said, "before long you will be asked to accept her god, and her science, and her clothing, and her customs."

"Her science is what created Kirinyaga and flew us here," said Ngobe. "How can it be bad if it made Kirinyaga possible?"

"It is not bad for the Europeans," I said, "because it is part of their culture. But we must never forget why we came to Kirinyaga in the first place: to create a Kikuyu world and reestabish a Kikuyu culture."

"We must think seriously about this," said Koinnage. "For years we have believed that every facet of the Europeans' culture was evil, for we had no examples of it. But now that we see that even a female can cure our illness faster than Ngai can, it is time to reconsider."

"If her magic could have cured my withered arm when I was still a boy," added Ngobe, "why would that have been evil?"

"It would have been against the will of Ngai," I said.

"Does not Ngai rule the universe?" he asked.

"You know that He does," I replied.

"Then nothing that happens can be contrary to His wishes, and if she could have cured me, it would *not* have been against Ngai's will."

I shook my head. "You do not understand."

"We are trying to understand," said Koinnage. "Enlighten us."

"The Europeans have many wonders, and these wonders will entice you, as they are doing right now . . . but if you accept one European thing, soon they will insist that you accept them all. Koinnage, their religion only allows a man to have one wife. Which two will you divorce?"

I turned to the others. "Ngobe, they will make Kimanti attend a school where he will learn to read and write. But since we do not have a written language, he will learn to write only in a European language, and the things and people he reads about and learns about will all be European."

I walked among the Elders, offering an example to each. "Karenja, if you do a service for Tabari, you will expect a chicken or a goat or perhaps even a cow in return, depending on the nature of the service. But the Europeans will make him reward you with paper money, which you cannot eat, and which cannot reproduce and make a man rich."

On and on I went, until I had run through all the Elders, pointing out what they would lose if they allowed the Europeans a toehold in our society.

"All that is on the one hand," said Koinnage when I had finished. He held his other hand out, palm up. "On the other hand is an end to illness and suffering, which is no small achievement in itself. Koriba has said that if we let the Europeans in, they will force us to change our ways. *I* say that some of our ways *need* changing. If their god is a greater healer than Ngai, who is to say that he may not also bring better weather, or more fertile cattle, or richer soil?"

"*No!*" I cried. "*You* may all have forgotten why we came here, but *I* have not. Our mandate was not to establish a European Utopia, but a Kikuyu one!"

"And *have* we established it?" asked Karenja sardonically.

"We are coming closer every day," I told him. "*I* am making it a reality."

"Do children suffer in Utopia?" persisted Karenja. "Do men grow up with withered arms? Do women die in childbirth? Do hyenas attack shepherds in Utopia?"

"It is a matter of balance," I said. "Unrestricted growth would eventually lead to unrestricted hunger. You have not seen what it has done on Earth, but *I* have."

Finally it was old Jandara who spoke.

"Do people *think* in a Utopia?" he asked me.

"Of course they do," I replied.

"If they think, are some of their thoughts new, just as some are old?"

"Yes."

"Then perhaps we should consider letting the witch tend to our illnesses and injuries," he said. "For if Ngai allows new thoughts in His Utopia, He must realize they will lead to change. And if change is not evil, then perhaps lack of change, such as we have striven for here, *is* evil, or at least wrong." He got to his feet. "You may debate the merits of the question. As for myself, I have had pain in my joints for many years, and Ngai has not cured it. I am climbing Koriba's hill to see if the god of the Europeans can end my pain."

And with that, he walked past me and out of the *boma*.

I was prepared to argue my case all day and all night if necessary, but Koinnage turned his back on me—on *me*, his *mundumugu*!—and began carrying his son back to Kibo's hut. That signaled the end to the meeting, and each of the Elders got up and left without daring to look me in the face.

There were more than a dozen villagers gathered at the foot of my hill when I arrived. I walked past them and soon reached my *boma*.

Jandara was still there. Joyce Witherspoon had given him an injection, and was handing him a small bottle of pills as I arrived.

"Who told you that you could treat the Kikuyu?" I demanded in English.

"I did not offer to treat them," she replied. "But I am a doctor, and I will not turn them away."

"Then *I* will," I said. I turned and looked down at the villagers. "You may not come up here!" I said sternly. "Go back to your *shambas*."

The adults all looked uneasy but stood their ground, while one small boy began climbing up the hill.

"Your *mundumugu* has forbidden you to climb this hill!" I said. "Ngai will punish you for your transgression!"

"The god of the Europeans is young and powerful," said the boy. "He will protect me from Ngai." And now I saw that the boy was Kimanti.

"Stay back—I warn you!" I shouted.

Kimanti hefted his wooden spear. "Ngai will not harm me," he said confidentally. "If He tries, I will kill him with *this*."

He walked right by me and approached Joyce Witherspoon.

"I have cut my foot on a rock," he said. "If your god will heal me, I will sacrifice a goat to thank him."

She did not understand a word he said, but when he showed her his foot she began treating it.

He walked back down the hill, unmolested by Ngai, and when he was both alive and healed the next morning, word went out to other villages and soon there was a seemingly endless line of the sick and the lame, all waiting to climb my hill and accept European cures for Kikuyu ills.

Once again I told them to disperse. This time they seemed not even to hear me. They simply remained in line, neither arguing back as Kimanti had, nor even acknowledging my presence, each of them waiting patiently until it was their turn to be treated by the European witch.

I thought that when she left, things would go back to the way they had been, that the people would once again fear Ngai and show respect to their *mundumugu*—but this was not to be. Oh, they went about their daily chores, they planted their crops and tended to their cattle . . . but they did not come to me with their problems as they always had done in the past.

At first I thought we had entered one of those rare periods in which no one in the village was ill or injured, but then one day I saw Shanaka walking out across the savannah. Since he rarely left his *shamba*, and *never* left the village, I was curious about his destination and I decided to follow him. He walked due west for more than half an hour, until he reached the landing area at Haven.

"What is wrong?" I asked when I finally caught up with him.

He opened his mouth to reveal a serious abcess above one of his teeth. "I am in great pain," he said, "I have been unable to eat for three days."

"Why did you not come to me?" I asked.

"The god of the Europeans has defeated Ngai," answered Shanaka. "He will not help me."

"He will," I assured him.

Shanaka shook his head, then winced from the motion. "You are an old man, and Ngai is an old god, and both of you have lost your powers," he said unhappily. "I wish it were otherwise, but it is not."

"So you are deserting your wives and children because you have lost your faith in Ngai?" I demanded.

"No," he replied. "I will ask the Maintenance ship to take me to a European *mundumugu*, and when I am cured I will return home."

"*I* will cure you," I said.

He looked at me for a long moment. "There was a time when you could cure me," he said at last. "But that time has passed. I will go to the Europeans' *mundumugu*."

"If you do," I said sternly, "you may never call on me for help again."

He shrugged. "I never intended to," he said with neither bitterness nor rancor.

Shanaka returned the next day, his mouth healed.

I stopped by his *boma* to see how he was feeling, for I remained the *mundumugu* whether he wanted my services or not, and as I walked through the fields of his *shamba* I saw that he had two new scarecrows, gifts of the Europeans. The scarecrows had mechanical arms that flapped constantly, and they rotated so that they did not always face in one direction.

"*Jambo*, Koriba," he greeted me. Then, seeing that I was looking at his scarecrows, he added, "Are they not wonderful?"

"I will withhold judgment until I see how long they function," I said. "The more moving parts an object has, the more likely it is to break."

He looked at me, and I thought I detected a hint of pity in his expression. "They were created by the God of Maintenance," he said. "They will last forever."

"Or until their power packs are empty," I said, but he did not know what I meant, and so my sarcasm was lost on him. "How is your mouth?"

"It feels much better," he replied. "They pricked me with a magic thorn to end the pain, then cut away the evil spirits that had invaded my mouth." He paused. "They have very powerful gods, Koriba."

"You are back on Kirinyaga now," I said sternly. "Be careful how you blaspheme."

"I do not blaspheme," he said. "I speak the truth."

"And now you will want me to bless the Europeans' scarecrows, I suppose," I said with finely wrought irony.

He shrugged. "If it makes you happy," he said.

"If it makes *me* happy?" I repeated angrily.

"That's right," he said nonchalantly. "The scarecerows, being European, certainly do not *need* your blessings, but if you will feel better . . ."

I had often wondered what might happen if for some reason the *mundumugu* was no longer feared by the members of the village. I had never once considered what it might be like if he were merely tolerated.

Still more villagers went to Maintenance's infirmary, and each came back with some gift from the Europeans: timesaving gadgets for the most part. Western gadgets. Culture-killing gadgets.

Again and again I went into the village and explained why such things must be rejected. Day after day I spoke to the Council of Elders, reminding them of why we had come to Kirinyaga—but most of the original settlers were dead, and the next generation, those who had become our Elders, had no memories of Kenya. Indeed, those of them who spoke to the Maintenance staff came home thinking that Kenya, rather than Kirinyaga, was some kind of Utopia, in which everyone was well-fed and well-cared-for and no farm ever suffered from drought.

They were polite, they listened respectfully to me, and then they went right ahead with whatever they had been doing or discussing when I arrived. I reminded them of the many times I and I alone had saved them from themselves, but they seemed not to care; indeed, one or two of the Elders acted as if, far from keeping Kirinyaga pure, I had in some mysterious way been hindering its growth.

"Kirinyaga is not *supposed* to grow!" I argued. "When you achieve a Utopia, you do not cast it aside and say, 'What changes can we make tomorrow?'"

"If you do not grow, you stagnate," answered Karenja.

"We can grow by expanding," I said. "We have an entire world to populate."

"That is not growing, but breeding," he repled. "You have done your job admirably, Koriba, for in the beginning we needed order and purpose above all else . . . but the time for your job is past. Now we have established ourselves here, and it is for *us* to choose how we will live."

"We have *already* chosen how to live!" I said angrily. "That is why we came here to begin with."

"I was just a *kehee*," said Karenja. "Nobody asked me. And I did not ask my son, who was born here."

"Kirinyaga was created for the purpose of becoming a Kikuyu Utopia," I said. "This purpose is even the basis of our charter. It cannot be changed."

"No one is suggesting that we don't want to live in a Utopia, Koriba," interjected Shanaka. "But the time has passed when you and you alone shall be the sole judge of what constitutes a Utopia."

"It is clearly defined."

"By *you*," said Shanaka. "Some of us have our own definitions of Utopia."

"You were one of the original founders of Kirinyaga," I said accusingly. "Why have you never spoken out before?"

"Many times I wanted to," admitted Shanaka. "But always I was afraid."

"Afraid of what?"

"Of Ngai. Or you."

"They are much the same thing," said Karenja.

"But now that Ngai has lost His battle to the god of Maintenance, I am no longer afraid to speak," continued Shanaka. "Why should I suffer with the pain in my teeth? How was it unholy or blasphemous for the European witches to cure me? Why should my wife, who is as old as I am and whose back is bent from years of carrying wood and water, continue to carry them where there are machines to carry things for her?"

"Why should you live on Kirinyaga at all, if that is the way you feel?" I asked bitterly.

"Because I have worked as hard to make Kirinyaga a home for the Kikuyu as you have!" he shot back. "And I see no reason to leave just because my definition of Utopia doesn't agree with yours. Why don't *you* leave, Koriba?"

"Because I was charged with establishing our Utopia, and I have not yet completed my assignment," I said. "In fact, it is false Kikuyu like you who have made my work that much harder."

Shanaka got to his feet and looked around at the Elders.

"Am I a false Kikuyu because I want my grandson to read?" he demanded. "Or because I want to ease my wife's burden? Or because I do not wish to suffer physical pain that can easily be avoided?"

"No!" cried the Elders as one.

"Be very careful," I warned them. "For if *he* is not a false Kikuyu, then you are calling *me* one."

"No, Koriba," said Koinnage, rising to his feet. "You are not a false Kikuyu." He paused. "But you are a mistaken one. Your day—and mine—has passed. Perhaps, for a fleeting second, we did achieve Utopia—but that second is gone, and the new moments and hours require new Utopias." Then Koinnage, who had looked at me with fear so many times in the past, suddenly looked at me with great compassion. "It was *our* dream, Koriba, but it is not *theirs*—and if we still have some feeble handhold on today, tomorrow surely belongs to them."

"I will hear none of this!" I said. "You cannot redefine a Utopia as a matter of convenience. We moved here in order to be true to our faith and traditions, to avoid becoming what so many Kikuyu had become in Kenya. I will not let us become black Europeans!"

"We are becoming *something*," said Shanaka. "Perhaps just once there was an instant when you felt we were perfect Kikuyu—but that instant has long since passed. To remain so, not one of us could have had a new thought, could have seen the world in a different way. We would have become the scarecrows you bless every morning."

I was silent for a very long time. Then, at last, I spoke. "This world breaks my heart," I said. "I tried so hard to mold it into what we had all wanted, and look at what it has become. What *you* have become."

"You can direct change, Koriba," said Shanaka, "but you cannot prevent it, and that is why Kirinyaga will always break your heart."

"I must go to my *boma* and think," I said.

"*Kwaheri*, Koriba," said Koinnage. *Good-bye*, Koriba. It had a sense of finality to it.

I spent many days alone on my hill, looking across the winding river to the green savannah, and thinking. I had been betrayed by the people I had tried to lead, by the very world I had helped to create. I felt that I had surely displeased Ngai in some way, and that He would strike me dead. I was quite prepared to die, even willing . . . but I did not die, for the gods draw their strength from their worshippers, and Ngai was now so weak that He could not even kill a feeble old man like myself.

Eventually I decided to go down among my people one last time, to see if any of them had rejected the enticements of the Europeans and come back to the ways of the Kikuyu.

The path was lined with mechanical scarecrows. The only meaningful way to bless *them* would be to renew their charges. I saw several women washing clothes by the river, but instead of pounding the fabrics with rocks, they were rubbing them on some artificial board that had obviously been made for the purpose.

Suddenly I heard a ringing noise behind me, and, startled, I jumped, lost my footing, and fell heavily against a thorn bush. When I was able to get my bearings, I saw that I had almost been run over by a bicycle.

"I am sorry, Koriba," said the rider, who turned out to be young Kimanti. "I thought you heard me coming."

He helped me gingerly to my feet.

"My ears have heard many things," I said. "The scream of the fish eagle, the bleat of the goat, the laugh of the hyena, the cry of the newborn baby. But they were never meant to hear artificial wheels going down a dirt hill."

"It is much faster and easier than walking," he replied. "Are you going anywhere in particular? I will be happy to give you a ride."

It was probably the bicycle that made up my mind. "Yes," I replied, "I am going somewhere, and no, I will not be taken on a bicycle."

"Then I will walk with you," he said. "Where are you going?"

"To Haven," I said.

"Ah," he said with a smile. "You, too, have business with Maintenance. Where do you hurt?"

I touched the left side of my chest. "I hurt *here*—and the only business I have with Maintenance is to get as far from the cause of that pain as I can."

"You are leaving Kirinyaga?"

"I am leaving what Kirinyaga has become," I answered.

"Where will you go?" he asked. "What will you do?"

"I will go elsewhere, and I will do other things," I said vaguely, for where *does* an unemployed *mundumugu* go?

"We will miss you, Koriba," said Kimanti.

"I doubt it."

"We will," he repeated with sincerity. "When we recite the history of Kirinyaga to our children, you will not be forgotten." He paused. "It is true that you were wrong, but you were necessary."

"Is that how I am to be remembered?" I asked. "As a necessary evil?"

"I did not call you evil, just wrong."

We walked the next few miles in silence, and at last we came to Haven.

"I will wait with you if you wish," said Kimanti.

"I would rather wait alone," I said.

He shrugged. "As you wish. *Kwaheri*, Koriba."

"*Kwaheri*," I replied.

After he left I looked around, studying the savannah and the river, the wildebeest and the zebras, the fish eagles and the marabou storks, trying to set them in my memory for all time to come.

"I am sorry, Ngai," I said at last. "I have done my best, but I have failed you." The ship that would take me away from Kirinyaga forever suddenly came into view.

"You must view them with compassion, Ngai," I said as the ship approached the landing strip. "They are not the first of your people to be bewitched by the Europeans."

And it seemed, as the ship touched down, that a voice spoke into my ear and said, *You have been my most faithful servant, Koriba, and so I shall be guided by your counsel. Do you really wish me to view them with compassion?*

I looked toward the village one last time, the village that had once feared and worshipped Ngai, and which had sold itself, like some prostitute, to the god of the Europeans.

"No," I said firmly.

"Are you speaking to me?" asked the pilot, and I realized that the hatch was open and waiting for me.

"No," I replied.

He looked around. "I don't see anyone else."

"He is very old and very tired," I said. "But He is here."

I climbed into the ship and did not look back.

Oracle
Greg Egan

Looking back at the century that's just ended, it's obvious that Australian writer Greg Egan was one of the Big New Names to emerge in science fiction in the nineties, and he is probably one of the most significant talents to enter the field in the last several decades. Already one of the most widely known of all Australian genre writers, Egan may well be the best new "hard-science" writer to enter the field since Greg Bear, and he is still growing in range, power, and sophistication. In the last few years, he has become a frequent contributor to *Interzone* and *Asimov's Science Fiction* and has made sales as well as to *Pulphouse, Analog, Aurealis, Eidolon,* and elsewhere; many of his stories have also appeared in various Best of the Year series, and he was on the Hugo Final Ballot in 1995 for his story "Cocoon," which won the Ditmar Award and the Asimov's Readers Award. He won the Hugo Award in 1999 for his novella "Oceanic." His first novel, *Quarantine,* appeared in 1992; his second novel, *Per-*

mutation City, won the John W. Campbell Memorial Award in 1994. His other books include the novels *Distress, Diaspora*, and *Teranesia* and three collections of his short fiction, *Axiomatic, Luminous*, and *Our Lady of Chernobyl*. His most recent book is a novel, *Schild's Ladder*. He has a Web site at http://www.netspace .netau/^gregegan/.

In the strange and eloquent story that follows, he takes us to a slightly altered version of our own familiar Earth in the days just after World War II, for a memorable battle of ideas between two of the smartest humans alive—a deceptively quiet battle of science versus superstition and rationality versus mysticism, fought with words broadcast over the radio, that could nevertheless change our view of the universe forever and perhaps even change the universe itself.

1

On his eighteenth day in the tiger cage, Robert Stoney began to lose hope of emerging unscathed.

He'd woken a dozen times throughout the night with an overwhelming need to stretch his back and limbs, and none of the useful compromise positions he'd discovered in his first few days—the least-worst solutions to the geometrical problem of his confinement—had been able to dull his sense of panic. He'd been in far more pain in the second week, suffering cramps that felt as if the muscles of his legs were dying on the bone, but these new spasms had come from somewhere deeper, powered by a sense of urgency that revolved entirely around his own awareness of his situation.

That was what frightened him. Sometimes he could find ways to minimize his discomfort, sometimes he couldn't, but he'd been clinging to the thought that, in the end, all these fuckers could ever do was hurt him. That wasn't true, though. They could make him ache for freedom in the middle of the night, the way he might have ached with grief, or love. He'd always cherished the understanding that his self was a whole, his mind and body indivisible. But he'd failed to appreciate the corollary: through his body, they could touch every part of him. Change every part of him.

Morning brought a fresh torment: hay fever. The house was somewhere deep in the countryside, with nothing to be heard in the middle of the day but bird song. June had always been his worst month for hay fever, but in Manchester it had been tolerable. As he ate breakfast, mucus dripped from his face into the bowl of lukewarm oats they'd given him. He stanched the flow with the back of his hand, but suffered a moment of shuddering revulsion when he couldn't find a way to reposition himself to wipe his hand clean on his trousers. Soon he'd need to empty his bowels. They supplied him with a chamber pot whenever he asked, but they always waited two or three hours before removing it. The smell was bad enough, but the fact that it took up space in the cage was worse.

Toward the middle of the morning, Peter Quint came to see him. "How are we today, Prof?" Robert didn't reply. Since the day Quint had responded with a puzzled frown to the suggestion that he had an appropriate name for a spook, Robert had tried to make at least one fresh joke at the man's expense every time they met, a petty but satisfying indulgence. But now his mind was blank, and in retrospect the whole exercise seemed like an insane distraction, as bizarre and futile as scoring philosophical points against some predatory animal while it gnawed on his leg.

"Many happy returns," Quint said cheerfully.

Robert took care to betray no surprise. He'd never lost track of the days, but he'd stopped thinking in terms of the calendar date; it simply wasn't relevant. Back in the real world, to have forgotten his own birthday would have been considered a benign eccentricity. Here it would be taken as proof of his deterioration, and imminent surrender.

If he was cracking, he could at least choose the point of fissure. He spoke as calmly as he could, without looking up. "You know I almost qualified for the Olympic marathon, back in forty-eight? If I hadn't done my hip in just before the trials, I might have competed." He tried a self-deprecating laugh. "I suppose I was never really much of an athlete. But I'm only forty-six. I'm not ready for a wheelchair yet." The words did help: he could beg this way without breaking down completely, expressing an honest fear without revealing how much deeper the threat of damage went.

He continued, with a measured note of plaintiveness that he hoped sounded like an appeal to fairness. "I just can't bear the thought of being crippled. All I'm asking is that you let me stand upright. Let me keep my health."

Quint was silent for a moment, then he replied with a tone of thoughtful sympathy. "It's unnatural, isn't it? Living like this: bent over, twisted, day after day. Living in an unnatural way is always going to harm you. I'm glad you can finally see that."

Robert was tired; it took several seconds for the meaning to sink in. *It was that crude, that obvious?* They'd locked him in this cage, for all this time . . . as a kind of ham-fisted *metaphor* for his crimes?

He almost burst out laughing, but he contained himself. "I don't suppose you know Franz Kafka?"

"Kafka?" Quint could never hide his voracity for names. "One of your Commie chums, is he?"

"I very much doubt that he was ever a Marxist."

Quint was disappointed, but prepared to make do with second best. "One of the other kind, then?"

Robert pretended to be pondering the question. "On balance, I suspect that's not too likely, either."

"So why bring his name up?"

"I have a feeling he would have admired your methods, that's all. He was quite the connoisseur."

"Hmm." Quint sounded suspicious, but not entirely unflattered.

Robert had first set eyes on Quint in February of 1952. His house had been burgled the week before, and Arthur, a young man he'd been seeing since Christmas, had confessed to Robert that he'd given an acquaintance the address. Perhaps the two of them had planned to rob him, and Arthur had backed out at the last moment. In any case, Robert had gone to the police with an unlikely story about spotting the culprit in a pub, trying to sell an electric razor of the same make and model as the one taken from his house. No one could be charged on such flimsy evidence, so Robert had had no qualms about the consequences if Arthur had turned out to be lying. He'd simply hoped to prompt an investigation that might turn up something more tangible.

The following day, the CID had paid Robert a visit. The man he'd accused was known to the police, and fingerprints taken on the day of the burglary matched the prints they had on file. However, at the time Robert claimed to have seen him in the pub, he'd been in custody already on an entirely different charge.

The detectives had wanted to know why he'd lied. To spare himself the embarrassment, Robert had explained, of spelling out the true source of his information. Why was that embarrassing?

"I'm involved with the informant."

One detective, Mr. Wills, had asked matter-of-factly, "What exactly does that entail, sir?" And Robert—in a burst of frankness, as if honesty itself was sure to be rewarded—had told him every detail. He'd known it was still technically illegal, of course. But then, so was playing football on Easter Sunday. It could hardly be treated as a serious crime, like burglary.

The police had strung him along for hours, gathering as much information as they could before disabusing him of this misconception. They hadn't charged him immediately; they'd needed a statement from Arthur first. But then Quint had materialized the next morning, and spelt out the choices very starkly. Three years in prison, with hard labor. Or Robert could resume his wartime work—for just one day a week, as a handsomely paid consultant to Quint's branch of the secret service—and the charges would quietly vanish.

At first, he'd told Quint to let the courts do their worst. He'd been angry enough to want to take a stand against the preposterous law, and whatever his feelings for Arthur, Quint had suggested—gloatingly, as if it strengthened his case—that the younger, working-class man would be treated far more leniently than Robert, having been led astray by someone whose duty was to set an example for the lower orders. Three years in prison was an unsettling prospect, but it would not have been the end of the world; the Mark I had changed the way he worked, but he could still function with nothing but a pencil and paper, if necessary. Even if they'd had him breaking rocks from dawn to dusk he probably would have been able to daydream productively, and for all Quint's scaremongering he'd doubted it would come to that.

At some point, though, in the twenty-four hours Quint had given him to reach a decision, he'd lost his nerve. By granting the spooks their one day a week, he could avoid all the fuss and disruption of a trial. And though his work at the time—modeling embryological development—had been as challenging as anything he'd done in his life, he hadn't been immune to pangs of nostalgia for the old days, when the fate of whole fleets of battleships had rested on finding the most efficient way to extract logical contradictions from a bank of rotating wheels.

The trouble with giving in to extortion was, *it proved that you could be bought*. Never mind that the Russians could hardly have offered to intervene with the Manchester constabulary next time he needed to be rescued. Never mind that he would scarcely have cared if an enemy agent had threatened to send such comprehensive evidence to the newspapers that there'd be no prospect of his patrons saving him again. He'd lost any chance to proclaim that what he did in bed with another willing partner was not an issue of national security; by saying yes to Quint, he'd made it one. By choosing to be corrupted once, he'd brought the whole torrent of clichés and paranoia down upon his head: he was vulnerable to blackmail, an easy target for entrapment, perfidious by nature. He might as well have posed *in flagrante delicto* with Guy Burgess on the steps of the Kremlin.

It wouldn't have mattered if Quint and his masters had merely decided that they couldn't trust him. The problem was—some six years after recruiting him, with no reason to believe that he had ever breached security in any way—they'd convinced themselves that they could neither continue to employ him, nor safely leave him in peace, until they'd rid him of the trait they'd used to control him in the first place.

Robert went through the painful, complicated process of rearranging his body so he could look Quint in the eye. "You know, if it was legal there'd be nothing to worry about, would there? Why don't you devote some of your considerable Machiavellian talents to that end? Blackmail a few politicians. Set up a Royal Commission. It would only take you a couple of years. Then we could all get on with our real jobs."

Quint blinked at him, more startled than outraged. "You might as well say that we should legalize treason!"

Robert opened his mouth to reply, then decided not to waste his breath. Quint wasn't expressing a moral opinion. He simply meant that a world in which fewer people's lives were ruled by the constant fear of discovery was hardly one that a man in his profession would wish to hasten into existence.

当

When Robert was alone again, the time dragged. His hay fever worsened, until he was sneezing and gagging almost continuously; even with freedom of movement and an endless supply of the softest linen handkerchiefs, he would have been reduced to abject misery. Gradually, though, he grew more adept at dealing with the symptoms, delegating the task to some barely conscious part of himself. By the middle of the afternoon—covered in filth, eyes almost swollen shut—he finally managed to turn his mind back to his work.

For the past four years, he'd been immersed in particle physics. He'd been following the field on and off since before the war, but the paper by Yang and Mills in '54, in which they'd generalized Maxwell's equations for electromagnetism to apply to the strong nuclear force, had jolted him into action.

After several false starts, he believed he'd discovered a useful way to cast gravity into the same form. In general relativity, if you carried a four-dimensional velocity vector around a loop that enclosed a curved region of spacetime, it came back rotated—a phenomenon highly reminiscent of the way more abstract vectors behaved in nuclear physics. In both cases, the rotations could be treated algebraically, and the traditional way to get a handle on this was to make use of a set of matrices of complex numbers whose relationships mimicked the algebra in question. Hermann Weyl had catalogued most of the possibilities back in the twenties and thirties.

In spacetime, there were six distinct ways you could rotate an object: you could turn it around any of three perpendicular axes in space, or you could boost its velocity in any of the same three directions. These two kinds of rotation were complementary, or "dual" to each other, with the ordinary rotations only affecting coordinates that were untouched by the corresponding boost, and vice versa. This meant that you could rotate something around, say, the x-axis, and speed it up in the same direction, without the two processes interfering.

When Robert had tried applying the Yang-Mills approach to gravity in the obvious way, he'd floundered. It was only when he'd shifted the algebra of rotations into a new, strangely skewed guise that the mathematics had begun to fall into place. Inspired by a trick that particle physicists used to construct fields with left- or right-handed spin, he'd combined every rotation with its own dual multiplied by i, the square root of minus one. The result was a set of rotations in four *complex* dimensions, rather than the four real ones of ordinary spacetime, but the relationships between them preserved the original algebra.

Demanding that these "self-dual" rotations satisfy Einstein's equations turned out to be equivalent to ordinary general relativity, but the process leading to a quantum mechanical version of the theory became dramatically simpler. Robert still had no idea how to interpret this, but as a purely formal trick it worked spectacularly well—and when the mathematics fell into place like that, it had to mean *something*.

He spent several hours pondering old results, turning them over in his mind's eye, rechecking and reimagining everything in the hope of forging some new connection. Making no progress, but there'd always been days like that. It was a triumph merely to spend this much time doing what he would have done back in the real world—however mundane, or even frustrating, the same activity might have been in its original setting.

By evening, though, the victory began to seem hollow. He hadn't lost his wits entirely, but he was frozen, stunted. He might as well have whiled away the hours reciting the base-32 multiplication table in Baudot code, just to prove that he still remembered it.

As the room filled with shadows, his powers of concentration deserted him completely. His hay fever had abated, but he was too tired to think, and in too much pain to sleep. This wasn't Russia, they couldn't hold him forever; he simply had to wear them down with his patience. *But when, exactly, would they have to let him go?* And how much more patient could Quint be, with no pain, no terror, to erode his determination?

The moon rose, casting a patch of light on the far wall; hunched over, he couldn't see it directly, but it silvered the gray at his feet, and changed his whole sense of the space around him. The cavernous room mocking his confinement reminded him of nights he'd spent lying awake in the dormitory at Sherborne. A public school education did have one great advantage: however miserable you were afterward, you could always take comfort in the knowledge that life would never be quite as bad again.

"This room smells of mathematics! Go out and fetch a disinfectant spray!" That had been his form-master's idea of showing what a civilized man he was: contempt for that loathsome subject, the stuff of engineering and other low trades. And as for Robert's chemistry experiments, like the beautiful color-changing iodate reaction he'd learned from Chris's brother—

Robert felt a familiar ache in the pit of his stomach. *Not now. I can't afford this now.* But the whole thing swept over him, unwanted, unbidden. He'd used to meet Chris in the library on Wednesdays; for months, that had been the only time they could spend together. Robert had been fifteen then, Chris a year older. If Chris had been plain, he still would have shone like a creature from another world. No one else in Sherborne had read Eddington on relativity, Hardy on mathematics. No one else's horizons stretched beyond rugby, sadism, and the dimly satisfying prospect of reading classics at Oxford then vanishing into the maw of the civil service.

They had never touched, never kissed. While half the school had been indulging in passionless sodomy—as a rather literal-minded substitute for the much too difficult task of imagining women—Robert had been too shy even to declare his feelings. Too shy, and too afraid that they might not be reciprocated. It hadn't mattered. To have a friend like Chris had been enough.

In December of 1929, they'd both sat the exams for Trinity College, Cambridge. Chris had won a scholarship; Robert hadn't. He'd reconciled himself to their separation, and prepared for one more year at Sherborne without the one person who'd made it bearable. Chris would be following happily in the footsteps of Newton; just thinking of that would be some consolation.

Chris never made it to Cambridge. In February, after six days in agony, he'd died of bovine tuberculosis.

Robert wept silently, angry with himself because he knew that half his wretchedness was just self-pity, exploiting his grief as a disguise. He had to stay honest; once every source of unhappiness in his life melted together and became indistinguishable, he'd be like a cowed animal, with no sense of the past or the future. Ready to do anything to get out of the cage.

If he hadn't yet reached that point, he was close. It would only take a few more nights like the last one. Drifting off in the hope of a few minutes' blankness, to find that sleep itself shone a colder light on everything. Drifting off, then waking with a sense of loss so extreme it was like suffocation.

A woman's voice spoke from the darkness in front of him. "Get off your knees!"

Robert wondered if he was hallucinating. He'd heard no one approach across the creaky floorboards.

The voice said nothing more. Robert rearranged his body so he could look up from the floor. There was a woman he'd never seen before, standing a few feet away.

She'd sounded angry, but as he studied her face in the moonlight through the slits of his swollen eyes, he realized that her anger was directed, not at him, but at his condition. She gazed at him with an expression of horror and outrage, as if she'd chanced upon him being held like this in some respectable neighbor's basement, rather than an MI6 facility. Maybe she was one of the staff employed in the upkeep of the house, but had no idea what went on here? Surely those people were vetted and supervised, though, and threatened with life imprisonment if they ever set foot outside their prescribed domains.

For one surreal moment, Robert wondered if Quint had sent her to seduce him. It would not have been the strangest thing they'd tried. But she radiated such fierce self-assurance—such a sense of confidence that she could speak with the authority of her convictions, and expect to be heeded—that he knew she could never have been chosen for the role. No one in Her Majesty's government would consider self-assurance an attractive quality in a woman.

He said, "Throw me the key, and I'll show you my Roger Bannister impression."

She shook her head. "You don't need a key. Those days are over."

Robert started with fright. *There were no bars between them.* But the cage couldn't have vanished before his eyes; she must have removed it while he'd been lost in his reverie. He'd gone through the whole painful exercise of turning to face her as if he were still confined, without even noticing.

Removed it how?

He wiped his eyes, shivering at the dizzying prospect of freedom. "Who are you?" An agent for the Russians, sent to liberate him from his own side? She'd have to be a zealot, then, or strangely naive, to view his torture with such wide-eyed innocence.

She stepped forward, then reached down and took his hand. "Do you think you can walk?" Her grip was firm, and her skin was cool and dry. She was completely unafraid; she might have been a good Samaritan in a public street helping an old man to his feet after a fall—not an intruder helping a threat to national security break out of therapeutic detention, at the risk of being shot on sight.

"I'm not even sure I can stand." Robert steeled himself; maybe this woman was a trained assassin, but it would be too much to presume that if he cried out in pain and brought guards rushing in, she could still extricate him without raising a sweat. "You haven't answered my question."

"My name's Helen." She smiled and hoisted him to his feet, looking at once like a compassionate child pulling open the jaws of a hunter's cruel trap, and a very powerful, very intelligent carnivore contemplating its own strength. "I've come to change everything."

Robert said, "Oh, good."

Robert found that he could hobble; it was painful and undignified, but at least he didn't have to be carried. Helen led him through the house; lights showed from some of the rooms, but there were no voices, no foot-steps save their own, no signs of life at all. When they reached the tradesmen's entrance she unbolted the door, revealing a moonlit garden.

"Did you kill everyone?" he whispered. He'd made far too much noise to have come this far unmolested. Much as he had reason to despise his captors, mass murder on his behalf was a lot to take in.

Helen cringed. "What a revolting idea! It's hard to believe some-times, how uncivilized you are."

"You mean the British?"

"All of you!"

"I must say, your accent's rather good."

"I watched a lot of cinema," she explained. "Mostly Ealing come-dies. You never know how much that will help, though."

"Quite."

They crossed the garden, heading for a wooden gate in the hedge. Since murder was strictly for imperialists, Robert could only assume that she'd managed to drug everyone.

The gate was unlocked. Outside the grounds, a cobbled lane ran past the hedge, leading into forest. Robert was barefoot, but the stones weren't cold, and the slight unevenness of the path was welcome, restoring circulation to the soles of his feet.

As they walked, he took stock of his situation. He was out of cap-tivity, thanks entirely to this woman. Sooner or later he was going to have to confront her agenda.

He said, "I'm not leaving the country."

Helen murmured assent, as if he'd passed a casual remark about the weather.

"And I'm not going to discuss my work with you."

"Fine."

Robert stopped and stared at her. She said, "Put your arm across my shoulders."

He complied; she was exactly the right height to support him comfortably. He said, "You're not a Soviet agent, are you?"

Helen was amused. "Is that really what you thought?"

"I'm not all that quick on my feet tonight."

"No." They began walking together. Helen said, "There's a train station about three kilometers away. You can get cleaned up, rest there until morning, and decide where you want to go."

"Won't the station be the first place they'll look?"

"They won't be looking anywhere for a while."

The moon was high above the trees. The two of them could not have made a more conspicuous couple: a sensibly dressed, quite striking young woman, supporting a filthy, ragged tramp. If a villager cycled past, the best they could hope for was being mistaken for an alcoholic father and his martyred daughter.

Martyred all right: she moved so efficiently, despite the burden, that any onlooker would assume she'd been doing this for years. Robert tried altering his gait slightly, subtly changing the timing of his steps to see if he could make her falter, but Helen adapted instantly. If she knew she was being tested, though, she kept it to herself.

Finally he said, "What did you do with the cage?"

"I time-reversed it."

Hairs stood up on the back of his neck. Even assuming that she could do such a thing, it wasn't at all clear to him how that could have stopped the bars from scattering light and interacting with his body. It should merely have turned electrons into positrons, and killed them both in a shower of gamma rays.

That conjuring trick wasn't his most pressing concern, though. "I can only think of three places you might have come from," he said.

Helen nodded, as if she'd put herself in his shoes and catalogued the possibilities. "Rule out one; the other two are both right."

She was not from an extrasolar planet. Even if her civilization possessed some means of viewing Ealing comedies from a distance of light-years, she was far too sensitive to his specific human concerns.

She was from the future, but not his own.

She was from the future of another Everett branch.

He turned to her. "No paradoxes."

She smiled, deciphering his shorthand immediately. "That's right. It's physically impossible to travel into your own past, unless you've made exacting preparations to ensure compatible boundary conditions. That *can* be achieved, in a controlled laboratory setting—but in the field it would be like trying to balance ten thousand elephants in an inverted pyramid, while the bottom one rode a unicycle: excruciatingly difficult, and entirely pointless."

Robert was tongue-tied for several seconds, a horde of questions battling for access to his vocal chords. "But how do you travel into the past at all?"

"It will take a while to bring you up to speed completely, but if you want the short answer: you've already stumbled on one of the clues. I read your paper in *Physical Review*, and it's correct as far as it goes. Quantum gravity involves four complex dimensions, but the only classical solutions—the only geometries that remain in phase under slight perturbations—have curvature that's either *self-dual*, or *anti-self-dual*. Those are the only stationary points of the action, for the complete Lagrangian. And both solutions appear, from the inside, to contain only four real dimensions.

"It's meaningless to ask which sector we're in, but we might as well call it self-dual. In that case, the anti-self-dual solutions have an arrow of time running backward compared to ours."

"Why?" As he blurted out the question, Robert wondered if he sounded like an impatient child to her. But if she suddenly vanished back into thin air, he'd have far fewer regrets for making a fool of himself this way than if he'd maintained a façade of sophisticated nonchalance.

Helen said, "Ultimately, that's related to spin. And it's down to the mass of the neutrino that we can tunnel between sectors. But I'll need to draw you some diagrams and equations to explain it all properly."

Robert didn't press her for more; he had no choice but to trust that she wouldn't desert him. He staggered on in silence, a wonderful ache of anticipation building in his chest. If someone had put this situation to him hypothetically, he would have piously insisted that he'd prefer to toil on at his own pace. But despite the satisfaction it had given him on the few occasions when he'd made genuine discoveries himself, what mattered in the end was understanding as much as you could, *however* you could. Better to ransack the past and the future than go through life in a state of willful ignorance.

"You said you've come to change things?"

She nodded. "I can't predict the future here, of course, but there are pitfalls in my own past that I can help you avoid. In my twentieth century, people discovered things too slowly. Everything changed much too slowly. Between us, I think we can speed things up."

Robert was silent for a while, contemplating the magnitude of what she was proposing. Then he said, "It's a pity you didn't come sooner. In this branch, about twenty years ago—"

Helen cut him off. "I know. We had the same war. The same Holocaust, the same Soviet death toll. But we've yet to be able to avert that, anywhere. You can never do anything in just one history—even the most focused intervention happens across a broad 'ribbon' of strands. When we try to reach back to the thirties and forties, the ribbon overlaps with its own past to such a degree that all the worst horrors are *faits accompli*. We can't shoot *any* version of Adolf Hitler, because we can't shrink the ribbon to the point where none of us would be shooting ourselves in the back. All we've ever managed are minor interventions, like sending projectiles back to the Blitz, saving a few lives by deflecting bombs."

"What, knocking them into the Thames?"

"No, that would have been too risky. We did some modeling, and the safest thing turned out to be diverting them onto big, empty buildings: Westminster Abbey, Saint Paul's Cathedral."

The station came into view ahead of them. Helen said, "What do you think? Do you want to head back to Manchester?"

Robert hadn't given the question much thought. Quint could track him down anywhere, but the more people he had around him, the less vulnerable he'd be. In his house in Wilmslow he'd be there for the taking.

"I still have rooms at Cambridge," he said tentatively.

"Good idea."

"What are your own plans?"

Helen turned to him. "I thought I'd stay with you." She smiled at the expression on his face. "Don't worry, I'll give you plenty of privacy. And if people want to make assumptions, let them. You already have a scandalous reputation; you might as well see it branch out in new directions."

Robert said wryly, "I'm afraid it doesn't quite work that way. They'd throw us out immediately."

Helen snorted. "They could try."

"You may have defeated MI6, but you haven't dealt with Cambridge porters." The reality of the situation washed over him anew at the thought of her in his study, writing out the equations for time travel on the blackboard. "*Why me?* I can appreciate that you'd want to make contact with someone who could understand how you came here—but why not Everett, or Yang, or Feynman? Compared to Feynman, I'm a dilettante."

Helen said, "Maybe. But you have an equally practical bent, and you'll learn fast enough."

There had to be more to it than that: thousands of people would have been capable of absorbing her lessons just as rapidly. "The physics you've hinted at—in your past, did I discover all that?"

"No. Your *Physical Review* paper helped me track you down here, but in my own history that was never published." There was a flicker of disquiet in her eyes, as if she had far greater disappointments in store on that subject.

Robert didn't care much either way; if anything, the less his alter ego had achieved, the less he'd be troubled by jealousy.

"Then what was it, that made you choose me?"

"You really haven't guessed?" Helen took his free hand and held the fingers to her face; it was a tender gesture, but much more like a daughter's than a lover's. "It's a warm night. No one's skin should be this cold."

Robert gazed into her dark eyes, as playful as any human's, as serious, as proud. Given the chance, perhaps any decent person would have plucked him from Quint's grasp. But only one kind would feel a special obligation, as if they were repaying an ancient debt.

He said, "You're a machine."

2

John Hamilton, Professor of Medieval and Renaissance English at Magdalene College, Cambridge, read the last letter in the morning's pile of fan mail with a growing sense of satisfaction.

The letter was from a young American, a twelve-year-old girl in Boston. It opened in the usual way, declaring how much pleasure his books had given her, before going on to list her favorite scenes and characters. As ever, Jack was delighted that the stories had touched someone deeply enough to prompt them to respond this way. But it was the final paragraph that was by far the most gratifying:

However much other children might tease me, or grown-ups too when I'm older, I will NEVER, EVER stop believing in the Kingdom of Nescia. Sarah stopped believing, and she was locked out of the Kingdom forever. At first that made me cry, and I couldn't sleep all night because I was afraid I might stop believing myself one day. But I understand now that it's good to be afraid, because it will help me keep people from changing my mind. And if you're not willing to believe in magic lands, of course you can't enter them. There's nothing even Belvedere himself can do to save you, then.

Jack refilled and lit his pipe, then reread the letter. This was his vindication: the proof that through his books he could touch a young mind, and plant the seed of faith in fertile ground. It made all the scorn of his jealous, stuck-up colleagues fade into insignificance. Children understood the power of stories, the reality of myth, the need to believe in something beyond the dismal gray farce of the material world.

It wasn't a truth that could be revealed the "adult" way: through scholarship, or reason. Least of all through philosophy, as Elizabeth Anscombe had shown him on that awful night at the Socratic Club. A devout Christian herself, Anscombe had nonetheless taken all the arguments against materialism from his popular book, *Signs and Wonders*, and trampled them into the ground. It had been an unfair match from the start: Anscombe was a professional philosopher, steeped in the work of everyone from Aquinas to Wittgenstein; Jack knew the history of ideas in medieval Europe intimately, but he'd lost interest in modern philosophy once it had been invaded by fashionable positivists. And *Signs and Wonders* had never been intended as a scholarly work; it had been good enough to pass muster with a sympathetic lay readership, but trying to defend his admittedly rough-and-ready mixture of common sense and useful shortcuts to faith against Anscombe's merciless analysis had made him feel like a country yokel stammering in front of a bishop.

Ten years later, he still burned with resentment at the humiliation she'd put him through, but he was grateful for the lesson she'd taught him. His earlier books, and his radio talks, had not been a complete waste of time—but the harpy's triumph had shown him just how pitiful human reason was when it came to the great questions. He'd begun working on the stories of Nescia years before, but it was only when the dust had settled on his most painful defeat that he'd finally recognized his true calling.

He removed his pipe, stood, and turned to face Oxford. "Kiss my arse, Elizabeth!" he growled happily, waving the letter at her. This was a wonderful omen. It was going to be a very good day.

There was a knock at the door of his study.

"Come."

It was his brother, William. Jack was puzzled—he hadn't even realized Willie was in town—but he nodded a greeting and motioned at the couch opposite his desk.

Willie sat, his face flushed from the stairs, frowning. After a moment he said, "This chap Stoney."

"Hmm?" Jack was only half listening as he sorted papers on his desk. He knew from long experience that Willie would take forever to get to the point.

"Did some kind of hush-hush work during the war, apparently."

"Who did?"

"Robert Stoney. Mathematician. Used to be up at Manchester, but he's a Fellow of Kings, and now he's back in Cambridge. Did some kind of secret war work. Same thing as Malcolm Muggeridge, apparently. No one's allowed to say what."

Jack looked up, amused. He'd heard rumors about Muggeridge, but they all revolved around the business of analyzing intercepted German radio messages. What conceivable use would a mathematician have been, for that? Sharpening pencils for the intelligence analysts, presumably.

"What about him, Willie?" Jack asked patiently.

Willie continued reluctantly, as if he was confessing to something mildly immoral. "I paid him a visit yesterday. Place called the

Cavendish. Old army friend of mine has a brother who works there. Got the whole tour."

"I know the Cavendish. What's there to see?"

"He's doing things, Jack. *Impossible things.*"

"Impossible?"

"Looking inside people. Putting it on a screen, like a television."

Jack sighed. "Taking x-rays?"

Willie snapped back angrily, "I'm not a fool; I know what an x-ray looks like. This is different. You can see the blood flow. You can watch your heart beating. You can follow a sensation through the nerves from . . . fingertip to brain. He says, soon he'll be able to watch a thought in motion."

"Nonsense." Jack scowled. "So he's invented some gadget, some fancy kind of x-ray machine. What are you so agitated about?"

Willie shook his head gravely. "There's more. That's just the tip of the iceberg. He's only been back in Cambridge a year, and already the place is overflowing with . . . wonders." He used the word begrudgingly, as if he had no choice, but was afraid of conveying more approval than he intended.

Jack was beginning to feel a distinct sense of unease.

"What exactly is it you want me to do?" he asked.

Willie replied plainly, "Go and see for yourself. Go and see what he's up to."

The Cavendish Laboratory was a mid-Victorian building, designed to resemble something considerably older and grander. It housed the entire Department of Physics, complete with lecture theaters; the place was swarming with noisy undergraduates. Jack had had no trouble arranging a tour: he'd simply telephoned Stoney and expressed his curiosity, and no more substantial reason had been required.

Stoney had been allocated three adjoining rooms at the back of the building, and the "spin resonance imager" occupied most of the first. Jack obligingly placed his arm between the coils, then almost jerked it out in fright when the strange, transected view of his muscles and veins appeared on the picture tube. He wondered if it could be some kind of hoax, but he clenched his fist slowly and watched the image do the same, then made several unpredictable movements which it mimicked equally well.

"I can show you individual blood cells, if you like," Stoney offered cheerfully.

Jack shook his head; his current, unmagnified flaying was quite enough to take in.

Stoney hesitated, then added awkwardly, "You might want to talk to your doctor at some point. It's just that, your bone density's rather—" He pointed to a chart on the screen beside the image. "Well, it's quite a bit below the normal range."

Jack withdrew his arm. He'd already been diagnosed with osteoporosis, and he'd welcomed the news: it meant that he'd taken a small part of Joyce's illness—the weakness in her bones—into his own body. God was allowing him to suffer a little in her stead.

If Joyce were to step between these coils, what might that reveal? But there'd be nothing to add to her diagnosis. Besides, if he kept up his prayers, and kept up both their spirits, in time her remission would blossom from an uncertain reprieve into a full-fledged cure.

He said, "How does this work?"

"In a strong magnetic field, some of the atomic nuclei and electrons in your body are free to align themselves in various ways with the field." Stoney must have seen Jack's eyes beginning to glaze over; he quickly changed tack. "Think of it as being like setting a whole lot of spinning tops whirling, as vigorously as possible, then listening carefully as they slow down and tip over. For the atoms in your body, that's enough to give some clues as to what kind of molecule, and what kind of tissue, they're in. The machine listens to atoms in different places by changing the way it combines all the signals from billions of tiny antennae. It's like a whispering gallery where we can play with the time that signals take to travel from different places, moving the focus back and forth through any part of your body, thousands of times a second."

Jack pondered this explanation. Though it sounded complicated, in principle it wasn't that much stranger than x-rays.

"The physics itself is old hat," Stoney continued, "but for imaging, you need a very strong magnetic field, and you need to make sense of all the data you've gathered. Nevill Mott made the superconducting alloys for the magnets. And I managed to persuade Rosalind Franklin from Birkbeck to collaborate with us, to help perfect the fabrication process for the computing circuits. We cross-link lots of little Y-shaped DNA fragments, then selectively coat them with metal; Rosalind worked out a way to use x-ray crystallography for quality control. We paid her back with a purpose-built computer that will let her solve hydrated protein structures in real time, once she gets her hands on a bright enough x-ray source." He held up a small, unprepossessing object, rimmed with protruding gold wires. "Each logic gate is roughly a hundred Ångstroms cubed, and we grow them in three-dimensional arrays. That's a million, million, million switches in the palm of my hand."

Jack didn't know how to respond to this claim. Even when he couldn't quite follow the man there was something mesmerizing about his ramblings, like a cross between William Blake and nursery talk.

"If computers don't excite you, we're doing all kinds of other things with DNA." Stoney ushered him into the next room, which was full of glassware, and seedlings in pots beneath strip lights. Two assistants seated at a bench were toiling over microscopes; another was dispensing fluids into test tubes with a device that looked like an overgrown eyedropper.

"There are a dozen new species of rice, corn, and wheat here. They all have at least double the protein and mineral content of existing crops, and each one uses a different biochemical repertoire to protect itself against insects and fungi. Farmers have to get away from mono-cultures; it leaves them too vulnerable to disease, and too dependent on chemical pesticides."

Jack said, "You've bred these? All these new varieties, in a matter of months?"

"No, no! Instead of hunting down the heritable traits we needed in the wild, and struggling for years to produce cross-breeds bearing all of them, we designed every trait from scratch. Then we manufac-tured DNA that would make the tools the plants need, and inserted it into their germ cells."

Jack demanded angrily, "Who are you to say what a plant needs?"

Stoney shook his head innocently. "I took my advice from agricultural scientists, who took their advice from farmers. They know what pests and blights they're up against. Food crops are as artificial as Pekinese. Nature didn't hand them to us on a plate, and if they're not working as well as we need them to, nature isn't going to fix them for us."

Jack glowered at him, but said nothing. He was beginning to understand why Willie had sent him here. The man came across as an enthusiastic tinkerer, but there was a breathtaking arrogance lurking behind the boyish exterior.

Stoney explained a collaboration he'd brokered between scientists in Cairo, Bogotá, London, and Calcutta, to develop vaccines for polio, smallpox, malaria, typhoid, yellow fever, tuberculosis, influenza, and leprosy. Some were the first of their kind; others were intended as replacements for existing vaccines. "It's important that we create anti-gens without culturing the pathogens in animal cells that might themselves harbor viruses. The teams are all looking at variants on a simple, cheap technique that involves putting antigen genes into harmless bacteria that will double as delivery vehicles and adjuvants, then freeze-drying them into spores that can survive tropical heat without refrigeration."

Jack was slightly mollified; this all sounded highly admirable. What business Stoney had instructing doctors on vaccines was another question. Presumably his jargon made sense to them, but when exactly had this mathematician acquired the training to make even the most modest suggestions on the topic?

"You're having a remarkably productive year," he observed.

Stoney smiled. "The muse comes and goes for all of us. But I'm really just the catalyst in most of this. I've been lucky enough to find some people—here in Cambridge, and further afield—who've been willing to chance their arm on some wild ideas. They've done the real work." He gestured toward the next room. "My own pet projects are through here."

The third room was full of electronic gadgets, wired up to picture tubes displaying both phosphorescent words and images resembling engineering blueprints come to life. In the middle of one bench, incongruously, sat a large cage containing several hamsters.

Stoney fiddled with one of the gadgets, and a face like a stylized drawing of a mask appeared on an adjacent screen. The mask looked around the room, then said, "Good morning, Robert. Good morning, Professor Hamilton."

Jack said, "You had someone record those words?"

The mask replied, "No, Robert showed me photographs of all the teaching staff at Cambridge. If I see anyone I know from the photographs, I greet them." The face was crudely rendered, but the hollow eyes seemed to meet Jack's. Stoney explained, "It has no idea what it's saying, of course. It's just an exercise in face and voice recognition."

Jack responded stiffly, "Of course."

Stoney motioned to Jack to approach and examine the hamster cage. He obliged him. There were two adult animals, presumably a breeding pair. Two pink young were suckling from the mother, who reclined in a bed of straw.

"Look closely," Stoney urged him. Jack peered into the nest, then cried out an obscenity and backed away.

One of the young was exactly what it seemed. The other was a machine, wrapped in ersatz skin, with a nozzle clamped to the warm teat.

"That's the most monstrous thing I've ever seen!" Jack's whole body was trembling. "What possible reason could you have to do that?"

Stoney laughed and made a reassuring gesture, as if his guest was a nervous child recoiling from a harmless toy. "It's not hurting her! And the point is to discover what it takes for the mother to accept it. To 'reproduce one's kind' means having some set of parameters as to what that *is*. Scent, and some aspects of appearance, are important cues in this case, but through trial and error I've also pinned down a set of behaviors that lets the simulacrum pass through every stage of the life cycle. An acceptable child, an acceptable sibling, an acceptable mate."

Jack stared at him, nauseated. "These animals fuck your machines?"

Stoney was apologetic. "Yes, but hamsters will fuck anything. I'll really have to shift to a more discerning species, in order to test that properly."

Jack struggled to regain his composure. "What on Earth possessed you, to do this?"

"In the long run," Stoney said mildly, "I believe this is something we're going to need to understand far better than we do at present. Now that we can map the structures of the brain in fine detail, and match its raw complexity with our computers, it's only a matter of a decade or so before we build machines that think.

"That in itself will be a vast endeavor, but I want to ensure that it's not stillborn from the start. There's not much point creating the most marvelous children in history, only to find that some awful mammalian instinct drives us to strangle them at birth."

Jack sat in his study drinking whiskey. He'd telephoned Joyce after dinner, and they'd chatted for a while, but it wasn't the same as being with her. The weekends never came soon enough, and by Tuesday or Wednesday any sense of reassurance he'd gained from seeing her had slipped away entirely.

It was almost midnight now. After speaking to Joyce, he'd spent three more hours on the telephone, finding out what he could about Stoney. Milking his connections, such as they were; Jack had only been at Cambridge for five years, so he was still very much an outsider. Not that he'd ever been admitted into any inner circles back at Oxford: he'd always belonged to a small, quiet group of dissenters against the tide of fashion. Whatever else might be said about the Tiddlywinks, they'd never had their hands on the levers of academic power.

A year ago, while on sabbatical in Germany, Stoney had resigned suddenly from a position he'd held at Manchester for a decade. He'd returned to Cambridge, despite having no official posting to take up. He'd started collaborating informally with various people at the Cavendish, until the head of the place, Mott, had invented a job description for him, and given him a modest salary, the three rooms Jack had seen, and some students to assist him.

Stoney's colleagues were uniformly amazed by his spate of successful inventions. Though none of his gadgets were based on entirely new science, his skill at seeing straight to the heart of existing theories and plucking some practical consequence from them was unprecedented. Jack had expected some jealous backstabbing, but no one seemed to have a bad word to say about Stoney. He was willing to turn his scientific Midas touch to the service of anyone who approached him, and it sounded to Jack as if every would-be skeptic or enemy had been bought off with some rewarding insight into their own field.

Stoney's personal life was rather murkier. Half of Jack's informants were convinced that the man was a confirmed pansy, but others spoke of a beautiful, mysterious woman named Helen, with whom he was plainly on intimate terms.

Jack emptied his glass and stared out across the courtyard. *Was it pride, to wonder if he might have received some kind of prophetic vision?* Fifteen years earlier, when he'd written *The Broken Planet*, he'd imagined that he'd merely been satirizing the hubris of modern science. His portrait of the evil forces behind the sardonically named Laboratory Overseeing Various Experiments had been intended as a deadly serious metaphor, but he'd never expected to find himself wondering if real fallen angels were whispering secrets in the ears of a Cambridge don.

How many times, though, had he told his readers that the devil's greatest victory had been convincing the world that he did not exist? The devil was *not* a metaphor, a mere symbol of human weakness: he was a real, scheming presence, acting in time, acting in the world, as much as God Himself.

And hadn't Faustus's damnation been sealed by the most beautiful woman of all time: Helen of Troy?

Jack's skin crawled. He'd once written a humorous newspaper column called "Letters from a Demon," in which a Senior Tempter offered advice to a less experienced colleague on the best means to lead the faithful astray. Even that had been an exhausting, almost corrupting experience; adopting the necessary point of view, however whimsically, had made him feel that he was withering inside. The thought that a cross between the *Faustbuch* and *The Broken Planet* might be coming to life around him was too terrifying to contemplate. He was no hero out of his own fiction—not even a mild-mannered Cedric Duffy, let alone a modern Pendragon. And he did not believe that Merlin would rise from the woods to bring chaos to that hubristic Tower of Babel, the Cavendish Laboratory.

Nevertheless, if he was the only person in England who suspected Stoney's true source of inspiration, who *else* would act?

Jack poured himself another glass. There was nothing to be gained by procrastinating. He would not be able to rest until he knew what he was facing: a vain, foolish overgrown boy who was having a run of good luck—or a vain, foolish overgrown boy who had sold his soul and imperiled all humanity.

"A *Satanist*? You're accusing me of being a Satanist?"

Stoney tugged angrily at his dressing gown; he'd been in bed when Jack had pounded on the door. Given the hour, it had been remarkably civil of him to accept a visitor at all, and he appeared so genuinely affronted now that Jack was almost prepared to apologize and slink away. He said, "I had to ask you—"

"You have to be doubly foolish to be a Satanist," Stoney muttered.

"Doubly?"

"Not only do you need to believe all the nonsense of Christian theology, you then have to turn around and back the preordained, guaranteed-to-fail, absolutely futile *losing side*." He held up his hand, as if he believed he'd anticipated the only possible objection to this remark, and wished to spare Jack the trouble of wasting his breath by uttering it. "I *know*, some people claim it's all really about some pre-Christian deity: Mercury, or Pan—guff like that. But assuming that we're not talking about some complicated mislabeling of objects of worship, I really can't think of anything more insulting. You're comparing me to someone like . . . *Huysmans*, who was basically just a very dim Catholic."

Stoney folded his arms and settled back on the couch, waiting for Jack's response.

Jack's head was thick from the whiskey; he wasn't at all sure how to take this. It was the kind of smart-arsed undergraduate drivel he might have expected from any smug atheist—but then, short of a confession, exactly what kind of reply would have constituted evidence of guilt? *If you'd sold your soul to the devil, what lie would you tell in place of the truth?* Had he seriously believed that Stoney would claim to be a devout churchgoer, as if that were the best possible answer to put Jack off the scent?

He had to concentrate on things he'd seen with his own eyes, facts that could not be denied.

"You're plotting to overthrow nature, bending the world to the will of man."

Stoney sighed. "Not at all. More refined technology will help us tread more *lightly*. We have to cut back on pollution and pesticides as rapidly as possible. Or do you want to live in a world where all the animals are born as hermaphrodites, and half the Pacific islands disappear in storms?"

"Don't try telling me that you're some kind of guardian of the animal kingdom. You want to replace us all with machines!"

"Does every Zulu or Tibetan who gives birth to a child, and wants the best for it, threaten you in the same way?"

Jack bristled. "I'm not a racist. A Zulu or Tibetan has a *soul*."

Stoney groaned and put his head in his hands. "It's half past one in the morning! Can't we have this debate some other time?"

Someone banged on the door. Stoney looked up, disbelieving. "What is this? Grand Central Station?"

He crossed to the door and opened it. A disheveled, unshaven man pushed his way into the room. "Quint? What a pleasant—"

The intruder grabbed Stoney and slammed him against the wall. Jack exhaled with surprise. Quint turned bloodshot eyes on him.

"Who the fuck are you?"

"John Hamilton. Who the fuck are you?"

"Never you mind. Just stay put." He jerked Stoney's arm up behind his back with one hand, while grinding his face into the wall with the other. "You're mine now, you piece of shit. No one's going to protect you this time."

Stoney addressed Jack through a mouth squashed against the masonry. "Dith ith Pether Quinth, my own perthonal thpook. I did make a Fauthtian bargain. But with thtrictly temporal—"

"Shut up!" Quint pulled a gun from his jacket and held it to Stoney's head.

Jack said, "Steady on."

"Just how far do your connections go?" Quint screamed. "I've had memos disappear, sources clam up—and now my superiors are treating *me* like some kind of traitor! Well, don't worry: when I'm through with you, I'll have the names of the entire network." He turned to address Jack again. "And don't *you* think you're going anywhere."

Stoney said, "Leave him out of dith. He'th at Magdalene. You mutht know by now: all the thpieth are at Trinity."

Jack was shaken by the sight of Quint waving his gun around, but the implications of this drama came as something of a relief. Stoney's ideas must have had their genesis in some secret wartime research project. He hadn't made a deal with the devil after all, but he'd broken the Official Secrets Act, and now he was paying the price.

Stoney flexed his body and knocked Quint backward. Quint staggered, but didn't fall; he raised his arm menacingly, but there was no gun in his hand. Jack looked around to see where it had fallen, but he couldn't spot it anywhere. Stoney landed a kick squarely in Quint's testicles; barefoot, but Quint wailed with pain. A second kick sent him sprawling.

Stoney called out, "Luke? *Luke!* Would you come and give me a hand?"

A solidly built man with tattooed forearms emerged from Stoney's bedroom, yawning and tugging his braces into place. At the sight of Quint, he groaned. "Not again!"

Stoney said, "I'm sorry."

Luke shrugged stoically. The two of them managed to grab hold of Quint, then they dragged him struggling out the door. Jack waited a few seconds, then searched the floor for the gun. But it wasn't anywhere in sight, and it hadn't slid under the furniture; none of the crevices where it might have ended up were so dark that it would have been lost in shadow. It was not in the room at all.

Jack went to the window and watched the three men cross the

courtyard, half expecting to witness an assassination. But Stoney and his lover merely lifted Quint into the air between them, and tossed him into a shallow, rather slimy-looking pond.

Jack spent the ensuing days in a state of turmoil. He wasn't ready to confide in anyone until he could frame his suspicions clearly, and the events in Stoney's rooms were difficult to interpret unambiguously. He couldn't state with absolute certainty that Quint's gun had vanished before his eyes. But surely the fact that Stoney was walking free proved that he was receiving supernatural protection? And Quint himself, confused and demoralized, had certainly had the appearance of a man who'd been demonically confounded at every turn.

If this was true, though, Stoney must have bought more with his soul than immunity from worldly authority. *The knowledge itself* had to be Satanic in origin, as the legend of Faustus described it. Tollers had been right, in his great essay "Mythopoesis": myths were remnants of man's prelapsarian capacity to apprehend, directly, the great truths of the world. Why else would they resonate in the imagination, and survive from generation to generation?

By Friday, a sense of urgency gripped him. He couldn't take his confusion back to Potter's Barn, back to Joyce and the boys. This had to be resolved, if only in his own mind, before he returned to his family.

With Wagner on the gramophone, he sat and meditated on the challenge he was facing. Stoney had to be thwarted, but how? Jack had always said that the Church of England—apparently so quaint and harmless, a Church of cake stalls and kindly spinsters—was like a fearsome army in the eyes of Satan. But even if his master was quaking in Hell, it would take more than a few stern words from a bicycling vicar to force Stoney to abandon his obscene plans.

But Stoney's intentions, in themselves, didn't matter. He'd been granted the power to dazzle and seduce, but not to force his will upon the populace. What mattered was how his plans were viewed by others. And the way to stop him was to open people's eyes to the true emptiness of his apparent cornucopia.

The more he thought and prayed about it, the more certain Jack became that he'd discerned the task required of him. No denunciation from the pulpits would suffice; people wouldn't turn down the fruits of Stoney's damnation on the mere say-so of the Church. Why would anyone reject such lustrous gifts, without a carefully reasoned argument?

Jack had been humiliated once, defeated once, trying to expose the barrenness of materialism. But might that not have been a form of preparation? He'd been badly mauled by Anscombe, but she'd made an infinitely gentler enemy than the one he now confronted. He had suffered from her taunts—but what was *suffering*, if not the chisel God used to shape his children into their true selves?

His role was clear, now. He would find Stoney's intellectual Achilles' heel, and expose it to the world.

He would debate him.

3

Robert gazed at the blackboard for a full minute, then started laughing with delight. "That's so beautiful!"

"Isn't it?" Helen put down the chalk and joined him on the couch. "Any more symmetry, and nothing would happen: the universe would be full of crystalline blankness. Any less, and it would all be uncorrelated noise."

Over the months, in a series of tutorials, Helen had led him through a small part of the century of physics that had separated them at their first meeting, down to the purely algebraic structures that lay beneath spacetime and matter. Mathematics catalogued everything that was not self-contradictory; within that vast inventory, physics was an island of structures rich enough to contain their own beholders.

Robert sat and mentally reviewed everything he'd learned, trying to apprehend as much as he could in a single image. As he did, a part of him waited fearfully for a sense of disappointment, a sense of anticlimax. *He might never see more deeply into the nature of the world. In this direction, at least, there was nothing more to be discovered.*

But anticlimax was impossible. To become jaded with *this* was impossible. However familiar he became with the algebra of the universe, it would never grow less marvelous.

Finally he asked, "Are there other islands?" Not merely other histories, sharing the same underlying basis, but other realities entirely.

"I suspect so," Helen replied. "People have mapped some possibilities. I don't know how that could ever be confirmed, though."

Robert shook his head, sated. "I won't even think about that. I need to come down to Earth for a while." He stretched his arms and leaned back, still grinning.

Helen said, "Where's Luke today? He usually shows up by now, to drag you out into the sunshine."

The question wiped the smile from Robert's face. "Apparently I make poor company. Being insufficiently fanatical about darts and football."

"He's left you?" Helen reached over and squeezed his hand sympathetically. A little mockingly, too.

Robert was annoyed; she never said anything, but he always felt that she was judging him. "You think I should grow up, don't you? Find someone more like myself. Some kind of *soulmate*." He'd meant the word to sound sardonic, but it emerged rather differently.

"It's your life," she said.

A year before, that would have been a laughable claim, but it was almost the truth now. There was a de facto moratorium on prosecutions, while the recently acquired genetic and neurological evidence was being assessed by a parliamentary subcommittee. Robert had helped plant the seeds of the campaign, but he'd played no real part in it; other people had taken up the cause. In a matter of months, it was possible that Quint's cage would be smashed, at least for everyone in Britain.

The prospect filled him with a kind of vertigo. He might have broken the laws at every opportunity, but they had still molded him. The cage might not have left him crippled, but he'd be lying to himself if he denied that he'd been stunted.

He said, "Is that what happened, in your past? I ended up in some . . . lifelong partnership?" As he spoke the words, his mouth went dry, and he was suddenly afraid that the answer would be yes. *With Chris. The life he'd missed out on was a life of happiness with Chris.*

"No."

"Then . . . what?" he pleaded. "What did I do? How did I live?" He caught himself, suddenly self-conscious, but added, "You can't blame me for being curious."

Helen said gently, "You don't want to know what you can't change. All of that is part of your own causal past now, as much as it is of mine."

"If it's part of my own history," Robert countered, "don't I deserve to know it? This man wasn't me, but he brought you to me."

Helen considered this. "You accept that he was someone else? Not someone whose actions you're responsible for?"

"Of course."

She said, "There was a trial, in 1952. For 'Gross Indecency contrary to Section 11 of the Criminal Amendment Act of 1885.' He wasn't imprisoned, but the court ordered hormone treatments."

"*Hormone treatments?*" Robert laughed. "What—testosterone, to make him more of a man?"

"No, estrogen. Which in men reduces the sex drive. There are side effects, of course. Gynecomorphism, among other things."

Robert felt physically sick. *They'd chemically castrated him, with drugs that had made him sprout breasts.* Of all the bizarre abuse to which he'd been subjected, nothing had been as horrifying as that.

Helen continued, "The treatment lasted six months, and the effects were all temporary. But two years later, he took his own life. It was never clear exactly why."

Robert absorbed this in silence. He didn't want to know anything more.

After a while, he said, "How do you bear it? Knowing that in some branch or other, every possible form of humiliation is being inflicted on someone?"

Helen said, "I don't *bear it.* I change it. That's why I'm here."

Robert bowed his head. "I know. And I'm grateful that our histories collided. But . . . how many histories *don't?*" He struggled to find an example, though it was almost too painful to contemplate; since their first conversation, it was a topic he'd deliberately pushed to the back of his mind. "There's not just an unchangeable Auschwitz in each of our pasts, there are an astronomical number of others—along with an astronomical number of things that are even worse."

Helen said bluntly, "That's not true."

"What?" Robert looked up at her, startled.

She walked to the blackboard and erased it. "Auschwitz has happened, for both of us, and no one I'm aware of has ever prevented it—but that doesn't mean that *nobody* stops it, anywhere." She began sketching a network of fine lines on the blackboard. "You and I are having this conversation in countless microhistories—sequences of events where various different things happen with subatomic particles throughout the universe—but that's irrelevant to us, we can't tell those strands apart, so we might as well treat them all as one history." She pressed the chalk down hard to make a thick streak that covered everything she'd drawn. "The quantum decoherence people call this 'coarse graining.' Summing over all these indistinguishable details is what gives rise to classical physics in the first place.

"Now, 'the two of us' would have first met in many perceivably different coarse-grained histories—and furthermore, you've since diverged by making different choices, and experiencing different external possibilities, after those events." She sketched two intersecting ribbons of coarse-grained histories, and then showed each history diverging further.

"World War II and the Holocaust certainly happened in both of *our* pasts—but that's no proof that the total is so vast that it might as well be infinite. Remember, what stops us successfully intervening is the fact that we're reaching back to a point where some of the parallel interventions start to bite their own tail. So when we fail, it can't be counted twice: it's just confirming what we already know."

Robert protested, "But what about all the versions of thirties Europe that don't happen to lie in either your past or mine? Just because we have no direct evidence for a Holocaust in those branches, that hardly makes it unlikely."

Helen said, "Not unlikely *per se*, without intervention. But not fixed in stone, either. We'll keep trying, refining the technology, until we can reach branches where there's no overlap with our own past in the thirties. And there must be other, separate ribbons of intervention that happen in histories we can never even know about."

Robert was elated. He'd imagined himself clinging to a rock of improbable good fortune in an infinite sea of suffering—struggling to pretend, for the sake of his own sanity, that the rock was all there was. But what lay around him was not inevitably worse; it was merely unknown. In time, he might even play a part in ensuring that every last tragedy was *not* repeated across billions of worlds.

He reexamined the diagram. "Hang on. Intervention doesn't end divergence, though, does it? You reached *us*, a year ago, but in at least some of the histories spreading out from that moment, won't we still have suffered all kinds of disasters, and reacted in all kinds of self-defeating ways?"

"Yes," Helen conceded, "but fewer than you might think. If you merely listed every sequence of events that superficially appeared to have a nonzero probability, you'd end up with a staggering catalog of absurdist tragedies. But when you calculate everything more carefully, and take account of Planck-scale effects, it turns out to be nowhere near as bad. There are *no* coarse-grained histories where boulders assemble themselves out of dust and rain from the sky, or everyone in London or Madras goes mad and slaughters their children. Most macroscopic systems end up being quite robust—people included. Across histories, the range of natural disasters, human stupidity, and sheer bad luck isn't overwhelmingly greater than the range you're aware of from this history alone."

Robert laughed. "And that's not bad enough?"

"Oh, it is. But that's the best thing about the form I've taken."

"I'm sorry?"

Helen tipped her head and regarded him with an expression of disappointment. "You know, you're still not as quick on your feet as I'd expected."

Robert's face burned, but then he realized what he'd missed, and his resentment vanished.

"*You don't diverge?* Your hardware is designed to end the process? Your environment, your surroundings, will still split you into different histories—but on a coarse-grained level, you don't contribute to the process yourself?"

"That's right."

Robert was speechless. Even after a year, she could still toss him a hand grenade like this.

Helen said, "I can't help living in many worlds; that's beyond my control. But I do know that I'm one person. Faced with a choice that puts me on a knife-edge, I know I won't split and take every path."

Robert hugged himself, suddenly cold. "Like I do. Like I have. Like all of us poor creatures of flesh."

Helen came and sat beside him. "Even that's not irrevocable. Once you've taken this form—if that's what you choose—you can meet your other selves, reverse some of the scatter. Give some a chance to undo what they've done."

This time, Robert grasped her meaning at once. "Gather myself together? Make myself whole?"

Helen shrugged. "If it's what you want. If you see it that way."

He stared back at her, disoriented. Touching the bedrock of physics was one thing, but this possibility was too much to take in.

Someone knocked on the study door. The two of them exchanged wary glances, but it wasn't Quint, back for more punishment. It was a porter bearing a telegram.

When the man had left, Robert opened the envelope.

"Bad news?" Helen asked.

He shook his head. "Not a death in the family, if that's what you meant. It's from John Hamilton. He's challenging me to a debate. On the topic 'Can a Machine Think?'"

"What, at some university function?"

"No. On the BBC. Four weeks from tomorrow." He looked up. "Do you think I should do it?"

"Radio or television?"

Robert reread the message. "Television."

Helen smiled. "Definitely. I'll give you some tips."

"On the subject?"

"No! That would be cheating." She eyed him appraisingly. "You can start by throwing out your electric razor. Get rid of the permanent five o'clock shadow."

Robert was hurt. "Some people find that quite attractive."

Helen replied firmly, "Trust me on this."

The BBC sent a car to take Robert down to London. Helen sat beside him in the back seat.

"Are you nervous?" she asked.

"Nothing that an hour of throwing up won't cure."

Hamilton had suggested a live broadcast, "to keep things interesting," and the producer had agreed. Robert had never been on television; he'd taken part in a couple of radio discussions on the future of computing, back when the Mark I had first come into use, but even those had been taped.

Hamilton's choice of topic had surprised him at first, but in retrospect it seemed quite shrewd. A debate on the proposition that "Modern Science is the Devil's Work" would have brought howls of laughter from all but the most pious viewers, whereas the purely metaphorical claim that "Modern Science is a Faustian Pact" would have had the entire audience nodding sagely in agreement, while carrying no implications whatsoever. If you weren't going to take the whole dire fairy tale literally, everything was "a Faustian Pact" in some sufficiently watered-down sense: everything had a potential downside, and this was as pointless to assert as it was easy to demonstrate.

Robert had met considerable incredulity, though, when he'd explained to journalists where his own research was leading. To date, the press had treated him as a kind of eccentric British Edison, churning out inventions of indisputable utility, and no one seemed to find it at all surprising or alarming that he was also, frankly, a bit of a loon. But Hamilton would have a chance to exploit, and reshape, that perception. If Robert insisted on defending his goal of creating machine intelligence, not as an amusing hobby that might have been chosen by a public relations firm to make him appear endearingly daft, but as both the ultimate vindication of materialist science and the logical endpoint of most of his life's work, Hamilton could use a victory tonight to cast doubt on everything Robert had done, and everything he symbolized. By asking, not at all rhetorically, "Where will this all end?" he was inviting Robert to step forward and hang himself with the answer.

The traffic was heavy for a Sunday evening, and they arrived at the Shepherd's Bush studios with only fifteen minutes until the broadcast. Hamilton had been collected by a separate car, from his family home near Oxford. As they crossed the studio Robert spotted him, conversing intensely with a dark-haired young man.

He whispered to Helen, "Do you know who that is, with Hamilton?"

She followed his gaze, then smiled cryptically. Robert said, "What? Do you recognize him from somewhere?"

"Yes, but I'll tell you later."

As the makeup woman applied powder, Helen ran through her long list of rules again. "Don't stare into the camera, or you'll look like you're peddling soap powder. But don't avert your eyes. You don't want to look shifty."

The makeup woman whispered to Robert, "Everyone's an expert."

"Annoying, isn't it?" he confided.

Michael Polanyi, an academic philosopher who was well known to the public after presenting a series of radio talks, had agreed to moderate the debate. Polanyi popped into the makeup room, accompanied by the producer; they chatted with Robert for a couple of minutes, setting him at ease and reminding him of the procedure they'd be following.

They'd only just left him when the floor manager appeared. "We need you in the studio now, please, Professor." Robert followed her, and Helen pursued him part of the way. "Breathe slowly and deeply," she urged him.

"As if *you'd* know!" he snapped.

Robert shook hands with Hamilton then took his seat on one side of the podium. Hamilton's young adviser had retreated into the shadows; Robert glanced back to see Helen watching from a similar position. It was like a duel: they both had seconds. The floor manager pointed out the studio monitor, and as Robert watched it was switched between the feeds from two cameras: a wide shot of the whole set, and a closer view of the podium, including the small blackboard on a stand beside it. He'd once asked Helen whether television had progressed to far greater levels of sophistication in her branch of the future, once the pioneering days were left behind, but the question had left her uncharacteristically tongue-tied.

The floor manager retreated behind the cameras, called for silence, then counted down from ten, mouthing the final numbers.

The broadcast began with an introduction from Polanyi: concise, witty, and nonpartisan. Then Hamilton stepped up to the podium. Robert watched him directly while the wide-angle view was being transmitted, so as not to appear rude or distracted. He only turned to the monitor when he was no longer visible himself.

"Can a machine think?" Hamilton began. "My intuition tells me: *no*. My heart tells me: *no*. I'm sure that most of you feel the same way. But that's not enough, is it? In this day and age, we aren't allowed to rely on our hearts for anything. We need something scientific. We need some kind of *proof*.

"Some years ago, I took part in a debate at Oxford University. The issue then was not whether machines might behave like people, but whether people themselves might *be* mere machines. Materialists, you see, claim that we are all just a collection of purposeless atoms, colliding at random. Everything we do, everything we feel, everything we say, comes down to some sequence of events that might as well be the spinning of cogs, or the opening and closing of electrical relays.

"To me, this was self-evidently false. What point could there be, I argued, in even conversing with a materialist? By his own admission, the words that came out of his mouth would be the result of nothing but a mindless, mechanical process! By his own theory, he could have no reason to think that those words would be the truth! Only believers in a transcendent human soul could claim any interest in the truth."

Hamilton nodded slowly, a penitent's gesture. "I was wrong, and I was put in my place. This might be self-evident to *me*, and it might be self-evident to *you*, but it's certainly not what philosophers call an 'analytical truth': it's not actually a nonsense, a contradiction in terms, to believe that we are mere machines. There might, there just *might*, be some reason why the words that emerge from a materialist's mouth are truthful, despite their origins lying entirely in unthinking matter.

"There might." Hamilton smiled wistfully. "I had to concede that possibility, because I only had my instinct, my gut feeling, to tell me otherwise.

"But the reason I only had my instinct to guide me was because I'd failed to learn of an event that had taken place many years before. A discovery made in 1930, by an Austrian mathematician named Kurt Gödel."

Robert felt a shiver of excitement run down his spine. He'd been afraid that the whole contest would degenerate into theology, with Hamilton invoking Aquinas all night—or Aristotle, at best. But it looked as if his mysterious adviser had dragged him into the twentieth century, and they were going to have a chance to debate the real issues after all.

"What is it that we *know* Professor Stoney's computers can do, and do well?" Hamilton continued. "Arithmetic! In a fraction of a second, they can add up a million numbers. Once we've told them, very precisely, what calculations to perform, they'll complete them in the blink of an eye—even if those calculations would take you or me a lifetime.

"But do these machines *understand* what it is they're doing? Professor Stoney says, 'Not yet. Not right now. Give them time. Rome wasn't built in a day.'" Hamilton nodded thoughtfully. "Perhaps that's fair. His computers are only a few years old. They're just babies. Why should they understand anything, so soon?

"But let's stop and think about this a bit more carefully. A computer, as it stands today, is simply a machine that does arithmetic, and Professor Stoney isn't proposing that they're going to sprout new kinds of brains all on their own. Nor is he proposing *giving* them anything really new. He can already let them look at the world with television cameras, turning the pictures into a stream of numbers describing the brightness of different points on the screen . . . on which the computer can then perform *arithmetic*. He can already let them speak to us with a special kind of loudspeaker, to which the computer feeds a stream of numbers to describe how loud the sound should be . . . a stream of numbers produced by more *arithmetic*.

"So the world can come into the computer, as numbers, and words can emerge, as numbers, too. All Professor Stoney hopes to add to his computers is a 'cleverer' way to do the arithmetic that takes the first set of numbers and churns out the second. It's that 'clever arithmetic,' he tells us, that will make these machines think."

Hamilton folded his arms and paused for a moment. "What are we to make of this? Can *doing arithmetic*, and nothing more, be enough to let a machine *understand* anything? My instinct certainly tells me no, but who am I that you should trust my instinct?

"So, let's narrow down the question of understanding, and to be scrupulously fair, let's put it in the most favorable light possible for Professor Stoney. If there's one thing a computer *ought* to be able to understand—as well as us, if not better—it's arithmetic itself. If a computer could think at all, it would surely be able to grasp the nature of its own best talent.

"The question, then, comes down to this: can you *describe* all of arithmetic, *using* nothing but arithmetic? Thirty years ago—long before Professor Stoney and his computers came along—Professor Gödel asked himself exactly that question.

"Now, you might be wondering how anyone could even *begin* to describe the rules of arithmetic, using nothing but arithmetic itself." Hamilton turned to the blackboard, picked up the chalk, and wrote two lines:

$$\text{If} \quad x + z = y+z$$
$$\text{then} \quad x = y$$

"This is an important rule, but it's written in symbols, not numbers, because it has to be true for *every* number, every x, y, and z. But Professor Gödel had a clever idea: why not use a code, like spies use, where every symbol is assigned a number?" Hamilton wrote:

The code for "a" is 1.
The code for "b" is 2.

"And so on. You can have a code for every letter of the alphabet, and for all the other symbols needed for arithmetic: plus signs, equals signs, that kind of thing. Telegrams are sent this way every day, with a code called the Baudot code, so there's really nothing strange or sinister about it.

"All the rules of arithmetic that we learned at school can be written with a carefully chosen set of symbols, which can then be translated into numbers. Every question as to what does or does not *follow from* those rules can then be seen anew, as a question about numbers. If *this* line follows from *this* one," Hamilton indicated the two lines of the cancellation rule, "we can see it in the relationship between their code numbers. We can judge each inference, and declare it valid or not, purely by doing arithmetic.

"So, given *any* proposition at all about arithmetic—such as the claim that 'there are infinitely many prime numbers'—we can restate the notion that we have a proof for that claim in terms of code numbers. If the code number for our claim is x, we can say 'There is a number p, ending with the code number x, that passes our test for being the code number of a valid proof.'"

Hamilton took a visible breath.

"In 1930, Professor Gödel used this scheme to do something rather ingenious." He wrote on the blackboard:

There DOES NOT EXIST a number p meeting the following condition:
p is the code number of a valid proof of this claim.

"Here is a claim about arithmetic, about numbers. It has to be either true or false. So let's start by supposing that it happens to be true. Then there *is no* number p that is the code number for a proof of this claim. So this is a true statement about arithmetic, but it can't be proved merely by *doing* arithmetic!"

Hamilton smiled. "If you don't catch on immediately, don't worry; when I first heard this argument from a young friend of mine, it took a while for the meaning to sink in. But remember: the only hope a computer has for understanding *anything* is by doing arithmetic, and we've just found a statement that *cannot* be proved with mere arithmetic.

"Is this statement really true, though? We mustn't jump to conclusions, we mustn't damn the machines too hastily. Suppose this claim is false! Since it claims there is no number p that is the code number of its own proof, to be false there would have to be such a number, after all. And that number would encode the 'proof' of an acknowledged falsehood!"

Hamilton spread his arms triumphantly. "You and I, like every schoolboy, know that you can't prove a falsehood from sound premises—and if the premises of arithmetic aren't sound, what is? So *we* know, as a matter of certainty, that this statement is true.

"Professor Gödel was the first to see this, but with a little help and perseverance, any educated person can follow in his footsteps. *A machine could never do that.* We might divulge to a machine our own knowledge of this fact, offering it as something to be taken on trust, but the machine could neither stumble on this truth for itself, nor truly comprehend it when we offered it as a gift.

"You and I *understand* arithmetic, in a way that no electronic calculator ever will. What hope has a machine, then, of moving beyond its own most favorable milieu and comprehending any wider truth?

"None at all, ladies and gentlemen. Though this detour into mathematics might have seemed arcane to you, it has served a very down-to-Earth purpose. It has proved—beyond refutation by even the most ardent materialist or the most pedantic philosopher—what we common folk knew all along: no machine will ever think."

Hamilton took his seat. For a moment, Robert was simply exhilarated; coached or not, Hamilton had grasped the essential features of the incompleteness proof, and presented them to a lay audience. What might have been a night of shadowboxing—with no blows connecting, and nothing for the audience to judge but two solo performances in separate arenas—had turned into a genuine clash of ideas.

As Polanyi introduced him and he walked to the podium, Robert realized that his usual shyness and self-consciousness had evaporated. He was filled with an altogether different kind of tension: he sensed more acutely than ever what was at stake.

When he reached the podium, he adopted the posture of someone about to begin a prepared speech, but then he caught himself, as if he'd forgotten something. "Bear with me for a moment." He walked around to the far side of the blackboard and quickly wrote a few words on it, upside down. Then he resumed his place.

"Can a machine think? Professor Hamilton would like us to believe that he's settled the issue once and for all, by coming up with a statement that *we* know is true, but a particular machine—programmed to explore the theorems of arithmetic in a certain rigid way—would never be able to produce. Well . . . we all have our limitations." He flipped the blackboard over to reveal what he'd written on the opposite side:

If Robert Stoney speaks these words, he will NOT be telling the truth.

He waited a few beats, then continued.

"What I'd like to explore, though, is not so much a question of limitations, as of opportunities. How exactly is it that we've all ended up with this mysterious ability to know that Gödel's statement is true? Where does this advantage, this great insight, come from? From our souls? From some immaterial entity that no machine could ever possess? Is that the only possible source, the only conceivable explanation? Or might it come from something a little less ethereal?

"As Professor Hamilton explained, we believe Gödel's statement is true because we trust the rules of arithmetic not to lead us into contradictions and falsehoods. But where does that trust come from? How does it arise?"

Robert turned the blackboard back to Hamilton's side, and pointed to the cancellation rule. "If x plus z equals y plus z, then x equals y. Why is this so *reasonable*? We might not learn to put it quite like this until we're in our teens, but if you showed a young child two boxes—without revealing their contents—added an equal number of shells, or stones, or pieces of fruit to both, and then let the child look inside to see that each box now contained the same number of items, it wouldn't take any formal education for the child to understand that the two boxes must have held the same number of things to begin with.

"The child knows, we all know, how a certain kind of object behaves. Our lives are steeped in direct experience of whole numbers: whole numbers of coins, stamps, pebbles, birds, cats, sheep, buses. If I tried to persuade a six-year-old that I could put three stones in a box, remove one of them, and be left with four . . . he'd simply laugh at me. Why? It's not merely that he's sure to have taken one thing away from three to get two, on many prior occasions. Even a child understands that some things that appear reliable will eventually fail: a toy that works perfectly, day after day, for a month or a year, can still break. But not arithmetic, not taking one from three. He can't even picture *that* failing. Once you've lived in the world, once you've seen how it works, the failure of arithmetic becomes unimaginable.

"Professor Hamilton suggests that this is down to our souls. But what would he say about a child reared in a world of water and mist, never in the company of more than one person at a time, never taught to count on his fingers and toes. I doubt that such a child would possess the same certainty that you and I have, as to the impossibility of arithmetic ever leading him astray. To banish whole numbers entirely from his world would require very strange surroundings, and a level of deprivation amounting to cruelty, but would that be enough to rob a child of his *soul*?

"A computer, programmed to pursue arithmetic as Professor Hamilton has described, is subject to far more deprivation than that child. If I'd been raised with my hands and feet tied, my head in a sack, and someone shouting orders at me, I doubt that I'd have much grasp of reality—and I'd still be better prepared for the task than such a computer. It's a great mercy that a machine treated that way wouldn't be able to think: if it could, the shackles we'd placed upon it would be criminally oppressive!

"But that's hardly the fault of the computer, or a revelation of some irreparable flaw in its nature. If we want to judge the potential of our machines with any degree of honesty, we have to play fair with them, not saddle them with restrictions that we'd never dream of imposing on ourselves. There really is no point comparing an eagle with a spanner, or a gazelle with a washing machine: it's our jets that fly and our cars that run, albeit in quite different ways than any animal.

"*Thought* is sure to be far harder to achieve than those other skills, and to do so we might need to mimic the natural world far more closely. But I believe that once a machine is endowed with facilities resembling the inborn tools for learning that we all have as our birthright, and is set free to learn the way a child learns, through experience, observation, trial and error, hunches and failures—instead of being handed a list of instructions that it has no choice but to obey—we will finally be in a position to compare like with like.

"When that happens, and we can meet and talk and argue with these machines—about arithmetic, or any other topic—there'll be no need to take the word of Professor Gödel, or Professor Hamilton, or myself, for anything. We'll invite them down to the local pub, and interrogate them in person. And if we play fair with them, we'll use the same experience and judgment we use with any friend, or guest, or stranger, to decide for ourselves whether or not they can think."

The BBC put on a lavish assortment of wine and cheese in a small room off the studio. Robert ended up in a heated argument with Polanyi, who revealed himself to be firmly on the negative side, while Helen flirted shamelessly with Hamilton's young friend, who turned out to have a PhD in algebraic geometry from Cambridge; he must have completed the degree just before Robert had come back from Manchester. After exchanging some polite formalities with Hamilton, Robert kept his distance, sensing that any further contact would not be welcome.

An hour later, though, after getting lost in the maze of corridors on his way back from the toilets, Robert came across Hamilton sitting alone in the studio, weeping.

He almost backed away in silence, but Hamilton looked up and saw him. With their eyes locked, it was impossible to retreat.

Robert said, "It's your wife?" He'd heard that she'd been seriously ill, but the gossip had included a miraculous recovery. Some friend of the family had lain hands on her a year ago, and she'd gone into remission.

Hamilton said, "She's dying."

Robert approached and sat beside him. "From what?"

"Breast cancer. It's spread throughout her body. Into her bones, into her lungs, into her liver." He sobbed again, a helpless spasm, then caught himself angrily. "*Suffering is the chisel God uses to shape us.* What kind of idiot comes up with a line like that?"

Robert said, "I'll talk to a friend of mine, an oncologist at Guy's Hospital. He's doing a trial of a new genetic treatment."

Hamilton stared at him. "One of your *miracle cures?*"

"No, no. I mean, only very indirectly."

Hamilton said angrily, "She won't take your poison."

Robert almost snapped back: *She won't? Or you won't let her?* But it was an unfair question. In some marriages, the lines blurred. It was not for him to judge the way the two of them faced this together.

"They go away in order to be with us in a new way, even closer than before." Hamilton spoke the words like a defiant incantation, a declaration of faith that would ward off temptation, whether or not he entirely believed it.

Robert was silent for a while, then he said, "I lost someone close to me, when I was a boy. And I thought the same thing. I thought he was still with me, for a long time afterward. Guiding me. Encouraging me." It was hard to get the words out; he hadn't spoken about this to anyone for almost thirty years. "I dreamed up a whole theory to explain it, in which 'souls' used quantum uncertainty to control the body during life, and communicate with the living after death, without breaking any laws of physics. The kind of thing every science-minded seventeen-year-old probably stumbles on, and takes seriously for a couple of weeks, before realizing how nonsensical it is. But I had a good reason not to see the flaws, so I clung to it for almost two years. Because I missed him so much, it took me that long to understand what I was doing, how I was deceiving myself."

Hamilton said pointedly, "If you'd not tried to explain it, you might never have lost him. He might still be with you now."

Robert thought about this. "I'm glad he's not, though. It wouldn't be fair to either of us."

Hamilton shuddered. "Then you can't have loved him very much, can you?" He put his head in his arms. "Just fuck off, now, will you."

Robert said, "What exactly would it take, to prove to you that I'm not in league with the devil?"

Hamilton turned red eyes on him and announced triumphantly, "Nothing will do that! I saw what happened to Quint's gun!"

Robert sighed. "That was a conjuring trick. Stage magic, not black magic."

"Oh yes? Show me how it's done, then. Teach me how to do it, so I can impress my friends."

"It's rather technical. It would take all night."

Hamilton laughed humorlessly. "You can't deceive me. I saw through you from the start."

"Do you think x-rays are Satanic? Penicillin?"

"Don't treat me like a fool. There's no comparison."

"*Why not?* Everything I've helped develop is part of the same continuum. I've read some of your writing on medieval culture, and you're always berating modern commentators for presenting it as unsophisticated. No one really thought the Earth was flat. No one really treated every novelty as witchcraft. So why view any of my work any differently than a fourteenth-century man would view twentieth-century medicine?"

Hamilton replied, "If a fourteenth-century man was suddenly faced with twentieth-century medicine, don't you think he'd be entitled to wonder how it had been revealed to his contemporaries?"

Robert shifted uneasily on his chair. Helen hadn't sworn him to secrecy, but he'd agreed with her view: it was better to wait, to spread the knowledge that would ground an understanding of what had happened, before revealing any details of the contact between branches.

But this man's wife was dying, needlessly. And Robert was tired of keeping secrets. Some wars required it, but others were better won with honesty.

He said, "I know you hate H. G. Wells. But what if he was right, about one little thing?"

Robert told him everything, glossing over the technicalities but leaving out nothing substantial. Hamilton listened without interrupting, gripped by a kind of unwilling fascination. His expression shifted from hostile to incredulous, but there were also hints of begrudging amazement, as if he could at least appreciate some of the beauty and complexity of the picture Robert was painting.

But when Robert had finished, Hamilton said merely, "You're a grand liar, Stoney. But what else should I expect, from the King of Lies?"

Robert was in a somber mood on the drive back to Cambridge. The encounter with Hamilton had depressed him, and the question of who'd swayed the nation in the debate seemed remote and abstract in comparison.

Helen had taken a house in the suburbs, rather than inviting scandal by cohabiting with him, though her frequent visits to his rooms seemed to have had almost the same effect. Robert walked her to the door.

"I think it went well, don't you?" she said.

"I suppose so."

"I'm leaving tonight," she added casually. "This is good-bye."

"What?" Robert was staggered. "Everything's still up in the air! I still need you!"

She shook her head. "You have all the tools you need, all the clues. And plenty of local allies. There's nothing truly urgent I could tell you, now, that you couldn't find out just as quickly on your own."

Robert pleaded with her, but her mind was made up. The driver beeped the horn; Robert gestured to him impatiently.

"You know, my breath's frosting visibly," he said, "and you're producing nothing. You really ought to be more careful."

She laughed. "It's a bit late to worry about that."

"Where will you go? Back home? Or off to twist another branch?"

"Another branch. But there's something I'm planning to do on the way."

"What's that?"

"Do you remember once, you wrote about an Oracle? A machine that could solve the halting problem?"

"Of course." Given a device that could tell you in advance whether a given computer program would halt, or go on running forever, you'd be able to prove or disprove any theorem whatsoever about the integers: the Goldbach conjecture, Fermat's Last Theorem, anything. You'd simply show this "Oracle" a program that would loop through all the integers, testing every possible set of values and only halting if it came to a set that violated the conjecture. You'd never need to run the program itself; the Oracle's verdict on whether or not it halted would be enough.

Such a device might or might not be possible, but Robert had proved more than twenty years before that no ordinary computer, however ingeniously programmed, would suffice. If program H could always tell you in a finite time whether or not program X would halt, you could tack on a small addition to H to create program Z, which perversely and deliberately went into an infinite loop whenever it examined a program that halted. If Z examined itself, it would either halt eventually, or run forever. But either possibility contradicted the alleged powers of program H: if Z actually ran forever, it would be because H had claimed that it wouldn't, and vice versa. Program H could not exist.

"Time travel," Helen said, "gives me a chance to become an Oracle. There's a way to exploit the inability to change your own past, a way to squeeze an infinite number of timelike paths—none of them closed, but some of them arbitrarily near to it—into a finite physical system. Once you do that, you can solve the halting problem."

"How?" Robert's mind was racing. "And once you've done that . . . what about higher cardinalities? An Oracle for Oracles, able to test conjectures about the real numbers?"

Helen smiled enigmatically. "The first problem should only take you forty or fifty years to solve. As for the rest," she pulled away from him, moving into the darkness of the hallway, "what makes you think I know the answer myself?" She blew him a kiss, then vanished from sight.

Robert took a step toward her, but the hallway was empty.

He walked back to the car, sad and exalted, his heart pounding.

The driver asked wearily, "Where to now, sir?"

Robert said, "Further up, and further in."

4

The night after the funeral, Jack paced the house until three AM. When would it be bearable? *When?* She'd shown more strength and courage, dying, than he felt within himself right now. But she'd share it with him, in the weeks to come. She'd share it with them all.

In bed, in the darkness, he tried to sense her presence around him. But it was forced, it was premature. It was one thing to have faith that she was watching over him, but quite another to expect to be spared every trace of grief, every trace of pain.

He waited for sleep. He needed to get some rest before dawn, or how would he face her children in the morning?

Gradually, he became aware of someone standing in the darkness at the foot of the bed. As he examined and reexamined the shadows, he formed a clear image of the apparition's face.

It was his own. Younger, happier, surer of himself.

Jack sat up. "What do you want?"

"I want you to come with me." The figure approached; Jack recoiled, and it halted.

"Come with you, where?" Jack demanded.

"To a place where she's waiting."

Jack shook his head. "No. I don't believe you. She said she'd come for me herself, when it was time. She said she'd guide me."

"She didn't understand, then," the apparition insisted gently. "She didn't know I could fetch you myself. Do you think I'd send her in my place? Do you think I'd shirk the task?"

Jack searched the smiling, supplicatory face. "Who are you?" *His own soul, in Heaven, remade?* Was this a gift God offered everyone? To meet, before death, the very thing you would become—if you so chose? So that even this would be an act of free will?

The apparition said, "Stoney persuaded me to let his friend treat Joyce. We lived on, together. More than a century has passed. And now we want you to join us."

Jack choked with horror. "No! This is a trick! *You're the Devil!*"

The thing replied mildly, "There is no Devil. And no God, either. Just people. But I promise you: people with the powers of gods are kinder than any god we ever imagined."

Jack covered his face. "Leave me be." He whispered fervent prayers, and waited. It was a test, a moment of vulnerability, but God wouldn't leave him naked like this, face-to-face with the Enemy, for longer than he could endure.

He uncovered his face. The thing was still with him.

It said, "Do you remember, when your faith came to you? The sense of a shield around you melting away, like armor you'd worn to keep God at bay?"

"Yes." Jack acknowledged the truth defiantly; he wasn't frightened that this abomination could see into his past, into his heart.

"That took strength: to admit that you needed God. But it takes the same kind of strength, again, to understand that *some needs can never be met*. I can't promise you Heaven. We have no disease, we have no war, we have no poverty. But we have to find our own love, our own goodness. There is no final word of comfort. We only have each other."

Jack didn't reply; this blasphemous fantasy wasn't even worth challenging. He said, "I know you're lying. Do you really imagine that I'd leave the boys alone here?"

"They'd go back to America, back to their father. How many years do you think you'd have with them, if you stay? They've already lost their mother. It would be easier for them now, a single clean break."

Jack shouted angrily, "Get out of my house!"

The thing came closer, and sat on the bed. It put a hand on his shoulder. Jack sobbed, "Help me!" But he didn't know whose aid he was invoking anymore.

"Do you remember the scene in *The Seat of Oak*? When the Harpy traps everyone in her cave underground, and tries to convince them that there is no Nescia? Only this drab underworld is real, she tells them. Everything else they think they've seen was just make-believe." Jack's own young face smiled nostalgically. "And we had dear old Shrugweight reply: he didn't think much of this so-called real world of hers. And even if she was right, since four little children could make up a better world, he'd rather go on pretending that their imaginary one was real.

"But we had it all upside down! The real world is richer, and stranger, and more beautiful than anything ever imagined. Milton, Dante, John the Divine are the ones who trapped you in a drab, gray underworld. That's where you are now. But if you give me your hand, I can pull you out."

Jack's chest was bursting. *He couldn't lose his faith. He'd kept it through worse than this. He'd kept it through every torture and indignity God had inflicted on his wife's frail body. No one could take it from him now.* He crooned to himself, "In my time of trouble, He will find me."

The cool hand tightened its grip on his shoulder. "You can be with her, now. Just say the word, and you will become a part of me. I will take you inside me, and you will see through my eyes, and we will travel back to the world where she still lives."

Jack wept openly. "Leave me in peace! Just leave me to mourn her!"

The thing nodded sadly. "If that's what you want."

"I do! *Go!*"

"When I'm sure."

Suddenly, Jack thought back to the long rant Stoney had delivered in the studio. Every choice went every way, Stoney had claimed. No decision could ever be final.

"Now I know you're lying!" he shouted triumphantly. "If you believed everything Stoney told you, how could my choice ever mean a thing? I would always say yes to you, and I would always say no! It would all be the same!"

The apparition replied solemnly, "While I'm here with you, touching you, *you can't be divided*. Your choice will count."

Jack wiped his eyes, and gazed into its face. It seemed to believe every word it was speaking. What if this truly was his metaphysical twin, speaking as honestly as he could, and not merely the Devil in a mask? Perhaps there was a grain of truth in Stoney's awful vision; perhaps this was another version of himself, a living person who honestly believed that the two of them shared a history.

Then it was a visitor sent by God, to humble him. To teach him compassion toward Stoney. To show Jack that he, too, with a little less faith, and a little more pride, might have been damned forever.

Jack stretched out a hand and touched the face of this poor lost soul. *There, but for the grace of God, go I.*

He said, "I've made my choice. Now leave me."

Author's note

Where the lives of the fictional characters of this story parallel those of real historical figures, I've drawn on biographies by Andrew Hodges and A. N. Wilson. The self-dual formulation of general relativity was discovered by Abhay Ashtekar in 1986, and has since led to groundbreaking developments in quantum gravity, but the implications drawn from it here are fanciful.